Prologue

Date: 1/12/2025
From: KarmaChamelia@hotmail.com
To: Livvin_mybestlife@hotmail.com
Subject: Another bloke bites the dust

Hey Livvie,

Who knew it was possible to hate two blue ticks so much?

Yep, you've guessed it: yet another bloke has gone and done a runner and left me on read for over thirty-six hours now.

I hate this. It feels like all I ever email you about these days is seemingly decent men who end up ghosting me.

The latest one's called Billy, though telling you his name is pointless as he'll probably never come up in conversation again. But seriously, Liv, he seemed so bloody nice.

I got a good vibe from him the moment I saw him. Even his first-day mugshot that I uploaded to the intranet's staff directory caught my attention as he was actually smiling, rather than trying to look all cool and aloof like so many other new starters here.

We were getting along great. And spent the whole day (and night...) together on Saturday. But, since

Sunday morning, I've heard n-o-t-h-i-n-g from him. Zilch. And now, on this freezing Monday night at the start of December, I find myself on my sofa weeping along to those American made-for-TV Christmas movies in an attempt to distract myself from those chirpy little checkmarks. I've stared at them so much I can even see them when I blink, as if they've seared themselves onto the insides of my eyelids.

I know I used to make fun of you for watching these cheesy festive films on Channel 5 on Sunday afternoons when you should've been doing your homework, but I'll admit there is something about them that seems to make me forget about All Of The Shit. Despite the fact they're all pretty much the same, I can't help but invest in the tropey character arcs, gasp when they tell me to gasp (OMG, he's secretly SANTA?!) and swoon when they tell me to swoon.

As ever, the one I'm watching as I'm writing this email features a seemingly carefree and career-focused single woman who's despatched to a picture-perfect town for some obscure December work assignment. After spending mere days there, she concludes – of course – that her life in the big city she was perfectly content with the previous week is now utterly meaningless compared to the small-town simplicities presented to her by a kind-hearted local fellow.

I've watched so many of these identikit films over the last few years that I've even devised my own bingo-based drinking game to play as I watch them. I must admit I never thought ticking off Christmas movie clichés with nothing but blankets, cushions and a sticky shot glass for company would be my

It's Beginning To Look A Lot Like Christmas

It's Beginning to look a lot like Christmas

HAYLEY DUNLOP

hera

Penguin
Random
House

First published in the United Kingdom in 2025 by

Hera Books, an imprint of
Canelo Digital Publishing Limited,
20 Vauxhall Bridge Road,
London SW1V 2SA
United Kingdom

A Penguin Random House Company
The authorised representative in the EEA is Dorling Kindersley Verlag GmbH.
Arnulfstr. 124, 80636 Munich, Germany

A CIP catalogue record for this book is available from the British Library.

Print ISBN 978 1 83598 153 5
Ebook ISBN 978 1 83598 155 9

Printed and bound in Great Britain by Clays Ltd, Elcograf S.p.A.

Look for more great books at
www.herabooks.com | www.dk.com

For my children, Elliott and Maisie.

And for myself.

life's greatest joy just a couple of years off my 40th birthday.

I just wish that… fuck, what is it that I wish? I have no bloody idea. Except for one thing, of course. But that's the only thing I can never have.

Right, I'd better go. I'm out with Elle after work tomorrow, which, as you know, means I ought to bank as much sleep as possible while I've got the chance.

Missing you, as always.

Love,

Me xxx

Chapter 1

☑ **Story opens in city**

I knew the table would be sticky, but I rested my forehead on it anyway.

'The absolute fucker.'

Elle's instant summation took me by surprise – especially since I'd only given her a ten-word overview (I-slept-with-Billy-but-haven't-heard-from-him-since) of my predicament – but I couldn't deny its accuracy.

I cocked my head to the side and looked up at her out of one eye.

'Huh, don't hold back, Elle.'

'Sorry, Mally, but I just can't believe it. I thought he was one of the good ones.'

'I know, right? But apparently not. I can't figure out what the hell I've done wrong this time.'

I peeled my face off the surface and took my time dragging my wine glass towards me to avoid Elle's commiserative gaze for as long as possible. I drained the liquid slowly but determinedly as her anti-Billy castigation continued. I'd been relying on Elle's venomous take to exorcise any remaining fondness I had for him, and I hadn't been disappointed so far.

'Elle?'

'Mmm?'

'We're going to need more alcohol.'

'On it.'

Elle called over the waitress in Val Taro, our favourite West End wine bar that was possibly the only undiscovered drinking hole left in this corner of London's theatreland. It was handily located in the basement underneath our office on Orange Street, a narrow and distinctly un-orange road between Trafalgar Square and Leicester Square.

Setting the world to rights in here after a rough day of office politics always made me feel like my life had morphed into an episode of *Ugly Betty*. Albeit without the chaotic yet loving family waiting for me at home.

We were sitting in our usual discreet spot – tucked away yet with our seats on the small, circular table angled outwards so we could keep an eye on new arrivals and ensure we weren't overheard by any mutual colleagues. The walls behind us were adorned with Blu-Tacked theatre posters, curly-cornered wine charts and vintage Campari mirrors. Dusty strands of fairy lights were strung around the bar as a reluctant nod to the time of year.

'Hey, can we get another bottle, and two carbonaras?' Elle asked.

I'd been about to order a pizza. But with the wine – and Elle – in full flow, I knew there was no point in objecting.

The Italian waitress of the family-run business smiled and nodded, placing a shallow wooden bowl on the table containing some odds and ends of crisps. I smiled back at her and passed her my unopened menu while Elle continued talking.

'I mean, I could see you were getting close to him, but I didn't want to say anything as I knew that would've freaked you out. It seemed like it was all happening naturally.'

'That's how it felt, too.'

The ease with which Billy and I had hit it off had felt like a big deal, since the only other thing that seemed to come naturally to me was watching telly from a horizontal position.

'Right, you need to tell me absolutely everything, right from the start. Then we can strategise.'

It took three hours (and the same number of wine bottles) to tell Elle about the office romance that had been bubbling away between me and Billy over the past few months.

I divulged every detail Elle asked for. How, after he'd joined *The Helix* – where Elle and I both worked – it'd started off with Billy and I sharing awful puns over Slack and had ended in a day-long pub crawl around the cosy drinking holes of Greenwich on Saturday. It'd been a nippy, zips-up day that had turned into a tipsy, toes-touching dinner, followed by a 'nightcap' at mine... and a swift breakfast the next morning before he had to leave for the airport to fly to his cousin's wedding.

I concluded my tale of woe with the visual agony of those two blue ticks that had tormented me for three days now. Three agonising days in which that floaty yet ever-so-slightly nauseating feeling of possibility had mutated into its ugly opposite: pure, all-consuming self-pity... and one actual anxiety vomit. Three days' worth of tears that my favourite custard cream-shaped cushion had dutifully absorbed as I filled my brain with predictable yet comforting made-for-TV Christmas movies. Three days since I'd enquired via WhatsApp as to whether Billy had managed to source caffeine before his early-afternoon flight, since we'd run out of time for coffee back at mine.

'Run out of time, eh?' Elle topped up my wine glass and pushed it towards me. She was enjoying this way too much for my liking. Even back at school, she'd always gotten a kick out of taking the piss out of me. 'So, you sent him that message about coffee and then… nothing since?'

'Yup.'

'This feels off to me. Give me your phone.'

I hated it when she did this. The last time she'd got her hands on it she'd sent my brother Josh an offensive GIF that had ripped the piss out of his dedication to veganism. I'd managed to administer a swift deletion, but not before he'd seen it.

After twenty-five years of friendship, I was used to mopping up the messes Elle tended to leave in her wake. She'd always been the confident one who courted attention, and these days loved nothing more than gossiping in the office kitchen with her cliquey underlings in the editorial features team. I, meanwhile, loved nothing more than escaping to the work loos for some alone time every now and then to take a break from my busy internal comms role. Elle had put me forward for the job a year or so after she'd joined *The Helix*. Being invited for a selection day at one of the world's leading online publishing companies – when I hadn't even applied for the position – had been a unique experience, that's for sure. Especially since my limited digital presence meant I didn't have a clue what half the interview questions had been about. But, apparently, my 'obvious lack of journalistic ambition'

– as referenced in my formal job offer – had worked in my favour in the end. They'd wanted someone who was focused on the corporate duties outlined in the job description, not distracted by the lure of a ruthless editorial career.

Working with Elle had never been the plan after uni. In fact, I'd always intended to carve out my own path, bit by bit. But, in fairness to her, I was now on a much bigger salary than before. I owed her a lot.

I handed over my phone, metaphorical mop at the ready. Elle unlocked it and fired up WhatsApp, quickly finding the last message in the conversation with Billy:

> **Mally:**
> Has that flat white been acquired? xx

She started scrolling upwards.

'Elle, come on – that's private.'

I held out my hand to get it back, but instead she rolled her eyes and shut down WhatsApp before swiping through my paltry collection of apps. Defeated, my hand reached for my wine glass instead.

'You know,' Elle said, 'it would take me like two minutes to set you up with a Hinge profile. I can do it right now if I could just figure out how to download apps on this piece of junk…'

My choice of mobile phone – a basic pay-as-you-go model from Argos and the cheapest smartphone in whatever the digital equivalent of their iconic paper catalogue was these days – was always a source of amusement to anyone who noticed it. Yes, it was clunky, but it ran all the apps I needed. And a dating app certainly didn't fall into that category. I reeled off my pre-rehearsed answer whenever this subject came up.

'I can't be arsed with it, Elle. The blokes on there are mainly on the prowl for one-night stands. And the ones who claim to be "open-minded" tend to dismiss anything you care about while trying to frame it as an "intellectual debate".' My over-exuberant air quotes brushed the wine glass and it started to topple. Elle swooped in to save it.

'That's a literal summary of all our male colleagues,' she said, moving my glass out of harm's way.

Except Billy. Or maybe I'd been wrong about him all along. It wouldn't have been the first time I'd scared a bloke off by – as one ex had succinctly summarised – 'expecting too much, too soon'. Although, in his case, it'd been my quite reasonable suggestion that I leave a mini tube of Sensodyne toothpaste at his place that had sent him running for the hills.

'C'mon, Elle, let me have my phone back.'

She sighed and skidded my phone along the table towards me.

'And he didn't say anything about doing a digital detox while he was away or anything like that?' she asked.

'Nope, in fact...'

I looked down at the screen to review its tortuous insights.

'...yup, look – he's online right now. And only a couple of hours ago he posted a Reel of himself with one of those ironic unicorn inflatables. Argh, what am I even saying?' I briefly re-introduced my forehead to the tacky table – it really could do with some Purdy & Figg. 'I don't want to spend my spare time obsessing over the online exploits of a man who's treated me like shit. I'm thirty-eight years old, for fuck's sake – I shouldn't be reduced to this! I just want to meet someone, Elle. Someone who I can meet at home after work and binge-watch telly with. Is that really too much to ask for?'

'Strong life goals there, Mally.'

'Oof, you know what I mean. I want to connect with someone who… gets me. Like what you and Rory have.'

Talking about relationships and the deep connections I craved didn't come easily to me, unless I was pouring everything out in one of my emails to my younger sister, Livvie. Elle was the opposite. Back at school, our conversations had revolved around her latest crushes – yes, plural – and seemingly endless love-life dilemmas. Finding a life partner was less of a mission for her and more of a YO! Sushi-esque conveyor belt of blokes, practically begging for her to select them.

She'd met Rory during freshers' week as soon as we'd arrived at uni and he'd followed her around like a lost puppy from the outset. But, unlike all the others, she'd permitted him to stay on the scene. And he had, despite Elle messing him around endlessly for three years.

They'd finally made things official shortly before graduation and had been together ever since, though it took Rory an age to convince Elle to move in with him, and even longer to have a kid. But she was always at her most relaxed in his company. And he was blatantly still so smitten with her. It was easy to see why: even without her perfectly proportioned figure, flawless porcelain skin, poker-straight glossy brown hair and almost obscenely large almond-shaped hazel eyes, her magnetic personality alone was enough to get her noticed. Success was always going to come easily to Elle – professionally *and* romantically.

Unlike me. What I lacked in charisma I tried to make up for with my self-deprecating humour and unshake-able reliability. And while I had no real qualms with my pale, mousy but pleasant-enough appearance, I wasn't in possession of that carefree girl-next-door vibe that would attract attention from anyone who didn't already know me. I was very much the 'kooky yet weirdly organised best friend' to Elle's chaotic yet magnetic 'main character'. No wonder I found meeting decent men so bloody labour-intensive.

'More than anyone you deserve some luck on the rela-tionship front. Look, we need to get to the bottom of this. And we will. But I don't have any answers for you right now. What are you up to Friday night?' Elle asked.

'Friday? I thought Tuesdays were your only child-free night?'

'They are, but Rory's going to be out until God knows when on Friday for his work Christmas do and it'll just be me and Frannie. So why don't you come to mine for the night? You can give me a hand getting her to bed and then we can have a cosy night in with a film and a takeaway and try and figure out your next move.'

'I swear we had this exact conversation when we were like fifteen – minus the toddler element.'

'Yeah, except this time we won't be drinking my mum's sherry while miming to "Lady Marmalade" in my bedroom mirror. We can upgrade to a nice bottle of pinot grigio I've been saving, watch whatever you fancy on Netflix and hope Frannie doesn't wake up and insist we watch *Olaf's Frozen Adventure* for the sixty-eighth time this year.'

I shivered at the prospect of watching anything from the *Frozen* canon. I used to love watching Disney films, but these days they triggered way too many difficult memories. And I wasn't sure I'd ever be able to watch one that centred around the unbreakable bond between two very different sisters.

'Yeah, go on then.'

'And maybe we can also have a teeny-weeny chat about that article you keep promising to write for me and never do?'

These 'teeny-weeny' chats about writing an article for our employer, *The Helix* – one of the UK's leading lifestyle, entertainment and features websites – were a regular fixture of our conversations. Elle was always on the lookout for ways to commission cheap – or, let's be honest, free – content.

'Here's me thinking we'd made it through a night without you bringing that up,' I said. 'I still can't think of anything remotely interesting to write about. The people you commission for *The Helix* all have so much to say, whereas I've got nothing. Unless you want me to write about chocolate-based breakfast cereals, in which case I can have an article with you by nine a.m. tomorrow.'

'Let's pop a pin in that particular idea, eh, Mally?' Elle placed her wine glass down and grabbed my hands firmly. 'Seriously, though. You know I'm the features editor, right? And I could simply commission you to write something with no questions asked?'

She squeezed my hands tightly as if to emphasise her clout.

'I know, but I don't even work in editorial. It'd be awkward – everyone would assume I'd been commissioned because we're friends. I swear most people still think that's how I got my job anyway.'

She sighed and released her grip, sliding her glass towards her. I did the same.

'We commission non-editorial employees all the time, you know that! I swear I've been approached by 95 per cent of people who work for the company. Only yesterday, Colin from the canteen asked if he could write a piece about his top ten favourite hand dryers.'

'I'd read that.'

'Yeah, I know *you'd* read that, but I reckon the topic's a tad niche, even for *The Helix*. Plus, the draft he insisted on sending me read like an actual hand dryer catalogue, not a wry feature. Whereas the intranet piece you wrote today about next week's health and safety training genuinely made me cackle.'

'Huh. I think the pun in the headline is probably my career highlight.'

Elle sighed. 'You're doing that thing again.'

'What thing?' I don't know why I bothered to play dumb with Elle; she knew me better than anyone.

'You're selling yourself short. How many times do I need to say this, Mally Allister? You're an amazing writer, but your talent's going to waste. You need to free your voice! Who knows, if you play your cards right, you could be moved up to editorial! Whatever it is that's holding you back needs to do one.'

Was I being held back, though? Or was I simply content with a quieter life than hers? Even when we were teenagers, Elle had always been chomping at the bit to move to London and grow into the person she was born to be. She'd had her life and career mapped out from the start, whereas mine seemed to be playing out like a fading vapour trail behind her flaming booster jets. And I didn't mind it that way – I'd rather evaporate than burn.

'Yeah, I know. But my heart doesn't lie in journalism; it never has. Actually' – I took a larger-than-average swig of wine for courage – 'I've been thinking about it a lot recently, and what I'd really like to do next year is start focusing on the ideas I've got for my children's books. If I start writing clickbaity features, I worry that I'm going to end up distracted and pigeonholed, so...'

'Stop. Listen to me. In the kindest possible way, you're some way off from having kids. I mean, think about it: do you honestly believe you'll be able to write anything that will resonate with that audience and that market?'

My stomach flipped at Elle's words, my throat swelling. Despite always knowing what I needed to hear to boost my confidence, she also had a knack for slapping it back down again. But she was right, of course. Meeting someone who I might be able to start a family with one day was definitely on my ultimate to-do list, but if I wanted to even have a shot at having kids this side of forty, I'd have to meet someone immediately. Like, this month. And she was probably right about my pathetic book ideas, too. I tried to maintain my composure but my glossy eyes must have given me away.

'Urgh, don't look at me like that,' Elle said. 'I feel crap enough as it is. It's been a shitty week at work – you wouldn't believe some of the stuff that's going down in editorial at the moment.'

'It's fine. I just thought... you know, with Billy, maybe I'd finally met someone who I could...' The rest of the words got lodged in my neck. I downed the remainder of my wine in an attempt to wash them away.

'Like I said: what an absolute fucker.'

'Yeah.'

I looked at my phone and did a double-take at the time.

'Shit, I've got to go or I'll miss my train.'

I wiped my eyes quickly and grabbed my stuff. I had eight minutes to sprint from Leicester Square to platform three or five – I could never remember at this time of night – at Charing Cross station. It was just about doable based on previous drunken dashes but it was going to be tight.

'Okay, go, go, go. I'll sort the bill and you can pay me back. I've got a busy couple of days coming up so I might not see you around the office. But come by my desk on Friday just before five and we'll head to mine from there, yeah?'

'Will do. And, Elle?'

'Mmm?'

'That elf and safety training is *mandatory*, okay?'

I missed the train by about four seconds. It was a freezing thirty-minute wait on the concourse for the next one to Hither Green. And, as much as I respected his enthusiasm, I wasn't sure I could hack the resident saxophone busker playing the same four bars from 'Last Christmas' on an endless loop.

Shivering on the platform bench, I put my earmuffs on and decided to re-read the email I'd sent to Livvie last night. After all, re-reading our historical correspondence was one of my life's biggest comforts these days. I logged into my ancient inbox, which I only ever used for Livvie.

The sight that greeted me caused every millilitre of blood in my body to plummet to my feet. Because, for the first time in twenty years, there was a reply. I had to hold back the urge to plunge my thumb through the screen to read it as quickly as possible, forcing out a restrained tap instead.

An unfamiliar noise escaped from my voice box as it all became clear:

> Address not found
>
> Your message wasn't delivered to
> Livvin_mybestlife@hotmail.com because the
> address couldn't be found or is unable to receive
> email.

I was shocked by the intensity of my reaction to the automatically generated reply. I knew, after all these years, it was inevitable this would happen at some point. But part of me had never really let myself believe it.

By the time I'd pulled myself together I almost missed the next train, too. Settled into my usual spot in my usual carriage, I re-read the bounce-back message. It was so brutal. So final. And I knew I never wanted to get one of those blunt emails ever again. But that meant one thing: I would have to stop emailing Livvie. And I wasn't sure I was ready for that. Because I always liked to imagine that, in some alternative universe, she'd replied to every single one of my messages over the last two decades in her usual no-nonsense manner. In the case of Billy, she'd have said something along the lines of 'just call him, FFS!'. Instead, I'd spent two decades having to imagine her advice.

She'd always been that rare kind of person who'd never cared what anyone had thought of her. She'd always been unashamedly herself – and had made me feel *I* could be unashamedly *myself*, in a way that no one else had since.

My little sister had been my confidante, my best friend, my favourite human – by quite some margin. But then we lost her when she was just fifteen.

And losing her was the catalyst that, eventually, caused the rest of my family to lose each other, too.

Chapter 2

☑ **Solo Christmas ahead**

'Hey, Mum.'

'Hi, sweetheart. How's work today?'

A total write-off, Mum, but I'm hiding it well.

I swiftly swallowed my gut response; Mum always had enough on her plate without my woes piling her worries up even higher. Even discounting my hangover, everything about today was hard after last night's email thunderbolt and the resulting sleepless night I'd had. Not that I could ever talk to Mum – or anyone – about that, of course. No one knew I'd been emailing my dead sister every single day for two decades.

'It's fine. My boss is away so it's pretty full-on this week. I'm about to go into a meeting so I can only talk for a minute. Is it urgent?'

'Oh, I was hoping to catch you on your lunch break.'

I stifled a sigh. No matter how many times I told my parents that I left my flat at seven in the morning each day and rarely stopped until I got back twelve or so hours later, they still operated under the assumption that I enjoyed a daily lunch hour and got home in time for tea at five thirty. After all, that's what my dad's full-time working routine had been like at my age. They couldn't get their heads around the concept that the working practices of a small-town accountancy office in the twentieth century and an international online publication in the twenty-first didn't overlap in the slightest.

'Yeah, Mum, like I've said before, I don't often get time to have a—'

'I'll keep this brief, then. Your dad and I – well, this is kind of awkward…'

'Just say it, I'm sure it's fine.'

'Okay, well, we've been invited to Auntie Sandra's place in Florida…'

Oh wow, this was big. Mum and Dad had barely slept in a different bed for the last twenty years, let alone gone overseas.

'Ooh, at last – get you!'

'…for Christmas.'

Ouch. Not that our family Christmases were particularly joyful occasions these days. But they still felt important, somehow.

'Oh.'

'Yes, I know. Not the best timing, hmm?'

'You're going, then?'

'Well, we've not made up our minds yet. We'd hate to let you and your brother down, but you know how much we've been meaning to get out there at some point. Her friends Neil and Nina have had to pull out – something about Nina's inner ear – and we think it's finally the right time to go. Your dad and I were just saying that it may even be the last chance we get.'

'Mum, you're sixty-five, not ninety-five. Have you spoken to Josh about this yet?'

'He just replied to my message. He's fine with it. Got the impression he's been under some pressure from Saskia to spend Christmas with the in-laws, anyway.'

I rolled my eyes as I squashed my handset between my ear and my shoulder while topping up my stainless-steel water bottle ready for my meeting.

'Fair enough. Have you spoken to him recently?'

'Not on the phone, no. You know what he's like.'

Like me, my older brother, Josh, had moved to London after graduating from uni. But even though we only lived a few miles apart, we never met up outside of family occasions. I mean, why would we? His wellness lifestyle of fitness, 'clean eating' and online influencing couldn't be further away from my sedentary instincts, shameless sugar addiction and unwillingness to engage in any social media platforms at all.

'So, what are you thinking, love?'

'Oh, you should totally go. I'll be fine. I'm sure I'll find a plan B easily enough.'

I didn't tell her that my plan B would probably involve a day weeping in the bath while eating a three-day-old festive sandwich from Pret.

'Are you sure? I can always ask Sandra if there's room for one more?'

I grimaced. The thought of spending a week with Mum and her well-meaning but overbearingly wealthy sister – their relationship revolving around the unspoken agreement that they'd never acknowledge, let alone discuss, their political differences – filled me with imme-diate existential dread.

'No, no, no, no, no.' *Did I say 'no' too many times? Oh well.* 'It's fine. I'll be fine. It'll be… character-building.'

'Hmm, if you say so. Well, to make up for the change of plan we'd love you and Josh to come round for a Sunday roast this weekend. I'll send you both the details on WhatsApp.'

Unlike other families, we'd ice-skated around the convenience of forming a collective WhatsApp group. I think we all knew that the banality of GIFs and emojis would be completely at odds with everything else that would undoubtedly go unsaid.

'I'll invite Saskia, too, but you know what she's like,' Mum said.

Huh, well, that would be a wasted invitation. Josh's wife had made it perfectly clear that she couldn't find us less interesting if she tried. I couldn't help but think that the news of my parents' last-minute December trip would probably be the highlight of her year.

'She won't come, Mum.'

'Hmmm. Well, I've got to keep trying, haven't I? Right, I've got to go, your dad's got his finger hovering over the mouse to buy flights and he's paranoid the prices are going to shoot up if we leave it too long. You know how jumpy he gets after that time he held off from booking Portugal until payday only for the prices to have doubled by then.' Ah, 'Algarve-gate'. We'd ended up going to Weymouth that year instead.

'Well, tell Dad to complete that transaction. Honestly, I'll be fine. I've got to head into that meeting now so...'

'DO IT, BOB. Huh? Oh yes. Look, let's speak about this properly later, okay?'

'Sure. Bye, Mum.'

'Bye, love.'

I slid my phone into my skirt pocket and started climbing the staircase towards the executive offices. Mum's phone call had caught me totally off guard. On the one hand, I was thrilled they were finally going on this long-overdue trip. But, on the other, I had absolutely no clue what I was going to do with myself in their absence. The routine of going to Mum and Dad's for the festive period was hardwired into me, and the thought of *not* going there felt massively discombobulating, especially after last night.

I reached the corridor of *The Helix*'s transparent 'collaboration cabins' (the trade press had had a field day with that one) and double-checked the room number that I'd scribbled at the top of my notepad before sliding the heavy, glass door open. The meeting had been put into my calendar last-minute by the director of operations – a damp and permanently harangued-looking man in his early fifties called Ian – after he realised my boss, Maggie, was on leave.

'Ah – Mally, is it?'

Charming, I'd only worked there for almost ten years. Though I did have a carefully cultivated air of forgettability about me, so I couldn't really blame him.

I activated smiley-Mally mode. 'That's me!'

'Right. Sorry to put this on you, but in Maggie's absence Izzy thought you'd be the best person for this.'

Izzy, Ian's executive assistant, who was expected to attend every meeting with him, confirmed his summation with a flicker of a smile and a nod. Was it me or were they both looking even more grim than usual?

'Mally,' Ian said, placing his hands either side of his laptop and looking at me intently as if he was about to tell me that Santa wasn't real. 'We need to send an all-staff email about an... unexpected office closure before Christmas.'

Well, this was a surprise. I lowered my eyebrows as quickly as I could and shifted my expression into one that I hoped emanated professional intrigue.

'Sure, no problem. What are the key messages we want to get across to employees?'

I turned to a fresh page in my notebook, my pen poised. Everyone else took their laptops into meetings but I preferred the traditional note-taking method. Izzy shot Ian a look before he replied.

'Ah, well, we were hoping we could use your comms expertise to help us with that.'

Ian was now wearing a hopeful expression that reminded me of the way Elle's three-year-old daughter, Frannie, looked at me when I was eating something sugary in her presence. I eventually deduced that he was waiting for me to talk.

'Oh, right, so let's start with the basic info,' I said. 'What date is the office closing and for how long?'

'Of course, of course. So – where are we now, Izz?'

'It's Wednesday 3 December... 2025.' Izzy shot me an amused look as she said the year after a perfectly timed comedic beat. I grinned as I exaggeratedly underlined the full date, including the year, in my notebook. Ian didn't react.

'The third, then. So, let me see, let me see... yes, here we go. The office *was* due to be closed for the annual festive shutdown between Wednesday 24 December and Friday 2 January. But we need to close the week before that this year, so that'll be Monday 15 December.'

In less than two weeks? Shit, this would get tongues wagging. I jotted down the dates.

'Okay, got it. So, why is that?' I asked.

'We've got some… operational issues to take care of in the office that week.'

Oh God, this was like pulling teeth. No wonder Maggie referred to him as 'Iancompetent' after a drink or two.

'I see.' I didn't see. 'But, ha ha, you know what they're like down in editorial; the rumour mill will go into overdrive. So I reckon it might be good to tell staff a bit more than that, if that makes sense?'

'I told you that wouldn't be enough, Ian. Shall I…?' Izzy said.

Ian sighed and nodded once at Izzy, looking defeated and downcast.

I took a long sip of water to avoid the atmosphere of awkwardness that had descended around us. Argh, too much water. I mopped my chin with the back of my hand, hopefully before either of them noticed the dribble.

'Mally.' Izzy was now leading the conversation. It was a poorly kept secret that Izzy Curtis was the person *actually* in charge of the day-to-day operational function of *The Helix* in the UK, not Ian. As a natural fixer, she'd quietly worked her way up the management ladder ever since she'd started working here as a receptionist straight out of uni. But when she'd returned from maternity leave a couple of years ago, the leadership pathway – which had previously been so clearly laid out before her – was suddenly littered with obstacles. When I say 'obstacles', I mean mediocre men. She'd been sidelined into executive assistant roles ever since. Elle had told me on the sly that she was constantly trying to resign, but they kept paying her more to stay because she 'knew too much'.

'We need employees to vacate the office a week early to carry out some unplanned maintenance work,' Izzy continued. 'As you know, key editorial and commercial staff usually work from home between Christmas and the new year on a rota basis, but this year we're asking those staff to commence their remote working slightly earlier than usual.'

I took some more notes. 'Okay, got it. What about the rest of us – I mean, the rest of the company?'

'They won't be required to work during the extended shutdown period.'

'Right. But… they'll still be paid?'

'Mmm-hmm.'

Oh! This was big. And potentially… not good. There'd been tons of speculation in recent months about the long-term viability of such a large UK presence for *The Helix*, especially since commercial revenues had dropped off a cliff in the last couple of years.

The business had grown exponentially since the UK-based arm of the global online publication had launched back in 2007. My own position had been created in 2016 as part of one of many waves of expansion as the website's audience traffic – and commercial revenue – had soared in the years that followed. Recruitment had tailed off recently, but the US-based owners had announced just this year that they had 'ambitious plans for growth and innovation'. But rumours had already been rife that all of this would come at the expense of the UK-based operation. Surely news of this sudden office closure would only add more fuel to the gossip fire in London media circles?

I thought carefully about what to say next so I could end this meeting as soon as possible and get back to my desk to give my co-manager, Lauren – who ran our PR team – an urgent heads-up about this potential comms inferno.

'Right, so – off the top of my head – it seems to me that maybe the message should be that everyone's getting a fully paid extra week off before Christmas?'

'Yes! That's it, Mally.' Ian suddenly had a bit of colour back in his face.

'Well, I'm not sure I'd put it like that...' Izzy was rubbing her temples and looking at me in a way that suggested she was trying to communicate via telepathy. I'm sure she was wishing it was Maggie in this meeting rather than me. The two of them always seemed to untangle these largely male-made knots, but with Maggie out of action for the rest of the year having a hysterectomy, contacting her was out of the question.

'No, this is perfect.' Ian placed what he obviously believed to be a reassuring hand on Izzy's shoulder as a signal that he was going to take over the reins of the meeting once more.

'Okay, Mally. Let's go with something like this: *As a thank you for the exceptional efforts that employees have put in this year, we're extending the annual festive shutdown for an extra week. During this time, essential maintenance work will be carried out in the office ahead of our return in the new year.* How does that sound?'

It sounds like a crock of shit, Ian.

'Perfect, got it. So, returning to the office as planned on Monday 5 January?'

'That's the plan, yes.'

The plan? Oh God, our employees were going to be coming to all manner of conclusions about this paper-thin email. *The Helix*'s management had always opposed the unionisation of its staff, insisting that its 'online start-up culture' – despite its one-thousand-plus employees both here and in the US – meant that there was 'no need' for employees to rely on collective representation. It left all of us vulnerable to the whims of management who lived the other side of the Atlantic, and inevitably resulted in a permanent frenzy of paranoia. I caught Izzy's eye furtively, eyebrows briefly raised, to indicate that I'd clocked her concern. She nodded almost imperceptibly to confirm that she'd received my message.

'Brill. Do you think we ought to link to some FAQs on the intranet to explain it all in a bit more detail?' I asked.

'Great question,' Ian replied. 'Izzy, what do you think?'

'You already know what I think,' Izzy retorted.

Christ, their working relationship was... intense. I couldn't figure out if they hated each other, or had recently ended an illicit affair.

'Oh, just ignore her: PMT strikes again!'

Izzy calmly pressed her laptop closed, smiled at me with tight lips and walked out of the room. Okay, she definitely hated him. And justifiably so.

'See what I mean?'

I fixed my face into a neutral expression and said nothing. He gathered up his things and stood to leave. 'Right, I'd better go and make amends before she reports me to HR!'

He seemed to have forgotten that I *was* HR – or 50 per cent HR, anyway. As internal communications officer, I jointly reported in to the head of communications – Lauren – *and* Maggie, the head of human resources, who I'd *definitely* be chatting to about this conversation in the new year.

Ian's head appeared around the door as I read through my limited notes from the meeting.

'Oh, and can you send me a draft by three o'clock? I need to leave at half three today for my youngest's nativity, but it really needs to go out in the next day or so to give everyone as much notice as possible.'

I wondered whether Izzy was ever permitted to leave early for nativity plays, and concluded that – if Elle's experience in editorial was anything to go by – she probably wasn't.

'Yup, I'll get on it straight away. Enjoy the show!'

After checking he'd definitely left this time, I turned to a separate page and wrote down his sexist comment while it was fresh in my mind. Keeping such notes was futile, but I did it anyway. I knew from the experience of other female colleagues that trying to get the company to change its culture of toxic masculinity was like trying to get my dad to stop doing the *Guardian* crossword, my mum to stop dusting and Josh to stop pulverising goodness-knows-what in his Nutribullet.

Back at my desk, it took me about twenty minutes to put together an initial draft for the all-staff email. Lauren wasn't around to consult, so I pasted the draft into an email to Ian and copied her in, marking it as 'urgent'.

Urgh, I hated that word. The relentless pace of life at *The Helix* – 'the world's leading digital smoothie for content, correspondence and culture' – had taken me the best part of a year to adjust to after I'd left the small south London children's charity I'd worked for previously. Both were internal communications roles, but communicating to an employee base of thirty – where a meme-based poster in the communal kitchen would usually do the trick – compared to a headcount in the hundreds, meant that the two jobs were poles apart in terms of what was expected of me. In fact, any internal posters at *The Helix* wouldn't only be ignored, they'd probably be defaced by some up-and-coming writer who walked around with an inkless fountain pen tucked behind his ear.

I read through my email one final time before pushing 'send'. I knew my boss well enough to predict that she'd stage a PR intervention before the internal comms about the sudden office closure went out. But the vibe I'd got from the meeting was that it would almost certainly go ahead, regardless of how they spun and disseminated the news. I wondered how the majority of employees would react to the prospect of an extra week of paid leave in the run-up to Christmas.

Presumably, most of them would be able to fill it with extra joy and merriment.

Presumably, most of them wouldn't be spending it alone.

Twenty years earlier

Date: 03/10/2005
From: KarmaChamelia@hotmail.com
To: Livvin_mybestlife@hotmail.com
Subject: Fresher('?)s('?) Week Hell

Where does the apostrophe even go, Livvie? WHERE?! It seems that nobody here at Cardiff Uni can decide (or cares), as there's a total lack of consistency on the various posters, flyers and banners around the campus. It annoys me every time I see it, but no one else seems to be bothered (least of all, Elle). I know you'll understand, though. Your grammar might not be your strong suit... but being right is, hehe. So please do some research so I can start to rest easy, safe in the knowledge that there's a right way and a wrong way! Ta.

OK, so the word 'hell' is a bit of an exaggeration when it comes to how I'm finding freshers'(???) week, but, blimey, it's been an intense start to university life. Elle is basically in her natural habitat, constantly surrounded by blokes while I awkwardly linger and try and make conversation with the mates of who(m)ever her latest conquest is. But it's hard enough for me to make small talk with sober people at the best of times, let alone with drunk people when 'Brown Eyed

Girl' by Van Morrison and the Baywatch theme tune are blaring through the speakers at the student union club on repeat. The only thing for it is to, well, drink. I've already had two hangovers that wiped out the entire day (do NOT tell Mum and Dad! Ha, as if I need to say that).

I'm sure Dad told you and Mum all about my room. It's pretty decent. I mean, it's tiny but it's nice to have a space to myself (finally!) and having an en suite feels proper posh, especially as loads of other halls around the campus don't have them. Mind you, it's so tight in there I could have a shower while pooing. Dad probably also told you that me and Elle are in the same flat, in adjoining rooms! In classic Elle style, she managed to pull some strings over the summer and kept it as a surprise for when I arrived. It's nice to have a familiar face around.

Lectures haven't started yet but I've had to select a few extra modules. Elle convinced me to sign up for some of the ones she's doing so we could go together. There are also lots of clubs and societies I can join. Elle has put our names down for the student newspaper, and I might look into the creative writing group once I've settled into university life a bit more.

How's good old Soarnbrook? I know I've only been gone for a week but I already miss it! Especially the view from our room. All I can see out of this window are a brick wall and a load of bins.

Right, I'd better go, I'm running out of time on this library computer and the person next in line is giving me evil looks from the doorway.

Please reply soooooon! I'll try and get another computer slot booked in for tomorrow so I can check.

Love from meeeeeee xxxx

Date: 03/10/2005
From: Livvin_mybestlife@hotmail.com
To: KarmaChamelia@hotmail.com
Subject: Re: Fresher('?)s('?) Week Hell

I can't believe the main thing on your mind right now is GRAMMAR.

Amelia Jane Allister: LET YOUR HAIR DOWN AND HAVE FUN!!!!!! THAT'S A LIVVIE ORDER!!!!!

Yes, Dad told me about the adjoining rooms. Like – is that what you even want?! I mean, it's one thing going to the same uni as Elle, but now you're going to be in the same lectures, doing the same newspaper thing AND practically sharing a room?

I know you don't like me bringing this stuff up, but pleeeeease promise me you'll do some stuff for YOURSELF, yes? That creative writing club sounds amazing, for starters, and you should sign up for it immediately WITHOUT TELLING ELLE. You do know that's allowed, right?!

Scarnbrook is Scarnbrooking, but home isn't the same without you, Mills.

Right, I've got some STUPID HOMEWORK to do before double science tomorrow.

Reply when you can!!!

Liverrrrrrrrrrrrrs xxxxxxx

P.S. As soon as you've read this, walk away from that library computer and go and sign up for the creative writing club!!!!!

P.P.S. The possessive apostrophe goes after the 's' in 'freshers' because there is more than one fresher – I asked Mr Anderson in English today. He was in shock as it was the longest conversation I'd ever had with him that didn't involve the word 'detention'.

Chapter 3

☑ **Annoying best friend**

Twenty years later

'You're bound to find something to do. I'd invite you to spend it with us, but we'll be in Stevenage with' – Elle shuddered – 'Rory's parents. I bet they've already highlighted the *Mrs Brown's Boys* Christmas special in their *Radio Times*.'

'Crikey, good luck. Pass me a poppadom, would you?'

By the time we'd managed to coax Frannie to switch her stubborn 'on' switch to the 'off' position, ordered food and waited for it to arrive, it was approaching ten o'clock and I was beyond hungry. Having foreseen these exact circumstances, I'd suggested to Elle earlier in the week that we pre-order our takeaway, but she wanted to see what she fancied there and then. Curry it was.

I snapped off a poppadom shard and spooned on a selection of chutneys. I could feel every hangry cell in my body relax the instant the salt-sweet food hit my tastebuds.

'It's fine. I'll figure something out.' I spoke between enthusiastic mouthfuls of mushroom rice and butter chicken. My chaotic eating style was in complete contrast to Elle's precise bites of sauceless tandoori king prawn, plain okra and a restrained spoonful of vegetable biryani.

'Although it doesn't help that I've got this extra week to fill.'

The all-staff email hadn't been sent out yet. As predicted, Lauren had raised some concerns and wanted to spend the weekend 'tightening it up' before it went out first thing Monday. I'd filled Elle in nonetheless.

'All right, don't rub it in,' she said, between dry nibbles of naan. 'I could've really done with that extra week off – I still haven't done any Christmas shopping. I swear I'm going to end up like Arnold Schwarzenegger in that kids' Christmas film. You know the one I mean?'

'Ooh, *Jingle All the Way*, truly a piece of underrated satire thanks to its horrifying depiction of a world in which love itself has been commodified.'

'Mally, you're *such* a nerd.'

To me, this was a compliment rather than an insult, and Elle knew it. I'd inherited my geeky tendencies from Dad – he kept detailed records of every penny he'd ever spent, even going so far as digitising his archived paper receipts as soon as he bought his first computer. I preferred a more analogue approach, my lists meticulously organised in a growing collection of notebooks, one of which was indeed dedicated to every Christmas movie I'd ever watched.

Despite Elle's protests about the office closure, she seemed strangely unbothered about what it might mean. As features editor, she'd be one of the few editorial employees who'd need to work over Christmas, and I knew she'd be feeling excited about the extra visibility with senior US execs the longer-than-usual shutdown would give her. Since having Frannie three years ago, she'd catapulted herself into her job more than ever. She was a workaholic anyway, but motherhood seemed to have pushed her ambition levels into overdrive, which wasn't surprising given *The Helix*'s notorious family-unfriendly culture.

'Right, then, what to watch...' Elle picked up the remote and opened up Netflix, the familiar sonic logo greeting us like a virtual hug.

'Can I suggest something?' I'd been looking forward to this moment all night.

'I'm listening.'

I made quick work of another mouthful of curry before lifting the remote control to my mouth and activating the microphone: '*A Christmas Reunion*.'

'I had no idea my remote did that,' Elle said. 'And why are you speaking in such a deep voice?'

'Because voice technology favours male voices. Don't get me started...'

Elle scribbled something down on her ever-present notepad – no doubt an idea for a feature had popped into her head, as it often did mid-conversation.

I selected the first film on the menu.

'Er, Mally, that's *A Family Reunion Christmas*, not *A Christmas Reunion*.'

'Doesn't matter. They're all the same. As long as you use the prefix "Christmas" or "holiday" you can pretty much choose any word and a film will show up. Try it!'

'Umm, okay. *Christmas Grope*.'

'Elle!'

But, despite Elle's attempts to defeat the system, the words 'Hope at Christmas' appeared, accompanied by an image of a couple standing in front of a Christmas tree fashioned from a huge stack of books. The woman was wearing a deep red winter coat, while the man sported one in a dark shade of green. They looked disconcertingly alike.

'That'll do nicely,' I said. 'Right, first, we need stronger alcohol.'

'This is getting better and better.' Elle placed a bottle of artisan sloe gin on the table and two glasses.

'Ooh, classy. Right, then. This is not only a film. It's a game. I've taken the liberty of creating some accompanying viewing notes.'

'Are you going to test me afterwards or something?'

'Not this time. Here's your worksheet. And here's your pen.'

'Only you would bring a selection of stationery to a girly night in.'

'I mean business. Because tonight, Elle, we're playing: Christmas movie bingo!'

'I've not seen you this excited about watching something since they announced the first "late night" *Hollyoaks*. I'm definitely going to need more information to go on.'

'Of course. You see, every single one of these American made-for-TV festive films follows an almost identical formula. There'll be a single woman in her thirties with a successful career who ends up in a picture-perfect small town for some convoluted reason. She'll fall in love with a warm-hearted chiselled chap while she's there and jack in her job to start a new life with him.'

'Jesus, Mally. I knew you loved all the Christmas classics but I had no idea you'd descended into the realm of TV movies. Surely there are better ways to spend your time?'

Not everyone's living their perfect life, Elle. But I didn't let my face give away my feelings.

'Life's about balance! Are you seriously telling me you've never watched any of these films before?'

'Not knowingly, no.'

Unlike me, Elle had never been the type of person to laze about watching shows like *Homes Under the Hammer* and *Say Yes to the Dress* for hours on end, so it didn't surprise me that she hadn't ever stumbled across these weirdly addictive movies on wintry weekend afternoons.

'It doesn't matter,' I continued. 'So, whenever one of the tropes on your sheets happens you a) tick it off and b) drink a finger of your alcoholic beverage.'

'Okay, I'll humour you. So let me get my head around my list.'

Christmas movie bingo! Elle's card

- Fake snow
- Reconnecting with the past
- A man and a woman wearing red and green
- Cosy fire
- Christmas concert
- Story opens in city
- Annoying best friend
- Baked goods
- Unexpected reunion
- Decorating a Christmas tree
- Small-town guy is secretly talented
- Awkward farewell
- Festive-themed contest
- Relatable klutz
- The actress Lacey Chabert
- 'Inn' or 'lodge'
- The lure of Manhattan

- A festive freebie
- Seeing someone in a new light
- Bad news piles up

Christmas movie bingo! Mally's card

- Solo Christmas ahead
- Steaming mug of delicious cocoa
- Car drama
- Festive train journey
- Sentimental item from childhood
- Little white lie
- A hasty departure
- Failing family business
- Character confronts loss
- Old family home
- A Christmas wish
- Near-miss kiss
- Creativity rediscovered
- Small-town guy falls for big-city woman
- A cold house
- Outsider saves the day
- Local scoundrel
- Coming together to solve a problem
- Mistaken identity
- New year ahead, new life ahead

She glanced at the lists and looked at me as if I was someone who'd turned up at her doorstep asking if she wanted to buy any seafood from the back of a van.

'You're saying all these things are going to happen, regardless of what film we watch?'

'Most of them, yeah! Wanna know my favourite tropes?'

'Sure…?'

I looked down each list to refresh my memory.

'Ooh, "festive train journey" is a good one. My favourite one of these films has a magical train that takes a career-focused woman back in time to her hometown so she has another chance with the one who got away. I also love seeing how the filmmakers attempt to make a warm summer's day look like a nippy winter's one with whatever fake snow they can muster.'

'Right… and what's with everyone wearing red and green?'

'Everyone wears red and green, constantly! Just wait! Oh, and "near-miss kiss" is practically guaranteed in every film. They're about to snog and then a reindeer farts or something, and they jump apart.'

'Can't wait for the farting festive creatures.'

'Elle, c'mon, it'll be fun!'

'What's my motivation, here? What do I win with a full house?'

'*This.*'

I reached into my backpack at the side of the sofa and thrust a faded miniature trophy in her direction.

'Oh my God, Mally, is that your… Year Nine PE effort award?'

'It is! I was clearing out some cupboards the other day and found it languishing at the bottom of a box. It's still the only thing I've ever won.'

'Ha! I remember your maroon face when you had to get up on that stage to accept it and you made that ridiculous speech.'

Given that a microphone had been stuck into my teenage hand with zero warning, I'd thought my brief remarks at the time – 'Here's to trying – and failing' – had been pretty witty. Embarrassingly, only one guffawing but unknown pupil in the otherwise silent audience had agreed with me.

'It was honestly one of the most hilarious things I've ever witnessed,' Elle said, inspecting the statuette. 'But the trophy's actually nicer than I remember. Let's play.'

Eighty-four minutes later, the credits began to roll.

'Well, that ended suddenly. Er, Mally, are you crying?'

I was. I dabbed at my eyes with one of the frustratingly unabsorbent takeaway napkins.

'I can't help it! I could binge-watch these films all night, even though I know exactly what's going to happen. It's probably what I'll end up doing when I spend Christmas alone this year.'

Elle grinned and reached for her notepad and pen, but stopped mid-action.

'Oh my God, Mally. This is it!'

'This is what?'

'This is the feature that's been waiting for you!'

Whatever she was thinking, I could pretty much guarantee she was wrong.

'I have no idea what you're talking about.'

'Okay, hear me out. You're a successful, big-city career woman. You're single and, as recent events with a certain Billy-the-bastard have proven, unlucky in love…'

'Ouch.'

'Sorry, but it's true. And I – your ever-so-slightly annoying best friend and kind-of boss – am about to send you off on an absurd Christmas assignment!'

She began writing frantically in her notepad. She finished with a flourish and a dramatic full stop.

'Honestly, Mally, this is brilliant. Here's what I have in mind: I book you a cute little cottage out in the sticks in the run-up to Christmas…'

I had no idea where this was going. But I detected danger.

'…I can expense the accommodation and you can take these bingo sheets and try and tick off as many tropes as you can manage in real life. And, best of all, you can write me an amazing feature all about your awkward English attempt to recreate the plot of a cheesy Christmas movie!'

Why did this always happen? All I wanted from tonight was to be consoled and plied with food and alcohol to try and distract me from my pathetic man-related misery. Yet right now I was feeling less at ease than I had been ever since Billy – and Livvie's email account – had ghosted me.

'This is the worst idea I've heard in quite some time. How strong *is* this sloe gin?'

I busied myself with the pretence of reading the label, my quickening heartbeat pounding in my ears.

'I'm serious, Mally. This could be a really fun feature. You could befriend some of the locals and find out what ridiculous regional traditions they insist on holding on to at this time of year. You might even stumble across one of those "winter wonderland" immersive experiences that always end up being hilariously underwhelming.'

I tried to swallow the lump of anxiety in my throat while I put the bottle back on the table among our bingo sheets and shot glasses. Elle had won the trophy, having ticked off almost all her tropes.

'Yeah, it's a great idea for a feature,' I said, keen to let her down gently. 'And I'd love to read it. But – and please don't hate me – I just don't think I'm the best person to *write* it. You know what I was like back when I tried journalism during our student newspaper days: I couldn't even pick up the phone, let alone conduct an interview.'

And Elle should remember this. While she'd always relished being the student paper's centre-of-attention music editor, I'd ended up as a desk-bound subeditor so I didn't have to risk making an idiot of myself in front of important people. All people, in fact. Plus, the thought of talking to well-meaning strangers only to send them up in a wry feature taking the piss out of the place they called home sounded, well, more than just a little bit cruel.

'And this is all why it'll make such a brilliant piece!' Elle said. 'Think about how you're feeling right now: you're cynical and full of doubts. You're resenting me for even suggesting such a ludicrous idea. Know who you remind me of? Hotshot advertising executive Sydney at the start of *Hope at Christmas* before she went back to Hopewell and discovered that box of ornaments at her dead grandma's home she'd just inherited!'

Yeah, but Sydney was a beautiful, confident, independent mum who had everything going for her. That description couldn't be any further away from my own existence.

'I'm impressed you remembered her name,' I said.

'What can I say, I enjoyed her character arc. I mean, who *wouldn't* turn down that once-in-a-lifetime Manhattan job for the sake of a puppy-eyed English teacher, who she *also* discovered was a secret world-renowned novelist? Seriously, though, you're the perfect person to write this, Mally. You *know* you are. You're even planning to spend Christmas alone.'

'I'd rather be home alone than in some random town, Elle.'

She waved a hand dismissively and continued talking. Her mind was made up, wasn't it? 'You already have an encyclopaedic knowledge of Christmas movies, and... well...'

'"Well" what?'

Elle put down her pen, turned to face me and placed her hands on my shoulders. 'How to say this without coming across as a total bitch...'

'That's never stopped you before, pal.'

'Fair. So... you're stuck in a massive rut and it's stressing me the fuck out.'

I braced myself for the onslaught to continue, as it always did.

'You've been at *The Helix* for, like, nearly ten years now?'

I nodded.

'And in that time, you've not gone for a single promotion or asked for any kind of pay rise?'

'I'm happy with my salary, and the annual incremental increases are pretty...'

Elle removed her hands from my shoulders, scrunched up her face and knocked her balled-up fists against her head a few times.

'Mally! Just, stop! Okay, I'm going to be honest with you here, and this information cannot – leave – this – room: Kyle called a crisis editorial meeting earlier this week.'

'Oh. Right. Shit.'

'Yeah. Our readership figures are dropping. Fast. The US team thinks we've reached peak irony and our audience is bored. They want fresh perspectives. Authenticity over eyerolls. Stories with heart that we can syndicate to other media outlets for extra revenue. And Kyle has told me that I'm one of the people who has to find all of that. Reading between the lines, I get the impression he's desperate to turn things around and justify his position as editor-in-chief.'

Kyle had been a surprise hire from *The Helix*'s primary UK rival about six months ago. He and Elle didn't have the greatest working relationship given that Elle had had her eye on a promotion before Kyle was parachuted in without so much as a cursory job interview. In truth, Elle *still* had her eye on the role.

'You don't think this is related to the extra week off in December, do you?' I asked.

'I do, yeah. And, seriously, you cannot tell anybody this, but I think jobs are on the line. Lots of jobs. In fact, a skeleton editorial team might be the only thing that survives.'

'Fuck.'

'Yeah. Fuck. So, you can see why putting yourself out there now could be a wise move for you, right?'

'I honestly had no idea things were this bad.'

'They're bad, all right. The editorial team's practically climbing over each other to prove they can create viral content. But, as Kyle reminded us this week, so far our December traffic is even worse than normal. Apparently we're in desperate need of "festive feels with a *Helix* twist".'

She pretended to be sick. Yet my own nausea was very much genuine. Not only was I at an ever-growing risk of having to write this feature for her, but my job security was plummeting by the minute. I made a mental note to dig out my CV this weekend.

'Can you now see why I'm basically begging you to do this, for both of us? I know it's totally out of your comfort zone, but I wouldn't ask if I wasn't absolutely on my knees here to try and save our jobs. Every original voice and fun idea I can commission at the moment will really help to keep Kyle off my back – especially if it's got a Christmas angle. And if you make enough of a mark, there's a chance I could make you a permanent part of the features team.'

I took a long sip of my sloe gin, giving Elle's tirade the chance to settle in my bloodstream alongside the growing concentration of alcohol. Did I want to become 'a permanent member of the features team'? No. But did I have any other employment prospects or professional connections whatsoever that I could fall back on in this horrendous job market? Also no. As much as I hated to admit it, writing this article would – at the very least – help to keep my options open if the shit did indeed end up hitting the fan.

'Jesus, this is a lot to get my head around. Okay, so say I agree to do this – which I haven't, by the way. What if I didn't strike the right tone? All your usual writers would put some witty spin on all of this. But going somewhere new would be a big deal for me. And I'd feel really uneasy putting my name to something that could end up hurting the people who actually lived there.'

I drained the rest of my drink, watching Elle as she turned something over in her mind.

'I reckon we can work around that.'

'How?'

'We won't name the town. Thinking about it, we could even come up with a fictional name to add an element of mystery. And you can change the names of anyone you happen to encounter to protect their privacy.'

'Hmm.'

'And, if it was the dealbreaker, you could even write the piece anonymously. Come to think of it, all these secretive elements might even make it more compelling and shareable as readers try and figure out what small town we visited.'

'You're not going to let me say no, are you?'

'Probably not. But, c'mon: what else are you going to do with all this time off work before Christmas? I really think you can do this, Mally. Even if you won't do it for yourself, will you do it for me? Please?'

I blew out the air from my lungs while pouring myself another extra-large measure. I downed it in one go, so I could at least later pretend I'd agreed under the influence of too much booze.

'Fine. But those anonymity conditions are non-negotiable, okay?'

Elle squealed and bundled me into a tight hug. Uncomfortably tight.

'Thank you, thank you, thank you! This is going to be so much fun to organise! Right, first of all we need to figure out where I can send you. Does anywhere spring to mind?'

'Nah, not really.'

But I wasn't telling the truth. Because, if I was the leading lady in a made-for-TV Christmas movie, the obvious place for me to go to would be my hometown: Scarnbrook, a sprawling village on the very furthest outskirts of Bristol, where Elle and I had grown up. Despite the painful memories it held, I'd been thinking about my hometown more than ever this year, since it was the twentieth anniversary of What Happened – not that anyone had bothered to acknowledge it. And, now that the digital connection I'd had with Livvie had been unceremoniously severed by a faceless Silicon Valley algorithm, it suddenly felt as if Scarnbrook might be the only thing I had left of her.

But I knew that sharing this ice chip of an idea before it had fully taken shape would backfire. Elle would quickly melt it with a blast of hot air, just like she'd done with all my other attempts to suggest a trip there in recent years. She'd always insisted I wasn't 'ready' to return after what happened back then. My family had always made it abundantly clear through their actions, as well as their total absence of words, that they had no desire to show their faces there again. And Elle herself no longer had a reason to go back, since her mum had moved out of the area a couple of years ago. As far as Elle was concerned, Scarnbrook was a mere footnote to the ever-growing tome of her exciting life. Whereas for me it was the formative prologue and opening chapters.

Was I ready to return now? Yeah, probably not. But I reckoned it was more or less impossible to ever be 'ready' to go back to the place I'd been so happy for the first eighteen years of my life, before my sister died, my family dispersed and everything changed.

I rolled the notion around in my head while Elle yabbered on. The longer I did so, the more frozen matter it collected that hadn't seen the light of day for years. By the time I turned in for the night, drunk and apprehensive about what the hell I'd agreed to, the idea was no longer an ice chip, but a snowball-sized plan.

The question was, would I ever be brave enough to throw it?

Chapter 4

☑ **Sentimental item from childhood**

Frannie was an early riser, and I was a light sleeper, so a lie-in at Elle's was never an option. But, hey, that's what Saturday afternoon naps were for.

I lay in bed for a while, checking my work emails to see if there'd been any developments on 'all-staff-email-gate' since yesterday (there hadn't), before pulling my clothes on, having a major falling-out with the ridiculously unfoldable futon in their home office box room and making my way down to the kitchen. As expected, Elle was nowhere to be seen – Saturdays were her lie-in days and Rory got Sundays. Though looking at Rory's hungover pallor as he attempted to coax Frannie to eat her gluey Ready Brek, I was surprised he hadn't managed to negotiate a swap this weekend.

'Morning, little one. Oh, and Frannie,' I said, with perfect comedic timing. Dad humour is the best humour.

Rory groaned at the classic gag. 'Very funny, Auntie Mally. Say good morning, Fran.'

'Nor-nin, Nally!'

'Big night, then?' I asked.

'Ha. You could say that.'

'What time did you get in?'

'Only a few hours ago. We haven't woken you, have we?'

'Nah, you're good. So where did you go?'

'Oh God, it was this awful bar near the hospital. The food was dire. Honestly, come and look at this.' Rory unlocked his phone and opened up his photo gallery, swiping to the relevant image.

'What am I looking at here? The only thing that's even vaguely recognisable is a plate.'

'Believe it or not, Mally, residing upon said plate is – allegedly – Christmas pudding.' Rory's face had turned worryingly green.

'I'm sorry – what?!'

I looked at the image again – the pudding resembled an ungenerous slice of malt loaf that had been drizzled with watered-down salad cream, and then punched by a very large fist.

'Did you *eat it*?'

'Course not. *Look at it!* Honestly, though, the whole night was a total shambles. We had no choice but to drink our way through it.'

'Sometimes it's the only way. I'll get some coffee on.'

'Mally, you fucking—' Rory glanced down at Frannie and exaggeratedly clapped his hand to his mouth. She giggled. 'I mean *flipping* legend. Yes, please. I swear you know your way around this kitchen better than I do. You'll stay for breakfast?'

'Ah, thanks, but once this caffeine's coursing through my veins I'm going to head off and grab something en route.' A perfect 3D image of a Greggs Steak Bake popped into my head, spinning seductively to show me every greasy, oozing angle of deliciousness. I reluctantly dismissed the meaty mirage: there was an unacceptable absence of a conveniently located Greggs branch between here and my flat.

'Hey, Mally.' Rory glanced at the kitchen door behind me and lowered his tone before continuing. 'I wondered if Elle's said anything to you about this stuff going on at work?'

'Well, just a little. But I probably know as much as you do, to be honest.'

'Which is…?'

'Oh, just that – like the whole online media industry, really – we need more clicks and more revenue. Same old story.'

'Cool. And, er, she hasn't mentioned anything else to you that's on her mind?'

I knew better than to mention the pending office closure. Rory had always been a natural worrier and I knew Elle would tell him what he needed to know and when.

'Like what?'

'Oh, nothing in particular. She just seems extra-stressed at the moment and I know she sometimes confides in you.'

'Nope, all good.'

His shoulders slumped a little. He knew something was up, deep down.

'Right, I'd better be off. See ya, munchkin,' I said to Frannie, taking a gulp of my coffee before kissing the top of her head.

'Do you have your baby, Auntie Nally?'

Rory's brow contracted in confusion. 'Baby? Is there some news you'd care to share with me?'

I reached into my coat pocket and showed him a clump of moss she'd proudly handed me when Elle and I had picked her up from nursery the evening before. I winked at Rory before crouching down to conspire with my goddaughter.

'Of course I do, poppet! I'm going to take him back to my place and find a lovely cosy spot for him. I'll send your mummy a photo later so you can see his new home.'

'Yay! Look, Daddy, Nally has a baby!'

I chuckled, but her words cut deep. Let's be honest, taking care of this crumbly green lump would probably be the closest I'd ever get to starting my own family.

The journey from Bounds Green in North London to Hither Green in the south-east of the capital was rarely a straightforward one on weekends. With various Tubes and trains to contend with, engineering works could easily scupper the entire trip.

As my final mode of transportation pulled into Hither Green station – thankfully not a rail replacement bus this time around – I was reminded how at ease I always felt in this village-esque pocket of the borough of Lewisham. Especially at this time of year, when the community-funded Christmas tree greeted me at the bottom of the station ramp, its branches proudly bearing the colourful, laminated handiwork of the local schoolchildren.

As I wandered past the ranks of independent stores, I admired their festive window displays, breathing in the comforting scent of mulled wine wafting from the pub on the corner. In the many years since I'd lived here, the pubs had gradually all been renovated and gastronomised, the greasy spoons and old-school carpet shops giving way to craft beer bars and brunchy cafes. Shame, really – I missed my weekly full English breakfast with fried slice. Almost all the rat-run residential streets were now cordoned off with bollards that the local residents' association had transformed into well-maintained planters as part of the local council's 'low-traffic neighbourhood' scheme. Property prices had soared accordingly. These days, there'd be no way people like me would be able to afford to live in this pleasant Zone 3 conservation area – which was practically gated off from the surrounding A-roads – if they were trying to get on the property ladder as I'd done all those years ago. In fact, the only reason I'd been able to get a mortgage back then was thanks to the credit crunch, an unexpected inheritance from my grampy and the guaranteed rental income from Elle as my lodger. Elle still treated my place like her second home, letting herself in every so often with the set of keys she still had.

I entered the draughty communal hallway, which I shared with the flat upstairs. Their enormous running stroller always took up most of the space to save them lugging it up the staircase to the first floor of our converted Victorian terrace. I glanced down and spied two little be-wellied feet poking out of the buggy's blackout blanket: often Sophie or Kay had to walk or jog little Oscar around the nearby Manor House Gardens to get him to nap. Then they'd park him at the foot of the stairs with their flat door open, one of them perched on the stairs to keep an eye on him.

I bent my head down low enough to see who'd drawn the short straw today and mouthed 'Hi' to Sophie, who looked up from her phone and smiled through her obvious exhaustion and waved back silently. I'd been trying to pluck up the courage to speak to them about the increasingly loud pre-dawn noises that woke me up every morning – at the very least a rug on the wooden floors would absorb some of Oscar's toy-throwing antics – but I figured they already had enough on their plate without having to factor in a fussy downstairs neighbour.

I let myself into my flat as quietly as possible, which wasn't easy given the stiffness of my ancient lock. I'd been meaning to get it replaced for a while now, but the prices I'd been quoted had been ridiculous. If only the hardware shop on the corner of my street was still there. They used to stock everything – from rat poison to rat food – and they would've popped up the road and replaced my lock in a jiffy for next to nothing. But these days the shop was a high-end 'concept store' where every 'carefully curated' item of clothing and homeware appeared to have had its saturation colour level dialled right down until it was almost – but not quite – greyscale. I'd only been in there once, but had swiftly left when one of the owners had flared her nostrils in the direction of the bottle of 7UP I'd been swigging from at the time.

I headed straight for the mantelpiece in the living room to open today's advent calendar window.

Mum still sent me a calendar every December, though she'd stopped sending them to Josh a few years back after he'd taken her aside to 'impart his wisdom' about single-use plastic and the plight of the world's cocoa farmers. But she knew my weakness for anything that contained that heady mix of chocolate and countdowns, so they'd kept on coming.

I peeled back the sixth cardboard door of the *Doctor Who*-themed calendar and dug through the foil to reveal a Dalek-shaped milk chocolate treat. As it melted on my tongue, I wondered whether anyone had ever thought about developing a Dalek-shaped ice lolly. I subconsciously composed a message to Livvie in my mind:

Idea: Dalek-shaped ice lolly called 'Dalick'.
Or maybe 'Licksterminate'. Preference?

I pierced the pointless thought as I kicked off my boots and dumped my coat on the bed of the spare room, carefully removing the moss from my pocket before I did so. I'd been thinking about converting Elle's old bedroom into a fancy living room ever since she'd moved out when she and Rory got engaged. It was the largest room in the flat – square and light with a stunning original fireplace and beautiful bay window.

But everything was still as it was after Elle had gone, meaning it remained a functional two-bedroom flat rather than the amazing one-bedroom property it had the potential to be. Projects like this, which would undoubtedly involve making countless decisions and changes, always sent me into a tailspin. Over the years, I'd managed to convince myself that having a spare room had handy dumping ground, storage and washing-drying benefits, as well as serving as an actual spare bedroom on the rare occasions my parents came to stay. It was easier to just shut the door on the mess and keep the flat the same as it'd always been.

I carried the moss past my much-smaller double room, which was sandwiched in between the spare room and the bathroom, right in the middle of the property. It always felt safe and snug in there, like my own little nest. The long and low window looked out over the flat's narrow, concrete side return, which led to my measly patch of grass and rotting garden shed / spider sanctuary at the end. Mum always tried her best to whip the garden into shape whenever she was here, but she was fighting a losing battle. It was fair to say that I hadn't inherited her horticultural instincts at all. It wasn't exactly an inspiring view out of my bedroom, unlike the one I'd had in Scarnbrook while growing up, but it was private and the room wasn't overlooked from any direction, thanks to the busy railway line that bumped up directly against the garden.

The living space was at the back of the flat — an awkwardly shaped room that somehow managed to house a kitchen, sitting and dining area. Even though it was creaky, tired and rough around the edges, this was the room that had grabbed my heart back when we'd first viewed the flat all those years ago. While Elle had always had designs on the front bedroom, it was this dark and enclosed living space, with original stripped floorboards, bare-bricked chimney breast housing a woodburning stove and shelves creaking with the previous owners' books and trailing succulents that immediately made the flat seem like a place I could feel comfortable in.

I made an offer straight after our first viewing. At Elle's insistence, it'd been a cheeky one since the financial crisis had suddenly put buyers like me on the front foot. She'd coerced the estate agent into letting slip that the owners were desperate to move to secure their dream countryside project, and I'd ended up getting a bit of a bargain by today's London property standards.

I removed a saucer from a kitchen cupboard and placed it on a shelf among some neglected house plants and creased-spined books. I laid the moss on the plate and put a small, torn square of kitchen roll over half of it, as if it was tucked up in bed. I took a photo of it and sent it to Elle.

Mally:
For Frannie (she'll understand). Thanks for a fun night. Might see you in the office on Monday x

Elle (voice message):
Ha, she loves it! Best godmum ever. Oh, and don't think I was too drunk last night to remember about your Christmas movie article. I've had some more ideas so I'll find you on Monday to talk it over. Argh it's so exciting!

Maybe there were some people who found Elle's fondness for sending voice messages endearing, but I wasn't one of them. Especially when she was sharing vital logistical information and I had to listen to them over and over again, always knowing they could disappear at any moment due to her tendency to randomly delete them, too.

I'd been hoping that all that gin-induced chat about me writing this feature would've been forgotten. But who was I kidding? This was Elle. When it came to her ideas and plans, she never let them go until they became a reality.

I needed to chew over this some more. I decided that physical chewing would help.

I plonked myself on the sofa with a big bowl of Weetos – delighted it was the end of the pack, which meant I got the bonus addition of the extra-sweet cereal dust – and stuck *Saturday Kitchen* on. I rolled my eyes as an antler-wearing TV chef served up a plate of raw scrambled eggs under the pretence of having cooked a speedy omelette in order to have their face slapped onto a meaningless leaderboard.

I aimlessly flicked through the channels until I landed midway through a Christmas movie on Channel 5, as I'd known I would. My whole body relaxed as I stretched out on the sofa, balanced the bowl of cereal on a cushion and settled in for forty-five minutes or so of safe storytelling. According to the TV guide, this one was called *Christmas Wonderland* and it was about a budding artist who'd put her creative dreams on hold for the sake of a glittering career in the city. I watched with renewed interest as the protagonist told repeated lies to her horrible boss so she could return to her hometown for some emergency babysitting, only to bump into her high-school ex.

I had no high-school ex, but as the rest of the film played out exactly in line with my bingo sheets, it made me think more about the possibility of returning to Scarnbrook.

Scarnbrook. Even the silent utterance of the word in my mind seemed slightly foreign and unreal, as if it had faded from my vocabulary over the last two decades and I had to teach myself how to get my mouth around it again.

My parents had cut all ties with the village since Livvie's death, and neither Josh nor I had had any obvious reason to return since her funeral. But I'd always missed the place I'd once called home, despite everything that had happened.

From the outset, Livvie had been the anomalous sibling. While never explicitly confirmed by our parents, her appearance three years after me was widely accepted to have been… unexpected. It was always as if she subconsciously knew this and applied it to every way she lived her life. She was absolutely determined to exist.

She'd been the total opposite to each and every one of us other Allisters. Even her colouring – her copper hair, bright blue eyes and dusting of freckles over her pale skin – had seemingly come out of nowhere. Mum eventually tracked it back to some ginger-bearded great-uncle on her side.

Whatever kind of ease each of us had established before her arrival, she totally disrupted. Where my mum was conflict-averse and fastidiously tidy, my sister was contrary and seemed to thrive among mess and chaos. Where my dad was numbers- and details-oriented, my sister lived for big ideas and zany projects. Where my brother was athletic and unshakably serious, she was unabashedly clumsy and an emotional open book. And where I was dry-humoured yet ultimately rule-abiding, she was completely fearless, actively seeking out extravagant ways to draw attention to her musical talent and whimsical nature.

Despite her endless schemes, everybody – and I mean *everybody* – loved her. From the moment she was born, she slowly but surely pulled each of us out of ourselves. I could talk to her about anything; with full faith I could trust her with all my secrets big (like my huge, out-of-character crush on the most popular boy in school that even Elle had never known about) and weird (like my irrational fear of the *Thomas the Tank Engine* theme tune). Me, Livvie and Josh had always looked out for each other. Mum and Dad were thrilled at the wholesome dynamic of their offspring, as they could trust us to stay at home by ourselves once Josh was a fully-fledged teenager without having to find babysitters to keep up with their active roles in the community.

Livvie had truly been the glue that bonded each of our relationships with each other together. Especially the one between me and Josh, which had always been a bit strained. That's why the two years after Josh left home for university, even though he was only twenty-five minutes up the road at the University of the West of England, were practically the happiest years of my life. Just me and Livvie, loafing about at home after school every day, while Mum and Dad were busy with their own jobs and social lives.

Livvie was the beating heart of our family. It was impossible not to be tugged towards her spirit and love of life. There was no doubt in my mind that she'd do something significant with her talents, most likely through the cello that she loved playing so much, and that – regardless of whatever she did with her life and wherever she ended up – Scarnbrook wouldn't forget Livvie Allister in a hurry.

And, well, it never did – for all the wrong reasons. Because Livvie's departure was as unexpected as her arrival.

But thinking about that stuff – let alone talking about it – was instinctively out of bounds. I blinked away my tears and opened up my coffee-table drawer to retrieve my Christmas movie notebook. I added the details of the film that had just ended, along with the one I'd watched with Elle last night. I'd watched twenty-nine of them last December, and it was my intention to beat that figure this year.

After I'd tallied up my latest viewing total, I decided I might as well put up my Christmas tree. These days, 'putting up the tree' was a pretty depressing affair. It involved retrieving my miniature fibre-optic spruce from its tatty box, bending the bristly wires into vaguely branch-like positions and shoving it on top of the space-saving dining table in the corner of my living room, which was permanently folded away into its smallest position these days. As my outstretched hand scrabbled about under my bed for the box in question, it landed on another box, instead – the one that had housed my PE effort award for all those years.

It was the kind of box that had moved around with me ever since I'd left Scarnbrook, shoved into the corners of understairs cupboards alongside the never-used steam cleaner that had been bought on a wine-induced whim after watching soothing late-night infomercials. I wrapped myself in my dressing gown, sat on the floor and dragged it over to have another rifle of its contents. It was a hodge-podge collection of late-nineties tweenage memorabilia that my parents had hastily scooped up from my bedroom when they'd moved out of our Scarnbrook home not long after Livvie's funeral.

Among yellowed Point Horror and Sweet Valley High books, a bottle of Exclamation perfume ('make a statement without saying a word!'), chipped ornaments from family holidays to the Balearics and a sealed sandwich bag of shrivelled bath pearls, I discovered an old snow globe. I gave it a little shake and watched as the artificial flakes drifted downwards through the murkiness of the yellowing glass. I could just about make out Tower Bridge nestling amidst the floating glitter. Annoyingly, it played a plinky-plonky version of 'London Bridge is Falling Down' when you twisted its crank. The mismatching of the iconic landmark with a song that related to a completely different bridge grated, but the tune did bring back memories of a December trip to London to visit

Auntie Sandra back when we were kids. She'd taken the three of us to Hamleys and had let us choose anything we wanted for our Christmas presents, which had basically been the best moment of our lives up until that point.

Not wanting to take advantage, I'd selected the modest snow globe as a nice memento of a happy winter weekend. Typically, Livvie had absolutely taken advantage and – much to my parents' dismay – had chosen one of those giant floor pianos, as popularised by the film *Big*. The only room large enough for it at home had been the garage. She used to spend hours in there, running up and down the light-up keys in a surprisingly tuneful way. I had no idea what had happened to it when they decided to sell up. From what I remembered, Josh had chosen a Formula One quiz book.

I carried the dusty snow globe into the living room and put it on the mantelpiece, hoping it might add an extra element of festive magic to the place. Nope.

I returned to my room and unscrewed the lid of an ancient kiwi fruit lip balm from The Body Shop. I took a big sniff, the familiar but long-forgotten aroma immediately transporting me back to school corridors and dashing through the gauntlet of communal showers after PE. Teenage sleepovers and hours-long phone calls behind the curtain in the dining room, fingers occupied by a curly cord. Friendship dramas – usually with Elle at the heart of them – and Tom Brinton. Ah, Tom Brinton – the cool boy a quiet girl like me should never have had a crush on, but absolutely did.

It's fair to say I'd been pretty smitten with Tom Brinton for almost the entirety of my time at Scarnbrook Community School. Even today, I still dreamt about a fictionalised adult version of him every so often, which was testament to the depth of my formative crush.

I screwed the lid back onto the ancient lip balm, amazed at the flurry of memories a simple sniff had triggered. I was surprised at how many of them were happy ones.

I placed the pot in my dressing-gown pocket and climbed up onto my bed, wrapping myself in the covers as more and more memories broke through the surface. I thought about the last normal time I'd been in Scarnbrook: I'd been in the car with my dad on a drizzly September morning, with a kettle on my lap and a boot full of clothes and crockery, on my way to Cardiff, my mum crying as she faded into the distance in the rear-view mirror. I remembered having to push down the emotional bubble in my own teenage throat. Because, the truth was, I'd never wanted to move away. I'd have been perfectly happy to stay in Scarnbrook for the rest of my life, just as my parents had intended to do themselves. But Elle had convinced me that three short years at a university just forty-five minutes up the M5 wouldn't do any harm, so off I went. Little did I know that I was unwittingly severing my bond with Scarnbrook forever.

Because the next and most recent time I'd been in Scarnbrook, Livvie was gone and everything had changed. And instead of arriving in a place where I'd always felt nothing but ease and comfort, I returned to find nothing but a raw atmosphere of sickening shock that had pervaded the entire village.

I unscrewed the lip-balm lid once more and took another inhale from my horizontal position, trying to disperse the sad memories with the ancient fragrance. When it came to writing this article, I had no idea what to do for the best – and I was annoyed at myself for even considering the possibility of going back to Scarnbrook. All this pain was in the past. Wasn't that where it belonged?

Chapter 5

☑ **Baked goods**

I was right: Josh's wife, Saskia, declined Mum's invitation to Sunday lunch, so it would be just the four of us at my parents' place that day. It was a shame I didn't know my sister-in-law better – or at all, truth be told. My reluctance to wade into the world of social media – around which Saskia's life appeared to revolve – no doubt meant that establishing any kind of relationship with her was a non-starter. But, from what Elle relayed to me about Saskia's online influencing exploits, it wasn't as if we had anything in common, anyway.

It'd taken me ages to figure out what to wear for the occasion; Josh always had something to say about fast fashion and how capitalism would be the death of us all. I mean, he probably wasn't wrong, but he was always so bloody preachy about it. And he didn't seem to mind that capitalism was working out pretty damn well for him and Saskia in their luxurious Chelsea apartment overlooking the River Thames.

Eventually, I settled on a pair of vintage dungarees over the top of one of Mum's old Sweater Shop turtle-necks, which I'd been thrilled to discover languishing at the back of her wardrobe last Christmas. I pulled on my go-to Clarks ankle boots, grabbed my coat and ran for the station.

The train pulled into Crowborough station where I was due to meet Dad for the final leg of the journey to their remote cottage. The house had once been Auntie Sandra's second home back when she'd still worked in finance, but they'd bought it from her for a knock-down price after everything that happened. They'd needed a fresh start.

As I waited in a short queue at the exit, I noticed a tall, familiar figure threading his paper ticket through the barrier a few people ahead of me. It was my brother, Josh, with a huge suitcase and various tote bags. I tapped him on the arm once I'd emerged out the other side.

'Hey! We must've been on the same train!'

He removed his earbuds and turned around, probably expecting to encounter one of his online followers, rather than his uninteresting younger sister.

'Oh, hi. What did you say? I was just listening to a cut of my latest podcast.'

Eww. He'd launched his *You Only Get One Body* podcast about a year ago as an offshoot to his burgeoning Instagram account. I'd managed to make it through about three minutes of the first episode before I'd had to switch off. Yes, I only had one body. And I was quite content for it to wobble and be filled with Wagon Wheels, thank you very much.

Looking at us side by side, you'd never put us together as siblings. He was the quintessential golden-boy, sporty type: blue-eyed, tall and muscular – while I was the quint-essential mousy, average type: murky-green-eyed, short and insulated by a layer of doughy softness that I never moved enough to shed. I liked to think of it as 'stored energy'. Sure, I might not be able to outrun the zombies, but I could hole up somewhere without withering away until the rapturous commotion had (hopefully!) passed.

After Livvie's funeral, Josh had thrown himself into his final year of studying sport and exercise science at university and, as the years went on, his body continued to harden – followed by his mind. I guessed it was only to be expected that, once Livvie had gone, mine and Josh's connection would suffer, but the gap between us had widened so far that, these days, it felt like Clayton / Eastwood Ravine with no way across. And the fact that I worked for what he described as 'a media outlet that purports to be progressive yet happily accepts advertising from brands who continuously exploit the earth's resources' only hindered my occasional efforts to construct a rickety bridge.

'I said, "we must have been on the same train".'

'Oh, right. Yeah, I guess so.'

'What's with all the luggage? Trouble in paradise?'

He looked at me and blinked slowly before turning his gaze back to the car park.

'I'm doing an intensive PT programme with a client nearby so I'm staying at Mum and Dad's for the week.'

'Gotta look fit for Santa!'

For a second I thought I saw him smile, but the expression vanished as quickly as it had appeared.

'It's an actor prepping for a role.'

As well as running his online training sessions, Josh also had a bunch of celebrity clients who he coached in person thanks to his high profile on social media.

'Ooh, can you say who it is?'

'You know I can't.'

Josh claimed to guard his clients' privacy with the utmost professionalism, but Elle reckoned he must offer discounts to those who tagged him in their social media workout humblebrags, since they were constantly doing so.

Josh put his earbuds back in. Charming. We stood in silence on the kerb of the collection bay. I scanned the car park, but couldn't pick out Dad's car among the drizzly sea of dark grey vehicles. It was unlike him to be late – he had countless train apps and always knew what time I'd arrive to the minute. He probably knew about any impending delays before the train driver did.

'Can't see Dad's car, can you?' I asked, in an attempt to jump-start another conversation.

Josh sighed and removed a single earbud.

'Can you see Dad's car?' I repeated.

'Nope.'

'So, how's Saskia?'

'She's fine.'

'Why couldn't she come?'

'Some work stuff.'

By 'work stuff' I could only presume she was working on her latest TikTok by contorting her ridiculously flexible body into letters to spell out a generic wellness statement to a trending remix of 'Lifted' by Lighthouse Family. Elle – who hate-followed Saskia on Instagram and kept me in the loop of the main developments of her and my brother's increasingly public life – had deduced her influencing niche existed at the intersection of veganism, yoga and mental health. What a Venn diagram that was.

Mind you, it was better than Josh's. He was also something of a 'wellness influencer' these days, with upwards of 500,000 followers. The trouble was that, alongside promoting plant-based smoothie subscriptions and his virtual strength-training programme, his content seemed to be gradually mutating into anti-science nutribollocks – all under the guise of promoting natural alternatives, individual choice and 'holding authority to account'.

Although Josh had never confirmed it, Elle and I were pretty sure that he and Saskia had met through social media. It was all too easy to imagine them sliding into each other's DMs, swapping meat-free sweet nothings and mutually cooing over their combined following of almost a million.

'It's a shame she couldn't come. I don't think I've seen her since your wedding.'

Silence from Josh. For once, I was relieved it was raining, as the sound of it drumming on the tin roof above us gave my ears something to focus on. I didn't know why I even bothered to instigate chitchat with him these days. It was like trying to converse with a traffic cone – albeit a six foot two traffic cone with its own range of personalised eco-merch.

Dad arrived a couple of minutes later to fill the conversation vacuum. He swung into the collection bay and wound down the passenger window.

'Ah, well, this all worked out, then. I was hoping the stars would align and I could do one journey instead of two. Come on, kiddos, climb in.'

I wondered how Dad would've felt if his own parents had referred to him as a 'kiddo' as he approached his fortieth year on the planet. Deep down, though, I liked the familiarity and warmth of the collective nickname. Even if one kiddo was missing.

I climbed into the back of the car through reflex. It's not like I needed the extra legroom.

'Still sticking with diesel, then?' Josh asked from the front passenger seat.

I could see my dad bristle in the wing mirror as he checked his blind spot and pulled away into the puddle-strewn road. He knew that Josh would say something like this, but it still wounded him every time it happened.

'Joshua, as you know, your mother and I don't go out very much or drive very far. This car really does have very few miles on the clock for its age, and if we sold it, its new owner would undoubtedly clock up more. Our carbon footprint really is as small as we can manage.'

'That's not stopping you from getting on a plane next week, though, is it? Did you read that article I sent you about aviation emissions yet?'

My body tensed to signal that my anti-conflict mode had activated.

'Please, Josh. We've literally just got in the car. Dad. How are you?' I asked, trying to inject as much chirpiness into my tone as possible.

'Very well thanks, love. Your mum's cooking us all a proper feast —'

Josh opened his mouth to interject but Dad knew it was coming.

'Yes, Joshua, all vegan, of course. That's why I'm three minutes late – your mum sent me on a mission to source a vegan Christmas pudding.'

Shit, shit, shit.

Dad's utterance of the C-word made me suddenly realise that this 'Sunday lunch' was effectively a substitute for a family festive gathering. I hadn't thought this through at all. Their gifts were all on order, but I'd brought nothing with me to give anyone, not even Christmas cards.

My pulse quickened as I racked my mind for a solution to my festive faux pas. I didn't have much time since the station was only a ten-minute drive away from their cottage. I looked across at the large canvas bag that Josh had placed on the backseat next to me and gently sifted through its contents as subtly as I could manage, grateful that Dad was filling the silence with his usual chat about temporary traffic lights, potholes and flooding hotspots. Josh had predictably segued the conversation to the climate emergency at the first mention of the word 'flood'. In his bag, underneath his crocheted scarf, I could definitely detect the presence of a modest selection of fabric-wrapped gifts and a couple of bottles of wine.

Argh, I hadn't even brought a sodding bottle.

'Yes, she's very much looking forward to seeing you both.'

The conversation was suddenly involving me again, so I removed my hand from the bag as speedily as I could while Dad tried to catch my eye in the rear-view mirror.

'Believe it or not it'll be the first time the four of us have been together since last Christmas.'

The realisation that we'd not spent any time together for practically a year compounded my daughterly guilt even further. I mean, I'd popped down for the odd weekend or two by myself in the last twelve months, but those trips had – quite deliberately – never coincided with Josh. It was easier for everyone that way.

Mum was waiting for us at the front door when we arrived, sporting her Alpine-themed pinny. The cottage was aglow with fairy lights in the dull late-morning light, and I felt a faint festive tingle spark up inside me.

'Come here, sweethearts.' She bundled us both into an awkward hug and Josh tensed up even further. He definitely wasn't the hugging type. He was barely the touching type.

'Let's get you inside, out of this horrible rain. It just hasn't let up, has it, Bob? I'll pop the kettle on so we can all have a cup of tea with some gingerbread men I've just taken out of the oven.'

My mouth moistened at the mere thought of Mum's legendary festive biscuits that she used to sell for charity every year in Scarnbrook. I took off my boots and hung up my damp jacket and scarf in the hallway above the scalding-hot cast-iron radiator.

'Josh!' I hissed, as he began following Mum through to the kitchen.

'Hmm?'

'I haven't brought any presents!'

He rolled his eyes. 'And you're telling me this because…?'

'Because it suddenly feels like this is effectively our family Christmas. Can we say one of your gifts is from me, too, just for today?'

'Sorry, won't work – Saskia got our gift tags made up by a contact who does customised calligraphy so your name will stick out like a sore thumb.'

I rolled my eyes and muttered 'Of course she did' under my breath.

'Listen, "Mally"…'

You could hear the inverted commas around my name as he said it.

'…you can think what you want about me but please leave Saskia out of it, okay? You know nothing about her.'

Yeah, and that was the problem. Since they'd got together a couple of years ago, I'd barely had a conversation with her. It was obvious she felt superior to us and had no intention of wasting her time getting to know her extended family. In fact, the first time I'd ever heard about Saskia was when they'd announced their engagement.

I sighed.

'Fine. Sorry. Can I at least have one of your bottles of wine to give them, then? Please? You know I wouldn't ask if I didn't feel so guilty about it.'

He thought for a few seconds before reaching a conclusion.

'Okay, hang on.' He took three bottles out of the bag one by one and inspected each label.

'Right, you can give them this one. But you'll need to pay me back for it. And it's not cheap.'

'Mum, this is really delicious. Where did you get this recipe from?'

Josh took a photo of his plate while asking the question and tapped his screen for a minute or so – audible keyboard clicks and all – before placing his phone back on the table. I assumed he'd cropped out the untouched – and unacknowledged – place at the table that Mum had set opposite him, as always. The presence of their best Portmeirion crockery – given to my parents when they got married – confirmed that this meal was indeed an early Christmas dinner.

'Oh, it was one from that cookbook you gave us last Christmas,' Mum replied.

Yeah, it was probably a gifted PR product – he'd given the same one to me.

'The Jamie Chops book? Nice. Yeah, his recipes are great. Top guy, too.'

'I forgot you knew him. Strange name, though – *Jamie Chops*,' Mum said.

Josh cast a glance at me as if to say, *Can you believe her?* but I had no idea what she'd said wrong this time. I furrowed my brow and shrugged.

'Mum, Jamie Chops isn't his name! I mean, his first name is Jamie, but his surname isn't Chops. It's "Jamie chops", as in, "Jamie chops vegetables". That's his user-name on Instagram and TikTok – Jamie, underscore, Chops.'

'Oh, I see. That does make more sense, I suppose.'

This was a classic Mum gaffe. A bit like the time she thought the chicken chasseur recipe had called for 3 *or* 4 pints of water, rather than 3/4 pint. She'd opted for four, and we'd ended up with enough (tasteless) sauce to feed the entirety of Scarnbrook.

I helped Mum carry the dishes into the small but perfectly formed country kitchen – complete with Aga, Welsh dresser and original flagstone floor – and started loading the dishwasher.

'Honestly, Amelia, you don't have to do that.'

A chill shot down my spine. I couldn't remember the last time someone had called me that. I'd never specifically told them that I'd chosen to go by Mally in an attempt to start afresh in London. But I'd never tried to hide it, either.

Elle had started calling me Mally – a mash-up of Milly and Allister – not long after she'd moved next door with her mum when her parents got messily divorced. My family and other friends at the time had been bemused by it, but the moniker had stuck. I used the name on all my greetings cards and had proudly given them my business card when I'd started working at *The Helix*, which bore the name Mally Allister above my job title. But if they'd ever had any questions about my decision, they'd never asked them. Not in front of me, anyway.

'It's fine, Mum, I'd like to help. It's a luxury being able to shove it all in a dishwasher, to be honest.'

'You've still not got that new kitchen, then?'

I'd been saving up for some indistinct 'renovations' since I bought the flat, but the very act of existing had been eating into my funds slowly but surely ever since Elle had moved out.

'Nah, the flat's still the same as when you and Dad last visited.'

Which must have been around eighteen months ago when they stayed at mine for Josh and Saskia's 'intimate and low-key' wedding they'd practically livestreamed on social media.

'You're still happy there?'

'Happy' was a bit strong. But... 'settled'? Sure.

'Yeah, although the baby upstairs has just started to walk and seems to enjoy jumping about above my head from about five o'clock each morning.'

'He won't be little forever, love.'

'I know.'

'And work's going well?'

I swallowed. Why were these chit-chatty interactions with Mum some of the hardest conversations I ever had?

Because you have to hold back so much.

'Everything's fine, Mum. Although Elle keeps saying I should be trying to push for a promotion.'

Mum sighed, but still didn't look up from the dishes. 'And is that what you want?'

'I mean, maybe? Why do you say it like that?'

Mum didn't answer immediately. She kept scrubbing the baking tray, which was caked in a layer of hardened polenta. The insides of my stomach could relate.

'I'd just love you to find your own way a bit, love, you know? Do something for yourself rather than doing whatever Elle wants you to do all the time. From what I remember, you didn't even want to work there in the first place.'

We'd had different versions of this conversation over the years. The worst of which had been when she'd discovered I'd turned down an offer to stay home and study English literature at Bristol University in favour of going to Cardiff with Elle.

Mum wasn't the shouting type. But she'd shouted at me, voice quivering, that day: 'You'll regret it, Amelia! One day you'll look back at this conversation and see that I was right.'

If only she knew just how much I regretted it, for all the reasons in the world. My plan had been to move straight back home after graduating, but by the time I'd left university, home no longer existed. Mum and Dad had sold the house, Josh had gone travelling and Elle had convinced me to move straight to London with her, where she'd secured an entry-level job at a teen magazine.

Armed with not much beyond my underwhelming 2:2 degree and some initial temping leads, I followed Elle to the Big Smoke – and I didn't even step foot in Scarnbrook on the way. The week of Livvie's funeral had been the last time I'd been there. Did I really want *that* to be the final time I'd ever visited the place that had once been so special to me?

I pushed the question back down, switching my mind back to Mum.

'I've done okay for myself, don't you think?'

'Of course, and you know how proud we are of you. But yours and Elle's paths do still seem to be very much… aligned, don't they?'

'It's just the way things worked out, I guess.'

She and Elle had never got along very well. It wasn't helped by the fact that she and Elle's mum had never clicked when the two of them had moved next door back in 2000. My parents had been really community-minded back then, but despite their repeated efforts to get Elle's mum involved in their endless social activities, she'd never accepted any of their invitations. Mum had never said as much, but it was obvious that she'd taken the rejection personally.

'It's fine, Mum. I've got a great job, I'm financially independent, I've got a foot on the property ladder unlike most of my generation. It's all good – you don't need to worry about me.'

Apart from the fact that I'm lonely as hell.

Mum finally turned to me, fixed her mouth in a straight smile and nodded. 'I know I don't. You've always been the steady one, haven't you?'

She dropped her gaze and turned away quickly, upping the speed at which she went at it with a scourer on the stubborn pan. I wanted to give her shoulder a gentle squeeze – or give her an unexpected full-on bear hug from behind, Joey-and-Chandler-style – but I knew it'd tip her over an edge that none of us ever wanted to confront. So, instead, I silently loaded up the rest of the dishwasher, spritzed the surfaces with that familiar citrus-laced chemical scent and wiped them down to the soundtrack of scrubbing. As she busied herself with dessert, I could see she was trying her hardest to hold it together. I left her to it: over the years I'd learnt that she, Dad and Josh preferred to falter privately. I preferred not to falter at all.

Before I went back to the table, I took a detour to the downstairs cloakroom. As I sat on the loo, massaging my temples to calm myself after yet another conversation with Mum that was somehow both empty of everything yet overflowing with so much, I remembered the time a few Christmases ago – under the influence of at least one too many snowball cocktails – I'd brought up the subject of Scarnbrook with Dad once Josh and Mum had gone to bed.

'Will you ever go back, do you think?' I'd asked gently.

Dad got up and shut the living-room door before answering. 'No, love, we won't.'

He told me about how the pain had been too much for Mum. She'd tried her best to continue her life in Scarnbrook after the funeral and in the run-up to the inquest. Like Dad, she'd been born and bred there and had been such a lynchpin of the community that the thought of leaving had never crossed her mind. But, despite all her friends' best intentions to balance their ongoing sympathy with a desire to 'keep things normal' for her in the months that followed Livvie's death, Mum simply couldn't face the prospect of either. She hated the pitying looks and soft shoulder squeezes wherever she went. But she was also floored when her friends spoke about mundane things, too. It was the seemingly innocuous comments about teenage mischief that crushed her the most. About birthday parties Livvie should've gone to, mock exam results she should've received, hearts she should've had a chance to break. Staying in Scarnbrook became a melting pot of triggers, and cutting ties became the only way to escape them.

Dad's primary focus became their escape. I could imagine how he would've filled his mind with budgets and plans and spreadsheets to do what he could to shelter her from as much pain as possible – and distract himself from his. They'd escaped to Auntie Sandra's holiday cottage in time for Christmas that year. They hadn't moved – or sent out one of their Christmas round-robin updates – since.

As I washed my hands, I came to a definitive realisation: if I was ever going to go back to Scarnbrook, I would have to do it alone – and without Mum and Dad finding out. If they ever discovered I'd been back without them – even though they had no intention to return – it would fill them with guilt and anguish I couldn't even bear to think about. And the thought of going there with Josh felt like a scenario that belonged in another timeline altogether.

With my parents going away just as I had this oppor-tunity – more than that, this *urge* – to revisit the place we'd all once called home, I felt in my polenta-lined gut that the stars would never align like this again. By the time I returned to the table and Dad set alight the Christmas pudding (vegan, ofc), my mind was made up. Sure, I'd write this article for Elle – but I was going back to Scarnbrook for *me*.

Twenty years earlier

Date: 04/10/2005
From: KarmaChamelia@hotmail.com
To: Livvin_mybestlife@hotmail.com
Subject: Cardiff visit sooooooooooon?

Hey little sister who is actually taller than me! Thanks for the apostrophe clarification. Mr Anderson loves a good grammar-based conversation so hopefully you're in his good books (for once!).

Can't write much as I've only got five minutes of Internet time left, but what about this for an idea… how about you come and stay with me in my halls for a weekend soon? I'm thinking the weekend after next? You could come after school on the Friday and head back to Scarnbrook on Sunday.

Strictly speaking, under 18s aren't allowed but I'm sure it won't be a problem given that you look older than me! I reckon Dad could give you a lift to the station and pick you up etc and it's only a short train journey. What do you think?!

A xxx

Date: 05/10/2005
From: Livvin_mybestlife@hotmail.com
To: KarmaChamelia@hotmail.com
Subject: Re: Cardiff visit soooooooooon?

Ummmm yesssss! Checked it all over with Mum and Dad and they're happy for me to take the train to Cardiff by myself (!) as long as you can meet me at the station?

OMG, I also have some biiiiig gossip for you. Guess who I saw in town on the weekend? That boy you used to fancy at school! Tom Brinton!! He was in Cafe Amoré having lunch with his mum :))))))) She looked familiar but I couldn't put my finger on why.

ANYWAY. They were having some kind of tiff, and she ended up storming out???? It was like an episode of Hollyoaks or something! Tom looked really sad and embarrassed, before he paid the bill and ran after her. What do you think that could have been about????

Anyway, thanks so much for the invite. Can't wait to see the view out of your window… tee hee.

Liv xxx

P.S. Also excited to try pooing and showering at the same time.

Date: 06/10/2005
From: KarmaChamelia@hotmail.com
To: Livvin_mybestlife@hotmail.com

Subject: Re: Re: Cardiff visit soooooooooon?

Amazing, I'll get planning!

God, that's so random you mentioned Tom Brinton – I hadn't thought about him in ages and then only a few nights ago I had a dream about him?!

I haven't seen him since he randomly dropped out of sixth form after just a couple of months. Sad times.

No idea why he'd be arguing with his mum. Tempted to ask Elle but that would no doubt involve her figuring out I'd had a monumental crush on him and I'd never hear the end of it.

Hope he's OK, though.

Gotta go, will email Cardiff info soon!

xxxxx

Chapter 6

☑ **Little white lie**

Twenty years later

As anticipated, Elle had initially rejected my idea to return to our old stomping ground to write the article in one of her trademark voice messages:

> **Elle (voice message):**
> Mally-Wally. Urgh. Not loving this idea.
> Why put yourself through it? Please let me
> find somewhere less shit!

Standing up to her was never easy, but with the pressure on Elle to commission Christmas features, I knew I had a rare ace up my sleeve. Eventually, we'd reached a compromise: Elle would do all the research and book me somewhere to stay in Scarnbrook, and all I had to do was figure out how to get there. And I'd still be writing it under a pseudonym.

A week later, having tied up all my loose ends at work before the office closure, I was back in East Sussex, having convinced my parents to let me drive them to the airport for their Sunday afternoon flight. As far as they were concerned, the plan was this:

I'd give them a lift to Gatwick Airport in Dad's car.

I'd drive back to theirs and housesit for a few days.

At some point, I'd get the train back to London for Christmas itself.

But the more I repeated this fake plan to myself to get my story straight, the more I was tempted to make it my *actual* plan. The idea of holing up here in this picture-perfect cottage, surrounded by stunning countryside and not being perceived by anyone at all for days on end felt like absolute bliss. Just *imagine* how many corny Christmas movies I could get through!

But the timing of the airport run and easy access to Dad's car felt like yet another way fate was funnelling me towards Scarnbrook; travelling there on public transport would've been a monumental faff, with no useful train stations at the end of the journey. Having a car would make it loads easier to get around while I was there and, most importantly, would mean I could leave whenever I wanted. The holiday rental was booked for a full week, but I figured I'd only need to be there for two nights – three, max – to visit old haunts and write the article before getting out of there and back to normal life.

Deceiving my parents went against every single one of my instincts, but strictly speaking they *had* said I could use the car while I was at theirs. I just needed to remember to keep the fuel gauge at a similar level.

I got them to the airport in good time – unsurprising, given that Mum had insisted we leave four hours before the flight despite the fact it was only a forty-five minute journey – and enjoyed the solo drive back to the countryside with Radio X blaring, using the steering wheel as a makeshift drumkit.

Josh, who was travelling back to London later that day, was making himself some kind of fluorescent orange hot drink when I got back.

'Want one?' It could very well have been the first question he'd asked me in two decades.

'Depends what it is. It looks like hot Lucozade or something?'

Was that a twitch of a smile? Nah, probably wind from his bean smoothie earlier – or whatever it was he poured down his throat each morning.

'It's turmeric and ginger tea.'

I instinctively mimed a gagging motion before catching myself halfway through and attempting to transform it into a cough.

'No, thanks anyway, though.'

'Fair enough. I'm going to be heading off soon, by the way – there's a taxi coming to pick me up at ten thirty.'

'Oh, really? I can drop you off at the station; it's no bother.'

He took a small sip of his 'tea' and shook his head. 'No, thanks. It's actually taking me to my client's place for a final session, then I'll head back to London from there.'

'Fair enough. The cab's an electric car, I presume? Or hybrid at least?'

I could see his jaw clench in exactly the same way Mum's sometimes did, but I couldn't help myself. He hated being caught out in his own hypocrisies.

'Well, it's not ideal but—'

'Josh, it's okay – you don't have to defend yourself to me; I couldn't care less. But maybe give Dad a bit of an easier time on his car choices next time, hmm?'

'Yeah, all right.'

I gave him a double thumbs up, but he looked at me blankly before turning away with his tea and gazing out the kitchen window.

'Right, I'm going to jump in the shower as I didn't get the chance before the airport run. You'll probably be gone by the time I get back, so… merry Christmas, I guess! Oh, and you still haven't told me how much I owe you for that wine.'

'I'll message you the details.' Just like Mum, he didn't even turn to face me as he spoke.

I trudged up the narrow staircase, the seventh one always catching me out with its ginormous creak.

Josh had left a modest-looking gift outside my bedroom door. To be fair, the calligraphic label – tied to the rectangular present with mustard-yellow string – was beautiful.

I grabbed the towel from the chair in my bedroom and headed to the bathroom for my shower. But then the freestanding bathtub caught my eye. Sod it, I was going to have a nice, long soak instead.

A few minutes later I sank into the water, which was hot enough for every nerve ending in my body to go *ooh!* before they went *aah*, producing a satisfying all-over tingle. I luxuriated in the bubbly depths for a good ten minutes, inhaling the lavender-scented oil. Eventually, I heard the gentle crunching of a car on the gravel driveway outside and the thud of the front door closing.

I heaved myself into a sitting position and began to wash my hair. The smell of the highlight-activating shampoo, not that my single-tone mousy hair had any highlights to activate, reminded me of my mum. A rush of apprehension possessed me as I thought about the days ahead.

I knew my decision not to tell my family I was going back to Scarnbrook was the right one. After all, it was the place that had crumbled our very foundations. Plus, with Mum and Dad being out of the country for the first time in forever, they'd *never* need to know I'd even been back. It felt like this would be the most opportune moment I'd ever get to return home.

Home.

Twenty years away and I still called it that. Thought of it like that. The question was, would it still feel like home after everything that had happened? I'd waited two decades to find out. It was now or never.

Chapter 7

☑ **Unexpected reunion**

Scarnbrook was about twenty minutes from the motorway, thanks to the ring road that had been built during my childhood. Back then the smooth, efficient bypass had saved me from the previously winding and travel-sickness-inducing route we'd always taken on our way to Auntie Sandra's swanky apartment in West London.

The dual carriageway eventually gave way to familiar A-roads, followed by B-roads, followed by residential streets too insignificant to be identified by letters and numbers.

And then I was there. Scarnbrook. A tucked-away pocket of suburban Bristol that liked to call itself a village but, in reality, was a hodgepodge collection of vast residential estates – with occasional clusters of cottages – that had gradually absorbed farmland either side of a valley over the course of the last century or so.

Driving along the high street as my dad's ancient satnav indicated I was approaching my destination, I clocked the village hall where Mum and Dad had once organised community dinners for the local senior citizens. It was weird to think that they themselves were now old enough to attend such an event. Over the road was the dog groomer's where I'd inexplicably done work experience in Year Eight, despite having zero interest in canines. Oh, and there was the old sweet shop that Mum used to take us to after the dentist as a paradoxical reward for keeping our teeth relatively clean. The sweet shop now appeared to be a luxuriously appointed residential property boasting sage window frames and a fancy-pants festive wreath on the front door. My expectations for my holiday cottage jumped up a couple of notches.

Seeing these places – which were somehow so different yet achingly familiar at the same time – brought home to me just how long I'd been away. How much the place had moved on. How much the people here must've moved on, too.

I took a deep breath and turned right down a narrow lane between the fish and chip shop and The Star, a pub I'd only been to once on a memorable night out with Elle just before we left for university. In the noughties, it'd been one of those pubs where underage drinkers could sneak into the function room through the beer garden entrance and spend the evening crammed around a pool table while the eldest-looking members of the party were despatched to the bar to fetch drinks. But that's not the context in which Elle and I visited on that single occasion. No, that would've been far too normal. Instead, Elle had managed to wangle a gig on the local mystery shopping circuit and had talked me into going 'undercover' with her. And so, one humid Friday night in August, the two of us had rocked up to undertake our strict mission of ordering two cocktails, a plate of chips and inspecting the toilets for cleanliness. After doing our duty by ordering two cosmos from the cocktail menu – and burning our mouths on the hottest chips in the world – we'd left, and never returned.

Despite the fact that the story had gone on to become one of mine and Elle's favourite Scarnbrook anecdotes – largely because the pub had ended up with a perplexingly high mystery shopping score due to the automated diligence of the staff – I remembered feeling disappointed at how the night had panned out. Because, at the back of my mind, I'd been half-hoping – fine, three-quarters-hoping – to see Tom Brinton there, since I knew he and his friends went there quite a bit.

Elle and I had only heard about their riotous nights at The Star from snatches of overheard conversations on Mondays at school. Week after week, the two of us secretly updated our ever-growing 'saliva chain' diagram based on who had snogged whom that particular weekend. Eventually, we were able to prove that, in a roundabout way, practically everyone in that particular friendship circle had snogged everyone. Including themselves.

But little did Elle know that I had a vested interest in the saliva chain. Because each week I waited with silent fretfulness to find out if Tom Brinton had entered the DNA-based mix in any shape or form. As far as I could tell, he'd always remained beyond the boundaries of the flow(!)chart.

As I drove alongside the pub, I noticed it'd been smartened up since then. I pulled into Hollyhock Close, a modern-ish looking cul-de-sac that had cars mounted on every pavement due to the lack of sufficient parking. I double-checked the address that Elle had only got around to sending me this morning. It was definitely the right place. Huh.

Elle had described the holiday rental to me as a 'mews cottage on an exclusive private road', but really it was a two-bedroom end-terraced house on a nondescript development of new-builds. The house had a driveway, which I managed to squeeze onto in between two parked cars. Reversing out of there was *not* going to be fun.

As instructed, I unlatched the narrow gate to the side of the property to find the key access box, which was caked in a layer of grime. Following the passcode instructions, I tugged the plastic tab upwards to find a key nestling inside and let myself in through the yellowed UPVC door.

First impressions? It was… underwhelming. The heating must've been off for quite some time, and there was a distinct aroma of bleach in every room. Well, at least it was clean.

Elle had said something about the place being more basic than she'd have preferred due to recently imposed expenses constraints, which was fair enough. I was only going to be here for a couple of nights, anyway. And I couldn't help but think that the crappy standard of accommodation would probably give me at least one funny thing to write about in my article. Speaking of which: I really needed to come up with an efficient trope-ticking plan for the next couple of days.

I heaved my suitcase up the stairs and dumped it in the only room with a bed in it before sticking my head round the door to the bathroom. Bloody hell, there wasn't even any loo roll in this place! A trip to the shops was definitely in order.

I considered wandering along to the nearby Co-op to pick up a few bits, but then I remembered about the Big Tesco with the petrol station off the ring road. I needed to top up Dad's tank, and the BP garage that used to be at the end of Scarnbrook's high street had been turned into a Lidl.

I somehow managed to reverse off the narrow driveway without needing to leave my insurance details on anyone's windscreens, and headed back to the dual carriageway, my inner satnav remembering the way to the supermarket. The car park was starting to empty given there were only forty-five minutes until closing. I'd have to be quick.

I grabbed a shallow trolley and headed inside. A blast of industrial heating hit me as I crossed the threshold, the glare of the harsh, fluorescent lighting burning my tired eyes following all the day's driving. And that's when the realisation hit me, too. The realisation that people might stare if they recognised me. After all, I was connected to one of Scarnbrook's saddest historical chapters.

Unless they've all forgotten.

More than anything in the world at that moment, I wanted to be back in my draughty but familiar London flat, wrapped up in my bobbly slanket and watching a plasticine-faced man with a felt-like beard fix the broken-down car of a rosy-cheeked owner of a small-town inn. I considered performing a dramatic U-turn with the trolley and hiding outside to collect myself – or scarpering altogether – but the wind was picking up again and my stomach was growling with hunger. I took a shaky breath, cast my eyes upwards and glanced around. It wasn't too busy at all. I relaxed a little, and focused my attention on scooping up my essentials as quickly as possible, as if I was a contestant on *Supermarket Sweep* being cheered on over the Tannoy.

At the end of the final aisle, I guided the trolley to an empty till. And there he was: perhaps the only person I *hadn't* mentally prepared myself to bump into – Tom blimmin' Brinton – stood with his own full-sized trolley at the adjacent checkout.

As his eyes briefly met mine, my insides did a flippy-floppy thing I hadn't felt since school. I unloaded my collection of processed foods while trying to give off an air of calm indifference, while internally I was trying to figure out if my tummy had ever felt like this with any other man. I wasn't convinced it had. I'd always put that down to the fact that I was now, apparently, a fully grown woman rather than a stupid teenage girl with a ridiculous, unrequited crush. But perhaps not? I thought I detected a glimmer of recognition as Tom flashed his trademark dimply grin and continued to fill the conveyor belt in an admirably practical order with the heaviest item first – which appeared to be the world's largest frozen turkey – and a loaf of fresh bread at the very end.

Back at school, I'd always found him endlessly interesting to look at. He was attractive, but less conventionally so than some of his peers, with an angular, pointy face and strong, straight nose. His rich, conker-brown hair was always perfectly tousled – short round the sides but thick and wavy on top, just crying out to be mussed, though I reckon I would've struggled to reach it given the height difference. His understated eyebrows sloped down towards his slightly protruding ears, one of which had glinted with a small, gold stud. He had generous, mouth-hugging dimples under both cheekbones when he grinned, which was often.

But it was his piercing, ice-blue, almost silver eyes that had always entranced me the most. Constantly glinting with humour and ideas, if I happened to make eye contact with him my stomach would fizz with a high that I'd enjoy for the rest of that day, as if his energy was contagious.

Double English had always been the highlight of my week as it meant I got to sit opposite Tom Brinton for two entire hours – the most direct contact I ever had with him since neither our friendship groups nor any of our other lessons crossed over at all. It also happened to be the only class I didn't share with Elle.

Back then, I'd manage to convince myself that, sometimes, it felt as if he was looking in my direction. And, while we didn't have much in common on the surface, quite often we'd quietly chuckle at each other's witticisms.

Despite his rebellious streak – which often saw him in detention – I'd always sensed this underlying essence of niceness. He was the kind of person who could make anyone feel at ease, even people like me who he'd never even had a single conversation with.

But the very idea of him ever being interested in yours truly was frankly hilarious – even to me. Because you probably couldn't have chosen two people who were any less likely to fit together as friends, let alone anything more. There I was: short, clumsy and sat at the front of the coach on school trips thanks to my history of travel sickness. And there he was: tall, effortlessly confident and right at the back of the coach thanks to his innate popularity and cheekiness. Yet, he'd appeared to glide through any situation or academic challenge with an ease and self-assurance I could only dream of – until he left suddenly a term or so into sixth form, when we were seventeen.

Because I'd kept my secret infatuation to myself – with the exception of confiding in Livvie, who knew everything about me – I couldn't ask anyone where he'd disappeared to. So that was that – he'd instantly vanished from my life like an elusive bubble suddenly popping mid-air.

As we bagged up our respective groceries – his into one of those expandable, colour-coded shopping trolley bags – there was that undeniable fizz once more, as his eyes caught mine for the second time. For a moment, I forgot that the only thing that was likely to make me memorable to Tom Brinton was the stuff that had gone down with my family two decades ago.

I attempted to coax my hair to hang over my face to cloak the ever-deepening shade of crimson it was turning as all these memories swirled around my head. Meanwhile, Tom finished his transaction ahead of me – he was exceedingly nice to the chap on the checkout, of course – and turned to give me a gentle wave. In my attempt to casually wave in return, I managed to fling my debit card out of my hand and towards Tom Brinton's face. In a display of characteristic competence, he somehow caught it and handed it to me in one swift motion.

'And for your next trick?' What was I even saying?

I inattentively passed the card to the checkout lady as Tom chuckled and said, 'Trying to fit this lot in my car,' gesturing towards his overflowing concertina bags.

'Ha, good luck with that!'

'I'll need it!'

And he walked out of my life once more.

I sighed and turned back to my own conveyor belt, packing my groceries into my raggedy canvas bags.

The checkout lady passed me back my card. 'It's contactless, love.'

'Oh right, of course.'

As the receipt tumbled out of the till, she looked at me with kind eyes and smiled.

'I'm sorry, I don't know if I should say anything, but I'm Dawn, Gemma's mum – she was in your class at school?'

Oh God, bumping into Tom Brinton like that had completely distracted me from my plan to avoid this kind of encounter and resulting conversation.

I swallowed and smiled blandly as she continued to talk, most of her words not registering. 'And how are your parents? We still miss them at Supper Club! Completely understandable, of course.'

'Ah, the Supper Club's still running?'

'Oh yes, but we had to relocate it to The Star after they turned the village hall into flats.'

How tragic. My parents had had their first snog in that village hall, as Dad had once told us after a few too many limoncellos one Majorcan holiday.

'Well, here's your receipt, sweetheart. Do pass them my love, won't you?'

'Of course. Thanks, Dawn. And say hi to Gemma from me.'

I pushed my trolley towards the exit, gripping the handle extra-tight to try and stop my hands from trembling. The news that I'd returned would now fly around the WhatsApp groups of Scarnbrook, I was sure of it. There was no hiding now.

I was still shaking as I pulled up to the pump in the supermarket's own-brand petrol station. As the fuel flowed into the vehicle, I tried to regulate my breath, inhaling the flammable yet soothing fumes as I did so.

The sudden judder of the nozzle jolted me back to the present. I paid at the pump and settled back into the driver's seat, relieved that the supermarket ordeal was finally over.

As I was about to put my key in the ignition, there was a sudden hammering on my window. It was Tom Brinton. And he was shouting, frantically.

Chapter 8

☑ **Car drama**

'STOP! DON'T START THE ENGINE!' Tom Brinton screamed, his delicate eyebrows contorted in panic.

What-in-the-forecourt-flip was happening? I froze and slowly moved my hands away from the steering wheel, the keys dangling from my right thumb.

Tom made a gesture for me to lower the window. Which, of course, I couldn't do without my keys in the ignition, so I opened the car door a couple of inches instead and angled my head in the general direction of the gap.

'Umm, hello?'

'Hey, oh God, I'm so sorry for acting like a lunatic here, but I promise you this will all make sense. Eventually. It's Amelia, right? You might not remember me but we were in the same year together at school. I'm Tom – Tom Brinton?'

'Oh yeah – Tom – of course. I knew you looked familiar at the checkout.' *Just give me the Best Actress Oscar now.* I was acutely conscious that not only was this the first time I'd ever spoken Tom Brinton's name to his face rather than round and round in my head, but it was also the only time I'd not followed 'Tom' up with 'Brinton'.

To me, Tom Brinton had reached household-name brand status, like Sugar Puffs or Cillit Bang.

'Okay, so please don't turn the engine on. I realise this whole scenario is, well, ridiculous on many levels, but I've got a bad feeling you might've just put petrol in your diesel car.'

'Diesel car? I... oh... fuck!'

This was so bloody typical of me. *Stupid, idiotic Mally.* The first time I'd ever done something even vaguely rebellious when it came to my parents and I'd flung myself into a steaming pile of manure at the very first hurdle. I remembered getting detailed, typed-out instructions from Dad the first time I'd borrowed his car, which had said something along the lines of: *NEVER fill it with unleaded fuel by mistake. This will COMPLETELY ruin the engine. You have been warned!*

'Huh, I don't think I've ever heard you swear before,' Tom said.

'Huh' indeed. Because it was true – I don't think I *had* ever uttered a swear word back at school. I added 'phenomenal memory for useless information' to my mental list of Tom Brinton's qualities. A list that, come to think of it, had probably once existed in top-secret physical form back in my school days.

'I guess that's what a decade and a half in London does to you,' I replied.

'The corrupting capital.'

Did he just...? Yes. He'd winked at me. I felt my insides threaten to melt into a puddle of serotonin. There was no doubt that my outsides were blushing furiously. And, by the looks of his be-dimpled face as he examined the ground between us, he'd clocked as much.

'Anyway... um, yeah, as you probably know, petrol doesn't tend to make diesel cars very happy. I noticed you filling up while I was sorting out my tyre pressure...'

He gestured towards a gleaming vehicle in the corner of the forecourt.

'...and then I saw the make of the car so I made a dash for it. Sorry, banging on your window was probably one of the weirdest things I've ever done but, with any luck, I might've just saved you a fair amount of money. Once that key gets turned and the fuel flows into the engine...'

He drew his finger in a horizontal line over his neck and stuck his tongue out of the side of his mouth.

Stop staring at said tongue, Mally.

'Shit, yeah, thanks. I'm not normally this scatty but it's my dad's car and I was on autopilot.'

I'm not sure I could've chosen a more inappropriate analogy. Autopilots were in control. I was already flying by the seat of my pants, and I'd only been back a couple of hours.

'Ah, I see. You're here with your family, then?'

'No, it's just me. My parents are abroad for a couple of weeks.'

I noticed a flash of surprise cross Tom's face, as if he was trying to compute something in his mind.

'Anyway, thanks for alerting me. I'd better get on to the AA.'

Lol, as if I had any roadside assistance to call on. I briefly thought about disguising my voice as my dad's in order to utilise his account and defraud their helpline, but the idea unravelled as quickly as it appeared.

'No worries. But, hey, if you're happy for me to make a quick phone call I might have a faster solution than the

AA. My mate Ryan – you might remember him from school, actually – Ryan Seldon?'

Woah, that name was a blast from the past. Ryan had been the mainstream heartthrob figure in our year group with his David Beckham-inspired mohawk, obscenely long, dark eyelashes and athletic physique. He and Elle had even had a day-long 'thing' in Year Ten. The three of us had been assigned to work together on a field trip to the local wetlands centre. Inevitably, I'd spent the entire day on lookout duty for teachers while they snogged among the bullrushes, leaving me to single-handedly search for wildfowl habitats in order to complete all three of our assignments. I think I'd even gone as far as using a different pen for each worksheet to ensure the deception was as convincing as possible.

He'd been pretty smitten with her from what I could remember. But she'd made some loud comment about his bad breath at school the following week and that was that – just one fellow in a long line of heartbroken chaps that Elle had casually discarded over the years.

'Ryan? Yeah, of course.'

'Cool, well, he owns a garage not far from here and can probably give you as decent a quote as you're going to get. I'll give him a quick call now if you like?'

'That would be amazing, but only if you've got nowhere to be?'

Tom ran his hand through his thick, wavy hair, which still had an underlying sheen of auburn, albeit with a new smattering of silver here and there. The gesture afforded him a quick glance at his watch. It was sweet of him to disguise it.

'It's no problem at all; I need to get this shopping back at some point but that can wait for a bit.'

'Thanks so much, this is so kind of you. I'll let the petrol station person know.'

As Tom walked back to his car to make the call to Ryan, I took a moment to review my appearance in the sun visor's vanity mirror. Reality mirror, more like. I concluded that, yes, I definitely should've put some make-up on today. I popped some lip salve on, and even went as far as smearing a little on my eyebrows to smooth them down, as if the lack of rogue micro-hairs might suddenly make Tom Brinton – or Tom – see me in some new, revelatory light.

I put the hazard lights on and placed my dad's reflective triangle thingy behind the car to give off the impression I'd been in this kind of situation before and knew exactly how to handle it, and walked towards the small payment booth. The teenage employee just shrugged and pointed towards a traffic cone, which I placed next to the triangle, just as Tom wandered back over.

'Wow, I reckon the rear of your car is definitely safe from harm now.' He looked down at the myriad of plastic safety measures.

I covered my eyes with my hands, shaking my head in cringy amusement.

'Any luck with Ryan?' I asked.

'Yes, he—'

The rain had eased but it was getting increasingly cold in the fast-fading December light, so I attempted to wrap my scarf around my neck a couple more times as he spoke. The tassels caught Tom's left eye on the second rotation.

'Argh!'

'Oh my God, I'm so sorry. Are you okay?'

'I'm fine, just wasn't expecting any scarf *or* debit card-related injuries tonight. That's a really long scarf by the way.'

'I bought it from Lenny Kravitz.'

What on earth were all these phrases that were coming out of my mouth?

'Sensible. The bigger the scarf, the less likely it is to "Fly Away".'

A Lenny Kravitz pun? Okay, this conversation was taking an interesting turn. A *pleasing* turn.

'I can fetch you my emergency foil blanket from my boot if you like,' Tom continued. 'You'll match your reflective triangle, that way.'

I couldn't help but emit a very loud snort. 'I think I'll survive under the protection of Lenny's knitwear.'

'Ha ha. Anyway, Ryan lives in one of the new-builds nearby so can be here in a few minutes.'

'Amazing, thanks again. I'm fine to wait for him here so there's no need to hang around.'

Please hang around.

'Nah, you're good. I might as well wait until he gets here – been meaning to catch up with him for a while. So, London, then?'

'Yeah, after sixth form I went to Cardiff Uni—'

'With Elle, right?'

'That's right, we ended up in the same halls, which was nice.'

I still had no idea how Elle had managed to wangle us adjacent rooms in the same block. I'd been a bit miffed at the time – going to the same uni as her was one thing, but living in such close quarters had somewhat dampened my hopes to mingle and meet new people. But, in the end, the relief of having her next door the day it'd mattered most – the day I found out about Livvie – had overridden all of that.

'Did you live with Elle throughout?'

'I did. We studied different degrees – she did media and journalism and I did English literature – but there were a couple of modules that crossed over so we got to spend quite a lot of time together. It was nice to have a familiar face around.'

'Yeah, I can imagine.'

There was a pause. I took a deep breath and continued. 'Yeah, so, um, while I was at uni there was obviously that… stuff with my sister.'

'Yes, of course, I'm so sorry.'

'Thanks. So, yeah, by the time I'd finished my degree my parents had moved away and I could kind of start afresh wherever I liked, so I ended up heading to London with Elle.'

'The Big Smoke. Do you like it there?'

'I guess. But it can be quite intense and just a bit…' I didn't quite know how to finish the sentence. But Tom did.

'…much?'

'Exactly. But I don't have any connections anywhere else so it was as good a place as any. And it's been great for my career so I can't really complain. Anyway, how about you? You still live around here, then?'

He shrugged and looked at his feet, tapping his toes together a couple of times as if trying to wish himself back to Kansas. Had I touched a nerve? I could totally see how my question about his choice to stay here might have come across as belittling, whereas – if anything – I was jealous.

'I guess I'm one of those people who's destined to stay in one place, you know?'

'I used to feel the same.'

There was a pause that should've felt awkward but actually felt quite comfortable.

And there were those eyes again, glancing up from the ground and locking on to mine – just for an instant, but an instant nonetheless.

'So, what have you been up to since school?' I asked.

'This and that. You might remember that I never did finish my A levels – what with one thing and another. I ended up getting an apprenticeship at an office in town. I'm still at the same company now, though I've worked my way up a bit.'

'Ah, nice. What kind of work is it?'

'Oh, it's pretty dull: we do facilities management for some local businesses. But we've been getting some pretty big contracts recently and we're hoping to expand to other locations in the next couple of years so, yeah, it's all worked out quite nicely.'

'That's really great – I'm pleased for you.'

'The feeling's mutual, Amelia.'

I felt heat in my face again, and was grateful that this particular part of the forecourt was poorly lit.

'I, er, actually go by Mally these days.'

'Noted. Suits you.'

At that moment a tow truck pulled into the forecourt, a rhythmic honk interrupting the conversation.

'Amelia Allister! The Double-A!' It was Ryan Seldon, reminding me from his wound-down window about a horrific school nickname that'd been bestowed upon me when I'd been late to blossom in the boob department.

As with any attempts to bully me – which had been pretty frequent when I started secondary school given my in-built awkwardness – I'd always laughed it off. I'd figured that a smiling victim's not really a victim, are they? I instinctively applied my idiot-repellent grin as Ryan wound up his window and switched off his engine.

Tom spoke quickly under his breath. 'Yeah, Mally, best if you ignore the vast majority of stuff that comes out of Ryan's mouth. Deal?'

I nodded once. 'Deal.'

Ryan hopped down from the cab and elbowed Tom in the ribs by way of greeting.

'She goes by Mally these days, Seldon. And it's a hard no on that fucked-up nickname, okay?'

'Righty-o. Well, what are the chances eh, Tom?'

Ryan gave Tom an imperceptible look that lasted maybe half a second longer than felt normal. There was definitely an element of a smirk to it and I swear I saw Tom's neck go ever-so-slightly blotchy.

I spoke first to break the perplexing moment that seemed to be passing between them. 'Thanks so much for this, Ryan.'

'No worries at all. Good job your knight in shining armour was here to rescue you, eh?'

Wow, did Ryan fancy a job at *The Helix*? Iancompetent would probably hire him in a heartbeat. On the flip side, perhaps I'd just had a sufficiently 'awkward encounter' for my trope-seeking article? After all, this ridiculous situation with my car could've come straight out of a Hallmark movie.

Tom spoke before I even had the chance to chuckle blandly.

'Ryan, seriously, do I need to sign you up to another "casual misogyny" workshop?'

What was happening? A man calling out his unenlightened mate's sexist remark? This felt... refreshing.

Tom mouthed 'Sorry' to me and rolled his eyes.

'Oh, she doesn't mind, do you? You look different, by the way – I mean I'd still recognise you. But, yeah, you look different.'

Ryan's West Country accent was much stronger than Tom's. While Tom's was more of a gentle twang, a bit like mine, Ryan's was unabashed, proud Bristolian. Lots of people found the accent harsh or grating, but I'd always loved it. It sounded like home.

'Umm, you also look different...?'

He... really did.

'Yes, yes, I lost all my hair in my early twenties. A painful blow. Thankfully I was already married by then – to Carly, one of the twins? The fun one.'

Oh my God, he was married to Carly? I couldn't wait to tell Elle about this.

'Nice – congrats!'

'Ta! Yeah, unlike Tom, I didn't get much luck in the ageing department – he's truly Scarnbrook's very own Paul Rudd.'

I laughed at the reference but... Ryan was totally right. Tom really didn't seem to have aged a bit. Apart from those dashes of greying hair around his temples, and some laughter lines around those mesmeric eyes, it was almost as if the last two decades had skimmed right over him.

We removed my shopping from my boot before attaching Dad's beloved car to Ryan's truck.

'Right, then, I'll give you a call in the morning once I've had a gander at the damage. Tom said you didn't start your engine after the misfuel?'

'Thankfully not.'

'Yeah, if that petrol had worked its way through the system it could've caused a right old mess in there. Hopefully I can give the tank a straightforward flush and that'll be that.'

'Phew, thanks so much, Ryan.'

'Not a problem, not a problem at all. Need a lift anywhere?'

Tom spoke quickly again before I could answer. 'It's fine, Ryan, I've got this.'

'I bet you do, Brinton.'

The blotches crept ever-so-slightly further up Tom's neck.

Ryan climbed back into the truck and fastened his seatbelt. As he started the engine, he leant out of the window once more and said, 'See ya, Tomelia!' before driving away.

'*Tomelia?!*'

Tom shrugged and shoved his hands in his pockets. 'Just one of his less funny puns, I guess. Anyway, where can I take you?'

Pretty much anywhere, Tom Brinton.

'I'm staying in Scarnbrook, believe it or not. I've got the address on my phone; let me just find it…'

I followed Tom to his car, which was still connected to the now-dormant tyre pressure pump. As I searched through my emails to dig out the postcode, one thought kept running through my head: Tom Brinton had remembered me. But it didn't mean anything, of course. Because, for the grimmest reason, *everyone* in Scarnbrook would remember me.

Chapter 9

☑ **Decorating a Christmas tree**

I opened the passenger door, only to find the seat was already occupied... by an enormous frozen bird.

'Umm, shall I sit in the back?'

'Huh? Why would you... fuck, the turkey!' He lifted it up to reveal a conspicuous puddle on the passenger seat.

'Shit!'

'Is it... melting?'

'Yup. Fuck! I totally forgot about my heated seats. I'm going to have to get this to my mum's ASAP before it starts gobbling again.'

'Your mum's?'

'Yeah, I do her food shop every Sunday. I keep trying to set her up with online shopping but she's convinced they'll try and fob her off with sub-par veg and fresh food that hasn't come from the very back of the shelf.'

'I agree with your mum.'

'Ha. Do you mind if we swing by hers before I drop you off? That's if you don't have your own deceased and defrosting poultry in the boot?'

I thought about my Super Noodles and selection of sugary cereals. 'Nah, I'm good.'

'Phew. Okay, let me just grab a towel from the boot and give this seat a wipe...'

He shrugged off his coat and chucked it on the back seat as he set to work on absorbing the turkey juices, revealing long, firm arms contained neatly in a light grey fitted cardigan over the top of a faded black T-shirt. The cardigan-wearing guys at work usually gave me the ick – their ironic charity-shop knitwear looked so contrived, not to mention itchy – but Tom's cardigan looked soft and practical, as if he'd chosen it for how it felt rather than how it looked. Which made it look all the more excellent. I swallowed the excess saliva that had pooled in my mouth as he tossed the towel into the footwell of the backseat.

'Right, all done. Your carriage awaits.'

I sank into the luxurious passenger seat, which was still slightly damp with carcass moisture, though I couldn't bear to tell him that.

'You know, if someone had told me earlier today that I'd be driving Amelia – sorry, Mally – Allister round to my mum's, I wouldn't have believed them.'

'If someone had told me I'd be sat in a car with Tom Brinton tonight, the words "fuck the turkey" ringing in my ears, I wouldn't have believed them either.'

He turned to me briefly and grinned with his whole face before turning his attention back to the road. 'So, what brings you back to Scarnbrook?'

I'd rehearsed an answer for this precise question, but his smile had rendered my brain momentarily useless. I issued a placeholder response to buy me some time.

'Oh God. It's a long story.'

'We've got time – my mum's place is the far side of Scarnbrook. It's lucky I bumped into you – I normally do her shopping at Morrison's, but she prefers the Tesco turkeys.'

'Blimey, where to start. Okay, so I'd usually be at work in London next week, but they've given us all an extra week off…'

'Woah, that's generous. Where do you work?'

'Oh, the same place as Elle, actually. It's—'

'You work at *The Helix*?!'

Explaining my way out of this was going to be way harder than I thought.

'Yep. You still follow Elle's movements, then?'

'It's hard not to when she's constantly posting about her high-flying life on social media.'

'I had no idea she was still in touch with everyone here.'

Elle and I never discussed any of our old schoolmates in Scarnbrook. I'd presumed she'd lost touch with everyone, just like I had.

'Well, it's not like she interacts with any of us or anything, but let's just say she appears to be very keen for everyone to know how successful she is.'

Ha, that sounded like Elle.

'She *is* pretty successful, to be fair.'

'So are you. But I don't see you plastering endless photos of your London lifestyle online.'

'I'm not really on social media.' I left out the part where I still checked Billy's Instagram page seventeen times a day.

'I keep thinking about quitting, myself. Social media has, well, broken the world a bit, hasn't it?'

My brain lit up and I beamed at him. 'Omigod yes. Social media is like forbidden fruit; it tastes good to begin with, but ultimately unleashes a torrent of worms from the rotten core that appear to be hellbent on devouring us all.'

'Yup. But, unlike you, I guess I couldn't resist taking a deep bite of that tempting apple.' He smiled as he watched the road, and completely involuntarily I felt myself quiver. *Oh dear.*

'Have you ever thought about deleting your accounts?' I asked.

'I have, but TikTok and Instagram have been game-changers at work. Our content has really helped to get our name out there. Anyway, we've gone off on a bit of a tangent – you were about to tell me why you're back in Scarnbrook?'

'Oh. Right. Well, I've been meaning to come back for a while, but it never seemed to work out. But with this extra time off work and no other plans it kind of felt like it was finally the right time, you know?'

'That makes sense. But you've come alone?'

I licked my lips and rubbed them together. 'Yeah. I don't think my parents will ever come back. And my brother – well, to be honest I never have any idea what's going on in that head of his.'

'You're not close?'

'Not any more, no.'

'I'm sorry, Mally.'

If he knew about my brother's online 'fame', he certainly wasn't letting on. I had to presume he did, though.

'Thanks.'

'So, what do you do at *The Helix*?'

'Oh, nothing particularly exciting. I work in the comms team and spend most of my time sending emails and organising employee events and stuff. Although I'm just starting out doing some freelance writing bits on the side, too, and would love to be a children's author in the future.'

My mouth was operating way faster than my brain. There was no way I wanted anyone in Scarnbrook to find out about the real article I was writing. But there was a part of me that wanted Tom to know that I hadn't completely abandoned my creative writing ambitions, which had always been a big part of my identity when I'd been at school.

'Wow, so you write for *The Helix*? That's amazing. I mean, I always knew you'd be successful so I don't know why I'm acting all surprised.'

I filed away the knowledge that Tom Brinton had once had any thoughts about me at all for detailed analysis in the very near future.

'Strictly speaking, I don't write for them… yet. But I've been given my first commission. I'm hoping to write it here while I've got some extra time.'

Careful, Mally.

'What's it going to be about?' he asked, pushing my internal alert system up to amber.

I tried to think of an explanation that, at the very least, orbited Planet Truth.

'It's about… spending Christmas alone and trying to rediscover small-town festive joy. What better place to do that than where I grew up?'

Was he buying this? I bloody well hoped so.

'Hang on, you're spending Christmas alone? How is this even possible?'

'Oh, it's no big deal. I was meant to go to my parents' place like I do every year, but they've gone on this last-minute trip to Florida, and Josh has made other plans. So, yeah, it is what it is.'

'I couldn't do it. I'm so rubbish in my own company. My brain runs away with itself and I find it impossible to relax. I moved in with my mum when the pandemic kicked off. We drove each other batshit crazy, but it would've been so much worse by myself.'

'No family of your own, then?'

'It's… complicated. Well, I guess it's not actually that complicated since the divorce came through. But, no, it's not worked out that way. Yet. Hopefully one day.'

Ooh. Single.

'Sorry, Tom. Someone from school?'

'Ha! No. Work. Don't get married when you're twenty is all I'll say.'

'Wow, twenty's young.'

'As my mum kept telling me at the time. Abbie was quite a few years older than me when we met at work, and Mum warned me not to jump in with both feet but I didn't listen. Turns out she was right, as she likes to constantly remind me. Me and Abbie, we… well, we wanted different things at different times. We stuck with it for as long as we could. But it just got too hard. She's with someone else now. How about you – any divorces up your sleeve?'

Divorces? No. Any truly meaningful romantic relationships? Nada. Endless hope that it was all leading to something? Sure, but it was getting harder and harder to conjure up an image of what the hell that 'something' might ever look like.

'Not really anything up these sleeves other than arms, to be honest with you.'

'Ha. Right, we're just about here.'

Tom parked up in front of a small semi-detached bungalow on one of the ex-council estates on the very outer edge of Scarnbrook. There were inflatable light-up Santas, snowmen, reindeer and – randomly – Easter bunnies dotted around the small but perfectly maintained front garden.

'Your mum's definitely into Christmas, then?'

'Oh yes. Most of the decorations go up on the first of December every year, whatever day of the week it happens to be. It's been the same ever since I can remember.'

'And... the rabbits?'

'They were reduced in B&Q and she couldn't bear to leave them behind.'

'Fair.'

'Umm, Mally, before you come in, you should know that my mum, well, she's been struggling with multiple sclerosis for quite some time now. She's doing really well, considering, but the last couple of years have been especially hard for her — well, for both of us.'

I had an urge to wrap my arms around him tightly.

'Yeah, I bet. I can just wait here while you sort out her shopping,' I said. 'I imagine it might be a bit strange for a random woman to show up with her groceries on a Sunday evening.'

'No no no no, she'll be thrilled to see you, Mally. You might not remember this but back in the day she used to work at the local playschool that we went to before school.'

'Wait. What?'

'Yeah, remember Mrs B?'

'Of course!'

'Yeah, she's my mum. B for Brinton. Although she uses her maiden name these days.'

How did I not know this?

'I remember being in the same playgroup class as you, Ryan and the twins, but I had no idea Mrs B was your mum!'

'Yeah, she'll remember you for sure,' Tom said. 'Putting aside everything else, she remembers all the kids from back then.'

Putting aside everything else. I had an icy jolt of fear as we climbed out of the car. Would his mum want to talk to me about my sister and everything that happened back then? Oh well, it was too late to do a runner now. I followed Tom as he let himself in through the front door.

'Mum, it's me! And I've got a surprise visitor for you!'

He led me through to the living room, where his mum was sitting in what looked to be a relatively high-end adjustable armchair next to a small Christmas tree – undecorated with the exception of some multicoloured fairy lights that were switched off. She was leaning over a jigsaw puzzle, a pair of glasses on the tip of her nose. I absolutely recognised her from back then; she must've worked at the playschool for quite some time as she'd still been on the roster when Livvie had started going there. Her face lit up when she saw us, and I immediately felt safe.

'Amelia Allister, well I never!'

'See, I told you! Mum, Mally had some car trouble over at the Big Tesco so I said I'd run her back to where she's staying for the week. Then we had a slight turkey incident so we decided to swing by here on our way. Speaking of which, I'd better get the stuff in from the car.'

Tom headed outside while his mum kept chatting to me. She gestured for me to sit down on the sofa next to an old-looking suitcase.

'Oh, I'm so happy to see one of my little playgroup kiddies all grown up. You look marvellous. And it's Mally now, did I hear?'

'That's right, Mrs B. It's so nice to see you.'

'I don't think anyone's called me Mrs B for about thirty years, sweetheart. Please call me Jo.'

'Ha ha, thanks. I really don't want to put you out so I won't stay long. I've been benefiting from a lot of Brinton kindness today.'

'That's my boy. Could you be a sweetheart and pass me my walking frame?'

'Oh, of course, but please don't get up on my account...'

'Don't worry, I just really need a wee. I'll be back in a jiffy – make yourself at home. Thomas! Make our Mally a cuppa, would you? Then we can all sit down and have a nice little natter.'

Thomas! This was turning into a fun evening. I looked around the room while shopping-unpacking and kettle-boiling sounds emanated from the kitchen. Every single wall had floor-to-ceiling Billy bookcases from IKEA packed with all manner of objects ranging from *Puzzler* magazines to thimbles, Lilliput Lane ornaments to jigsaw puzzles. It would've been easy for it to have felt oppressive, but somehow it felt warm and fun. Everything seemed to be meticulously organised and I couldn't spot a speck of dust, unlike the permanent air swirls of the stuff back at my own flat in London.

All of a sudden, the cushion next to me moved, and a sleepy pair of eyes looked up at me with curiosity. It wasn't a cushion, after all – it was a little sausage dog. I instinctively scratched behind one of his ears.

'I see you've met Chippie, then?' Tom said, as he re-appeared.

I clocked he was wearing a well-worn pair of cosy slippers in lieu of his shoes. He set down a tray on the coffee table with three mugs of tea and a plate of chocolate Hobnobs. Ah, the king of dunkers.

'I think I've woken him up. Sorry, Chippie.'

'Ah, don't worry, he sleeps most of the time these days. He was born a sausage dog, but pretty much identifies as a cat.'

'That's my kind of dog,' I said, as Tom moved the old suitcase onto the floor and took its place beside me.

'Wow, your mum really loves... stuff, doesn't she?' I continued, looking around the cosy room, stroking Chippie as I did so.

'Yeah, she's an avid collector, that's for sure. Can't rest until she's completed every collection before moving on to the next fad. Recently it was those M&S Little Shop miniature things.'

He pointed to a shelf on the opposite wall of the room where, lo and behold, all the scaled-down groceries were proudly displayed in a branded collectors' case.

'Right now, it's...'

He leant over me – I had to actively restrain myself from confirming the softness of his cardigan – pulled out a canvas box from the shelf adjacent to his mum's chair and peered inside.

'Ha! Oh yeah. Pokémon cards. She's even set up a swap group on Facebook, keeps doing deals with all the local primary-school parents.'

'Seems perfectly reasonable.'

'Yeah. It makes her happy, so...' He stretched and scratched the back of his head.

Jo made her way back into the room and sat back down in her chair. 'Ooh, that's better. Hope Chippo's giving you enough space on there?'

'I thought his name was Chippie?' I asked, not sure if I was directing the question to Jo or Tom. Jo answered.

'Ah, Chippie, Chippo, to-may-to, to-mah-to. His proper name's Chipolata, y'see, since he's a…'

'…sausage dog!' I finished her sentence and cackled. I liked it here.

'Exactly! So where are you staying, Mally?'

'Oh, just a little holiday rental in the centre of the village for a few days.'

'And have you got anyone special waiting for you back there?'

Let's be honest, if there was 'anyone special' in my life, I wouldn't have ended up stumbling about, car-less, in Scarnbrook ten days before Christmas.

'Nah, I'm here solo, just for a quick work trip.'

'Well, I've never heard of anyone coming to Scarn-brook on business before, have you, Thomas?'

'I reckon it's a first. But Mally's been asked to write an article about childhood Christmases for a news website.'

'You're a writer! How wonderful. Thomas harboured dreams of writing when he was younger, didn't you, love?'

'Mum, I don't think Mally needs to know about this…'

'I most certainly do. Tell me more, Jo.'

'Oh yes, he used to have stories and poems coming out of his ears at one point. Pages and pages just scattered all over his room. I've still got it all somewhere…'

'*No!* Mum, that stuff is old and kind of… private. Let's change the subject. Please.'

'All right, all right, I'll shut up about it.' Jo's eyes twinkled at me conspiratorially, as if she'd known me for thirty-five years, rather than thirty-five years *ago*. 'But I tell you what I do have to hand. Let me see, let me see…'

Jo ran her thumb over a few book spines on the shelf above her burgeoning Pokémon card collection before pulling out the one she had in mind. It was a sun-faded scrapbook bearing a photo of the basic, prefabricated structure that had once served as Scarnbrook Village Play-school on the front. Jo flicked through its well-worn pages for a few seconds.

'Ah, here we go!'

She handed me the album and there it was – our 1990 class photo. I was sitting at the front, eyes scrunched up in the sunlight, wearing a miniature white track-suit and sporting the world's worst haircut. My blunt, uneven fringe would remain my trademark look for at least another few years thanks to Mum's insistence that she cut mine and Josh's hair herself to save money. It was only after Livvie was born with a mass of untameable curls that she finally admitted defeat and called upon the services of Snippy Snips on the High Street.

'Ah, wow. I haven't seen this picture for, well, decades.' I was well out of the habit of casually looking at old family photos. With the exception of a few precious images of me and Livvie back at my flat, all my old childhood photo albums were still at a storage unit that Auntie Sandra had hastily rented for us back in the noughties as a stopgap. The gap in question was still well and truly sealed.

I dismissed the thought, and instead scanned the other squinting faces in the photo, trying to place Tom on the back row among all the other taller kids.

'You're going to have to help me out here, Tom,' I said, handing him the scrapbook.

'I thought this might happen,' he said, pointing to the smallest child in the class on the front row.

'That's you?! Right next to me?'

'Oi, I was a summer-born baby, okay? And I had a pretty epic growth spurt just before secondary school.'

I peered closely at the tiny child next to mini Mally in the photo. His wavy hair had been slicked into a side parting and it looked like he was on the verge of crying, his thumb jammed firmly into his mouth, as if to stem the wails. With the other hand, he was clutching a bright orange soft toy of some kind to his chest, protectively.

'You don't exactly look happy to be there.'

'Our Thomas was always a sensitive soul, weren't you, love? Hated being left anywhere, which is partly why I ended up working there, so I could stop his little heart from breaking every day. And thank goodness for Marmalade, eh?'

'Marmalade?' I asked, baffled.

'She means the toy I'm holding in the photo,' said Tom, pointing at the out-of-focus bundle of orange fluff in the image. 'Me and Marmalade were best buds back then.'

'Oh, Thomas!' Jo's exclamation made me jump, but evidently she'd just remembered something. 'Speaking of Marmalade…!' She pointed at the suitcase on the floor next to Tom and bobbed up and down lightly in her chair.

'About that, Mum. I'll pop round later this week and we can finish off the tree then, yeah?'

Jo settled back into her seat, smiled and nodded, but her eyes looked disappointed. And suddenly it dawned on me why.

'Oh! You were meant to decorate your Christmas tree tonight? Gosh, I'm so sorry, I've really messed up your evening, haven't I?'

'Not at all, sweetheart. It's just something silly we usually do the second Sunday of December, isn't it, Thomas?'

'It's not silly, Mum! It's nice. But, yeah, it can wait for a couple more days this year.'

I glanced down at the suitcase. 'Wait. Is Marmalade in there?' I ventured, tilting my head towards the vintage-looking luggage.

'He is indeed,' Tom replied. 'He's been hibernating since the fifth of January, as he does every year.'

'Could I at least meet the little fella?'

Tom glanced at his mum, who nodded enthusiastically.

'Ach, go on then.' Tom clambered off the sofa and expertly released the two satisfyingly springy silver clasps on the suitcase. He rummaged about for a while before producing a now more-brown-than-orange toy cat, which he cradled delicately in his palms. Chippie looked up from his slumber, and I swear I saw him roll his eyes briefly as he caught sight of the toy cat, as if they were long-term rivals. He turned his head away and went back to sleep.

'Gentle, now,' Tom said, grinning widely and passing Marmalade into my own outstretched palms.

I didn't know it was possible to fall in love with an inanimate object, but there and then I would have done anything for soft, little Marmalade. One of his eyes had been replaced with a mismatched button, which had been inexpertly but lovingly sewn on slightly higher than the remaining original. Marmalade's neck had been reduced to just a few frayed strands of fabric, and mini clouds of stuffing were poking out from various strained stitches. Despite his many flaws, he was still perfect, and entirely embodied the word 'cherished'. I set him down on my lap and stroked him, like a real cat. He deserved it.

'He likes you,' Tom said.

'The feeling's mutual,' I replied, keeping my eyes firmly on my lap in the hope that Tom wouldn't notice my compliment-induced redness. 'So he comes out every year for Christmas, then?'

'Yeah, he's got a special little perch for the rest of the month. May I?' Tom reached out for Marmalade so I passed him over gently. Tom, in turn, placed his beloved toy among the branches of the unlit artificial spruce, facing outwards so his sweet, skew-whiff face could be admired by anyone who gazed at the tree.

'There you go, Marmy, back in your favourite spot for another Christmas,' said Jo, her face somehow aglow with delight as she gazed misty-eyed at her son's stuffed animal on the tree. Objectively, if you were an alien landing on earth for the first time witnessing this scene without any context, the whole thing would appear to be totally bizarre. But, there and then, all I felt in that room was love and magic. And my own eyes suddenly felt dangerously hot with liquid.

'He looks right at home,' I said, blinking all the wetness away before anyone noticed.

'Well, he *is* home!' Jo exclaimed, absorbing the dampness from her eyelashes with a tissue. 'We don't bother with tinsel or Christmas baubles here these days; we just put all our Christmas memories on the tree, don't we, Thomas?'

'Yep, our micro-family tradition.'

My eyes burnt once more. What the hell was coming over me? *Just keep talking and stop feeling, Mally.*

'What else is in the suitcase, if you don't mind me asking?'

Tom nudged the suitcase towards me with his foot.

'Go for your life. It's mainly Christmas stuff I made when I was a kid. Just tat, basically. But special tat, you know?'

'Yeah,' I murmured absentmindedly, since my attention was entirely absorbed by the treasure trove at my feet. The suitcase didn't contain any of the usual superficial sparkly things that most people would decorate their Christmas trees with. Instead, it contained precious memories of a childhood joyfully lived.

As I carefully removed each hand-made decoration from the suitcase, Tom and Jo shared a brief history of its significance before it was placed on the tree with Marmalade. Before I knew it, every branch was full, including the protruding one at the top that now featured a disintegrating toilet roll flanked by two flaps of tracing paper that had once been an angel that Tom had made in Sunday school when he was five.

'There!' Jo proclaimed. 'The best one yet, I reckon. Just one thing left! Thomas, could you…?' Before she'd even finished the sentence, Tom had walked over to the doorway and switched off the big light. Jo turned to me, a silhouette outlined in orange by the glow from the street-lights that seeped into the room through the net curtains.

'Go on, Mally – you do the honours.'

'Oh, gosh, no I couldn't—'

Jo reached over and squeezed my arm. 'Please, love, it would make my year.'

'Okay. Erm, Tom, where's the switch?'

Tom guided me to the plug socket using the torch on his phone.

'Right, then. Here goes. Three, two, one…'

At the click, the tree came to life. All the colours, all the memories, all the love. All that was special about

Christmas was, somehow, right there, in an unsuspecting corner of this small Scarnbrook bungalow, lit up with the simplest string of fairy lights.

And right in the centre of it all was lovely little Marmalade. Wonky, imperfect and defective, but adored by everyone, regardless. Perhaps with the exception of Chippie.

Chapter 10

☑ Awkward farewell

We stayed at Tom's mum's place for another hour or so after the tree had been fully adorned and illuminated. But the start of *Antiques Roadshow* – which Jo said she watched every week in the hope that she'd spot something from one of her many collections – gave us a natural moment to leave.

'Could you remind me where we're heading?' Tom asked, as he fastened his seatbelt.

'Sure, here you go, Tom. Or should that be Thomas?' I handed him my phone with the postcode.

'You know, she's never called me Tom in her entire life.' He checked my phone and chuckled. 'You're staying right next to The Star! Think I can manage to find my way there – not been for a while, mind. Have you been in to say hello?'

I didn't tell him that I'd only arrived earlier that evening, or ask why he thought it'd be appropriate for me to announce myself to a drinking establishment I hadn't stepped foot in since body glitter was all the rage. Anything to give off the air of someone who knew precisely what they were doing here. Which, I was beginning to realise, I absolutely didn't.

'Umm, not yet. But I'm heading there for dinner tomorrow night.'

I wasn't looking forward to dining alone, but hopefully the food would be marginally fancier than tonight's Pot Noodle plan. Plus, I was hoping to shoehorn in some subtle Christmas movie trope-ticking while I was there.

'Ah, nice. The food's brilliant. They'll be chuffed to see you.'

I could only assume that the pub wasn't exactly popular if they were likely to be excited about an early evening booking for a solo diner. A thought crept in. *Should I…?* No. Of course I shouldn't bloody ask him if he fancied joining me there. As if he wouldn't have better things to do. I changed the subject to prevent the irrelevant thought from lingering.

'Have you got a busy week coming up?' I asked.

'Yeah, always busy at this time of year. Don't get me wrong, it's great that business is booming, but my days just end up being filled with endless meetings. And it doesn't help that the venue we'd booked for our Christmas party later this week has cancelled on us and I've got a couple of days to sort a plan B.'

'Yikes! But think of it this way: plan Bs sometimes end up being better anyway.'

Tom puffed his cheeks and blew out the air slowly. 'I appreciate the positive spin, Mally, but finding a decent venue for twenty people at this time of year? Tough gig.'

'Ha, yeah, Good luck.'

Silence. *Shit, Mally, say something.*

'Your mum's so great! Funny story, though: I always thought her actual name was Mrs Bee – as in "bumblebee".'

129

Oh God, there was that all-over grin again. The shape of his head seemed to alter entirely when he broke into it. I'd never seen a smile so face-changingly wonderful before. And I couldn't get enough of the fact that something I'd said had caused it.

'Of course you did!'

'What does that mean?'

'I… just like the way your brain works, that's all.'

I had absolutely no idea what to say to that. So I carried on talking as if he hadn't said it at all.

'And your mum's home is lovely. Believe it or not, I'd never even seen that part of Scarnbrook before.'

I noticed his knuckles blanch slightly as he tightened his grip on the steering wheel.

'I mean, why would you have done? None of your mates lived on the estate, did they?'

Oh dear. The nerve I'd unwittingly brushed up against earlier when I mentioned his decision to stay in Scarnbrook seemed to be getting closer to the surface of Tom's skin. How to make it clear that none of this was intended as a dig at him?

'Well, I didn't really have that many friends. Mainly just Elle, in fact, especially after Year Nine when—'

He interrupted me – mouth smiling, but his face not changing its angles at all. 'Mally, you really don't have to explain. I'm just saying – we had pretty different upbringings, that's all.'

Shit, did he think me and my family were, like, wealthy or something back then?

'You reckon? I don't think they could have been that different, since we went to the same school and lived in an almost identical postcode.'

'Can we just, er, change the subject? Those days weren't exactly, well, the happiest of times for me and my mum.'

Not even a mouth-only smile this time. Accidentally triggering my secret teenage crush's childhood trauma definitely hadn't been part of today's plan. Mind you, neither had accidentally decorating a Christmas tree with him and his mum.

'Oh, God, I'm so sorry, Tom, I didn't mean to—'

He interrupted me again, talking quickly as if the words themselves were in charge. 'It's fine. It's just that my life wasn't like yours when we were at school. Even before Mum got diagnosed, I never got to do the family package holidays or French exchange trips or swimming lessons at dawn. And then my dad just upped and left us one day because he couldn't be arsed to deal with Mum's MS any more. That's why I had to drop out of sixth form – I had no choice but to go out and start earning money at seventeen. I couldn't just swan off to uni with my best mate and land on my feet in London.'

Pain pierced through my chest as I processed his words. I thought we were having a nice evening. But now it felt wrong. Every millimetre of my skin prickled with discomfort, my heart racing with adrenalin as I tried to think of a way to defuse this increasingly tense situation. I just wanted to be back in my Hither Green flat, on my sofa, under a blanket, watching a Christmas movie on Channel 5. Not here with someone who I was fast realising I barely knew – and who barely knew me. I had to steer this conversation back to safe ground again.

'That's… not an accurate description of my life, Tom.'

'Fuck. I'm so sorry, Mally, of course it isn't.'

'Yeah, I *never* went swimming at dawn. What maniac would choose swimming lessons over an extra two hours in bed? Well, except for my robotic brother, obviously.'

I caught a glimpse of Tom's dimples reappearing, which I hoped was a safe sign.

'It all just poured right out of me, didn't it?' he said. 'I'm so sorry. Are you okay?'

I looked down at my hands and picked at a piece of dirt that had lodged itself beneath my thumbnail.

'Yeah, I'm just a bit tired. It's been a long day.'

The silence stretched out. And this time I didn't have the energy to fill it, to change the subject, to act like I wasn't wounded. Tom eventually spoke.

'Mally, I'm really sorry about suggesting your life has been easy. That was so, so shit of me.'

'Yeah, it was a bit.'

Tom pounded the inside of his wrist against the steering wheel once, muttering, 'Fuck, I'm such an insensitive twat,' as he did so.

'You're not. Not for the most part anyway.' I caught his eye and nudged his gearstick-clutching arm gently to make it clear this was a joke. 'And I can see how my life must've looked that way to you – at one stage, anyway. But privilege comes in all shapes and forms, you know? Sometimes it's not about money, but all the other ways people feel comfortable without even realising it.'

Neither of us broke the silence that followed this time. I noticed we were practically at the house anyway.

'Okay, yeah it's just down this lane.'

Tom pulled into the narrow private road and cleared his throat before speaking.

'There was uproar when the developers put the planning application in for these new-builds, you know? Do you remember there used to be allotments here?'

Gosh, I did. My grampy had had one. He'd practically lived on it after my nan had died. I wondered if Mum knew they'd been tarmacked over – the allotments had been a special place for her, too. But it's not like I could just drop her a casual message to ask. It would be the equivalent of an atomic bomb for her.

'That was here?'

'Yeah, it was a sad day when they got flattened.'

Tom helped carry my shopping to the performative porch as I searched my handbag for the key, not easy with shaking hands.

'I'd better be off, Mally. I've got a long day tomorrow and need to get my own shopping in the fridge so…'

'Yeah, of course, of course.'

I was still fumbling around my handbag for the key when I remembered it was in my coat pocket all along.

'Aha! Got it. That really would've been the cherry on top of this evening.'

He flashed me a two-dimensional grin as he walked back towards his car.

I began to carry my shopping through to the kitchen. By the time I returned to the porch to fetch the final lot of bags, Tom Brinton and his shiny car had gone.

Chapter 11

☑ **Small-town guy is secretly talented**

Before I'd even opened my eyes the next morning I was consumed by an overriding sense of unease. It wasn't helped by the fact that I'd slept badly, desperately missing my non-lumpy pillows back at my flat.

My loose plan for today had been to go on a little drive around the village to see what else had changed – and what hadn't – while also keeping my eyes peeled for any provincial festive shenanigans for my article. But with the car at Ryan's garage for goodness knows how long, and torrential rain that didn't appear to be going anywhere, I had no idea what the hell I was meant to do until dinner at The Star later, which Elle had booked for me.

I decided I might as well stay in bed for as long as possible before my urge to crack into my stash of cereal would inevitably force me into a more vertical position. While horizontal, I replayed the previous night's conversations with Tom over and over in my head. Until the subject of his upbringing came up, it had been a really nice evening with him and Jo. Then I'd gone and put my foot in it and the night had derailed from there. The awkwardness with which we'd parted ways weighed heavily on me. But it wasn't as if we had any kind of friendship that I felt the urge to repair, and I didn't even have any way of contacting him. Which was probably for the best.

I stretched the consuming waves of cringing away and reached for my phone.

There was a message from Josh, who'd finally got around to sending me the details of that bottle of wine. I baulked at the cost – forty-five bloody quid!

I sent him the money online while scowling, put my phone back on the bedside table and reached for my laptop, awaking it from its perennial snooze mode. I figured I might as well try and make a start on this sodding article – the sooner it was done, the sooner I could get back to my memory foam mattress topper. And, truth be told, I already had some decent fodder for it after last night's car drama, the world's weirdest school reunion in the Tesco car park and an unexpectedly festive evening at Jo's house with the Christmas tree. A plan for that morning's writing scribbled itself in my brain's virtual notebook: write about last night in as vague a way as possible so nowhere and no one were identifiable *at all*. After that, I could legitimately spend a bit of time doing some background research about Christmas movies. Which would no doubt involve watching Christmas movies. Nice. I could also check out some local news sites and social media to see if any seasonal events were happening in the village over the next couple of days. At the very least, this would help me work out where to *avoid* going if I didn't want the risk of bumping into anyone else.

But, before I'd even opened a new Word document, the Instagram tab caught my eye. I refreshed Billy's page through muscle memory – if there was one thing this less-than-mediocre Airbnb had got right it was the broadband speed. A couple more photos had been posted in the last twelve hours or so. And I could see from the illuminated perimeter around his profile image that he'd also shared some new stories, but of course I couldn't access those without creating an account.

I loaded my brother's page next. His latest post was a paid partnership with a company called @TheVeganSleepCo. He and Saskia had been gifted an 'organic-certified vegan mattress' in return for 'an honest review' on Instagram. Weirdly, there was no sheet atop the mattress as the two of them lay on it in their matching Mocha Mousse-coloured pyjamas, faces consumed with fake laughter and their honey hair tastefully tousled. I assumed this was so the mattress logo was visible. I tried to permanently delete the mental image of a tripod and camera at the foot of their bed. I was about to close down the tab when I had a thought. I typed Tom's name into Instagram's search bar. Just for a brief gander, of course. It was a common name but I eventually found him. Private account. Darn it.

I noticed that he'd linked to what was presumably his business profile from his bio. I clicked the link, which took me to @WeFacilit8. The account's posts were reliant on memes and humour, all wryly connected to the dull humdrum of facilities management. I was impressed – the business had tens of thousands of followers, with several of the posts having gone viral. There was an entire series of TikToks explaining UK workplace legislation via the storylines, characters and locations of *Schitt's Creek*. As a massive fan of the show – which I'd binge-watched in a single week – I could vouch for the fact that the posts were very, very funny.

Now I could understand why the business would be reluctant to give social media up. I clicked on the company's website link and navigated to the About Us section. The welcome message from the CEO was written in the same witty yet friendly tone that shone from the company's Instagram account. I took a mental note to refer back to this page the next time I needed creative inspiration to convince eye-rolling colleagues to attend their compliance workshops. The CEO's name was at the bottom of the page.

Tom Brinton.

He was the CEO?! What was it he'd said last night? Something about having stuck around at the company? He'd obviously downplayed his success, which didn't surprise me in the slightest. He'd always been modest about his natural aptitude at school, often deflecting any attention away from his intelligence with mischief and backchat.

I devoured the rest of the website over the course of the next half an hour. It had clearly all been written by Tom himself. He appeared to be a natural writer *and* sales-person. I mean, I had no reason to procure the services of WeFacilit8 but even I was tempted to contact them to find out how they could support me with my non-existent facilities management needs.

My laptop's low battery alert startled me out of a photocopier-based daydream. I plugged it into the mains, finally opened up that Word document and flexed my fingers in preparation for a morning of writing.

I woke up two hours later, my body apparently having demanded that I catch up on the sleep it'd missed out on from all the tossing and turning the night before. Oh well. The article would have to wait.

Feeling significantly more refreshed and microscopically less icky about the previous evening, I opened WhatsApp on my phone and tapped out a message to Elle:

> **Mally:**
> You're not going to believe what happened to me last night. Can I call?

My phone rang almost immediately after I pressed 'send'.

'So, guess who I bumped into at Tesco yesterday...' I said.

'Was it Tom Brinton, perchance?'

Argh, it wasn't Elle. It was Ryan blimmin' Seldon. Presumably with car news.

'Sorry, thought you were someone else!'

'Obviously. Okay, so we've just checked over your car and, luckily for you, the damage is minimal.'

'Oh, thank God.'

'It's Lord Brinton, thy saviour, you should be thanking.'

'Ha, true.'

'So I'll try and get it sorted by Saturday.'

'The twentieth?!' I squeaked.

That was the last day I had my rental booked for – and I intended to be long gone by then.

'Yeah, sorry, I've got a pretty full schedule this week with lots of "we really need the car for Christmas" jobs. I'm going to have to squeeze it in after hours as it is. I can see if any of my contacts at other garages could do it

138

any sooner if you really need it, but they'll probably be booked up too.'

'No, it's fine. Thanks so much again. Just let me know when it's done.'

'Coolio, I'll give you a call when it's ready to collect. In the meantime, could you do me a favour and send me a message with your home address? I need to set you up as a new customer on the system.'

'Sure, no problem. Thanks again, Ryan.'

I hung up and navigated back to WhatsApp. Elle had replied:

> **Elle:**
> Can't talk – Frannie's got a fever, nursery won't take her and Rory couldn't take the day off. Plus, I've got six features on deadline and writers who all seem to have Christmas party hangovers. Still on track with your article?

> **Mally:**
> Oh no, good luck! Give her a get-better-soon kiss from me. No worries. Yup, all on track. Let's just say that, in typical Mally fashion, there have already been a number of ridiculous incidents…

> **Elle:**
> Great, can't wait to read. Don't forget the booking at The Star tonight.

Mally:
I won't!

I checked the time: 12.04 p.m. So many hours to fill before then. I sent Ryan a quick message with my London address, ate my cereal and decided to have a shower.

There was no hot water, obviously. I'd put off the inevitable for long enough: it was time to figure out the thermostat.

Chapter 12

☑ **Failing family business**

As I entered The Star twenty years after that infamous mystery shopping night, I was greeted by the sight of an unrecognisable establishment.

The layout was exactly the same as I remembered, but gone were the scruffy carpets, sticky Marmite-brown tables and flashing quiz machines, and in their place were beautifully restored parquet floors, mismatched shabby-chic furniture and filament bulbs as far as the eye could see. An ironic Queen Vic-esque bust took pride of place at the end of the bar, a Santa hat perched atop her head and tinsel around her neck. It was like being in one of South East London's gentrified ex-working men's clubs – old-school but on-trend. I loved it, and felt immediately at home.

I wandered up to the fairy-lit bar and cleared my throat to get the attention of the bartender.

'Hi, I've got a dinner reservation for Allister at six? It's, uh, a table for one…'

A head suddenly appeared out of the kitchen behind the bar. 'Oh my God, Milly, it *is* you!' It was Carly – Ryan's now-wife, which I still couldn't get my head around. I'd forgotten how insular a place Scarnbrook was.

'Oh, um, Carly, isn't it? I had no idea you worked here! Yes, that's me, though I go by Mally these days so...'

'Yeah, Ryan said something about that. Wasn't that Elle's weird little pet name for you at school?'

'That's the one, yeah.'

'How funny! Oh, we haven't seen you in *years*. What are you doing back here? Alone? And on pub quiz night?!'

Pub quiz? Oh God. This wasn't part of the plan.

'I'm staying nearby. For a work thing. Needed a bite to eat, so...'

'So you booked a table for one at six o'clock on a Monday night in Scarnbrook? Hilarious!'

I opened my mouth to explain that it hadn't actually been me who'd made the booking, but realised that would just sound even stranger.

'Ha, yeah, I suppose it is. Just used to busy pubs in London, I guess.'

'Oh my God, I have to tell Becky you're here. Becky! I was right! Look, it *is* Milly!'

Carly's identical twin appeared from the kitchen.

Becky and I had always got on well, especially in primary school, but had drifted apart as we'd grown up. We hugged warmly.

'Milly! It's so, *so* good to see you. But why the hell are you here?'

Becky never had been one to beat around the bush. But she was also one of those people who I could instantly feel at ease around, even after so many years apart.

'Ah, just a random work thing. You both work here, then?'

'We co-manage the place!' Carly replied. 'The old brewery pulled out about, what was it, Becky – eight years ago now?'

'Yeah, I reckon so. They had some horrible plan to sell it to this twat of a developer called Christian Woods, who wanted to convert it into flats. And after what he did with the allotments we couldn't let that happen – just too many good memories from back in the day. Plus, the rest of the pubs in Scarnbrook had gone by then, believe it or not. So, a bunch of us got together and launched a campaign to save it, and we now run it as a community pub.'

The name Christian Woods sounded familiar but the pub's phone interrupted my chain of thought before I could put my finger on why. Becky went off to answer it while Carly kept talking.

'Ryan said you bumped into Tom last night – something about your car?'

'Yes, I had no idea the two of you were married! Anyway, I thought driving to Scarnbrook would save me the hassle of a public transport mission, but I seem to attract hassle regardless.'

Carly cocked her head to the side. 'We've got a Bristol postcode, Milly, we're not exactly hard to get to!'

Oh God, had I offended her in the same way I'd put my foot in it with Tom last night? My mind started to race as I tried to figure out a way to make it clear that I absolutely did *not* think Scarnbrook was the arse end of nowhere, but before I could formulate the words, Carly's warm hand squeezed mine for a brief moment before she kept talking.

'Milly Allister, I refuse to let you spend the evening here alone. Ryan's already on his way from work, but let me see who else I can gather together. It's rollover night on the pub quiz, too. You're a clever-clogs – join the right team and you could be in for a big win!'

Every part of me wanted to do a runner. But the bingo sheets had imprinted themselves on my mind. Maybe an impromptu school reunion would give me some more material for the article. Hell, maybe it would give me *enough* material, and then I could hide myself away and write the damn thing until my car was fixed.

'I mean, don't go to any trouble or anything – I was just going to have a quick dinner before heading back…'

Carly's palm appeared disconcertingly close to my face. 'Enough. Let me handle this. You just go and sit at any table you like and I'll bring you a glass of fizz on the house. I'll get the kitchen to rustle you up one of our legendary Christmas dinners with all the trimmings. Unless… you're not vegan like your brother, are you?'

I made a mental note that Carly was aware of Josh's online profile. If *she* knew he'd started to veer into conspiracy theory territory, everyone probably did. It made me sad to think that the people here might presume that *all* the Allisters had lost their minds since we'd left. That said, perhaps we had.

'No, no – all good. Sounds perfect.'

'Great. Oh, it's just so good to see you, Milly!'

I opened my mouth to correct her, but closed it. It was kind of nice to be called Milly again.

Over the next forty-five minutes or so I somehow managed to polish off most of a bottle of Prosecco by myself while savouring my delicious dinner. Despite the slate tiles instead of regular plates, it was genuinely one of the tastiest pub meals I'd ever had. Becky came out from behind the bar as often as she could, and in snatches of conversation I learnt more about her and Carly's pub venture.

'Basically, me and Carly get paid to manage it as a job-share – we take it in turns to be here – but strictly speaking we're not the landlords. Instead, anyone in the community can buy a membership to get a share of the profits, and all the members also get an equal say in how we run the place.'

'Oh wow, so all the other staff here co-own the pub?'

'Mostly, yeah. We've got some paid employees – mainly in the kitchen – but we rely on member volunteers for pretty much every shift.'

'What an amazing story. I don't think I've ever been in a community pub before – not knowingly, anyway.'

'It got quite a bit of publicity at the time. We made the front page of the *Western Daily Press*!'

'I've got to say, Becky, you've worked wonders. I never came in here much before, but you and Carly have turned it into such a cosy and welcoming place. You should be really proud of yourselves.'

'Argh, you know I've never been good at taking compliments. But thanks – it means a lot you saying that. Especially at the moment.'

'What do you mean?'

Becky let out a long sigh and took a look over her shoulder before continuing quietly. 'Well, everything was going great here for the first few years, but then the pandemic kicked off, the bottom dropped out of the business and we started to get approached by that developer again – the same one who tried to close the pub down before we took over.'

'This Christian Woods bloke?' I asked. I still couldn't pinpoint where I'd heard that name before.

'Yes! Total twat. Over the last few months, he's crawled back out of the woodwork and seems hell-bent on getting his grubby little mittens on the pub again. It's as if he's some kind of parasite sucking all the community spirit out of Scarnbrook and we're the only independently owned business left for him to conquer. And his latest trick has been to launch a hate campaign against us.'

'In what way?' I asked.

'Oh, you know, the usual: complaining to the council about non-existent lock-ins and writing horrific online reviews about us on Google and Tripadvisor to put off any potential customers.'

'That's awful! Can't you report him to someone?'

'We've got no proof. But we know it's him. He even comes in for a meal or a drink now and then, leaving vastly inflated tips for the staff so they greet him like a celebrity whenever he's here. The pub members are even starting to turn against us themselves given how much quieter the place has been this Christmas. His strategy is blatantly to run us into the ground, gaslight at least two-thirds of the members into siding with him and make a vastly underinflated offer that, one day, we'll be brow-beaten enough to accept. I can't tell you how much I hate him.'

'I'm not surprised. He sounds like a total arsehole. I'm going to look him up – his name sounds so familiar but I can't figure out why.'

I tapped his name into Google accompanied by the word 'Scarnbrook'. Countless results popped up, including his social media accounts. I opened his LinkedIn page and zoomed in on his photo. Everything clicked into place.

'Aha,' I said.

'You recognise him? I'm not surprised, to be honest – he's something of a local figurehead with all these connections in high places. I swear that's how he ended up getting permission to flatten the allotments even though there was so much local opposition.'

'Yeah, he was in my brother's football team. His name rang a bell as I think he quite often comments on my brother's social media posts.'

'Huh. Small world.'

I was fast realising just *how* small. I put my phone away, but made a mental note to do some more digging on Christian Woods later since a 'local scoundrel' would come in handy for my article – especially one who appeared to be hell-bent on destroying a family-run business.

'I'm so sorry he's making life hard for you, Becky. I'd offer to do some promo on social media but I'm afraid I'm the very opposite of Josh when it comes to anything like that.'

'I know, I get it. Me and Carly are just so happy to see you back in Scarnbrook again.'

I smiled while pressing my spoon into a gooey chocolate fondant that had just been placed in front of me by the smiling bartender. Hearing nice people say nice things to me while eating nice food? This trip was turning out all right! *Oh bravo, clever, confidence-boosting alcohol.*

'Hang on a sec,' I said to Becky. 'If you and Carly take it in turns to manage the place, how come you're both here tonight? Or did I just happen to choose the right Monday for a solo dinner?'

'Well… to be honest with you, Ryan told Carly all about your surprise appearance at Tesco yesterday, and then we put two and two together with tonight's booking. We were a bit intrigued to see if it was actually you. So

Carly's kids are having a sleepover at our parents' as a Christmas holiday treat.'

Shit. A spontaneous Scarnbrook get-together was one thing, but a night hooked to my presence alone was quite another. What would everyone ask me? What would they want to know? I'm sure everyone meant well, but this level of attention was way beyond my comfort zone at the best of times. Why was I putting myself through this?

'Oh. Blimey.'

'Yeah, sorry, don't mean to be nosy or anything. It's just, well, we haven't seen you in so long and everything…'

'I know, I know. I'm sorry I've not been back before now.'

'Oh God, that's not what I mean, please don't apologise… shit, I need to go and get that phone. I'll be right back.'

I was fast remembering not only how close-knit Scarnbrook was, but how stifling it could be, too. And how visible I was here. A blast of cold air disturbed me from my increasingly anxious thoughts.

'There she is!' It was Ryan, and he was accompanied by a stocky, square-jawed man who – if the tightness of his T-shirt and lack of a coat in the middle of winter were anything to go by – was keen to let everyone know he frequented the gym. I got the impression that the 'nice' part of my evening had come to a juddering halt. Only more booze would get me through this.

Carly appeared and gave her husband a peck on the cheek.

'Yay! Ooh and you brought Darren! Good to see you, Dal.'

'Oi, Darren.' Ryan was pointing at me as if I was the largest piece of battered cod in a chippy's heated display cabinet. 'This is who I was telling you about – the one and only Miss Fuel.'

The new nickname went over my head. I could only hope that it was less offensive than Double A. The confusion on my face wiped the grin off Ryan's.

'Y'know, *Miss. Fuel*. Because of the misfuel of your motor?'

'Oh, yeah, of course, ha ha.'

Darren grunted 'All right?' in my vague direction and headed towards the bar.

'Don't mind him,' Ryan said, as he settled into a chair opposite me. 'He's the strong and silent type. He'll warm up after a couple of pints. Hope you don't mind us gate-crashing your night like this, Milly? Sorry, I mean Mally – can't get used to that!'

'Just call me whatever's easiest.'

'Ha, Miss Fuel it is, then. It's just that Carly said on the WhatsApp group that you were here on your tod, so we thought it would only be fair to join you, especially since it's quiz night and all.'

So, the WhatsApp rumour mill about a returning Allister was indeed working at full throttle. Great. I couldn't help but wonder whether Tom was also in the group in question. I hoped not. There was no way of knowing what he might've told everyone about my floundering last night.

At that moment a slosh of beer landed in my lap.

'Sorry, love,' mumbled Darren as he slammed the pint on the table in front of Ryan.

'Um, no worries. I'm just going to get this dried off in the loos. Back in a sec.'

Locking myself into a cubicle felt like a reprieve. I wondered how long I could get away with being in here before anyone noticed my absence. The thought made me ponder whether anyone in Scarnbrook had actually noticed my absence in the last twenty years. Probably not, otherwise I would've heard from them, surely?

By the time I got back to the table, a couple more members of the WhatsApp group had turned up – women I recognised after a moment as being Gemma Winters and Amy Cook. Or whatever their surnames were these days. The pub in general was starting to fill up, but it wasn't exactly bursting at the seams.

I took my seat next to Darren, who – judging by the empty glasses in front of him – was somehow already on his third pint. He took another large gulp before belching loudly and turning to me.

'So you're related to Josh Allister, then?'

There was a distinct thud from under the table.

'Fucking ouch, Seldon. I was asking about her *brother* not her sister—'

Ryan kicked him again and my stomach plummeted. I'd been back for just twenty-four hours and here I was, sat in a pub next to a rude stranger, and he'd mentioned my sister in his very first interaction with me. I pulled a beermat to the edge of the table and attempted to flip and catch it on repeat in the hope that it would give my frayed nerves something to focus on.

'Um, yeah, that's right…'

'Ah, awesome. So you must know Saskia Barnard, too. She's well fit. How'd those two meet, then?'

'I'm not sure, to be honest.'

'Oh. You're not close?'

The whole table was listening now. This was exactly the kind of scenario that Elle had warned me about whenever I brought up the subject of coming back. It annoyed me no end that she'd been right.

I shrugged as I drained my glass of its remaining Prosecco. There was more in the glass than I was expecting, which gave me extra time to formulate a response. 'He's just really busy with his work and everything. In fact, if you follow him on social media you probably see him more often than me.'

'You don't follow him yourself?'

'I don't do social media full stop,' I said, pouring myself the dregs of my bottle. I needed another one, and quickly.

'Huh. That surprises me.'

'Why?'

'Y'know, I kind of assumed you'd be pretty tight after everything that happened. He seems like a decent bloke.'

Silence descended around the table once more. Thankfully Darren kept talking, my ears ringing protectively as he rambled on about big pharma and individual freedom. The thing was that Josh *was* a decent bloke – he always had been. And he was usually right about most things – like climate change and the vital role of veganism in resetting our reliance on unsustainable food sources. The trouble was that he was starting to blur the boundaries between 'asking important questions' and 'questioning medical professionals and scientific experts about every word they'd ever uttered'. Elle had even noticed that Saskia was sharing her husband's content less and less.

'Hey, I said, can I get a selfie with you?'

Darren's repeated question brought me back to the room. He was already holding his phone aloft, arm outstretched, but before I could figure out how to say no in the nicest way possible, another cold blast of wind diverted the table's attention. A solo figure looked quickly around before heading our way. I didn't know if I was relieved or nervous to see him. Somehow, both?

It was Tom.

Chapter 13

☑ **Festive-themed contest**

'Tom!' Carly was carrying a big plate of chips, which she set down in the middle of the table. Maybe there was a mystery shopper among us.

She gave him a tight hug as I had another go at mastering the beer mat flip.

'Haven't seen you in yonks!' Carly continued. 'We weren't expecting to see you tonight?'

'Well, I saw your WhatsApp message and thought I might as well call in since it's on my way home. Can't stay long, though.'

'Amazing! And look who it is!' Carly gestured towards me as if I was a speedboat prize on *Bullseye*.

'Hey again, Mally.'

I glanced up for as brief a moment as possible and flashed a smile. 'Hey, Tom.'

'Oh yeah, I forgot you two had your own little reunion in the Morrison's car park last night.'

'Tesco,' we replied in unison and caught each other's eye as we did so. We both looked away quickly.

'Yeah, my mum said she saw you at the checkout, Milly,' said Gemma. 'Said it looked like you'd seen a ghost!'

Amy hissed 'Shh' in Gemma's direction.

'Shit, sorry. I didn't mean it like that,' Gemma mumbled, blushing.

This was all getting way too awkward. There was only one thing for it: more alcohol. I stood up to make my way to the bar.

'Anyone need a drink?' I asked. Hopefully the slurring was just in my head.

Darren held aloft his half-empty pint glass and wiggled it in my direction, without smiling.

'I'll give you a hand, Mally,' said Tom.

I smiled with gratitude – probably my most genuine smile ever since Darren had arrived – hoping that Tom's offer of help meant there was a chance we could put the tension at the end of last night behind us.

'Thanks, Tom. Drink?'

'Sure. Just a Coke, please – like I said, I'm on my way home so need to drive in a bit.'

'A Coke and another bottle of Prosecco please, Becky,' I said. 'Oh, and a pint of whatever Ryan's mate's having.'

We stood at the bar in silence while Becky poured the drinks. Tom tapped the bar nervously with his fingers while lightly bouncing up and down on the balls of his feet.

'Here you go, you two! Shall I add them to your tab, Mally?'

'Perfect, thanks.'

Becky walked to the other end of the bar to serve another customer.

'Cheers.' We clinked glasses, formally.

'Yeah, cheers. Thanks for the drink,' he said.

'It's the least I could do after your help yesterday.'

'Honestly, it was no bother.'

More sips, more silence. Argh, the cringe.

'Any luck finding somewhere for your Christmas do?' I ventured.

'That's a negative. We've decided just to have some drinks in the office tomorrow evening instead, Wernham Hogg-style.'

I smiled at *The Office* reference, took a long swig of Prosecco and topped up my glass to replenish the void. Tom cleared his throat.

'So, umm, I wanted to say sorry for how last night ended.'

'Argh, no, I'm the one who should be saying sorry,' I replied.

'Whatever for?'

'For saying such insensitive stuff about your upbringing and everything. It came out all wrong.'

'Yeah, maybe it did, but my reactions came out even worse. I hurt you, and I'm so sorry about that. I barely slept last night thinking about it, but I didn't even have your number to apologise. So, yeah, thought I'd swing by here to grovel in person.'

Before I knew what I was doing, I squeezed his forearm gently. 'Thanks, Tom. That really means a lot.'

'So, can we just forget about the tail end of last night, then?'

'I think "forget" might be a bit of a stretch. How about we chalk it up as part of our mutual and ongoing personal development?'

'Deal.'

We clinked glasses again. I started heading back to the table but Tom gently tugged me back to the bar by my elbow. 'Hey, who's that guy sat next to Ryan?'

'You don't know him? Someone called Darren – works at the garage, I think.'

'Oh right. Christ. Yeah, I've heard of him, but I've never met him in person. Think he's only worked there for the last six months or so.'

'Yeah, he's not exactly covered himself in glory so far tonight.'

He let out a long breath. 'That doesn't surprise me. Just know that he is *not* my friend, okay? He's not even an acquaintance, to be honest. Look, how long are you planning to stay tonight?'

'Gotta be honest with you, my instinct in these types of big social situations is always to escape as early as possible. But everyone seems to be having this rare child-free night out in my honour, so I feel like it'd be rude for me to leave anytime soon.'

He did his hair-rub-watch-check thing again. 'Okay, so how about we stay for a couple more drinks until the quiz gets going…'

I felt my cheeks flush at the notion of me and Tom being grouped together as 'we'.

'I thought you needed to head off soon?'

'Yeah, well, that's before I realised Darren Chambers was here.'

'I don't need a chaperone, Tom. But it'd be nice if you stayed anyway – if only to convince Ryan to change our team's name from Quiz In My Pants.'

'Oh no, he didn't?'

'He did.'

We made our way back to the table, where a heated debate was taking place about the picture round that had been distributed to each participating table. Each of the ten images featured an obscure still from a classic Christmas movie. Or at least, obscure to anyone except fellow Christmas movie geeks.

'I'm telling you, Gem, there's absolutely no way that *Groundhog Day* is a Christmas film,' Amy said.

I glanced down at the fuzzy yet indisputable image of Bill Murray.

'Ah, that's *Scrooged*,' I said. 'Probably the most eighties movie ever made. An underrated classic.'

'Told you! Here you go, Milly, see if you can fill in any of the other blanks.'

I did, and without effort. Tim Allen's swollen stomach in *The Santa Clause*, Arthur Christmas's musical slippers, Kevin's uneaten plate of macaroni cheese from *Home Alone* (surely he could've squeezed in at least *one* mouthful?), an aghast Alan Rickman as he toppled from the tower in *Die Hard* – they were all there. Disappointingly, none of the made-for-TV classics had made it onto the sheet, but all those images would've looked the same anyway.

The rest of the quiz passed by in a bit of a booze-fuelled blur. Dare I say it: I had fun. I had vague memories of sports, TV and literature categories – all of which Tom aced – and the obligatory Christmas number one music round. And, at some point, someone invented a drink called a Prosecco blitzer, which involved adding a shot of vodka to each glass of fizz.

Our team ended up winning, much to the displeasure of the other tables, who claimed that nepotism was at play given that Ryan was married to one of the managers.

Becky came over with our winnings, which came to £11.50 each. For some reason, my inner drunken calculator was trying to work out how many packets of Space Invaders that would've paid for from the leisure centre vending machine where I used to watch Josh's swimming galas. It therefore took me way longer than it should have to notice that Becky looked fed up.

'What's the matter, Becks?' Amy asked.

'Oh, someone's just messaged me to cancel his volunteer shift for tomorrow and we've got a big party booked in for their work do.'

A blurry image of my Christmas movie bingo sheets flashed before my eyes. I'd been mentally ticking off the tropes throughout the evening, and here was another opportunity that had landed right in my lap – because this 'failing family business' needed help! I spoke quickly and squeakily before I could chicken out.

'Umm, maybe I could lend a hand?'

Becky smirked and raised her eyebrows. 'I'm not sure you're going to be doing anything other than recovering tomorrow, if I'm honest.'

'Ah, go on, Becky, let me help.' Why was I speaking in an Irish accent?!

'I mean, if you're being serious it would be *so* amazing if you could?'

'I'm being serious. Look at this serioush face.' I pointed at my face until I was poking it. 'I've got nothing better to do.'

'Amazing, thank you, thank you, thank you! It's going to be one of our busiest nights of the year, mind.'

'All good, all good. What time shall I come?'

'Would five o'clock work? The table's booked for six so you could give me a hand setting up the private dining room. And I'll feed you as recompense.'

'Free food! Even better.'

I stood up to give Becky what I intended to be a casual fist bump to seal the deal, but as I rose, my alcohol-infused blood plummeted to my feet and I began to topple. A tattooed arm grabbed me around the waist and yanked me back into my seat before I hit the ground. It was Darren.

He pressed the side of his head against mine as he took a selfie. The entire incident probably took fewer than four seconds, but in that time Tom had stood up with chair-scraping urgency, grabbed our coats and pulled me out of Darren's strong grasp.

'Not cool, mate. What the fuck was that about?'

'Chill out, *mate*. Just wanted a quick photo with Josh Allister's sister, that's all.'

Tom rolled his eyes and turned to me, proffering my coat. I went to grab it but missed.

'Do you want to get going?'

I managed a nod.

'I'll walk you back.'

Chapter 14

☑ **Relatable klutz**

The rain was coming down heavily again. I still didn't have a bloody brolly, but I did have a beer jacket. Or should that be a Prosecco poncho?

Tom rummaged in his boot for a few seconds and emerged with a giant golf umbrella. He pressed a button and a canopy for two silently unfurled.

Our feet crunched in unison on the disintegrated tarmac lane that ran directly between the pub and the cul-de-sac. The same lane that I now remembered used to lead up to the allotments.

A vein in Tom's forehead was making itself known as I stole a look at him out of the corner of my eye, his mouth set in a tight line. He was quite obviously furious about what had just happened with Darren. But I didn't want to dwell on it. I took a few deep breaths, my mind automatically flicking through its archive of random conversation starters to disperse the tension. My drunkenness made the available files more abstract than usual.

'So, Thomas. Riddle me this: do you reckon that if aliens landed on earth on a rainy day, they'd think that our umbrellas were part of our exoskeleton?'

Tom momentarily stopped walking, turned to me and shook his head, smiling his big Brinton smile, before continuing on. 'It's not something I've ever given much thought to. I mean, maybe. Also, I know you're trying to divert my attention from what just went down in there, Mal.'

'Huh. Busted.'

'You don't want to talk about it?'

'Gotta be honest with you, Thomas – I reckon I'm a bit too pissed for deep and meaningfuls right now.'

'Ha. I hadn't noticed. How much do you reckon you drank?'

'No bloody idea. Though I do seem to remember requesting a straw for my bottle of Prosecco at one point.'

'Classy.'

I elbowed him in the ribs.

'Ouch!'

'Sorry, I went for playful nudge...'

'Well, I think your elbows are pointier than you realise.'

'I sharpen them every night before bed. Ryman sell everything these days, you know.'

'You're weird.'

'I know. Thanks.'

I pulled up my honey-I-blew-up-the-scarf further around my face, and slipped on a patch of black ice as I did so. Tom grabbed my waist to stop me from falling.

'Cheers. These bloody shoes have...' I slipped again. '...no grip.'

'I think it might be easier if you just grab on to me.'

I did. I wrapped my right arm around his slender yet solid waist, noting how my head fitted perfectly in the nook where the top of his arm met his chest.

'Oh, I kind of meant hold on to my arm, but this works nicely too.'

I would normally have let go but I was pissed and wobbly and he was warm and it felt safe there. So I didn't.

We walked in silence to the front door. I'd made sure that my hand had found the key already this time. But when I tried to insert it into the lock my coordination repeatedly failed me.

'Sorry, I think I might need some help to…?'

I handed him the keys, trying my best not to fixate on the all-over goosebumps the sensation of his fingers touching mine for a nanosecond during the exchange had caused. He pushed the door open and stood aside to let me pass, handing me back my key.

'Fancy, er, coming in out of the cold for a bit?' It was a good job I didn't know the questionable lyrics to 'Baby, It's Cold Outside' as otherwise I'm pretty sure I'd have burst into drunken song.

He cocked his head to the right, appearing to think for a couple of beats. 'I'd like that. But I've got another early start tomorrow so I really can't stay for long.'

'Long enough for a hot chocolate?' Man, I was storming through the Christmas movie tropes tonight.

'Yeah, go on, then.'

He wiped his feet on the doormat and removed his shoes. I realised it was probably the first time I'd ever seen Tom Brinton's socks. They were bright red.

'Could you pull that curtain across the door?' I asked. 'Without wanting to sound like an awkward customer in a Brewers Fayre, there's a nasty draught and me and the thermostat appear to be mortal enemies.'

'Your accent is stronger when you're drunk.'

'Arrrrrk at 'ee! In what way?'

He pulled the thick material across the rickety front door. 'Well, you just said "naaaaasty draaaaaught". I'm pretty if you were sober you'd say "narsty draurght".'

I put my hands on my hips in mock outrage and swivelled on my heel. A little too quickly, as it turned out: I'd intended to walk towards the kitchen at the end of the hallway, but ended up turning ninety degrees too far and walking into the wall instead.

'Ow,' I said, rubbing my nose, noticing that my extremities were feeling numb and tingly.

'Right, come on, let's get you sorted out. Go and sit through there and I'll get you a glass of water.'

'But I was going to make you a steaming mug of delicious cocoa!'

'Calm down, Mrs Claus. I'll see what I can rustle up.'

I plonked myself down on the hardest sofa in the world and was suddenly conscious of the lack of places to sit in the room. There was only this leatherette two-seater tub settee and a glass coffee table, which someone had evidently attempted to wipe clean with an abrasive product that had left a permanent misty smudge on the surface.

'Hey, Mally?' Tom called through from the kitchen.

'Mmm?'

He walked into the living room. He was holding my bingo sheets with a bewildered expression on his face.

'What are these, then?'

My mind flashed to that moment at the end of *Bridget Jones's Diary* when Mark Darcy stumbles across Bridget's secret journal. I definitely didn't want to end up chasing him down the road dressed in nothing but my underwear and a flimsy cardigan. But fuck it, why shouldn't I tell him?

'Argh. Okay. I need to swear you to secrecy about this…'

'Oooooookay. Why? What's going on?'

'So, this is the assignment that Elle's given me for *The Helix.*'

He looked at the sheets again, a look of total bafflement on his face as he read through the lists.

'Yeah, I just don't get it.'

'Pay attention, Thomas, as this is a bit complicated and I'm not exactly at my most coherent right now. But. Fuck, where do I start? Right. Have you ever watched one of those corny Christmas movies on Channel 5? You know, the ones that start at about three o'clock in the afternoon?'

'Oh God, you know what? My mum *loves* those films. Yeah, I ended up watching one or two of those with her over lockdown. They were…'

'Fucking brilliant, right?'

'Ha, well I'm not sure I'd go that far, but I guess they're oddly compelling in their own way.'

'Well, your mum's got great taste because I love them too, and that's why I'm here.'

'To watch corny Christmas films?'

'Nope. To, er, try and experience one of them.'

'Oh. Ooh. This is all starting to make sense now. So that thing with your car – that was real, right?'

'Yes! But it fits the formula perfectly. I couldn't believe it when you started pounding on my car like that.'

'I tapped assertively on the window, Mal. I wouldn't describe that as a "pounding".'

Melting face emoji.

'So the "car drama" one's ticked off,' he continued, after a quick ruffle of his thick hair. 'What else… what

164

else… Oh, and you've got loads of ticks next to "relatable klutz".'

'Welcome to my day-to-day existence. At least two of my klutzy moments were with you.'

'You can add a couple more ticks after that walk back. What else can you check off after tonight?'

'Ooh, let's see.'

He handed over the sheets and disappeared back into the kitchen, appearing soon after with a pint of water and a Nutrigrain bar. He plonked himself down onto the miniscule sofa next to me. I scanned through the lists, my eyes finding it harder to focus than usual.

'Ooh! Here's one – "festive-themed contest". The pub quiz totally counts with those Christmas rounds, right?' I ventured.

'I'd say so.'

I fished a pen out of my handbag and put a giant tick mark next to it.

'This one sounds a bit dramatic – "a hasty departure",' Tom said.

'Oh, that's the best one of all. They always manage to shoehorn in some conflict between the romantic leads, prompting one of them to scarper back to the city. But it all gets magically resolved a few scenes later. Seriously, though, pleeeeease don't mention this to anyone else. I'm going to be writing the article anomy – anonynous – under a fake name.'

Tom snorted, his shoulders shaking in amusement. I shot him a look – aiming for faux annoyance but probably achieving something closer to drunken mess – before continuing.

'And Scarnbrook won't even be named. I've kind of been strong-armed into it, truth be told.'

'By Elle?'

'Mmm-hmmm. And I *really* can't have my parents finding out.'

'Shit, your family doesn't know you're here?'

I shook my head and placed my inexplicably sticky hands over my face in an attempt to smother my shame. And I didn't use that word lightly. 'Nope. Does that make me a really shitty person?'

'No, of course not. But you always seemed like the kind of family who would be open and honest with each other, that's all.'

I placed my hands onto my lap and stroked my trousers. 'Yeah, well, maybe we were once. But… things change, don't they?'

'They do.' He smiled sympathetically before stretching and looking around the room. 'Not exactly cosy this place, is it?'

'Nope. You should see the spare bedroom – there's nothing in it apart from a travel cot that seems to have caved in on itself. I was hoping Elle would find me a cute cottage like Kate Winslet's place in *The Holiday*.'

'Elle?'

'Yeah, she booked it. Easier for her to expense it that way.'

'Right, yeah. Do you mind if I put the fire on? It's bloody freezing in here.'

'Be my guest – not figured that out yet, either.'

Tom knelt on the floor and leant over to the side of the gas fire to locate the control panel. His jumper rode up a couple of centimetres as he did so, exposing the tiniest line of bare flesh. He was still long and lean like he'd been at school, but there was a softness there now that hadn't been there before.

He twisted the dial and pressed it in. The lighter clicked a few times before the gas caught and the fire whooshed into action.

'Legend, thanks for that. No match for a wood burner, mind.'

I'd never mentioned my kind-of-illegal woodburning stove to Josh – he'd probably come round to forcibly remove it given how much they contributed to air pollution.

Tom re-joined me on the sofa. Perhaps I was imagining it but he appeared to be a few centimetres closer. *Keep reeling him in, girl!* Oh God, I was so drunk. I packed my metaphorical fishing rod and inexplicable internal American accent away.

'Tell me about it,' Tom said. 'Just got one installed at my place. It's perfect for cold weekends.'

'Nice, whereabouts is your place? Near your mum's?'

'Not far – I've got this converted barn out in Langwood.'

'Ooh, fancy!'

It really was. It was the kind of area where the houses had names rather than numbers.

'Ha ha, yeah, it's pretty nice. I was lucky to buy it when I did – prices have gone nuts in the last few years.'

'Tell me about it – the London housing market is wild.'

'Do you rent?'

'No, I was also lucky to buy just as the property market crashed, so we lived there together.'

'Ah, so you were with someone back then?'

'Huh? Oh, no. Elle was my lodger up until she got engaged. After we graduated, we moved to London and rented a place for a while. But then my grampy died and left me some money, which gave me the chance to buy at the right time.'

I took a long gulp of water and made a start on the Nutrigrain bar. Hang on a second. A Nutrigrain bar? I definitely didn't have anything in the house that involved 'nutrients' – genuine or otherwise – the last time I checked.

'Where the hell is this bar from, by the way?'

'Don't laugh but I always keep a stash of them in my boot. For emergencies.'

'What kind of emergencies?'

'Let me see: broken-down car in a blizzard, zombie apocalypse warrants swift getaway, pissed intriguing woman from my past in need of efficient sustenance to absorb alcohol...'

'Intriguing? That's not an adjective I'd associate with myself.'

'Really? Which adjectives should I use, then?'

'Ooh, "unremarkable", "awkward" and "organised" feel about right. Or if you fancy a few more syllables, why not go with "conscientious"?'

'You're pretty hard on yourself, aren't you?'

'Oi! I'm very proud of my conscientiousness, thank you very much.'

'Conscientiousness is underrated, it's true. I admire it. I wish I'd had more of it myself when I was at school.'

'I think you probably had enough going on.'

'Yeah, I know. But I do wonder how things could've worked out differently for me if I'd been able to see out my A levels. I mean, I've done well enough for myself here—'

'You really have, Tom – CEO? I'm impressed.'

There was no denying it now, he was definitely blushing. 'Ah, who told you? My mum?'

'Nope. I may have briefly glanced at your online credentials.' I attempted to cover my face with my hands again but he grabbed them before they reached their destination.

'Ha! Sneaky. Especially when Google drew a blank when I tried to do the same in return.'

He'd googled me! And… he was still holding my hands. I withdrew them, slowly, increasingly conscious of their stickiness.

'But yeah, I often wonder what else I might have achieved if things had been different for me,' he said. 'Like, if my dad hadn't left when he did or I hadn't got married so young.'

'Do you miss your ex?' Jesus, I felt like Lauren Laverne on *Desert Island Discs* with all this probing. Hopefully I wouldn't make him cry.

'I miss the companionship, sure – like I said, I'm not great at living alone. But we just met each other at the wrong time. I kind of wish I'd met her now, you know? But she's having a baby next year. So good for her, I guess.'

I was trying to look sympathetic but I was mainly trying to muffle an intense set of hiccups that had just started.

'Here, try having some more water.'

I took another sip, but as I swallowed the latest hiccup morphed into an enormous belch. Worse still, my diaphragm was insisting on pushing something up to the surface. Oh God, I was going to be… scratch that, I was *actually* being… sick, though thankfully my reflexes had been quick enough to make it to the wastepaper bin next to the sofa.

'Oh, God, Mally… umm, here let me—'

His sentence was interrupted by the sound of another violent heave.

'Oh… my God. I'm so… so sorry.' I repeated the word 'sorry' in between spluttering into the bin. After each spit I felt progressively less drunk, and progressively more mortified. 'This is so embarrassing.'

'Uh, don't worry, don't worry. Are you okay? Let me grab you a… tea towel or something.'

'Yeah, I think I just need to…'

I stood up but lost my balance. Tom caught me.

'Umm, I think you should probably just lie down and sleep this off. Shall I help you upstairs?'

I nodded as I wiped my mouth with the back of my hand, gagging once more as the rancid smell from my mouth reached my nostrils.

I knew two things for sure as I ascended the stairs with Tom's help: this element of my trip was definitely *not* going into my article. And this was the *single* most embarrassing moment of my life – about a million times more so than when I'd been presented with my PE effort award.

At least this time I wouldn't have to give a speech.

Chapter 15

☑ **Outsider saves the day**

Oh God.

The vibration of my phone had woken me up. Rude. I unsealed my right eye followed by my left and blinked the room into unusually sharp focus, which confirmed my fear that my contact lenses were still in place. A sure sign of a big night – with a poorly judged end. I took a peek under the duvet and noted that I was still wearing yesterday's clothes, too. Just brilliant.

I propped myself up on the world's most inadequate pillows and took a lengthy gulp of water from the pint glass on the bedside table.

I placed it back down and examined it through my sleep-smeared lenses. I never would've put an open container of liquid there, even in a drunken state. Who had done that? And placed that washing-up bowl on the floor? And... and laid one of the sandpaper-rough towels from the bathroom on top of the bed sheet, which was now scrunched up in a sweaty ball beneath me?

Oh God. Oh shit. Oh fuck.

The events of the previous evening coated the entire surface of my brain in a single instant.

I slithered back down under the covers and groaned. I'd been sick, hadn't I? And Tom Brinton had witnessed *All Of It*.

I reached my hand out from the depths of the duvet and scrabbled about for my phone, only narrowly avoiding spilling that glass of water. I brought it under the covers with me to see what it was that had woken me up at this totally uncivilised hour of... ten forty-seven. Huh.

It was a message from Becky.

> **Becky:**
> How's the hangover?! Still on for later? I think we agreed on 5 p.m.? P.S. Got your number from the booking system – hope that's OK!

Later? What was she...? Oh. Oh no. I'd agreed to cover a shift at the pub, hadn't I? I wasn't even sure how I'd get out of bed today, let alone make my career debut in hospitality.

I replied:

> **Mally:**
> Bad. Sure. See you then x

I closed my eyes and welcomed in the familiar rush of regret that always trotted not far behind an unwise agreement that had been made while completely hammered. My phone buzzed again. I looked to see Becky's reply only to discover a message from Josh, instead:

My regret was swiftly replaced by terror as I sat bolt upright. Too quickly, apparently, given that my hangover-induced nausea intensified by a significant magnitude as I did so.

I downloaded the attachment to his message. It was a screengrab of an Instagram story that awful Darren bloke had posted earlier this morning. It was the selfie he'd snapped while I'd been Peak Pissed. The caption read:

> Smashed @TheStarScarnbrook pub quiz with @RealJoshAllister's sister. Off to do his latest weights workout to sweat out the hangover.

The absolute prick. My hands shook as I typed out a swift reply to Josh in an attempt to nip this in the bud:

Mally:
Hey, just catching up with some old friends here while I've got some unexpected time off work. Nothing to be concerned about. Mum and Dad don't know and there's no reason why they need to. Don't worry.

Josh:
So you know this Darren guy? Doesn't seem like the kind of person you'd be friends with.

173

Mally:
No, just some random bloke in the pub
who ended up joining our quiz team.
Barely spoke to him.

Josh:
So how does he know you're my sister?

Mally:
The woman behind the bar said something
– you know what it's like round here. Bit
annoyed he's posted this to be honest.

Josh:
Do you want me to ask him to delete it?

Mally:
Don't bother. He's just fishing for attention.

Josh:
OK. Well, if you're sure everything's fine?

Mally:
I'm sure. Speak soon.

But I knew Josh. Despite my efforts to mollify his concerns, I knew he'd be scrutinising the revelation I was in Scarnbrook with an intensity that even *Line of Duty*'s Steve Arnott would be bursting out of his waistcoat to contain. There was only one thing for it: I absolutely had to get back to London as soon as humanly possible to avoid any other screw-ups like this. I could make the article up when I was safely back in my familiar flat. Let's be honest, it would probably be a better piece that way, too. Elle wouldn't care, as long as it gave her the clicks she craved. I began composing one of my mental lists:

Step one of mission to escape Scarnbrook: hydrate.

Step two: somehow get through the shift in the pub (I couldn't let Becky down, now).

Step three: acquire car ASAP – go to another garage if needed.

Step four: get the hell out of here. For good.

I decided to get a head start on step three by sending a quick message to Ryan:

> **Mally:**
> Hey, Ryan! Fun night last night! Any
> update on the car?

It was a good ten minutes before he replied, which afforded me some extra sleep – after I'd downed the rest of the water.

> **Ryan:**
> Soz, still got a backlog. Hoping to get to it
> tomo or the day after but no promises.

Tomorrow was just about acceptable, but I made a mental note to research other mechanics as a back-up plan. My phone buzzed with a follow-up message:

Ryan:
Btw, Darren's asked for your number. Can I pass it on?

Urgh, absolutely not. Sure, a disastrous date would no doubt give me some useful material for my article, but there was no way I was going to go anywhere alone with someone like that. And he'd been quick to show his true colours last night.

Mally:
Sorry, I'm kind of seeing someone back in London.

I mean, it wasn't a total lie…? Who was I kidding. I had to accept that me and Billy were never going to happen.

Ryan:
Does Brinton know? ;)

I felt a little wobble of promise about what Ryan was insinuating here. Would Tom be interested in knowing this about me? That said, he might already be aware – I could've told him my entire life story last night for all I knew.

Mally:
?

Ryan:
Lol, forget it. I'll be in touch as soon as ur car's ready.

Hmmm. I needed to ruminate on this some more. But I needed to empty my bladder and fill my stomach first. I staggered out of the bedroom and almost tripped over a thick wad of material that had been neatly folded on the landing. A handwritten note lay on top of it, the stems of the letters long and straight, like masts on a yacht:

Good morning,

In case you need a summary of what happened when you got in last night:

We discussed adjectives.

You were a little bit sick (not a problem, please don't feel bad!).

I helped you into bed.

I stayed for a while to make sure you were OK.

Sorry about the curtain, but it was the only thing I could find…! Not sure how long you'll be around but the soonest I can pop round to put it back up is tomorrow morning so hope that's OK. Please message me when you wake up so I know how you're doing.

T x

07700 900174

P.S. I sorted the boiler for you – the pressure just needed topping up.

There was no denying that it was a sweet note, and the metallic clinks I could now hear from the radiators were definitely reassuring from a frostnip POV, but I was confused about the curtain. I eventually figured out it had been the one hung across the front door. Had he – or I – pulled it down at some point? I couldn't recall any drapery dramas, but the specific details of last night didn't really bear thinking about right now.

I added his number to my contacts and tapped out a quick reply while on the loo.

> **Mally:**
> Hey, Tom, it's Mally (Allister). Just woken up. Thanks for the note. I'm so sorry that you had to deal with all that. So embarrassing. Thanks for sorting out the heating. I'd almost forgotten what warm felt like. Have a good day. M x

I decided to leave out the information about Darren's Instagram story. I always found it was best not to give situations like this any unnecessary oxygen.

Tom replied instantly:

> **Tom:**
> Thanks for clarifying which Mally had messaged me. There are too many of you to keep track of. No apology needed. It was a fun night… overall! I'll be round at 9ish tomorrow morning to sort the curtain if that's OK? xx

I almost replied telling him that there was no need to go out of his way, but I couldn't ignore the warmth in my chest – boosted by the steady uptick of kisses per interaction – that seemed to indicate that it *would* be nice to see him one final time before I headed back to London, so I replied simply with *Yup, thank you! xx* instead.

I added some sub-tasks in between steps one and two of my mission to leave Scarnbrook as I navigated the stairs on shaky legs.

Hydrate. Fill stomach. Back to bed. Shower. Pub.

Mally Allister: you've got this.

Operation Escape Scarnbrook was going to plan so far. Although I'd nearly been thrown off-course by a voice message from Elle, asking how the assignment was going. For the first time in a long time, I didn't get back to her straight away. I had no idea what to say; if I told her it was going well, she'd want details that I wasn't quite ready to share, and if I told her it was going badly, she'd probably force me to visit Santa's grotto at the local garden centre in the hope that would give me something to write about. I'd reply to her later after the shift at the pub.

I arrived at The Star at five on the dot, as per my promise. Becky was already setting up the private dining room – the very room that Elle and I had once cowered in with our cosmopolitans that unforgettable mystery shopping night. A magnificent, real Christmas tree was lit up at one end, with an open fire just getting going at the other.

'Allister! Right on time, as ever. Headache rating?'

'A solid six out of ten. Much better than this morning, though.'

She smiled and gestured towards the open cutlery drawer in a vintage dresser, so I duly began laying it out on the table next to each Christmas cracker.

'Speaking of this morning,' she said, with a definite twinkle of mischief in her eye, 'I couldn't help but notice that Tom's car was in the car park all night...?'

All night? I'd assumed he'd stayed for an hour or so after the vomiting incident, setting me up with my horizontal sick station, before leaving the note and heading back to his.

'Got to be honest with you, Becky, I can't remember much beyond securing the extremely generous pub quiz jackpot.'

Becky raised her eyebrows.

'Stop it. All I'm saying is that I more or less passed out when we got back to my place.'

I decided to spare her the details of me throwing up and being put to bed fully dressed like a hyperactive toddler after too much Ribena at a family wedding.

'Oh, well, all I know is that our CCTV caught him driving off at about seven thirty this morning so... er, Mills, are you OK? You're not going to be sick, are you?'

I'd passed the point of queasiness, but my face did indeed feel like it'd lost some of its colour as I thought back to last night, the mysterious curtain and Tom's note. All of a sudden, everything made a lot more sense.

'No, it's just that – oh God – I reckon Tom must've slept on the landing underneath a curtain all night in the absence of any basic comforts in my practically unfurnished rental.'

Becky chuckled. 'That sounds like classic Tom.'

'Does it? I barely know him.' Did my voice sound as casual as I was trying to make it? Becky's snort suggested not.

'You're hilarious. You *must* know he had a soft spot for you at school, right?'

I swore my heart stopped beating for a moment as I attempted to process Becky's words.

'What are you talking about? Me and Tom, we… never even spoke back then.'

But had there been glances? Unspoken in-jokes? I always thought I'd imagined it. And that *still* seemed like the most realistic explanation for my silent tsunami of adolescent feelings.

'To be fair, you didn't really speak to anyone but Elle from Year Nine onwards.'

I opened my mouth to deny the accusation but nothing came out. I mean, she was right. Mine and Becky's friendship had fizzled out after Elle had moved next door just as we were on the cusp of our teenage years.

'Don't stress about it, mate,' she said. 'We were kids! Female friendships are weird and complicated. If it weren't for Carly and her strangely unsatiable appetite for spending time with people, I *still* probably wouldn't have any non-bloke pals.'

I could relate to that. Without Elle, I'd also have a grand total of zero mates of any gender.

'Anyway, back to more pressing matters: Tom *definitely* had a thing for you, okay? When the guys at school found out they used to rib him about it. They even had a nickname for the pair of you.'

'Tomelia' suddenly made a lot more sense.

'Yeah, I bet they did.' I kept my eyes firmly focused on the table-laying task at hand, kind of hoping that if I didn't catch Becky's eye, she'd somehow fail to detect the deep shade of mulled wine I was fast turning.

'Why do you say it like that?'

'Maybe something to do with the fact that I was a massive square and he was the total opposite?' I glanced up to catch Becky rolling her eyes before she walked over to the fire to give it a tactical prod and rearrange the tasteful festive garland that adorned the mantelpiece.

'Well, I guess back then the two of you were quite different on the surface. Though, years later, he told us that he'd managed to convince himself that you were way out of his league.'

Talk about the twilight zone.

'What?!'

'Yeah, he was pretty lacking in self-confidence back then, especially when it came to getting close to anyone. We used to have to beg him to come out most weekends.'

I was starting to detect the beginnings of a correlation between what Becky was saying and the brief insights Tom had given me about his tricky childhood. But 'lacking in self-confidence'? Surely not.

'What are you talking about? He was probably the most outgoing and popular person in our year!'

Becky shrugged. 'Appearances can be deceiving. Anyway. It's a shame, really, as I can now see that you're practically the same person.'

'The same person?' This was fast turning into the most unlikely conversation I'd ever had. And the table place I'd just laid had two dessert spoons where the knife and fork should have been.

'Oh, c'mon, stop acting all surprised. I could tell when you two were together last night that there's something there. Even Carly noticed, and she's not exactly known for her perceptiveness. We've not seen him that happy in ages. Since he and Abbie broke up, he's really not been around that much.'

I wanted all the details. But, also, none of them. I decided to poke about, just a little.

'Was it a mutual separation?'

'Think so. He's never really spoken about it. I know that she was keen to have kids straight away, but Tom wanted to wait because he was still so young. And then by the time he was ready for that chapter they'd drifted apart to the extent that it wasn't the right time for either of them any more.'

'That's sad.'

'Trust me – it was for the best. She really wasn't a great match for him. Unlike someone else I know...'

I felt all sparkly, as if someone had switched on my internal fairy lights.

'Becky, stop it! This is... a lot to get my head around, especially on such a hungover stomach.'

'Don't overthink it, mate.'

'"Don't overthink it"? But overthinking is my happy place!'

'Ha ha, yeah, of course it is. Because it's Tom's happy place, too. Okay, go ahead and overthink it, then. But don't let that get in the way of actually doing anything about it, hmm? Right, can you pass me those napkins? I've found this amazing video that shows you how to fold them into cute little Christmas trees and I've been itching to give it a go. Up for the challenge?'

'You do remember that I was effectively banned from textiles lessons after repeatedly slicing my fingers open with the pinking shears, right?'

'No scissors involved here. Just cloth, YouTube and misguided grit.'

At seven o'clock – an hour past their scheduled arrival time and in response to a series of increasingly irritated voicemails left by Becky – the organiser of the private room booking finally confirmed they were no longer coming. The no-show was a devastating one: the deposit the group had paid to reserve the space for the night came nowhere close to making up for what the pub should've raked in from the group on booze sales alone. And all the wasted food they'd bought in especially – and had already begun to prepare based on pre-orders – didn't bear thinking about.

There were a few other smaller groups and couples enjoying the festive set menu, but even I could tell that, for the only pub in a busy little village like Scarnbrook to be 75 per cent empty in the immediate run-up to Christmas, something was very awry.

After helping to clear a table – and praying that I would never have to handle a piece of jagged, heavy slate masquerading as a plate ever again – I found Becky slumped in a fireside armchair in the private dining room, her head in her hands.

I pulled up a chair next to her and squeezed one of her shoulders. She looked up at me through mascara-damp eyes.

'It's him. He's done this.'

'Who?'

'That bastard Christian Woods. I'm telling you.'

'But the deposit…?'

'A few hundred quid means nothing to him. He's playing the long game.'

'Shit, I'm so sorry, Becky.'

'Thanks. You might as well head off – it's not like we need the extra help any more.'

I looked at the open fire roaring where a *Who Wants to Be a Millionaire* quiz machine used to reside. Staying here in this cosy establishment was way preferable to heading up the lane to my distinctly unfestive and fluorescent-lit rental. More importantly, Becky needed a friend right now. And I got the impression my presence alone would mean something.

'Nah, it's warmer here than back at my place. In all senses of the word.'

She gave me a quick hug before standing, wiping underneath her eyes and tapping her cheeks a few times as if to dislodge her disappointment.

'Right, I'm going to head back out there. Maybe you could put the cutlery back in the dresser so it doesn't get dusty? God knows when it'll next see the light of day.'

I saluted my compliance with a sympathetic grin as she went back into the main area of the pub, leaving the door ajar behind her.

I looked around the beautiful room. What a fucking waste. And what a fucking bastard that Christian Woods bloke was if it was indeed him who'd planned all of this for his own greedy gain.

And then I remembered: tonight was the night Tom's company was having its Christmas party. I tapped out a quick message to him, my fingers shaking as the potential of the idea took hold.

> **Mally:**
> Hey, bit last minute, but are you still in need of a venue tonight? The private dining room at The Star is suddenly free and the kitchen is bursting with food that will otherwise go to waste?

Tom replied almost instantly.

> **Tom:**
> Er, are you serious? Because let's just say 'drinks in the office' is fast turning into 'awkward silences in the office' and I feel like David Brent.

> **Mally:**
> Yeah! Give Becky a quick call, see what she says. But they could really do with filling the place up tonight.

Tom:

Understood. And the local taxi firm owes me one. Fingers crossed!

Moments later, the pub's phone rang and I peered round the dining-room door to see Becky's face light up. While she spoke into the handset, she looked in my direction, grinned and gave me a massive thumbs up before hanging up, doing a little dance and dashing into the kitchen.

I turned back to the dresser, feeling all warm inside, and began to handle the cutlery for the third time that evening.

I'd just about finished setting up the room when I heard a loud male voice proclaim 'Hello, anybody there?' as he approached the end of the bar just beyond the private dining room. I peered out through the crack of the door to see who on earth would feel the need to announce their presence so loudly. It was the fucker himself: Christian Woods, accompanied by a picture-perfect family of an attractive wife and two tweenage daughters. The four of them were inexplicably wearing matching Aran wool jumpers, as if they were part of the same veteran cricket team. Even looking at them made my throat feel constricted and itchy. The three female Woodses were despatched to the other side of the pub to find a table. 'That's if you can make your way through the Christmas crowds!' he scoffed while looking around, as if he was surprised to see the place so empty.

Becky emerged from the kitchen, a winter storm brewing in her eyes.

'Bit quiet tonight, isn't it, Carly?' Christian said.

'I'm Becky, as you're well aware. And I know it was you, Christian. How could you do this? Everyone working here has got families, you know. You're killing us.'

'I've got no idea what you're talking about, Becks. I've just come here with my family for a bite to eat and a celebratory drink.'

'Celebratory?' Becky replied.

'Yep! Because, by the looks of things in here, we're not far off securing our next property development contract. So, a bottle of your finest champagne, if you don't mind?'

While Becky fetched the bottle from the fridge, slammed it down on the bar and snatched his £50 note to take payment, I realised I wasn't breathing, my entire body frozen as their dispute continued. I knew Tom and his colleagues would be arriving at some stage, but until then I felt as if I was watching a scene from *EastEnders* play out in real-time, with some dastardly Steve Owen-style character in the midst of quietly threatening Peggy in the Queen Vic.

Whenever we used to watch these dramatic episodes on Christmas night, Livvie had always shouted at the telly for someone to secretly record the conversation so they could use it as evidence down the line.

SHIT! THIS IS YOUR CHANCE! RECORD THIS, MALLY!

With fumbling hands, I took my phone out of my pocket, aimed the handset through the crack and tapped record just as Christian removed some rolled-up sheets of paper from the back pocket of his dark pink trousers. He straightened the stapled sheets out on the bar and pushed them towards Becky as she unceremoniously plonked the champagne in an iceless ice bucket.

'What's this?' she asked.

'A new offer for your perusal. And for all your little community pub elves – or whatever it is you call them – to vote on, of course. I think you'll find that, given tonight's no-show and the direction this business is quite evidently heading in, the figures I've proposed here are *more* than generous.'

He knows about the no-show! This is proof!

At that moment Becky looked right at me, and right at the camera. Her face changed into one of surprise so quickly that it caught me off guard and my phone clattered to the ground. Christian's face whipped round, but not before I'd glanced down to clock that my phone – which wasn't visible behind the door frame – was still recording.

'And who do we have here?' he sneered. 'One of your little helpers is having a nice eavesdrop, are they?'

I stepped out of the room, leaving the phone behind. He didn't recognise me. But why would he? It wasn't as if our paths had ever crossed on the rare occasions I'd dragged myself out of bed on Sunday mornings to cheer my brother on from the muddy sidelines of the football pitch over two decades ago. I took a deep breath, trying to focus on the fact that his cream jumper actually made him look more like a weirdly large nativity sheep than a cricket player. I kept the farmyard thought in my head as I took a small but decisive step out of the doorway and into the main bar area.

'Becky didn't tell you there'd been a no-show tonight,' I said, my voice shaking, but my thoughts as steady as they'd ever been.

His smile faded for a nanosecond. It was the chink I needed to see to bolster my confidence even more.

'Speak up, darling, I couldn't quite hear you.'

'I said, Becky didn't say anything about tonight's no-show. So how did you know that they didn't turn up?'

'Oh, I don't know, someone probably said something on Facebook or...'

'Seriously, just stop talking.' Apparently these words had come from my mouth. And there were more following fast behind. 'We know it was you. We know the shitty reviews are you. We know the calls to the council are you. For some reason, you seem absolutely determined to get your hands on this place. What's driving it, Christian? Did someone once refuse to serve you in here back in 1999, is that it?'

Becky stood open-mouthed behind the bar, her eyes widening. My raised voice had captured the entire pub's attention, with me at the heart of a David vs Goliath showdown. It felt... bloody brilliant. Livvie would've been proud.

Christian chuckled casually and raised a hand of calm towards the gawping punters, as if to say, *Nothing to see here, get back to your drinks, folks.* He turned back to us and smoothed down his side-parted hair with the heel of his hand and spoke quietly in a faux-relaxed voice so that only me, Becky... and my phone... could hear him.

'Didn't you know? There's a housing shortage. And it boils down to this: if I don't develop this place, someone else will. It's just a simple matter of time and economics. And, sure, maybe I've been trying to hurry things along a little, but that's for everyone's benefit in the long-run; surely you girls can understand that?'

It was the word 'girls' that pushed me over the edge. I was nearly forty, for fuck's sake. Who did he think he was?

'It's not going to happen, Christian,' I said, arms folded, standing as high as my five feet and two inches could possibly take me. 'Especially after everyone finds out what you've just said here tonight.'

He scoffed. 'You're so naïve. This is just how it works in the real world. Plus, why would anybody believe you?'

I picked up my phone from behind the door frame and held it aloft, clearly showing him that the device was still recording. 'Because we've got this whole conversation on camera.'

'Hey, let me see that!' he hissed.

As he lunged towards me to grab my phone, I sidestepped him and threw the phone to Becky, which she caught coolly with one hand and continued to film.

Christian shook his head a few times quickly, as if he was trying to convince himself this was all a bad dream.

'Whatever. It's not like anybody will care about your silly little video clip, anyway. I play golf with the head of the planning department. And I went to Cambridge with the editor of the *Western Daily Press*. My application will get waved through, just like all the others.'

I laughed. 'Sorry, am I meant to find that impressive? Because *I* work with the editor of *The Helix* in London, and I'm sure he'd be *very* interested in commissioning an article about sleazy small-town developers who are sucking the lifeblood out of lovely places like Scarnbrook to line their woolly little pockets.'

Becky snorted at my knitwear reference, and a look of genuine terror flew across his face. 'Hang on a sec, who did you say you were again?'

'I didn't. But I've been meaning to ask: have you been in touch with my brother, Josh Allister, lately?'

Christian froze. From the very little I knew about him, I could already tell he was the type of person who valued others in terms of what he perceived to be their transactional value. And, in his eyes at least, Josh was an influential asset – no doubt useful for namedropping every now and then – that he couldn't afford to lose.

'Shit, you're Josh's sister?'

I curtseyed for the first time in my life. 'One and the same.'

'Fuck. I had no idea. Shit, stop recording now, Becky, okay?'

'We'll stop recording if you promise to stop obsessing about getting your hands on this place,' she said. We were an unstoppable team, now, certain of victory.

'Yeah, yeah, fine. Whatever.'

I nodded at Becky, who tapped 'stop' and stowed the phone away in her pocket for safe-keeping.

Christian opened his mouth to say something. But at that moment the pub door opened to a cacophony of noise. Finally, it was the festive revellers from Tom's company, WeFacilit8, who immediately shifted the pub's atmosphere from tense, soap opera cliffhanger to something more akin to a *Gavin and Stacey* Christmas special.

Christian's top lip curled upwards in frustration. He swivelled 180 degrees, fetched his family from the other side of the pub and made a swift exit without looking back once.

I was rooted to the spot, but all of a sudden Becky was bouncing up and down in front of me like some kind of magic jumping bean, and handing me my phone.

'Fucking hell, Allister – I think that was probably the best thing I've ever seen in real life!'

'Did that… really just happen?' I said, still frozen.

Becky somehow leapt over the bar as if it was a move she practised in private every night, grabbed me by the shoulders and looked directly at me. 'YES!'

And, after a couple of seconds, I joined her in the magic jumping bean stakes as she ripped up the offer papers he'd left behind and threw the scraps in the air, which fell like confetti all around us. I had no idea where my sudden ability to hold my own in an argument had come from. But I was fucking proud of myself.

'Er, what the hell is happening?' It was Tom, who'd extricated himself from his throng of colleagues to order a round of drinks.

'This fucking legend here has just told Christian Woods to do one, once and for all!'

'You're kidding?! Tell me everything!'

'Oh, we will,' said Becky, whipping off the Santa hat from the bust's head on the bar and plonking it on mine instead. 'But first, I believe there's a bottle of undrunk but paid-for champagne with our names on it that we need to crack into. You know what? Sod it: FREE CHAMPAGNE FOR EVERYONE!'

Once everyone in the pub had been given their free bubbles and Becky had filled Tom in on my showdown with Christian, I ducked back into the private dining room with my own glass to give it a swift, final appraisal from the doorway. Before Christian had arrived, I'd gone to a fair amount of effort, giving all the cutlery and glasses an extra buff so they gleamed and glistened. I'd somehow got the fire crackling contentedly, and had lit all the tealights – even adding some more I'd managed to find in the dresser to every available surface. Once all the fairy lights in the room had been switched on, and the Christmas tree in the corner was aglow, I'd decided we could afford to switch off the overhead lights, resulting in the aesthetic of a sumptuous festive banquet room that wouldn't have looked out of place in one of Nigella Lawson's innuendo-laden winter cookery shows.

I stepped to one side to give space for the diners to enter, only for Tom to step in the same direction so that my nose was practically touching his chest. I looked up, sheepishly, neither of us taking a step back.

'Mally! Woah, this room has never looked so good.' He pulled me in for a quick hug. He smelt of beer, sambuca and a nameless but delicious aftershave I knew I would need to track down so I'd be able to relive this deeply pleasurable sensory moment in the near and frequent future.

We moved away from the doorway to allow his team to enter the room, which they all did while cooing and squealing at their unexpectedly luxurious surroundings. As they all took their seats, Becky came up beside me, grinning from ear to ear.

'Milly Allister, once again you've outdone yourself. The room looks amazing! You'd never know I'd had my first snog up against a pool table pretty much where we're standing right now!'

She winked at me before bundling me into another massive hug.

'Right, I'd better let the kitchen know to get the starters out. Reckon you could give me a hand bringing them through?'

'Amelia Allister, at your service!' I replied.

It was the first time I'd said my real name aloud in twenty years.

By eleven thirty, the pub was empty of all customers – I'd been given the honour of ringing the bell for last orders – with the exception of Tom and his WeFacilit8 colleagues. They were rambunctiously waiting for a minibus to take them on to Rotunda – a sticky-floored nightclub in the next suburb over, devoid of any positive attributes whatsoever beyond a dancefloor and a late licence.

Tom hung back from the throng, joining me at the bar that I was wiping down with a frankly magical potion called Bar Keepers Friend. Before I'd even clocked his presence, he slung one long arm around my shoulder, and tossed his grey tweed coat over his own with an ironic flourish. It was tempting to transfer my weight into what was fast becoming my favourite human nook, but I kept my core firm and continued wiping.

'They missed the apostrophe.' His words bumped up against each other in a way I hadn't heard before, his breath sweet with eau-de-whisky-and-mince-pie.

'Erm, who, what, where?'

Tom pointed at the bottle of cleaning product. 'Surely there should be a possessive apostrophe after the word "Keepers". Without it, the word "Friend" is grammatically redundant.'

I picked up the bottle and took a closer look at the copy. Huh, he was right.

'Is this how our chats work?' I placed the bottle back down and focused on rubbing the surface in a vaguely 'wax-on, wax-off' fashion.

'You what now?'

'Well, last night I drunkenly bored you to death with adjective-related chitchat, and now *you're* drunkenly talking to me about possessive apostrophes. I'm starting to detect a linguistic pattern.'

'You didn't bore me, Mal. But are you saying that *I'm* boring *you*?'

My breath caught, and I decided to chance an honest answer since he probably wouldn't even remember this conversation by the end of the night.

'You know you're not.' *Keep wiping, Mally.*

'Good.'

'Minibus is here!' someone called from the doorway to a cacophony of cheers and West Country 'wahey's.

He removed his arm from me and I exhaled, unaware my breathing had been in glitch mode.

'Now then, Miss Mally. I know you're still feeling delicate from last night's chundering, but are you *absolutely sure* I can't convince you to join us at the legendary establishment that is Rotunda? Even for a single orange juice and lemonade? It's just that I have so many other language-based observations I'd love to get off my chest.'

Tom's eyes were fixed on mine, but his pupils were dilated. And, as tempted as I was to say 'yes', even the thought of stepping into that place sober made my stomach churn and eardrums ache.

'Not this time, Thomas.'

He stuck out his bottom lip in exaggerated disappointment, and my brain immediately leapt back to that vulnerable little boy from the playschool picture.

'Next time, then?' he asked, swinging his coat back round from the faux-casual shoulder sling. I had to lean back at the waist to avoid the thick material whipping me in the face. He attempted to put the coat on but couldn't successfully locate the armhole.

I snorted and put down my cloth, finally – my arm was killing me. 'Tom, you piss-head. Let me help.'

Tom chuckled. 'Please.'

I guided his firm arms into their respective holes from behind, standing on my tiptoes. Once his arms were in, he turned to face me, and I instinctively rose up on my tiptoes again to turn up his collar to protect him from the cold.

'Why thank you, Mally, you hangover-head.'

'Any time. Right then, off you pop.'

As he walked to the door, he turned and blew me a drunken kiss, which I pretended to catch mid-air and place in my pocket. I patted said pocket to indicate it was safe and snug.

'See you at nine o'clock sharp tomorrow morning for some curtain hanging!' Tom shouted, as he was ushered out of the pub by his boisterous colleagues.

I laughed quietly before turning around to return to my bar-wiping duties, only to come face to face with a smirking, wide-eyed Becky, her arms folded in friendly challenge.

'"Curtain hanging"? Is that what they're calling it these days? Debrief. Now.'

Becky pointed to a pair of well-worn sofas next to the fire, which was gradually dying down but still deliciously warm. I sank into the softness of one of them, relieved to take the weight off my sore feet. Becky sat on the sofa opposite, leaning towards me with eagerness and intent. I prepared for an Elle-style interrogation.

'Firstly, thank you.'

Oh! Unexpected.

'You don't have to thank me, Becky, I just—'

'I'm gonna stop you there. You prevented all that food going to waste and helped us have our best night in bloody months. You stood up to that dickhead Christian Woods and finally got through to him. And you laid and unlaid that massive table like seven times. You did fucking loads and I'm obsessed with you.'

'Gosh. Er, thanks! I guess...'

'And can I tell you what else I'm obsessed with?'

Ah, here goes.

'I have this feeling you might tell me anyway?'

'Correct. I'm utterly obsessed with this thing between you and Tom. Turning up his collar and catching his cute little kiss? I mean, Jesus, I'm a sceptic when it comes to all things romance, but even I couldn't help but swoon at the sparks that are almost literally flying between you guys.'

'Argh, stop it!'

'I couldn't stop, even if I wanted to. This *has* to go somewhere! Speaking of which, why didn't you go with him just now?'

'Because he's smashed and I'm very much not.'

'Fair enough. Fledgling relationships often rely on drunken equality.'

The word 'relationship' gave me goosebumps, which made me feel hopeful and pathetic all at once.

'In that case, if the last couple of days are anything to go by, Tom and I may be forever doomed to remain on opposite sides of the sobriety fence.'

'Oh my God, you *do* like him, don't you?!'

I said nothing as I heaved myself off the sofa and began collecting up my things, but my internal fairy lights were now flashing at maximum speed, and – somehow – Becky could tell. She let out a squeal so high-pitched that it was almost inaudible.

'Oof. I dunno, Becky – I'm heading back to London soon. Even if what you're saying is true, it all just feels a bit futile. And I still can't figure out why on earth he would've been interested in me back then, let alone now.'

She drummed her fingers on the table and bunched her lips to one side.

'Okay, I reckon I've got something back at mine that might help to convince you. I can drop it round in the morning. What number Hollyhock Close are you staying at?'

'Eleven.'

'Cool. If I find it, I'll pop it through your letterbox first thing on my way to the wholesaler's. And trust me – it's conclusive.'

Chapter 16

☑ **Fake snow**

I could've slept for many hours more than I did, but I needed to be up and presentable by the time Tom was due to call round to put the curtain up. That said, I was half-expecting a no-show given that he'd probably only turned in a few hours ago.

Waiting for me on the doormat when I came downstairs was a padded envelope with a Post-it note attached:

> *Watch this from 42 mins. Believe me now?! Becky*
> *x*

I tore open the envelope and extracted a loose DVD. Scribbled on it in Becky's recognisable script – which I distinctly remembered she'd copied from *The Baby-Sitters Club* books – was *School Stuff + Concerts*.

I inserted the DVD into the dusty player under the TV and, after navigating the complex AV options, skipped the disc to the timestamp in question. It appeared to be a camcorder recording of a party from Year Eleven at Becky and Carly's house – yet another one I hadn't been invited to – the fifteen- and sixteen-year-old tipsy guests midway through a game of 'snog, marry, avoid'. And it was Tom's turn. I turned the volume right up to make out the muffled dialogue over the tinny soundtrack of 'Crossroads' by Blazin' Squad:

> Ryan: *Brinton, you're up! Okay, your choices are: Amelia Allister, Holly Jackson and Sammy Washington.*
>
> Tom: *Argh, okay. First up I'd avoid Holly Jackson.*
>
> Ryan: *Probably wise.*
>
> Tom: *Erm, I guess I'd snog Sammy, which would leave Amelia for the marriage option.*
>
> Ryan: *You'd marry Double A?!*
>
> Tom: *Stop calling her that. Yes, I would.*
>
> Ryan: *Okay, Brinton, we're going to need a better explanation. You... you don't like her, do you?*

I could feel my face burning, as if I had teleported to that early 2000s room with teenage Tom. The camera had zoomed in on his blotchy face for dramatic effect as he tried to collect his thoughts to answer the question as non-committally as possible but, before he could, a mass of male teenage bodies flung themselves on top of him.

A chant of 'Tomelia, Tomelia!' soon began.

From the bottom of the pile-on, some muffled protests struggled to make themselves heard.

> Tom: *I just think she's... interesting. That's literally all. And funny. That's it. It doesn't mean I fancy her.*
>
> Ryan: *I think we've hit a nerve. Time to move on, lads.*

Well, this was certainly some interesting information. Was it as definitive as Becky had indicated it would be? No, I didn't reckon so – as Tom himself had said in the footage, he was simply choosing from the options available. Even so, I couldn't shrug off the urge to *actually* teleport back to my teenage self and give her this nugget of promise.

I replayed the footage a couple more times and left the DVD on as I carried my cereal bowl into the kitchen and began washing up the precarious mountain of crockery from the last couple of days.

The rich, distinctive tones of a stringed instrument stopped me in my tracks.

I dashed through to the living room, my hands covered in soapy foam, my heart beating out of my chest. Before I even saw the source of the sound, I knew what – and who – I'd see on the screen.

It was Livvie. My beautiful teenage sister playing her beloved cello at some kind of Christmas concert, judging from the bunches of holly tied to her music stand. I choked on a sob and collapsed back into the sofa, bringing my hands to the side of my head with such force that the washing-up bubbles floated through the air like a brief flurry of simulated snowflakes.

As the suds settled onto the rock-hard sofa around me, her face filled the screen – the amateur videographer zooming in to capture the magical way she'd become one with the music, as she always did whenever she played.

Accompanied by a recorded piano backing track, she was playing the song 'Angel' by Sarah McLachlan – one of her (many) all-time favourite pieces of music. A song that had gone on to be played at her funeral – I hadn't been able to listen to it since.

The footage was grainy, the audio quality poor. But I could still *feel* the rich tone of her cello – a sound that had once vibrated around our Scarnbrook semi as she'd practised the piece for months. The warm melody of home. But I hadn't even gone to this concert. No doubt I'd probably gone somewhere with Elle, instead.

The footage cut out after her solo, the DVD moving on to a dance recital that Becky and Carly had taken part in. I skipped it back to the moment that Livvie appeared, and watched it over and over again.

I was mesmerised by her, but the more I watched it the more overwhelmed I felt.

Why hadn't I seen this footage before?

When was the last time I'd seen Livvie's animated face?

What was I even doing back in Scarnbrook?

I calculated from the shaky timestamp in the corner of the screen that the concert had taken place less than a year before the unthinkable had happened. Before my selfish actions had *allowed* the unthinkable to happen.

Twenty years earlier

Date: 09/10/2005
From: KarmaChamelia@hotmail.com
To: Livvin_mybestlife@hotmail.com
Subject: Re: re: Cardiff visit sooooooooooon?

Livvviiiiieee! So I've got your Cardiff visit all planned out.

I'll meet you at the station on Friday evening and we can walk back to my halls (I know packing light doesn't come naturally to you but pleeeeeease try and squeeze everything into a backpack cos there's barely any floorspace in my room!).

There's so much cool stuff to show you in the city – and of course there's THE X FACTOR to watch on the Saturday night!

Btw, Elle doesn't know if she's going to be around that weekend, so she might end up tagging along with us for some of it if she is.

Big sissss xxxx

Date: 09/10/2005

From: Livvin_mybestlife@hotmail.com

To: KarmaChamelia@hotmail.com

Subject: Re: re: re: Cardiff visit soooooooooooon?

Yay that plan sounds so amazing, I honestly can't wait!!!! Yes yes yes, FINE I'll try to pack light. I was planning on bringing the floor piano from the garage AND my cello, but I guess I'll have to save my instruments for when I visit you in your grand student mansion next year.

Yikes, gotta go, Mum needs the phoneline to call Auntie Sandra about Christmas plans.

SOOOOO EXCIIIIITEEEED!!!!

Liv xxx

Chapter 17

☑ **Character confronts loss**

Twenty years later

Everything changed that Saturday morning in October.

While I was still occupied by the throes of freshers' mayhem in Cardiff, Livvie had gone along to her weekly orchestra club, just like she always did. But, this time, she never made it home.

She'd been waiting outside the church hall for her lift from Josh. He picked her up every Saturday on his way home from the gym; it was their little weekly ritual. Sometimes she'd convince Josh to go home via the nearest McDonald's drive-thru so she could pick up a milkshake. Back when I'd still been living at home, she'd always bring one back for me, too.

But that Saturday was different. Josh had been running late – only by a couple of minutes, but those precious seconds altered our trajectory, forever. According to one of her friends who'd been waiting in a car on the other side of the road, Livvie had been sitting on the wall behind the bus stop when a bus had pulled in. As the bus pulled away, Livvie had begun to cross the road, her trusty cello on her back.

Josh saw the moment it happened. He saw her flash of red hair out of the corner of his eye, quickly followed by the oncoming van, hidden from Livvie's view by the back of the bus. And that was that. Life destroyed.

Lives destroyed, really. Because the remaining Allisters' souls leaked away with hers that day. Our family had never been perfect. But it was only with brutal hindsight that we could see that our lives before Livvie was taken from us had been so full of ordinary everythings and incredible nothings. We'd belonged to each other. We'd been at such oblivious peace.

That morning, after *that* phone call from Dad, I was bundled into a taxi back to Scarnbrook with Elle in tow, but our destination was no longer 'home'; it was hell itself. I knew as soon as Mum pulled me from the taxi and we wailed and contorted and collapsed onto the lawn of our small front garden that home was gone for good.

Once our tears had stopped flowing continuously, the funeral had passed and the lasagnes stopped arriving from neighbours, each of us retreated back into ourselves. None of us knew how to live without her. None of us had emerged again since. And, soon, each of us had left Scarnbrook for good. Separately, not together.

While Mum and Dad had attempted to start afresh and Josh had filled his mind with exercise and the Internet, I was left to figure things out for myself, more or less. Falling in slow motion, scrabbling for purchase. I still hadn't found it, although Elle had kept me hovering just above ground zero as best as she could.

As the DVD repeated and repeated, and Livvie played and played, twenty years of pent-up grief began to escape from me in the form of guttural sobs. I had a primal urge to step into the screen and bundle her into my arms. I'd steer her back through the concert hall corridors, through the streets of Scarnbrook, to our little cul-de-sac. Back to the bedroom we'd shared ever since she'd been a baby. I wanted to tuck her up in bed with her favourite soft toy – a scrappy puppy called Toffee Donut – and lock the door behind her so she'd be safe, forever fifteen. A frozen prison. And the rest of us could join her in her time-frozen bubble – our own permanent utopia.

A plasticky knock on the front door interrupted my vision, followed by a deliberate rattle of the letterbox. I paused the DVD, wiped my eyes with soap-sticky hands and tried to even my breaths as I opened the draughty door.

Right on schedule, it was Tom.

'Should've guessed this place wouldn't have a doorbell! Anyway, I heard you were in need of a hungover tall person to re-hang a curtain?'

I tried to produce a smile as I let him in, but there was something about his presence that felt safe, as if it was okay to be vulnerable. So my face did something it rarely did instead: it crumpled.

'Shit, what's the matter? Has something happened?'

I couldn't get the thoughts organised in my brain, let alone any words out of my mouth. I nodded instead, letting more sobs escape.

'Oh God, Mally, come here.'

Tom pulled me into a tight hug. I gave myself over to the embrace, completely. I couldn't remember the last time anyone had held me like this.

'Oh, Mal…'

He gently let me go and turned towards the TV that had caught his eye behind me. There on the screen was a frozen frame of my sister mid-bow stroke, her eyes closed and her eyebrows raised as she played. God, she was beautiful.

'Wow, this must be so hard to watch.'

I found the remote and switched it off. Livvie's face vanished into darkness, and it felt like I'd lost her all over again. I collapsed onto the sofa, my head in my hands, and sobbed.

Tom let me sob. He sat down next to me, not too close, but close enough to place a hand on my juddering shoulder until I'd cried myself dry. Eventually, I raised my head, my eyes still closed, and let my head rest on the back of the settee.

'I'll get you some water.'

I rubbed my eyes as he disappeared into the kitchen. I felt numb, raw, exposed. I wiped my dripping nose with my sleeve. So much for trying to make myself look presentable this morning. Though I was past caring.

'Do you watch this often?'

Tom's voice interrupted my vacant staring. I took a thirsty gulp of the water.

I shook my head.

'It's not even my DVD.' I swallowed, my throat aching from crying. 'Becky put it through my door this morning and...'

'Becky?'

Surely Becky hadn't known this was on the DVD? She hadn't mentioned Livvie once since I'd been back – no doubt because I hadn't, either.

'Oh God, I don't think she realised this was on it, Tom. There was... something else she wanted me to see.'

I'd completely forgotten about the 'snog, marry, avoid' footage. It felt beyond trivial, now.

'Do you want me to take it back to her and have a word?'

A rush of possessiveness engulfed me.

'No! God, sorry, I didn't mean to shout. It's just that now that I've seen this video of Livvie I don't think I could give it back, if that makes sense.'

'You never have to say sorry for any of this, okay? I'm here for you.'

My lip quivered as I met his gaze and nodded with genuine gratitude.

'Thanks for saying that. I guess I just feel a bit silly, you know? She's been gone for twenty years, for Christ's sake. Surely I shouldn't still feel like this?'

I tried to even analyse what 'this' feeling was, but it was impossible, because it was everything and nothing all at once.

'Grief is a weird thing, Mally. It can creep up on you when you least expect it. I mean, I know it's not the same thing at all, but I still cry about my grandad whenever I hear the *Sports Report* theme tune on the radio, and he's been gone for almost thirty years.'

I smiled for the first time since Tom's arrival, because my own grampy had loved that radio show, too.

'But it's never crept up on me like this before, Tom. Right now it feels as if it's just happened.'

But deep down I knew why that was. It was because I'd spent the last twenty years of my life dodging any chance of this happening. Avoiding any risk of feeling this kind of searing loss, of re-opening this wound. But it was well and truly open, now, and everything was pouring out. And in. I walked into the kitchen to splash some cold water on my face. It was the kind of thing that characters in films did when they felt distressed and I could never understand why. To be fair, it felt pretty invigorating. I patted my face dry with a tea towel while Tom hovered in the doorway.

'I know we've not talked about it, but I'm so sorry for what happened to Livvie back then. I can't imagine how horrific it must have been for you. Me and Mum were so shaken up by it at the time. I mean, the whole of Scarnbrook was.'

'Really?'

'Yeah, I keep forgetting you weren't here to see any of it after the funeral. There were endless tributes. School assemblies, candlelit vigils – the works. Your sister was so loved.'

'It just got too much. Everyone thought it was best for me to go back to uni and keep things as normal as possible.'

'Is that what you wanted, too?'

'I… I just wanted to block it all out for a bit. But, well, let's just say that "a bit" went on for rather a lot longer than planned. Oh God, I've handled all of this so, so badly, haven't I?'

'God, Mally, no, not at all. What you and your family went through was so fucking awful. I don't think there'd ever be a "good" way to handle it. So, whatever you're feeling right now – which is understandably a lot – is totally cool, all right?'

I nodded.

'Is there anything I can do to help you right now?'

I shrugged and leant against the oven to directly face him. 'Bring my little sister back?'

'I so wish I could.'

I locked my eyes on to his, which were bloodshot with tiredness but wide with care and concern. 'You know, I haven't seen any videos of her at that age for, well, forever. I can't actually remember the last time I saw a video of her at all.'

'You family doesn't have any home videos or stuff like that?'

'I mean, probably, somewhere. Dad loved his camcorder back then. But most of it's in a storage unit somewhere.' Locked away. Pushed down.

Tom puffed out his cheeks. 'I have an idea, but it might be the opposite to what you need right now.'

'I'm listening.'

'Tell me to stop talking at *any* time. But my mum is a bit of a hoarder as you've seen for yourself. She's got tons of newspaper clippings from back then — not just that year, but all the years before. Your sister used to be in the local paper quite a lot from what I remember?'

'Yeah, she was always involved in some shenanigan or another.'

'What do you reckon — shall I give my mum a call and see if she can find some stuff for you to look through?'

'Yeah, go on, then. Now?'

'If that's what you want?'

I nodded again, but in truth I didn't know what I wanted. Well, I did: I wanted Livvie to burst into the room right now and for the last twenty years to have been a horrific nightmare.

But she could never come back. And I realised that was precisely why it'd taken me so long to return to the village: because Scarnbrook could never be Scarnbrook without Livvie. It was as if the version of it I'd returned to this week was a cheap, soulless imitation of what it had once truly been: home.

My family wasn't my family without her, either.

And I missed my family so, so much.

Chapter 18

☑ **Reconnecting with the past**

Jo welcomed me into her bungalow and gave my hands a gentle squeeze with hers as she led me through to her living room.

'Mally, love, Tom said you'd like to look through some things about Livvie. I've got a box full of stuff if you think it would help?'

Hearing someone say her name was like a drug. I sniffed and nodded, sitting down on the same soft spot I'd occupied a few nights ago. Chippie immediately rested his head on my thigh, somehow sensing I needed the comfort of touch.

'Of course. Tom, could you go and fetch the pink shoebox from the spare bed?'

Tom nodded and left the room.

'I've already had a quick look through what I've got, and have pulled out some things you might like to see and put them at the top. Now, there is some… other stuff in there, too. But I'll leave you to decide whether or not you want to have a rummage. I'll leave you here for a bit and if you need me for anything you can just shout, okay?'

I nodded again. 'Jo?'

'Yes, love?'

'Before you go, can you tell me what you remember about her? You know, from when you knew her from playschool?'

Jo's face lit up with warmth. 'Oh yes! Well, let me think. Oh! I remember this one time, not long after a new boy had started, she came running to me to tell me that another boy had been poking him with a stick. I rushed over to see what was happening, and before I could intervene, your sister said, "Oh it's okay, Mrs B, I dealt with it. I just wanted you to know because I think you might need to keep an eye on *him* in the future." I looked down at the older boy she was pointing to, and there he was, sat there with tears streaming down his face, his beloved stick snapped clean in two. He never bothered anyone again.'

'That story is classic Livvie!' And it was. She never put up with any mind-games or nastiness from anyone. I laughed through my tears. It was amazing hearing someone else talk about her like this. Mentioning Livvie – even in passing – had become a no-go zone for the Allisters. If we didn't talk, maybe we wouldn't have to feel.

But I wanted to feel, now. I wanted to absorb the fondness that was emanating from Jo as she spoke about my sister, and connect it somehow to my own buried memories.

Tom returned, placing an impressively pristine Dolcis shoebox down on the coffee table and perching on the arm of the sofa next to me. He placed his hand gently on my shoulder as his mum shared more memories.

'What else do you remember about her?'

'Well, I remember thinking that she was nothing like her older siblings.'

'Yeah, she was properly special, wasn't she?'

'Oh I didn't mean it like that. It's difficult to explain, but I suppose what I'm trying to say is that, like all kids really, each of you had such different inbuilt personalities – even when you were little. Josh, for example, was always so quiet but deeply sensitive and loyal, too – and I only knew him for a few weeks after I started. And you, Mally, well, you were a little sweetheart. Always smiling, always sharing your toys and making sure everyone had someone to play with, and helping me tidy up at the end of the day.'

Always smiling. That sounded about right. Why did I always feel the need to make people feel good about themselves, no matter how *I* was feeling? Livvie had never been that way. If she'd lived long enough to hear the term 'resting bitch face', she'd have claimed it with pride.

Jo could see I was getting lost in my thoughts. She grabbed her walker and headed towards the kitchen. 'Anyway, I'll leave you two to it for a bit.'

Tom gave my shoulder a squeeze, still sat on the arm of the sofa. 'How are you doing?'

I puffed out my cheeks and smiled. 'Yeah, I'm all right. I think I'd like to look at all this stuff by myself – I hope you don't mind.'

'Of course not. You need to do this in your own way and in your own time. I've got some stuff I need to chat to Mum about anyway. I'll be back in a bit.'

'Thanks, Tom.'

He closed the door soundlessly as he left the room. I could hear them murmuring quietly to each other while I lifted the lid off the box and gently extracted the larger-than-expected pile of photos and clippings. I took a deep breath, catching the crooked but reassuring gaze of Tom's scraggly toy cat, Marmalade, on the branches of the

Christmas tree. There and then – despite the odds of me being sat on this sofa in Tom Brinton's mum's living room being slim-to-none – I knew for certain I was precisely where I was meant to be. I moved my eyes down and focused on the first photo.

It was Livvie's playschool photo, Jo – Mrs B – beaming from the side of the group. Looking at the faces of the children, I could immediately hazard a guess at which boy had paid Livvie's price for his stick-poking due to the sullen but slightly sheepish look on his face. Discovering this fresh detail about my sister and being able to picture this interaction in my head for the first time felt like time travel.

Next in the pile was an article from the *Western Daily Press* from the year Livvie had competed in her first eisteddfod contest with her cello. There was a photo of her playing on stage, her face turned away from the camera, but her hair giving her away, as always.

Then I came to a small clipping of a letter she'd written to the editor of the paper a year or so later, a vague memory of which shimmered on the edge of my recollection:

> '*Sir*',
>   *I'm writing in relation to the article you published last week – 'IS THIS SCARNBROOK ALLEYWAY THE MOST DEPRESSING PLACE IN BRISTOL?' – about the ongoing vandalism issues in the alleyway next to Scarnbrook Community School. The reporter claimed to have spoken to several local residents, and come to the wild yet completely unfounded conclusion*

that 'loitering pupils' from the school must be responsible for the state of the pathway. However, surely the lack of sufficient street lighting in the alleyway in question, the constant overgrown brambles that pupils like me have to battle our way through each day, plus the lack of upkeep of the tarmac (which, frankly, is an accident waiting to happen) means that the real responsibility for this sad state of affairs actually lies with our local council, who are failing in their duty to maintain it to a reasonable standard? May I suggest that is where you direct your 'journalistic' focus in the future? I also have it on good authority that a) the school itself was not approached for comment by the reporter b) one of the interviewees gave a false name, which was not acknowledged in the piece and c) your offices are probably way more depressing.

Yours (mine),
Livvie Allister, age 12

I snorted at Livvie's mic-drop final line, baffled as to why the paper had not only printed it in what appeared to be its original state, but also awarded it Letter of the Week. Local journalism at its finest. I leafed through a few other clippings of various prizes she'd won and concerts she'd performed in, noting in the back of my mind that they were ordered vaguely chronologically, and That Year was fast approaching the top of the pile. Should I continue?

If not now, then when? The silent question appeared involuntarily, as if it hadn't come from myself. I glanced up.

'Are you infiltrating my mind, Marmalade?'

He just looked at me. The question may not have come from a partially stuffed vintage toy, but it had come from *somewhere*. And I felt a kind of weird duty to keep going, even though I knew it'd be devastating.

I moved Chippie off my lap and thumbed through some irrelevant clippings before coming to a front page of the *Western Daily Press*, which had been folded in half.

SCARNBROOK GIRL DIES IN TRAGIC ROAD ACCIDENT

Accident. That word had always felt so insufficient. Despite the fact that it was Livvie's misjudgement that ultimately caused the fatal collision, everything that had led to that moment had been anyone's fault but her own.

If I'd been a better sister. If Josh hadn't been late. If she'd never started playing that cello. If, if, if…

I quickly leafed through the following clippings without reading any of them until I got to an article about Livvie's funeral. Never in my life had I read these articles or seen any photos from this day. And there was one image that took my breath away.

Because there was Josh, carrying the coffin alongside other family members, his face utterly consumed with a raw anguish that I didn't realise he was capable of.

Compared to the rest of us, Josh had always appeared to be less grief-stricken by Livvie's death. He was angry, that's for sure, but he directed most of that towards the police, as he believed they should have been prosecuting the van's driver. Me, Mum and even Dad had openly wailed for days, barely able to function, yet Josh had bottled everything up, even maintaining his training regime at the gym throughout. This photo was the very first time I'd seen his pain. How on earth had he managed to keep it hidden from us – then and since?

Josh and the other coffin bearers were flagged by Livvie's two best friends from orchestra club, who'd played their violins as the procession entered the church. The wicker coffin itself was artfully draped with all manner of colourful blooms. I remembered thinking at the time that it was way more beautiful than any coffin deserved to be.

After that, the clippings related to Livvie were mainly about the inquest into her death a few months later, an inhumane process that had only amplified our pain given that the driver of the van in question had never expressed any sorrow or regret to us about what had happened. Not that it was his fault, of course – and he was probably following some kind of legal advice – but, still, it would've helped.

I put the clippings back in the box, with the exception of one, and replaced the lid as Tom appeared from the kitchen carrying a tray with a mug of tea and a plate heaped high with jam-smeared toast. It was as if he'd read my mind – it was approaching eleven o'clock and I hadn't eaten breakfast yet, which was unheard of for me.

'Thanks so much. I can't express just how much I appreciate all of this.'

'There's nothing to thank me for. How's it all going?' He sat down next to me.

'Yeah, I'm done. I didn't linger over much of it to be honest.'

'I bet.'

I took a slurp of the deliciously sweet tea and made an enthusiastic start on the toast. Tom cocked his head to the side as he watched me. 'You eat toast upside down.'

I pointed to my working jaw before responding, mouth still half-full.

'It's so the sweet side hits my taste buds first. It's revelatory. Here, try it.'

I offered him the plate and he selected the smallest square, flipping it over in an exaggerated motion and placing it in his mouth whole. His eyes widened as the effect took hold.

'Shit, you're right.'

'Welcome to the rest of your life. More?'

'Nah, I'm good. I'm going to have to get going in a bit as I've got a couple of work things I need to sort out.'

Work? Oh God, I'd completely forgotten it was a Wednesday. Tom must've called into my place on his way to the office. Little had he known he'd be walking into a full-blown emotional crisis.

'Shit, Tom, I totally forgot what day it was. Honestly, you should get going. I quite fancy walking back to the cottage from here once I'm done.'

'You really need to stop calling that place a cottage, Mal. And only if you're not just saying that to ease my guilt for leaving you here?'

No one else called me Mal. I liked it.

'Honestly, no guilt needed. Yeah, I think it'll do me some good after looking at all this stuff. Since I've been back, the only places I've visited are Big Tesco, here, The Star and the definitely-not-a-cottage. I think it's time I saw some more.'

'Okay, if you're absolutely, absolutely sure?'

'I'm double-absolutely sure. But thanks for caring. I mean that, Tom. I have no idea how I would've got through the last few days if it hadn't been for you. And your mum, of course.'

There were those tell-tale blotches again. I suddenly remembered the 'Tomelia' clip I'd watched just a couple of hours earlier, which had somehow been relegated to the least important part of the day already.

'There's absolutely no need to thank me. Spending this time with you over the last few days is probably the nicest time I've had in years.'

I snorted. 'You mean, with the exception of me vomiting, wailing and injuring you with random objects?'

He shrugged and looked down at his hands, tapping his fingertips together rapidly. 'All of it.'

Crikey, that wasn't far off Mark Darcy's 'just as you are' comment in *Bridget Jones's Diary*.

'Oh. Thanks. That's nice of you to say.'

Tom seemed to be weighing something up in his mind.

To fill the pause, I reached for my cup of tea and took another sip, making the mandatory 'aah' noise once I'd swallowed. The motion appeared to have afforded him the time he needed before turning to me.

'Right, so, how about this for an idea. And please say no if this is really inappropriate timing… but I've got this Christmas thing with one of my clients tonight and you'd be doing me a massive favour if you fancied tagging along? He's the owner of the Tapas Den chain and each year he gifts me a slap-up dinner for two. I've tried to wheedle my way out of it this year but he refuses to take no for an answer – even after I told him that, well, there is no "two" any more and hasn't been for quite some time. So he's insisting on joining me for the meal instead, if I can't find anyone to take. Which is very generous of him but, well, honestly I don't know what I'd talk to him about all night. I mean, he's a lovely bloke and everything, but… argh, God, sorry, I'm rambling. Anyway. If you fancy a free meal with me tonight it's yours for the taking. What do you say?'

Was Tom Brinton asking me out on a date? Or was I just a convenient plus one? Either way, the prospect of eating out tonight was much more appealing than the tinned Fray Bentos pie that was waiting for me back at the rental.

'What about your mum? Would she not want to come with you?'

Oh God, did I just inadvertently turn down Tom Brinton and suggest he go out with his mother instead of me?

'Nah, sadly it's not the kind of place she can access easily. You'll see what I mean if you come. So, what do you reckon?'

'Yeah, go on, then. Where would I need to be and when?'

'Amazing. I'll book you a car – the table's booked for seven thirty so it'll pick you up at seven if that works?'

'Perfect.'

'Great! I'll WhatsApp you later to confirm the car details. And if you change your mind before then it's no problem at all, just let me know.'

'Will do.'

'You're sure you're all right?'

'Yep, I'm sure. Did you say tapas?'

The last time I'd been out for tapas had been with Elle, Rory and one of his colleagues, who they'd been trying to set me up with for months. As soon as he'd helped himself to four out of five calamari rings that we'd agreed to share, I'd known he wasn't the one.

'Yup, is that okay? You don't have any food allergies or anything?'

'Oh no, it's nothing like that… but I should probably warn you that I've never been on board with this whole "small plates" thing. So if I get all territorial over my food, please don't take it personally. I guess that's what growing up with a ravenous older brother… and a cheeky little sister… does to you.'

Dropping Livvie into conversation like this was unheard of. But I wanted to hear myself talk about her. I wanted others to hear it, too.

'Understood. Righty-o, I'll leave you to your topsy-turvy toast.'

'Your mum won't mind me staying here without you?'

'Of course not. I'll let her know I'm leaving. See you tonight, Mally.'

Jo came back in a couple of moments later and settled into her chair, exhaling with relief as she sat down.

'Ooh, that's better. How're you doing, love?'

'I'm okay. All done. Thanks so much for letting me look through these.'

'I hope you don't mind that I kept them all – I guess it might seem a bit morbid keeping every last clipping, but it was just my way of coping with it back then, you know?'

'There's nothing to apologise for, Jo – Tom told me you enjoy collecting things.'

Jo gestured around the room. 'You probably could've figured that out for yourself!'

I pulled my coat on as we approached the front door, relieved that I could leave my hood down: this was the first time the rain had let up all week.

'Mally, sweetheart, there's just one thing I wanted to let you know about before you head off... Tom said you're staying next to The Star?'

'Yes, that's right.'

'Okay, so I'm not assuming which way you're going to walk or anything like that, but given the most direct route between here and there I thought you should know that, well, love, your old house on Oldville Close has recently gone on the market.'

23 Oldville Close, Scarnbrook. Home. For a moment I couldn't believe the 'new' owners would be selling it so soon after they'd bought it from us. But then I realised it'd been two bloody decades – more than enough time for them to have made it their own, maybe even had a kid or two who'd be all grown up by now.

'Oh. Gosh.'

'I hope you don't mind me telling you, it's just that my good friend Jenny lives round the corner and she happened to tell me about the "for sale" sign last week. I just thought I should mention it if you did happen to wander that way.'

In truth, I hadn't thought about which way I was going to walk. But she was right – the obvious way would take me right past the end of my old cul-de-sac.

I puffed out my cheeks. 'Thanks, Jo. For everything, I mean. You and Tom have been so, *so* kind to me this week.'

Kindness that I hadn't really seen – or maybe even sought out – for many years.

'Oh, Mally love, you deserve so much kindness. I hope you know that. You were always the giver. I think it's about time you took a little back.'

I nodded, more tears escaping.

'Thanks for saying that. Do you mind if I take this?' I held up the lone newspaper clipping I'd only just noticed I was still clutching, dabbing my eyes with a sleeve-shrouded fingertip.

'Oh of course not. You can have them all if you like.'

'No, just this one.'

It was the one that featured the photo of Josh. As I said goodbye to Jo, I opened my backpack and tucked the clipping into an inner pocket that had its own zip. It was a satisfyingly perfect fit. It was as if I was meant to have it.

Chapter 19

☑ **Old family home**

The sun was still nowhere to be seen, but the lack of rain and relative stillness of the air felt almost balmy after at least a week of relentless downpours and hair-whipping winds.

I strolled steadily in the vague direction of my old secondary school, noting one of the closed-down pubs on my way. It'd been converted into what looked like perfectly serviceable flats, though I couldn't detect any green space or parking, which explained why the nearby kerbs were yet again crammed with pavement-mounted cars. I wondered if it was another development by Christian Woods, and made a mental note to look it up when I got back.

The school itself was almost unrecognisable. Gone were the 1960s concrete cubes, and in their place were angular glass structures, not a flat roof in sight.

From there, the route was automatic. Down to West Lane, which I crossed to begin my descent into the lower bowels of Scarnbrook. I mentally clocked my old friends' houses as I passed by them, fondly remembering those early days at secondary school when a gaggle of us used to arrive en masse each day, having called for each other and swelled our numbers the closer we got to the school gates.

No sooner was I at the flood-prone bottom of the valley, it was time to ascend the other side, up the zig-zag path that emerged at the edge of the 1980s-built housing development where I'd spent my formative years.

All too quickly, I was at the final turn. I made a conscious effort to slow my breathing as I took the last few steps, emerging into our cul-de-sac in Oldville Close.

Unlike the school, it looked exactly the same. The only noticeable difference was the 'for sale' sign outside number 23. And the ridiculous number of kerb-side wheelie bins in hues ranging from purple to brown that were outside each property.

My footsteps slowed to a crawl, but I didn't intend to stop, figuring it'd be odd for a random woman to stand in the street and stare at a stranger's house. Instead, I intended to walk down the lane next to Elle's old place, which would quickly bring me out into the equivalent cul-de-sac of the neighbouring road.

But, just as I was about to draw level with my old home, a suited bloke emerged, followed by a couple. I took a swift step backwards and paused behind a tall shrub, so I was out of sight. They were around my age, maybe a bit younger. She was visibly pregnant. The three of them chatted for a while before the couple made their way to their car.

After they drove off, the estate agent took his phone out of his pocket and scrolled for a while before yawning, turning on his heel, and heading back towards the front door.

Before I was even conscious of making the decision to do so, I stepped out from behind the bush and called out to him.

'Excuse me?'

He turned to me, eyebrows raised.

'Hi, sorry, are you the agent showing people around this property?'

'That's right. Er, are you here for the viewing? I didn't think I had the next one for another half an hour or so.'

'Oh, no, I haven't booked one. It's just that, well, I used to live here. And I wondered if there's any chance I could pop in for a quick look around, you know, for old times' sake?'

He shrugged, his ill-fitting suit jacket shifting awkwardly. 'Sure, like I said you've got about half an hour. I'll wait out here. Give me a shout if you need me.'

'Thanks so much.'

I ascended the steep driveway up to the storm porch, crossed the threshold and pressed the door shut behind me. The soft, metallic click of the latch jolted me back in time.

Click: Dad getting home from the office at five thirty on the dot, just in time for tea in the living room with *Neighbours* on the telly: Crispy Pancakes, fish fingers and chicken and mushroom pies were on rotation back then. When it came to pie night, Dad used to convince us they contained special 'children's mushrooms'. I'd felt like Jessica Fletcher when I'd figured out he was having us on.

Click: Josh getting in from football practice, caked in mud, the carpet between the hallway and the bathroom preventatively lined with plastic sheeting so he could access the shower without compromising Mum's high standards of cleanliness.

Click: Nanny and Grampy arriving on Christmas morning when Josh and I were tiny with a big sack embroidered with the word 'TOYS'. Nanny always used to wear her best red coat on Christmas Day, which we always used to make fun of her about since it looked very much like her regular red dressing gown.

Click: Livvie coming home from orchestra club on Saturday mornings, her cello case rustling with cost-price confectionery she'd bought to share with us from the tuck shop in the years before her beloved McDonald's drive-thru had existed.

I dismissed the sudden taste of Hubba Bubba and looked around. The house had been completely redecorated, but the layout was exactly the same.

I removed my shoes and walked into the living room. It now had one of those carpets that showed up all the vacuuming marks. Mum wouldn't be impressed with that. The shallow bay window housed a white Christmas tree, decorated in nothing but silver ornaments and neon blue lights. I closed my eyes and remembered the trees that had sat in the same spot when the Allisters had called this place home. We used to choose a real tree together every year from the local garden centre, decorating it in every colour, with all manner of garish baubles and scratchy tinsel adorning its branches. So many strings of fairy lights hugged it that it was almost ultraviolet. Mum used to leave the curtains open a few inches so it could be seen from outside, providing our neighbours with the merest of glimpses of our festive joy. One year, the tree had been so tall it'd poked a hole in the ceiling.

I thought of my measly little fibre-optic spruce, switched off back in London, which couldn't be any further away from the Christmas trees of my childhood.

I blinked my eyes open and made my way through the archway in the middle of the room towards the dining table. We'd always called it 'the dining room', despite the fact it was essentially a single, long space. I was thrilled to see that the hatch into the kitchen was still intact. The three of us had spent hours throwing increasingly risky items of food through the gap – a game we'd named 'hatch catch' – before Mum had banned it after the infamous time we'd done it with a raw egg. The sideboard had never been the same again.

The kitchen itself had been replaced, but weirdly it smelt the same: slightly damp, slightly sweet, slightly catfood-y. Which had always been a bit of a mystery as we'd never had a cat. I tried the back door handle but it was locked. I wandered back through to the dining room and peered out into the rear garden through the newly erected conservatory. Whoever lived here wasn't particularly green-fingered by the looks of it. The lawn was artificial. I shuddered: another reason not to tell Mum anything about this – that small patch of land had been her pride and joy.

The downstairs done and dusted, it was time to go upstairs. I did so with trepidation. Because there was one room I hadn't dared to enter since Livvie had been taken from us: the bedroom we'd always shared.

The house was a three-bed semi, which had been perfect for the four of us before Livvie had arrived. A spacious double room for Mum and Dad, a smaller double for Josh and the cosy box room for me. We were all perfectly content with our lot. Then Mum got pregnant. We couldn't afford an extension, and with all our friends nearby, our parents were reluctant to move, so we all swapped bedrooms to make it work. Josh moved into the box room, Mum and Dad downgraded to the smaller double, and me and Livvie shared the biggest room in the house once she was potty trained. We used to refer to it as 'the suite' as we had an armchair in the corner, which was never not covered in Livvie's clothes, and it randomly had a sink on the wall opposite our single beds.

But, after Livvie had died and I'd returned from Cardiff, I couldn't bear to step inside. I'd slept at Elle's up until the funeral, never once venturing into the space I'd shared with my sister. And then the house had been sold and my belongings scooped up into boxes on my behalf.

After brief glances into the other three upstairs rooms – the milky cocoa-coloured bathroom long gone – it was time.

I pushed the door open, the bottom of it brushing the carpet. It sounded like an inhale. The sink was gone, and the two single beds had been replaced by a super king-size – which was ever-so-slightly too large for the proportions of the room.

But it was the view from the window I was most interested in. The view wasn't spectacular, but it was special. The room looked out onto the rest of the street, but thanks to the elevated position of our house at the very end of the cul-de-sac, the view stretched beyond our road, down into the valley of Scarnbrook, and up the other side. Endless houses, endless lives, until they faded into the green of the countryside on the horizon.

When Livvie was too small to see over the window sill, she used to insist I lift her up so she could say good night to Scarnbrook before she went to bed. After a couple of years of this we called it 'the window ritual'.

Every evening, without fail, the ritual was an ingrained part of our bedtime routine. And the Christmas Eve window ritual was our favourite one of the year. I had tummy-warming memories of the wondrous awe on Livvie's face the year that Dad climbed up onto the roof and sprinkled polystyrene beanbag balls down past our window just as I lifted her up to look. It was the only white Christmas she ever got. Thankfully, Josh wasn't so militant about single-use plastic back then.

Even on the last night before I left for university, despite the fact that she was a good half a foot taller than me by then, I lifted her feet off the ground and she whispered, 'Good night, Scarnbrook' with all the earnestness she'd had ten years previously.

I touched the window gently before noticing the estate agent was on the phone outside, staring up at me while he was talking. It was time to leave. I walked down the staircase slowly, caressing the banister for what I knew would be the final time of my life. At the last step, I gripped the handrail tightly before releasing it – a silent goodbye to the spine of what had once been such a happy home. I put my shoes back on and said a breezy 'Thanks!' to the estate agent as I continued my walk, upping my pace and using the heel of my hand to absorb the tears that had leaked from my eyes like Emma Thompson in the best scene of *Love, Actually*.

I turned down the lane, emerging onto the neighbouring cul-de-sac, and that's when I saw it: the spire. And I knew where I had to go next.

Livvie's simple headstone still looked to be one of the newest in the graveyard. Leaning against it was a huge bunch of white chrysanthemums, slightly past their best, tied together with bright mustard twine. The blowsy flowerheads looked like giant snowballs. I lifted them gently to see if there was a message, but there wasn't. Even so, it comforted me to know that someone cared enough to leave flowers for her all these years later.

I sat on a bench a few metres away. It was damp, but I figured I was less than an hour off a hot shower by now. I didn't know what to do. Whenever I saw these graveside scenes in films, the protagonist always seemed to know exactly what to say to their departed loved one, as if they'd penned a perfect speech in advance and delivered it with gusto while the sun shone and the birds sang.

This definitely wasn't like the movies. I had no desire to say anything. The right words didn't exist. But I kind of felt like being here was enough, for now. I looked at the soggy flowers and closed my eyes, remembering long, hot days on Grampy's allotment plot during the school holidays, hands sticky with melted Mr Freeze pops. The three of us playing hide and seek among the corridors of hollyhocks and dahlias, while Grampy dug and smiled, sweaty and content, sipping a beef Oxo cube dissolved in hot water from his trusty flask. It was the only form of liquid he ever drank. Mum had been there some-times on the days she wasn't working on reception at the local GP surgery, busying about deadheading the sweet peas to encourage further flourishes, placing the colourful harvests in a basket to fill our home with the scent of summer throughout the school holidays.

But it was the chrysanthemums that Grampy had loved growing the most. Every year, he and his allotment buddies grew the brash blooms competitively against each other with spirited banter, entering them into the local horticultural show each autumn. He nurtured those chrysanthemums as if they were his offspring, enveloping each enormous flower head in a paper bag until it was ready to be exhibited. That contest had been my grampy's favourite thing to do ever since my nan had died from a sudden stroke before Livvie was even born.

But the day before Livvie's funeral, Grampy and his friends had chopped down every single chrysanthemum that was left on every allotment plot to ensure Scarnbrook's streets were lined with endless colour as the cortege passed by. Those chrysanthemums were the last things he ever grew. After those stems had been severed, he'd never stepped foot in the allotment again. The now tarmacked-over plot had gone to seed, much like our family. Each of us had been scattered by random winds to new places, living as best as we could, but no longer nurtured – and definitely not thriving.

I wiped my eyes as I thought of my lovely grampy, who'd spent his final years in a retirement village not far from my parents' cottage courtesy of Auntie Sandra, and took a quick photo of the grave for posterity. I stood and, very briefly, squeezed the headstone, still glistening from this morning's rain. As I did so, the clouds parted, the sun peeking out momentarily for the first time all week. I squinted, the rays gently warming my cheek, and a simple sentence popped into my head. I didn't speak it aloud but it was definitely there.

Hey, Livvie. I came home.

Chapter 20

☑ **A Christmas wish**

The rental felt like the opposite of home when I arrived back there, my bum damp from the graveside bench and my face now, apparently, permanently damp from two decades' worth of released emotions. As I climbed the stairs for a shower, I thought about the DVD, still dormant in the player, that had broken the seal.

Had Becky known the footage of Livvie was on it? I very much doubted it. Was I glad that I'd seen it? Probably, yes. But it'd been so unexpected that it'd knocked the wind out of me.

Thank God Tom had arrived when he had. If he hadn't, I'd probably still be watching the concert on a loop right now, my heart even more disintegrated than it already was.

Tom Brinton. Well, what a revelation he'd been. I'd always sensed at school that he had a kind heart, despite his cheeky exterior, but his steadfast sensitivity over the last few days had well and truly won me over. And here I was, just a few hours away from spending an entire evening alone with him.

It felt crass to admit this to myself what with all the pain that was still swirling around inside of me, but I felt kind of… excited at the simple prospect of being in his company. But then I realised that it wasn't excitement I was feeling at all. It was something both much simpler and more substantial than that. It was the feeling of belonging.

So why did I also feel a niggle of doubt? Sure, I felt a bit nervous about tonight given that I was guaranteed to end up doing or saying something to embarrass myself, but this particular feeling of fear ran way deeper than the usual tummy-dwelling butterflies.

I concluded it was partly because Tom – the entire day so far – had begun to unfurl me somehow. I knew it was an important process that was probably long-overdue, but I'd come quite accustomed to folding myself smaller. Because the smaller I was, the less surface area there was to harm.

But, as I rinsed out my shampoo, I found myself admitting that the niggle was also partly down to that game of 'snog, marry, avoid' on the DVD. It was curious that Tom had put me in the 'marry' column all those years ago. Yet it was also clear that everyone in that room at the time had known that the pairing of Tom and me was so unlikely that it'd warranted its own teasing nickname: 'Tomelia'. And, by the sounds of it, his mates had been using it to poke fun at him ever since. In all likelihood, all the game meant was that, out of the three names presented to him, Tom had been prepared to tolerate me for the longest.

I stepped out of the shower and began rubbing myself dry, trying to get my head around why this annoyed me so much. It didn't take long for me to reach the blindingly obvious conclusion: because my ultimate wish wouldn't be for him to tolerate me forever. It would be for him to want me forever.

I took a final look at myself in the bathroom cabinet's mirror – the only mirror in the house – in the minutes before the taxi was due to arrive. My hair had turned out pretty nicely, its natural wave working in my favour for once, and a generous upside-down spray of Silvikrin (Maximum Hold) finishing it off nicely. My make-up looked decent enough – tinted moisturiser and cream blush as per, but this time I'd upgraded my look with a thin line of jet-black eyeliner with the tiniest flicks at each end, mascara *and* a berry-red lip. I bared my teeth and scrubbed a dot of lipstick off a canine. There. Not bad, I suppose.

I took a few steps back onto the landing and smoothed down the skirt of my cold-shoulder midi-dress as I turned and twisted my neck to catch microscopic glimpses of myself from various angles. The dress was an old favourite – a dark emerald-green colour with a sweetheart neckline and skater-style skirt that skimmed and hugged in all the right places. Best of all, it had properly deep pockets, which made it perfect for work events when, more often than not, I had no idea what to do with my hands.

Elle called it my 'Mary Berry dress' as she'd seen her wear something similar on *The Great British Bake Off* Christmas special one time. But, unlike me, Elle never struggled to find clothes that looked good on her. She was one of those people who could throw on an oversized sweater and look effortlessly cool and stylish. Whereas, in the very same top, I'd end up looking like Miss Trunchbull teaching PE.

Like Dame Mary, my go-to dress was classy, reliable and timeless. I knew I looked all right in it. Best of all, its heavy fabric meant that it never needed ironing and still looked freshly pressed, despite being screwed up into a ball at the bottom of my suitcase all week. Hopefully, with my thick black tights and simple ankle boots, it struck the right balance between 'potential festive date' and 'just threw this outfit together, NBD'.

The car was right on time – a disconcertingly silent Prius, no less – the driver sporting a Santa hat and in chatty spirits as we began the twenty-five-minute journey into town.

Ten minutes into the drive, I spotted the old chocolate factory where my nan used to work in the on-site discount shop. Posh flats now, of course. A snort of hilarity erupted from my throat as an old memory catapulted itself to the front of my mind. The noise caught the driver's attention and he glanced at me in the rear-view mirror. 'You all right, love?'

'Yeah... I'm... good.' I was full-on cackling now. 'Sorry, I just remembered something really funny about the chocolate factory.'

'Well, go on, then, don't leave me hanging.'

I told him about the time my grandparents had been on holiday in Devon, and had decided to treat themselves to a 'mystery coach trip'. Ninety minutes later, the coach pulled into her work car park for a tour and chocolate tasting, her colleagues baffled as to why she was buying bargain bags of broken biscuits with a gaggle of tourists when she was meant to be on holiday.

The anecdote went down well with the driver, and I'd enjoyed sharing it. It'd been one of my grampy's favourite stories, which we'd begged him to re-tell, over and over. I'd always assumed that letting my frozen memories thaw would do nothing but remind me of everything that had broken in my life. But joy and comforting nostalgia were also beginning to fill in the cracks. And, just like Grampy used to say to us every time he brought home a massive bag of seconds for us from the chocolate factory shop, 'Broken biscuits might well be broken, but they're still delicious.'

Chapter 21

☑ **A man and a woman wearing red and green**

The pre-paid taxi dropped me off on Small Street, a narrow road in the heart of Bristol that had felt progressively familiar as the car nudged its way through the cobbled backstreets.

I'd never appreciated the architecture in this corner of the city before, its grandeur – inextricably entwined with Bristol's complex history – having been unquestionably accepted as normal while I was growing up. But twenty years' absence was more than enough time to see this place with fresh eyes. Despite the tightness of the road, the buildings on each side of it were impressive, with their Gothic honey-stoned facades and imposing wooden doors. And nestled in between them was an unassuming doorway, which bore a subtle Tapas Den logo.

Tom was waiting for me outside, hands stuffed into the pockets of his dark grey tweed jacket, his collar upturned in the continued absence of a scarf. Maybe I should cut mine in half and share it with him flirtatiously like a stick of chewing gum. He was doing his distinctive little bouncing thing, which could've signalled either coldness or nervousness – or both. As I clambered out of the taxi with as much grace as I could manage, which was very little, I noticed that his face was freshly shaven. There was the tiniest dot of nicked skin on his jaw between his chin and his right ear.

We hugged awkwardly, and I silently chided myself for imagining the hint of tenderness that seemed to be transmitting from his hand to the gap between my shoulder blades. He smelt bloody lush, the aroma of his distinctive aftershave lingering as we parted and headed towards the restaurant's entrance. It was then I realised I'd stepped into the bowels of this nondescript venue before.

'Hang on a sec. Didn't this used to be Spaghetti Tree?'

'Yes! I was wondering if you'd recognise it. I don't remember ever seeing you here back in the day?'

Spaghetti Tree had been another saliva-chain venue I'd only ventured into once.

'Ha, funny story actually. Though I'll need a drink or two inside me before I tell it.'

A thought as clear as daylight flashed inside my mind: *I feel like I could tell you anything.*

'I'm sure we can manage that. Just wait 'til you see what Mateo's done with the place.'

He opened the door for me, a gust of aromatic warmth beckoning us inside. We made our way down into the infamous cellar that had been the location for countless teenage drinking exploits in the nineties and early noughties.

But the basement room that welcomed us at the foot of the staircase was unrecognisable. Instead of cigarette-stained magnolia walls and oppressively low ceilings painted black, the cellar had been stripped back to its original bare bricks, with miniature festoon lights strung across the arched ceiling to and from every possible corner. The floor, once tacky with layer upon layer of spilt Bacardi Breezers and goodness knows what else, was now entirely coated in a stunning mosaic of obsolete peseta coins.

Huddled in every possible nook that was too small for a table were pyramids of brightly coloured Spanish tins, aglow with fairy lights as if they were miniature Christmas trees.

Each table – all of them snugly occupied with the exception of one at the far end of the room – was immaculately set with alternating scarlet and ochre tablecloths, long, elegant candles in old Rioja wine bottles and Christmas crackers adorned with the restaurant's logo. The place was like the world's classiest Santa's grotto. And, I couldn't help but observe, it looked incredibly romantic.

'Umm, wow.'

'Yeah, amazing, isn't it? It's well-known for having some of the most authentic tapas in the region. These days, Mateo's got six restaurants dotted all over the area – all of them way bigger than this place, but this is by far my favourite.'

'I can see why. It's beautiful in here.'

Tom kept looking ahead but brushed his dangling fingers against mine for the briefest of moments. Whether or not it was deliberate was unclear, but I swear a significant proportion of my internal organs melted.

'Yeah, it is. Ah, here's the man himself.'

A chap around our age approached us dressed stylishly in black chinos and a black shirt, a white cloth slung over his shoulder. A warm smile lit up his face as he recognised Tom.

'Tom! So good to see you, fella. And so glad you were able to find someone to join you in the end.'

They briefly embraced and smacked each other's backs in that weird way that blokes do.

'Mateo, this is Mally. Mally – Mateo.'

He squeezed the top of my arm. 'Mally, welcome, welcome. First time here, I think?'

'Mateo has a bit of a reputation for remembering faces,' Tom explained, sensing my confusion.

'Oh, I see. Yeah, I was just saying to Tom about how much this place has changed since I was last here.'

'Ah, another Spaghetti Tree fan, eh?'

'Ha – not sure that's the word I'd choose.'

Tom helped me out of my coat and handed it to Mateo along with his. Tom was wearing slim-fitting indigo jeans and a dark red shirt buttoned right to the top, which complemented his colouring – and his long, narrow physique – perfectly.

Mateo continued talking as he stowed them away in a small cupboard. 'You'll have to forgive me, Tom, but one of our servers has called in sick tonight so we're a bit rushed off our feet. It's a good job you didn't come alone as I'm not going to be able to talk as much as I'd like.'

'No worries, Mally and I always seem to find plenty to chat about.' Tom's eyes glinted with sincerity as he glanced at me.

'Ah, it must've been fate, eh?' Mateo winked at me before leading us to the only empty table in the far corner of the room, adjacent to the largest and most majestic tin-can tree of them all.

'Here you go, the best table in the house for you, Tom.' He shook out our napkins and draped them across our laps once we'd taken our seats. 'So, as you know tonight it's our winter warmer set tapas menu. Take a look at the dishes on the blackboard and if there's anything you don't fancy just let us know, and we can replace it with something else. But other than that we'll just bring the dishes out as and when they're ready if that's okay?'

'Sounds amazing. Mally, all good?'

My stomach rumbled as I briefly glanced at the menu over Tom's shoulder. Half the words were in Spanish, but the dishes I could understand – roast Cornish scallops, crab and lobster croquettes, quail's eggs and piquillo peppers – sounded divine. I was ravenous, having only eaten that toast at Jo's and a bowl of cereal over the course of the day.

'A conveyor belt of incredible food? I reckon I can handle that, yeah!'

'*Perfecto*. And a jug of the house crangria?'

Crangria? Had I heard that right? 'Sorry, the house what?'

'Oh my God, Mally, you're in for a treat,' Tom said. 'One of the things that Tapas Den is renowned for is their house sangria, and the winter cranberry version is incredible. Christmas isn't Christmas around here without crangria. Fancy trying it?'

'Hard yes.'

Mateo bowed theatrically to acknowledge the order. 'Perfect. I'll get a jug right over to you and will let the kitchen know you're all set for some appetisers. Enjoy!'

I relaxed back into my chair, smoothing out the ochre napkin to ensure it covered as much of my dress as possible – if I made it through the meal without an oil-based blob ending up on it, it'd be a Christmas miracle.

'What a lovely bloke,' I said. 'How long have you worked with him?'

'Tapas Den was the first account I was given responsibility for after my apprenticeship ended. So that would've been about – shit! – eighteen years ago already. We've been with him from the very start. You look great, by the way. The colour of your dress is an exact match for your eyes.'

Mally, breathe, I thought. *Accept the compliment normally. Return the compliment normally.*

'Ah, cheers! I used B&Q's colour-match system. You look very nice too, by the way.'

Oh well.

'Ha, thanks. I shaved and everything!' He ran a hand across his smooth, enticing chin.

'I noticed!' I tapped a finger on my own jawline to mirror the location of his nano-wound.

'Yeah, classic, eh? I should've known better than to shave when I was nervous.'

I was about to express surprise about his nervousness when Mateo placed a terracotta dish full of the plumpest, Kermit-green olives I'd ever seen on the table and glugged a generous amount of the mysterious crangria into each of our glasses from a matching terracotta jug.

He patted Tom's shoulder twice as he departed.

'Cheers, Mally.'

'Cheers, Tom.'

We tapped our glasses together and I took a sip of the festive cocktail, which was bursting with fresh cranberries and chunks of orange in among what tasted like red wine, Prosecco and some kind of spiced rum. It was delicious. But I made a mental note to keep an eye on my lips during the course of the night, since red wine had a tendency to stain my mouth so it resembled a deep portal into an unknown world.

'Oh wow, this is delicious,' I said, taking another large sip. 'Remind me to ask Mateo for the recipe.'

'Ha, he'll never give it to you! They make a bit of a thing about it on their social media. They run regular competitions for people to try and guess all the ingredients but no one ever has.'

'Smart.'

I sipped again, trying to think of something to say, though Tom beat me to it.

'So, how's your article coming along?'

Earlier in the evening, I'd been tempted to finally get back to Elle and tell her what had happened today to wangle my way out of writing the article at all. But I wasn't sure I could bear her inevitable sanctimony about the fact that her worries about me coming here had come to fruition.

'Urgh. It's not. The last few days have all been a bit of a blur. I've barely had a moment to sit down and write anything. But, well, I've got twenty-four hours before the deadline and I had an idea on my walk earlier that I hope might make the piece vaguely interesting.'

'You're way too modest, you know. Speaking of which, me and Becky were chatting about how much you smashed it at the pub yesterday. Not just by getting us in the private dining room, but also putting that bastard developer in his place.'

I didn't know if it was the crangria or the knowledge that Tom and Becky had been talking about me that was making my belly feel all warm and cosy.

'I'm always happy to help.'

'Yeah, you are, aren't you? So, how are you doing after, y'know, this morning and everything?'

I still couldn't believe that all of that had happened just this morning. Being in this restaurant with Tom felt like a different decade entirely.

'I'm okay. It was so helpful going round to your mum's place and chatting to her about everything – thanks for suggesting that.'

'Honestly, there's no need to thank me. Her years working at the playgroup were some of her happiest. I know she would've got a lot out of reminiscing about those times, too.'

'She's so amazing, Tom. I bet she made your childhood Christmases really special.'

'Yeah, she absolutely tried her best. But, well, as I unsubtly hinted at the other night, my dad was a twat, regardless of the time of year.'

'I'm guessing it's not something you talk about that much?'

'You'd be correct. But I kind of feel like I could tell you anything. Is that a bit weird?'

I felt a rush of recognition at his choice of words. The very words that had screamed themselves loudly inside my own head just a few minutes ago. I had the sudden compulsion to reach over the table, unbutton the top of his shirt and slip my hand down the back of it, rub the base of his neck with my thumb and tell him he could tell me anything, forever. I wanted him to rewind back to his earliest memory and share every thought he'd ever had. About his life. About all the books he'd read and words he'd written. About what he made of the world. About what he made of me. I'd quite happily sit here and listen to him all night – and some. Instead, I gripped my glass tightly with the hand in question and replied simply, 'No, I feel the same.'

'Cool.' He grinned widely and took another sip. 'So, yeah, Christmases were fine, but it was usually just the three of us, although every so often my uncle would join us for the day and drink himself into a stupor until he and my dad would come to drunken blows. Mum would always stay sober so she could drive my uncle home. In the meantime, I had to stay and listen to my dad mouth off about what a dick his brother was.'

'Urgh, not nice. Christmases can be a really shitty time for families, can't they?'

'Yeah, I mean they obviously had some unresolved stuff between them. But, in a way, I always admired my uncle for standing up to him.'

'Your dad... he... wasn't violent, was he? You don't have to answer if you don't want to.'

'Nothing like that, no. But he had this knack for making absolutely everything about him. I mean, believe it or not, at first he even managed to make my mum's condition about *his* bad luck.'

'Fuck.'

'Yeah, he's a prick. And then he convinced me to study business, maths and biology at sixth form instead of the arts subjects I was obviously more interested in. Never outright told me to do so, but there was this constant drip-drip-drip of derision about my writing and the "girly" books I used to read.'

The more Tom spoke about his past, the more it all started to make sense. His choice of A levels had been a massive disappointment for me at the time. I'd always fantasised about how we'd bond over books and poetry in English literature, maybe even getting put on a project together like some kind of American teen rom-com where the jock falls for the nerd. Alas, it hadn't happened that way. But was something happening now? Who knew.

I suddenly noticed my hand was resting on his. I gave it what, on reflection, was a rather motherly pat before helping myself to an olive. They really were the tastiest olives I'd ever eaten.

'I was always surprised you didn't pursue English, I must admit,' I said.

'Oh? How come?'

I fished out the olive stone and started panicking as I realised I didn't know where to put it. Tom noticed my floundering and casually spun the bowl around to reveal a small pit holder clinging to the side of it.

'Thanks. Well, you always just seemed to genuinely enjoy the books. I remember when we were studying *Pride and Prejudice* at GCSE and you'd finished reading it during a single weekend.'

'I've read it loads of times since, too. Always did have a bit of a soft spot for Elizabeth.'

I melted some more. I'd always identified with Lizzie Bennet. 'Ooh, a crush on a literary character. Were you a secret nerd all along, Mr Brinton?'

'I reckon I might have been, Ms Allister. C'mon, are you telling me you didn't have any of your own literary longings?'

'Well, there's one that springs to mind, but it's a little odd, to say the least.'

'I'm listening.'

Was I really going to tell him this? Yes. Yes, I was.

'Aslan.'

Tom snorted and collapsed into a fit of laughter, pounding his fist against the table, causing me to do the same.

At that moment the first flurry of dishes was brought to our table by one of the waiting staff, forcing us to collect ourselves. I was relieved to see there were even numbers of everything, which immediately assuaged my small plates anxiety. That said, if our fingers accidently brushed while reaching for the same croquette, I absolutely would not mind.

'Thanks so much.' We spoke the words simultaneously to the server through fading giggles.

'Wow, this all looks amazing.' I was already heaping my plate high with a selection of steaming yumminess.

'Yeah, they've won tons of local awards. A table here is usually quite hard to come by, especially at this time of year. Seriously, though, the fucking lion?!'

I attempted to kick him under the table, but he somehow managed to grip my shin between his own legs in a way that stilled me, instantly.

'I wouldn't go that far. But, yeah, you're out with a freak tonight.'

He looked right at me and released my leg. 'I guess I like freaks then.'

He likes me. But everyone 'likes' Mally Allister, right? I wanted to excavate his response more, but my subject-changing instincts got in there first.

'What a top client to have on your books, though. But I can't get my head around something – surely if he's *your* client, shouldn't you be the one wining and dining *Mateo*?'

'An excellent observation.' Tom glanced around before continuing in a quieter voice. 'Let's just say that we've had some tricky moments with this place over the years given that a restaurant in a flood-prone basement with zero accessibility for customers with disabilities isn't exactly the easiest of buildings to manage, facilities-wise.'

'Shit, yeah, that explains why your mum can't come here.'

'Exactly. We've been trying to convince Mateo to move this branch above ground for years, but he won't hear of it – it was his first one, and he's very fond of the place. So, yeah, we work hard for him and this is one of his ways of thanking us each year.'

We ate for a couple of minutes, every mouthful being accompanied by a hedonic sound indicating the depth of our mutual enjoyment of the food. Once we'd cleared the first few plates they were discreetly removed. I ordered another jug of crangria.

Tom called after the waitress. 'Oh, and a jug of water, please. So, how about your family Christmases? Would you be happy to tell me about them?'

Did I want to go there? I wasn't sure. But there was only one way to find out.

'Sure. They were, well, they were pretty simple, really. But there was something about them that felt really magical, too. It's a hard feeling to describe, but they just made me feel... tingly, I guess? Those three or four days from 23 December or so once my dad had finished work for Christmas were always so full of silly little traditions and endless banter. Oh, and we had this longstanding family gag that one of us would give someone else a VHS of the film *The Princess Bride* every single year.'

'Great film, but random tradition?'

'Yeah, it started off when my dad got given it two years running and exclaimed "Inconceivable!"'

'Ha, classic.'

Another flurry of plates arrived, along with the crangria and water.

'It was. And, of course, we all used to shout the word in unison whenever it got to that particular present on Christmas morning. Oh! And there was another year when Dad painstakingly devised a treasure hunt for his present to Mum. She was so excited to find out what it was… only to solve the final clue and discover a new iron in the boot of the car.'

'You're kidding?'

'Nope, and she was pregnant with Livvie at the time. It was one of those moments that became part of the Allister family lore before, well, our family got ripped to shreds.'

Now it was Tom's turn to place one of his hands on mine, rubbing his thumb across my knuckles. 'And it's never been the same since?'

My eyes stung with restrained tears but I kind of didn't mind if they spilt out. 'No, never. I mean, me and Josh were never that close to begin with, although once Livvie arrived we warmed up to each other a bit. She and him got on really well, as did me and her. So she was basically the glue between the two of us. But ever since the funeral we've barely had anything to do with each other.'

'I'm so sorry. And your parents?'

'They're plodding along okay. I see them a few times a year. They've created a small but pleasant-enough life for themselves in the middle of nowhere. Mum looks after a bunch of gardens in the local villages and Dad does some private accountancy work from home. They've got some stunning hikes from their front door. Nature helps Mum, especially.'

I often pondered what she thought about on those long, solo walks. Whether she ever smiled when she was alone. Whether her inner voice ever spoke of anything other than the child who'd been stolen from her. From all of us.

'That sounds peaceful,' Tom said.

I swallowed a particularly delicious mouthful of seared, tender entrecote and took a deep breath before responding.

'Honestly? I don't think they've ever been at peace since Livvie died. I don't think any of us have. I mean, you saw me this morning, right? Today's probably the most I've *ever* confronted what happened. We've got this unspoken rule between the four of us that we don't talk about it. Ever. I guess we all find it easier to carry on without having to go through the pain of acknowledging it all. And I can't stop myself from feeling like I'm to blame for all of it.'

I hadn't intended to say that final sentence, but once I'd started talking it'd leaked out.

'What on earth are you talking about?'

My voice trembled as I replied in a whisper. 'Yeah. Because the fact of the matter is, Tom, if I hadn't been so selfish in Livvie's final weeks, none of it would've happened.'

Twenty years earlier

Date: 12/10/2005
From: KarmaChamelia@hotmail.com
To: Livvin_mybestlife@hotmail.com
Subject: Re: re: re: re: Cardiff visit soooooooooon?

Hey Livvie, I'm so sooooooo sorry to do this but I'm going to have to postpone your visit this weekend. Elle's managed to wangle us backstage passes for some gig on the Saturday night. She reckons it'll help us make a good impression with the student newspaper editor, which is good experience to have on my CV I guess.

I know you'll be disappointed but I promise we'll rearrange it soon, OK? Gotta go – I've got an essay due tomorrow and I've only managed to write two paragraphs so far...(who even am I?!). Send everyone my love xxx

Date: 12/10/2005
From: Livvin_mybestlife@hotmail.com

To: KarmaChamelia@hotmail.com

Subject: Re: re: re: re: re: Cardiff visit sooooooooooon?

Oh. OK. Well, just let me know what weekends you're free, I guess. I'll get to see you before Christmas, right?

L x

Chapter 22

☑ **Near-miss kiss**

Twenty years later

'I never answered her question, Tom. And the weekend she was meant to come to Cardiff was the weekend the accident happened. I've never forgiven myself.'

I'd never said those words out loud before. I could feel my composure faltering so I stood up abruptly before I cracked, the chair scraping loudly against the mosaic floor of dormant coins.

'I'm just going to nip to the loo. I won't be a sec.'

'Wait, are you okay?' Tom's eyes were locked on to mine.

I nodded once, my mouth fixed in a straight, hard line. 'I will be.'

I asked a waitress to direct me to the toilet, which was nothing more than a broom cupboard-sized cubicle next to the bar.

I gripped the tiny sink and inspected my face in the mirror as I tried to regulate my breathing.

I looked at myself in the eye. I'd unintentionally told Tom about the worst thing I'd ever done. What was I thinking? Mum, Dad and Josh had spent those early days and weeks trying to reassure me that my decision to cancel her visit wasn't something I should tear myself apart over. But I could always sense the permanent question mark that seemed to hang like an imminent snowstorm above every conversation we ever had as a family from that era onwards: *What if Livvie had been where she was meant to be that day?*

But my own internal question was much louder and harsher: *What if I had been a better sister? A better* person? And now Tom knew who I really was underneath all the dry wit and self-deprecation and urge to help everyone all the time.

I took a few deep breaths before re-emerging, just as another platter of dishes arrived. There was barely any space left on the table now, nor in my churning stomach.

Tom waited until the waitress had departed before speaking. 'Hey, how are you doing?'

'Yeah, I'm okay. It's just that you're the first person I've spoken to about what I did.'

'You didn't "do" anything, Mal.'

I shook my head. 'But that's exactly it, isn't it? I could – and should – have done so much more! I could've actually stood up to Elle when she guilt-tripped me into cancelling Livvie's visit. I could've got back to her instead of trying to bury my guilt – who knows what might have happened if I had? I can't believe I left her hanging and never replied to that final email. Well, not when she was alive, anyway.'

Wow, I was really going to tell him this as well – as if my previous confession hadn't been shameful enough.

'What do you mean?'

'Well, that first Christmas after she'd gone, I finally did reply. And I've been emailing her every day since.'

Tom placed one hand on mine and cradled his own forehead with his other. His eyes were glistening with…

something, or maybe it was just the reflection of the seventy-nine million fairy lights in the subterranean restaurant.

'Fuck, Mally.'

I dropped my eyes back to the table.

'Yeah, what a loser, eh? Trying to make up for letting her down' – I swallowed the vibrating lump in my throat away – 'by sending a load of pointless emails into the digital ether. They've shut down her account now, anyway. I got an automated bounce-back at the start of the month. It's probably for the best.'

'Pointless? What are you talking about? This is, like, the saddest, sweetest, fucking loveliest thing I think I've ever heard. Jesus, you must've loved her so much. You must miss her so much. I'm so sorry this happened to you. To your family. It breaks my heart to think you've been living your life thinking that you played any role at all in what happened to your sister.'

I kept swallowing but my throat was burning with emotion. For twenty years I'd truly believed that I'd been sending those emails to Livvie from the coldest pit of guilt and despair. Never once had I even considered that they came from a place of warmth and love. Or that those two seemingly opposing places overlapped in any way. I'd always seen the emails as – shit – almost *shameful*, somehow. But maybe they weren't? Maybe they were... okay? Special, even? Both of Tom's hands were now on mine. I looked up from the cooling food slowly, cheeks wet with tears that I'd not even noticed falling.

'Thank you.' I spoke quietly. And right then was when I felt a shift between us. I had countless conflicting feelings rushing around inside me, and I could detect that Tom's own emotions were whizzing about as well. What he was feeling I had no idea. But I knew what my own feelings were as if they were shouting their names to me:

Pain. Loss. Fury. Safety. Hope.

Love.

I felt ripped open, yet fiercely alive.

Tom cleared his throat as we waited for our puddings after the final savoury plates had been cleared. I could sense he was scrabbling about for a less heartrending topic of conversation. 'So, er, has enough alcohol been consumed to share your Spaghetti Tree story yet?'

'Urgh, just about.' I took another large gulp of my festive cocktail before continuing. 'Buckle up. I guess I would've been fifteen and Elle would've just turned sixteen, as she'd gotten herself a Saturday job at Kookaï on the high street.'

'Kookaï? Very trendy.'

'And didn't she know it. She was properly smug about it, especially when the only Saturday job I could find a few months later was at BHS.'

'Ah, but you couldn't get a decent fry-up at Kookaï.'

'Exactly! Though Elle never seemed to quite under-stand why I thought the on-site self-service restaurant was such a bonus. But I digress. So I'm fifteen, and Elle suggests I meet her in town after work one Saturday for some late-night shopping and a bite to eat.'

'Oh God, I think I can see where this is heading...'

'Yup. So there I am on the bus into town early one Saturday evening, wondering why Elle told me not to wear a coat, despite the fact that it's freezing out, but also feeling ever so grown-up for heading out for what I thought would be a fun shopping trip and girly dinner before we got the bus back to Scarnbrook.'

'You lived on the same street, right?'

'Yeah, next door to each other. She moved in with her mum at the start of Year Nine. I'm surprised you remembered that.'

Tom tapped his temple to signal his excellent ability to recall information.

'Anyway, as soon as Elle's shift ended, we headed over the road to The Body Shop, where they used to give you free makeovers if you bought a couple of products. So we bought some body lotions and lip balms in return for a full face of make-up each. Then, in the shopping centre loos, Elle produces two "going out" tops from Kookaï – to this day I don't know if she paid for them. We got changed into those and zig-zagged our partings before making our way to the restaurant for this so-called girly dinner, and Spaghetti Tree was indeed the venue. Not that I'd ever heard of it before then, mind.'

'An early adopter.'

'Hardly. So as the waiter showed us to our table, I noticed that all the other tables also appeared to be occupied by teenagers our age, all of whom seemed to have ordered exactly the same pizza. Which no one was eating.'

'The infamous margherita.'

'Yes! And then, at eight thirty on the dot, the lights dimmed, and everyone started pushing their tables up against the wall.'

'Oh God, these are just the cringiest memories, Mal.'

My lips twitched at the mention of 'Mal' again, before I continued my tragic teenage tale. 'And – as you well know

– all of a sudden, the restaurant had transformed into some kind of dingy, underage nightclub. I was in shock. And I suggested to Elle that we should get out of there, but she just laughed and told me to relax. She said there was a well-known legal loophole that you could drink alcohol in a restaurant aged sixteen, as long as you drank it with food, hence all the stacks of uneaten cheap pizzas. Which sent me into a spin because a) I was pretty sure you still needed an adult to actually *buy* the booze and b) I wasn't even sixteen at that point anyway.'

'Blimey, what a way to be initiated into the Spaghetti Tree underbelly.'

'Tell me about it. By now, we're sat next to our table, pizzas untouched as that seemed to be the done thing, backs against the wall as all manner of things start happening on the dancefloor. Elle's swigging from her bottle of Metz, trying to look all aloof, but she wouldn't take her eyes off the entrance. Turns out some bloke had come into Kookaï the Saturday before, liked the look of her and had mentioned something about meeting him and his mates at Spaghetti Tree the following weekend.'

'So, she wanted you there as her wing woman?'

'Wing *child*, Tom.'

'Urgh, right. Did he show?'

'Yeah, about an hour after the restaurant underwent its nightclub transformation. He was half-cut and had obviously forgotten who Elle even was. Though she had no problem reminding him the instant she clapped eyes on him.'

'Was this meant to be a funny story? Because it sounds horrific. How old was this bloke?'

'In his early twenties maybe? I found out later that Elle had told him she was nineteen.'

'Well, he probably knew that was a lie, hence he suggested they meet up in a well-known underage drinking hole.'

'Urgh, I'd never even considered that angle before.'

'So how did the night play out?'

'Well, I basically just sat in that little corner over there…'

I pointed to the opposite side of the restaurant where a group of four girlfriends were donning red and yellow paper crowns from their Christmas crackers and taking group selfies as they did so.

'…nibbling away at our pizzas, which were actually quite delicious by the way—'

'Yeah, I always did feel sorry for the chefs.'

'—while Elle and this guy danced and snogged. I kept thinking to myself, *Surely she'll need the toilet at some point and I can reason with her in there*. But no. They just kept snogging for what felt like hours. Some of his mates kept hassling me to dance with them, and at one stage Elle and the guy she was with pointed at me and laughed at some inside joke, which is what tipped me over the edge into full-on survival mode. I just needed to make sure that the two of us got out of there and home in one piece. Which is, of course, exactly why she'd invited me along in the first place.'

'As a safety net?'

'Always the safety net.'

'Hmm. So how *did* you get home?'

'I found a landline phone on the bar and called my brother. I knew Mum and Dad would still be out at Supper Club and he'd just passed his driving test. I managed to remove Elle from the clutches of the sleazy bloke under the guise of feeling sick and needing some fresh air. Thankfully, Josh was waiting for us outside at just the right moment and helped me to bundle her into the car. He'd had to bring Livvie with him, obviously, though she found all the drama thrilling.' I smiled, remembering how the night had panned out, Josh and Livvie coming to my rescue. The three musketeers, helping each other out, just as we'd always done as kids. 'Elle was furious, mind you, since she'd not managed to get the guy's number. I told her that if he wanted to see her again, surely he'd come back into the shop to find her.'

'Let me guess, he never did?'

'Well, if he did I never heard about it. So I'm assuming not. And we never came back here again.'

'I'm not surprised. And did your parents ever find out about it?'

'Fuck, no. We got home before them, thank God. Elle didn't have such luck, though – her mum hadn't even known she was going out after work and had been frantic with worry. When she got home drunk she was grounded for a month. Elle refused to speak to me for the entire time.'

'Harsh. So this is your first time in this basement since that night?'

'Yup.'

'Ha, way to choose an inappropriate venue for a first date, Brinton.'

Hang on. *Hang on.* Had he just said the words 'first date'? Two thoughts immediately competed for attention in my head: firstly, Tom Brinton had confirmed we were on a *date*. Secondly, he'd specifically said the phrase 'first date', which... suggested there'd be *more*?!

This silent revelation had taken hold just as I'd spooned a delicious mouthful of dulce de leche mousse into my mouth and, frankly, it was a miracle it hadn't spluttered out of my nose in excitement. Once I'd successfully swallowed it, I licked my lips and looked up.

We caught each other's eye and both smiled shyly. I could feel my cheeks burn as he looked down quickly at his own mousse, grinning while stirring it around.

Tom cleared his throat again. I realised it was a thing he did when he was nervous.

'So… it's weird that we never really spoke at school, isn't it?' he said.

'Is it?'

'I think it is a bit, yeah. Why didn't we?'

'I was quite shy back then, I guess.'

'Shy?'

'You didn't think so?'

'No. I mean, you weren't loud or outgoing or anything like that. Just, well, quietly sure of yourself, I guess. And funny.'

'That's weird, because that's exactly how I used to think of you back then. With the exception of "quiet".'

'Ha. So why didn't we ever hang out?'

'Oh, come on, I think we existed on completely different planes back then. Plus, as much as I've appreciated his mechanical support this week, me and the likes of Ryan Seldon aren't exactly kindred spirits.'

Which reminded me that he might have started work on my car today. Though, right now, I didn't feel quite the same urge to chase him about it.

'Fair enough. But you shouldn't judge someone by the company they keep, you know?'

'Oh, God, no of course not. I didn't mean it like that, it's just that you two seemed to come as a bit of a package back then.'

'I can see how it looked that way. But so did you and Elle. I never quite understood how the two of you slotted together as mates. Why were you friends with her?'

Huh. I was *not* expecting that question.

'Do you mean why *am* I friends with her?'

'I… guess so, yeah. It's just that, well, she always seemed so… different to you. I mean, your Spaghetti Tree story hasn't exactly covered her in glory. Oh, and there was that weird thing with her and Ryan at school for a while. He was like putty in her hands for a bit, do you remember?'

'Yeah, he had this massive crush on her in, like, Year Ten, it must've been?'

'Round about that time. He was smitten. But then there was that whole "bad breath" incident after they snogged on that school trip…'

'That was a cruel thing for her to say. I said as much to her at the time.'

'But did she ever tell you what happened the weekend *before* she said that?'

'Not sure. Tell me what you know.'

'So they snogged at the wetlands centre and Ryan was on cloud nine and asked her to go to the cinema with him that weekend.'

'Oh, wow. No, I had no idea about that.'

'Yeah, and she said yes. So that Saturday they met at Showcase Cinema on the other side of town. She somehow managed to smuggle in a bottle of vodka with her, so by the time the film had finished she was wasted.'

This was all new information to me. I was shocked. She used to tell me every single detail about her non-stop romantic exploits back then – or so I thought.

'And so was Ryan, I imagine?'

'No, that's the thing – Ryan was being really earnest about it all. He'd even arranged for his dad to pick them up after the film and drop her home.'

'Oh God, I don't think I like where this is going.'

'Your trepidation is valid. So, his dad turns up and she's absolutely steaming, and I reckon Ryan probably endured the most painful twenty minutes of his life. Apparently, she openly flirted with his dad, made fun of Ryan in the third person as if he wasn't sat right next to her in the back and to top it all off then proceeded to vomit all over the car.'

I'd never felt any kind of affinity with Ryan Seldon, but I blushed on his behalf. Poor bloke – no one deserved that. What had Elle been thinking?

'Shitting hell.'

'So… she never told you anything about it, then?'

'No. Nothing. All I know was that they snogged on the school trip, and then on the Monday she said that stuff about his breath. That was it.'

'Right, that all makes sense now.' He looked disappointed and relieved at the same time, though I had no idea why.

'What does?'

'Ah, nothing, don't worry. Anyway, I've never been able to get my head around why she did it beyond it being some weird power trip for her. I only heard about this years later, mind. I think Ryan was too embarrassed to talk about it at the time, but once he and Carly got together in their twenties it all came out one night when we were pissed and reminiscing about our, er, teenage crushes. So, yeah, I guess I've never held her in the highest regard, to be honest.'

Well, it was all coming out tonight, wasn't it? I could understand why Tom would feel that way about someone who'd hurt his mate, but I had to stand up for my mate, too.

'What can I say? Other than she's my best friend. Has been since she moved next door.'

'Well, sure, but that's not necessarily a reason to stay friends with someone, is it?'

I poured myself another large glass of crangria, sploshing a not-insignificant amount onto the tablecloth, and breathed out slowly as I did so. I couldn't remember the last time anyone had delved into my soul like this before. I had to dig deep for my response, because the roots of mine and Elle's friendship were sprawling, and always would be.

'The truth is, Tom, that after everything with Livvie, Elle was the only person I could count on to be by my side. She kept me from crumbling more than once. We became each other's family – she's never been that close to hers, and I've drifted from mine, as sad as that makes me. And, no, Elle isn't perfect and our friendship isn't as... reciprocal... as maybe it could be. But I'm far from perfect, myself. So, yeah, that's why we've stuck together all these years. She seems convinced writing this article will give my career a boost, and I'm happy to help her whenever I can.'

'Her safety net.'

'Touché.'

'But who's *your* safety net?'

I swallowed and looked down. 'Oh, I'm pretty self-sufficient. Who's yours?'

'My mum, without question.'

'And do you still see your dad?'

'A little. It's hard. But he knows he can't manipulate us any more, so he mainly leaves us alone. These days it's much easier for me to see how some of his behaviours were never conscious choices on his part, but caused by stuff that went on when he was younger that he's probably never dealt with. I guess we all have stuff like that dragging us backwards, don't we?'

'Yeah, tell me about it. But Elle's always been pretty good at dragging me forwards, you know?'

'In what way?'

'Well, as soon as we got back to uni after Livvie's funeral she kept taking me out, night after night. I buried myself in my studies the rest of the time. Obviously looking back I can see that Elle had thought that hoisting me up onto some kind of carousel of distraction was the right thing to do. I mean, we were both so young. I think she'd just taken it upon herself to keep my life as "normal" and positive as possible.'

'I can see why she might have felt the need to do that, sure,' he said.

'Well, what was the alternative?'

'I dunno. Just let you feel what you needed to feel, maybe?'

'She was a teenager, not a grief counsellor. Anyway. Enough about all that. A drink for the road?'

'Absolutely.'

Our desserts had been just as delicious as everything else. This had undoubtedly been the best meal of my life. And not just because of the food.

268

'Hey, mate, can you wait here a sec while I see her in?'

The taxi driver sighed. 'Fine, but keep it quick – this is one of my busiest nights of the year and I'm already late for my next fare.'

'Understood.'

We jogged to the door, the icy wind that had picked up outside while we'd been in the bowels of Tapas Den making my eyes water. My tear ducts had had quite the workout today.

'No Nutrigrains needed this time, Mal?'

'Nope, I reckon my blood-sugar levels are pretty decent thanks to that incredible food. What an amazing place.'

'Yeah. Soooo... how much longer will you be here for?'

In the absence of any news about Dad's car, I had no idea.

'Not sure. I need to give Ryan a bell tomorrow. But I imagine I'll probably head back in the next couple of days.'

'Okay. So... I was speaking to my mum earlier – and please, *please* feel free to say no if this is way too much – but we wondered if you might be interested in staying in Scarnbrook a little longer so you can spend Christmas with us? That's if you still have no plans back in London?'

Play it cool, Mally. Play. It. Cool.

'Oh, Tom, that's really kind of you, but I really couldn't gate-crash your family Christmas like that.'

'You wouldn't be gate-crashing it at all. I mean, you've seen how big that turkey is, right? How are the two of us meant to munch our way through that alone? Also, I'd... I'd really like to spend the day with you.'

Say yes, Mally. Otherwise, it'll just be you, an empty advent calendar and that chewy Pret sandwich.

'It sounds nice, it really does, but Christmas is still a week away and I only have this place' – I gestured behind me – 'for a couple more days, so staying here for any longer than that isn't really an option, I'm afraid.'

'Yeah, you wouldn't have to worry about that, either. Mum said she'd be happy to put you up at hers for a few nights. When I told her you were a fan of her Channel 5 films, she could barely contain her excitement. I reckon you two would probably get on like a house on fire.'

Even removing the prospect of spending Christmas with *Tom Brinton*, the thought of snuggling up on Jo's soft sofa with Chippie to stroke, a steady stream of cuppas and cheesy films sounded like a pretty lovely plan in and of itself.

'Ha, you're probably right. Go on, then. I must admit it does sound more appealing than getting woken up at dawn on Christmas morning by the relentless bouncing of the toddler in the flat upstairs.'

He tugged his fist downwards in an ironic celebratory gesture.

'Whoop!' He was smiling widely.

The taxi revved its engine as an unsubtle signal to hurry the fuck up.

'Of course, it's not a problem if you change your mind.' He turned to the taxi and pleadingly held up his forefinger to indicate he just needed one more minute. 'Hey, would you be up for me swinging by after work tomorrow? It's the last day in the office until the new year so I reckon I should be done by four, if that's enough time for you to finish your article?'

Woah, he was talking about having *multiple* dates in the coming days, which would be a new personal best for me.

'Yeah, that'd be nice. And a deadline would also be really helpful for me to get the damn thing done.'

'Awesome. And I can finally hang that curtain back up. But, umm, as much as this place has its… charms… maybe we could head over to mine once that's done? I could fire up the log burner and we could get a takeaway or something? Or we could go to the cinema, or a pub for dinner? Totally your call.'

I had sudden visions of legs entwined underneath a fireside blanket. I *definitely* ought to shave my legs. I cleared my throat and shook the thought out of my head before responding.

'The takeaway plan sounds perfect. And, in all honesty, I could probably do with a night off the booze, too.'

'Yeah, same. Okay, well, thanks again for helping me out tonight. It was a lot of fun.'

'It was.'

Tom gazed down at me, my eyes level with his surprisingly delicate neck. I was close enough to him to notice a tiny dot on his left earlobe, where a small, gold stud used to reside back in our school days. His Adam's apple bobbed as he swallowed while placing his hands lightly on my shoulders. A sudden gust of wind caught my hair and smothered my entire face in it. Typical. I secured half of it behind one ear with one hand, while Tom simultaneously did the same on the other.

'Were you always this small?' he murmured, as he slowly stooped down to close the height gap between us.

I whispered, 'No, I shrank,' in response and was about to close my eyes in anticipation of contact… when the taxi honked its horn for at least three seconds to indicate the driver's patience had finally expired, jolting both of us apart.

'Ha. Here's to trying – and failing.'

Those words were always associated with embarrass-ment and a clammy-gripped microphone, because they were the words I'd uttered when I'd accepted my PE effort award all those years ago. Was it a coincidence, or had he remembered? Somehow, Tom knew what I was thinking.

'Effort's underrated, Mal.' My entire face became a grin. His did the same as he lightly squeezed my hand and locked eyes with me.

'Tomorrow,' he said.

I nodded once. My hair was now blowing in every single direction again.

'Yeah, tomorrow. Night, Tom.'

'Night, Mally.'

Just before he got into the taxi, he turned to me and roared, surprisingly loudly.

I made a *WTF* gesture with my hands to indicate an explanation for the random noise was required.

He lowered the window and stuck his head out of it as the car sped off. 'Aslan!'

Funny. Attractive. Smart. Well-read. Kind. Generous. Modest. Credit where credit was due: teenage Mally had had bloody good taste. I let myself in and closed the door softly behind me, leaning on the inside in a way that I'd seen countless female protagonists do in all those made-for-TV movies.

I wanted to send a message to the fifteen-year-old version of me and tell her that TOM BRINTON FANCIED HER and that she just had to wait a quarter of a century or so for the stars to align.

I probably wouldn't tell her about the shitload of pain in between.

I sighed with a mixture of contentment and emotional exhaustion as I kicked off my boots and shimmied out of my coat. Mine and Tom's first kiss hadn't happened tonight, but I knew that it'd happen tomorrow – I'd never been surer about anything in my life.

Chapter 23

☑ **Creativity rediscovered**

I'd woken up smiling for the first time in ages. Because it was the morning after my First Date with Tom Brinton. And the day of our Second Date. I rubbed my cheeks in a circular motion to try and soften my goofy grin and focus my mind on today's first task: I had an article to write. And, crikey, over the last few days I'd collected gallons of trope-flavoured syrup to wade through for inspiration.

When I sat down at my laptop, words flowed out of me with ease. I'd planned to write a fun little piece about all the (many) awkward ways I'd managed to tick off a surprisingly high number of Christmas movie clichés since I'd been in Scarnbrook. But, since I'd been here, another idea had been marinading. And now the flavours were searing themselves onto the page.

Because, despite Christian Woods scarpering away like a cartoon villain earlier this week, Scarnbrook remained at risk of losing one of the only pieces of its soul it had left: its last remaining pub. After my wander around the village yesterday afternoon, I'd seen more and more evidence of how Christian Woods – and no doubt countless other developers like him – were draining the lifeblood out of this place. Cramming tenants into substandard residential boxes with little in the way of parking, let alone gardens, and then – to add insult to injury – ridding the village of much of the only communal green spaces they had left by building even more below-par properties over the top of them.

The allotments, two pubs, the village hall, the sweet shop and even the original Victorian building of my primary school had all been turned into residential abodes of varying quality. If The Star were to also fall prey to Christian's Grinch-like game-plan, where would all the villagers be able to get together after that? The middle of Lidl?

This was the story that the words falling out of me wanted to tell. Because, while the plots of all the cheesy Christmas movies I couldn't get enough of were marketed as romances, their core themes were almost always about the same things: community; a cause behind which people can come together; discovering, or rediscovering, a place it feels right to call home. And Christmastime – regardless of someone's relationship with religion – was when all of this stuff had the best chance of converging.

It wasn't as if I had any plans to up sticks and move back to Scarnbrook – I wasn't that idealistic. But this place would always be my *childhood* home. And being here, and writing this piece, felt right. Fuelled by numerous instant coffees and bowls of Tesco Choco Malt Wheats, the article took just a few hours to write. I'd changed the names of everyone and everywhere, as agreed with Elle, and paid homage to my beloved movies by referencing all the bingo tropes I'd managed to tick off. But, hopefully, the article also struck the right balance between awkward festive lols and the deeper meaning hidden beneath the seemingly vapid red and green gift wrap. Because I could feel that this trip – as devastating as some of it had been – had begun to fix something in me. I'd reconnected with people in ways I'd never thought possible. I'd learnt that sugar-coated sentimentality and soul-destroying sorrow could co-exist. And, even though none of this was explicitly on the page, I weaved my love for Scarnbrook through my words, the closing sentence feeling incredibly satisfying and truthful:

> *Coming back here finally gave me the opportunity to say goodbye to the place I'd called home for the happiest years of my life.*

I read over it one final time. I was pleased with what I'd been able to come up with, and hopefully Elle would be, too. I composed an email to her and hit send, including a quick apology for not replying to her message from a couple of days ago. It was just before two o'clock, so I still had a decent amount of time to get ready for my date with Tom. My phone buzzed. I expected it to be an acknowledgement of my article from Elle. But it was Tom, instead.

Tom:
Hey, thanks again for last night. Can't stop grinning today. Still on for later? Thomas x

Mally:
Ha, same on the grinning front. Of course. Can't wait. Mal x

After a quick shower, I pulled on my favourite pair of jeans and a cosy Fair Isle knit with a grey vest top underneath. In case things got… hot.

I wrapped the bath towel – no longer crispy after a few uses – around my head and checked my phone before making a start on my make-up.

There was a voice message from Elle on WhatsApp. Oh God, I hoped she liked my piece. I pushed play:

> **Elle (voice message):**
> Hey, Ryan, she can have the car back now. Thank you so much for everything! Despite the Darren flop, I got exactly what I needed. I definitely owe you one! And Tom, by the sounds of it! Give my love to Carly and Becky, too.

What the…?

But before I could play it again, the message was gone.

Chapter 24

☑ **A hasty departure**

I didn't need to listen to the message again to understand the most likely explanation for Elle's words: my trip to Scarnbrook – and no doubt many of the encounters I'd had since I'd arrived – had somehow been an elaborate set-up from the outset.

The pub quiz. Trying to set me up with Darren. 'Bumping into' Tom and last night's supposed 'date'. I had no idea what – if anything – about this week had been real any more. Had they all been laughing at me behind my back?

I was mortified to my very core. Yet, somehow, it almost felt as if this moment had been inevitable ever since I'd had the idea to come back to Scarnbrook. I mean, returning here was never going to end with a Christmas movie-style 'happily ever after' moment against a snowy backdrop, was it? The harrowing past was always going to rear its head. Old wounds were always going to re-open. And I was always going to end up alone. What I hadn't foreseen, however, was that Elle would be the cause of it all. What the fuck was going on with her? With us? The only things I knew for sure right now were these: I couldn't trust anyone but myself. And I needed to leave. Now.

Right on cue, having no doubt received the message that'd been intended for him, Ryan called.

'Great news, Miss Fuel, your car's ready. Reckon you could make your way over here to pick it up before I close? I'm sure Brinton'll give you a lift, ha ha.'

My voice quivered as I replied. 'Tell you what, Ryan, how about you just bring it to me, hmm?'

'Oh, er, I guess I could try and make that work.'

'Seriously, you can drop the act. I know you've all been plotting with Elle the entire time I've been here. She just sent me a message by mistake that was quite obviously intended for you. And I know that my car was probably ready days ago. Can you bring it here or not? You know where I'm staying, I presume?'

'Yeah, but which number?' Ryan's voice sounded different, all hints of cockiness evaporated.

'Eleven. Just put the car keys through the letterbox when you get here. You've got my London address to invoice me so just stick it in the post.'

Ryan's breath crackled the line between us as he exhaled. 'There'll be no invoice, Mally. It was a simple job in the end. God, I feel awful. Honestly, Elle told me you wouldn't mind.'

Wouldn't mind?! Elle had thought that manipulating me – when she knew how anxious I'd been about writing this stupid article – was even within the realm of 'reasonable', for fuck's sake?

'Of course she did. That's how she operates. But you know all about that from Year Ten, don't you?'

He paused before he spoke again, an edge of panic to his voice. 'Please don't tell Carly I was in touch with her. She messaged me on Facebook out of the blue last week for a "quick favour" and it just escalated from there. You know what she's like – she's impossible to say no to.'

I knew one thing for sure: I wasn't going to hesitate to say no to her ever again.

'You honestly think I'm going to stay in touch with anyone from Scarnbrook after this? Don't worry, Ryan, your secret is safe with dull old Double A.' My voice broke open at my school nickname. I hung up before he had the chance to talk again. He deserved to feel shit for this. And, for once, I wasn't going to put myself out to make him – or anyone else, for that matter – feel better about themselves.

I ran upstairs, tears careering down my hot cheeks. I grabbed my wheelie suitcase and began hastily shoving my clothes inside. My Mary Berry dress, which still smelt of Tapas Den, mocking me as it refused to crumple. I knew I'd never want to wear it again.

My ears rang as I tried to work out what had driven Elle's scheme as I scooped my smellies into my toiletries bag. The only answer I kept coming up with was 'ambition': she wanted to strand me in Scarnbrook to get a more interesting article out of me. I was so disappointed in her. No, 'disappointed' wasn't strong enough. I was furious with her. Sure, this was exactly the kind of game she'd play on any of her other writers in order to get the 'best' out of them. But to fool *me* like this? Her best friend?

I gave the rental a cursory tidy, ignoring the curtain that was still neatly folded on the landing. While I was putting the crockery away in the kitchen, I heard the hard, sleigh bell-esque jingle of keys landing on the laminate floor. I peered out the living-room window to see Darren driving Ryan away, Dad's car on the driveway.

I grabbed my stuff and locked the door behind me, placing the key back in its grubby box. I chucked my stuff in the boot, annoyed to see a spare umbrella inside. Alanis Morissette could've written one of her ironic 'Ironic' lyrics about that. As I careened my way out of Scarnbrook on the ever-widening roads, I tried to ignore the fact that four o'clock was approaching and Tom would be arriving at Hollyhock Close at any minute. I'd left no note and his number was blocked, along with everyone else's here. Even if last night had been real, my relationship with Scarnbrook – and therefore any prospect of a relationship with him – was over, once and for all. Christian Woods could burn the pub to the ground for all I cared.

Chapter 25

☑ **Bad news piles up**

I swung into my parents' driveway and sat there with my music still blaring for a minute or so. I'd turned it up loud when I'd started driving east out of Scarnbrook, letting the We Are Scientists frontman do the expressing for me through his anguished vocals. I switched off the engine and sat in the dark interior of the vehicle, trying to figure out my next move. The obvious first step was to establish contact with Elle and figure out what the hell had possessed her to do this to me. I tapped out a message to her from the driver's seat:

> **Mally:**
> Call me. Please. I've left Scarnbrook. I
> know you set me up.

Two blue ticks. I waited in the car for a few more minutes but there was nothing in return.

It was approaching seven o'clock. If it hadn't been for Elle's accidental message, I could've been happily re-enacting *The Notebook*'s fireplace scene with Tom right now. The thought made me feel both violated and miffed, which was an unusual combination at the best of times.

God, I'd been such a moron. I felt disgusted that I'd allowed myself to be swept along with everyone's retrospectively obvious ruse. It was all so humiliating.

It was the stuff with Tom that was confusing me most. I was pretty sure I hadn't imagined the chemistry between us last night. But I couldn't rule out the possibility that Elle had somehow guilt-tripped him into asking me to spend Christmas with him and his mum. A relationship based on a foundation of pity and saviourism? No, thanks.

I mentally flicked whatever version of him I thought I'd got to know away as I clambered out of the car with my luggage and let myself into the cottage. I immediately felt calmer as the low ceilings and creaky floors enveloped me. With instant clarity, I knew that I would hide out here for Christmas, instead of travelling back to London to deal with Elle. I relaxed into my new plan a little. It was what I'd actually wanted to do after I'd taken my parents to the airport, after all.

I lugged my suitcase upstairs, grabbed the heavy duvet from my bed and let it tumble down the narrow staircase before descending behind it. I bolted the front door, closed all the curtains, lit the fire and put the telly on to fill the silence. A quick rummage in the kitchen's understairs pantry proved productive: a full packet of mince pies and some mini bottles of whisky I'd found in an unfinished boozy advent calendar from a couple of years ago, which I was sure wouldn't be missed. I took the comforting sustenance to the sofa with me and buried myself deep in togs. The timing was perfect – a Christmas movie had just started on Channel 5 and they were broadcasting them back to back for the next six hours. Evening sorted, mind instantly occupied, nerves soothed.

During the first advert break, I checked my work emails to see if Elle had replied to me there, instead. I had zero desire for my article to see the light of day now I knew the layers of manipulation that had led to its conception.

There was no email from Elle. But the state of my inbox made every hair on my body stand to attention with alarm.

A barrage of unofficial all-staff emails had been doing the rounds over the course of the last couple of hours, the first of which had been sent from one of our most high-profile writers. He'd circulated a link to a national newspaper article with a subject line that merely read *WTF?*

I tapped on the link and gasped. The headline read:

THE HELIX UK STAFF FACE REDUNDANCY AS LONDON OFFICE CLOSES DOWN

What the hell?

I read through the news story, discovering that the reporter had been tipped off about a commercial letting listing for *The Helix*'s entire West End office. She'd gone on to speak to numerous 'sources' who'd confirmed the publication was pulling out of the UK. I guessed that explained the early December shutdown, no doubt to spruce the place up ready for its next tenants.

The journalist had approached *The Helix*'s UK and US representatives for comment but had been 'unable to reach' anyone. But a 'source close to the publication' had been quoted stating that '324 UK staff at its London-based office would soon be receiving emails informing them that they face losing their jobs'. I'd worked with HR long enough to know that 'face losing their jobs' was a legally compliant way of saying 'are going to be made redundant after a perfunctory consultation period'. This was an internal – and external – comms disaster.

I did some quick mental sums based on the regular status of my bank accounts. I figured I had two – maybe three – months of savings to tide me over before my finances would get hairy. I called my co-manager Lauren in the hope she'd be able to provide me with some reassurance, but it went straight to voicemail:

'You've reached Lauren Rollinson at *The Helix*. If you're a reporter seeking a comment, please call my counterpart in the US because I know absolutely fuck-all. If you're not a reporter, leave a message.'

Oh God. This wasn't good at all. I left a quick voicemail. She called back within minutes.

'Mally, hi. Sorry: you're on my list of people to call but as you can imagine my phone hasn't stopped ringing. How are you doing?'

I was tempted to tell her about all the shit that had gone down in the space of the last few hours. But she probably had enough on her plate already.

'I think I'm in shock.'

'Yeah, me too.'

'You had no idea?' I asked.

'Well, I think lots of us could sense something fishy was going on. But not to this extent. Plus, no one had bothered to bring me in on any of it. If they had, we could've managed this shitstorm a whole lot better. But they decided not to trust us to be actual professionals about it all. Some smart alec at *The Helix* decided to leak the story to get a head start on their job hunt. So we're completely on the back foot and have got absolutely nothing lined up to tell employees – or anyone, for that matter.'

'Do you reckon we'll ever get to go back to the office?' It seemed like the last thing that should've been on my mind, but I couldn't stop thinking about my favourite umbrella lying abandoned under my desk.

'Yeah, I'm sure we will – even if it's just to box up our stuff.'

'Does Maggie know about any of this?'

I could barely bring myself to think about my co-manager Maggie, who'd been a loyal staffer at *The Helix* since the very start of its UK expansion. She was meant to be having a peaceful post-op recovery at home before a quiet Christmas with her first grandchild.

'Yeah, I spoke to her just now. She's beside herself. She wanted to call you but I insisted that I'd do it since she's still on leave.'

'So what can we do now, comms-wise? Should we be sending out something to staff?'

'That's the thing: I've been instructed to say nothing. They've apparently got some fancy-pants New York PR agency lined up to handle all internal and external comms. But their contract wasn't meant to start until the new year, when all of this was *supposed* to be communicated. Frankly, they can have their Christmas ruined, too, for all I care. I just can't believe how badly they've handled this.'

A selfish thought flew into my mind: *At least everyone else will also be having a shit Christmas, now.* I was a bad person.

'So there's literally nothing we can do?'

'Nope. I'm so sorry I don't have much to tell you, Mally. As soon as I've got any more information I'll be in touch. Have you got someone with you?'

I looked around the empty room, my eyes landing on the muted Christmas movie on the telly, which had now resumed after the ad break. A blandly attractive man and Christmas movie legend Lacey Chabert were decorating a Christmas tree. I thought about tree-dwelling Marmalade back in Jo's living room, my eyes welling up once more.

'Don't worry about me, I'm good.'

After hanging up and messaging Maggie, I gave social media a quick search. The consensus seemed to be shock at the timing of the non-announcement-announcement, and how poorly *The Helix*'s hundreds of UK staff were being treated with complete silence from the top. Tons of my colleagues were sharing their own disbelief and anger, tagging the online publication's US editors and execs to demand answers – all of whom had, so far, said absolutely nothing.

In short, it was a complete mess.

My personal drama with Elle now seemed trivial in comparison to this latest lightning bolt of information. I knew she'd be devastated about her job and would already be hustling for employment elsewhere. In fact, it wouldn't have surprised me if she'd been the one who'd leaked the story. If that was the case, however, she could've at least had the decency to tell me, first.

Regardless, the situation had gotten beyond the realms of WhatsApp. I took a deep breath and called her instead. It rang out and went to voicemail.

I sighed and waited for the message tone. 'Elle, it's Mally. I just found out about *The Helix* closing down. Let's forget about all the Scarnbrook stuff for now. Please call me back. I need to know you're OK.'

I sank back down on the sofa and yanked the duvet over me. As I did so, it caught my tumbler of whisky. The heavy-based glass clattered to the floor, somehow not shattering, the amber liquid making a beeline for a small collection of presents under the Christmas tree. I leapt off the sofa and brushed the gifts aside in the nick of time. But something about a couple of them caught my eye. They were the ones from Josh, which Mum and Dad must've opted to leave here to open when they got back. The two fabric-wrapped parcels bore those beautiful calligraphic labels... which were tied to the presents with a distinctive mustard twine. I grabbed my phone and zoomed in on the photo I'd taken of Livvie's grave yesterday. The twine was exactly the same. Had Josh been in Scarnbrook, too?

As I absorbed the puddle of whisky with a few sheets of kitchen roll, my heart pounded in my ears. Why on earth hadn't he said anything if he had?

I sent him a message.

Mally:
Were you in Scarnbrook? I saw the flowers you left for Livvie and recognised the string.

The amount of time the dots next to his name were wiggling about indicated he was either composing an essay, or kept writing and deleting various replies.

Josh:
Yes, I was.

Well, that was an anti-climax.

288

Mally:
When were you there?

...

Josh:
A quick visit last week.

Mally:
Why????

...

Oh, FFS. Enough of this cryptic shit. I pushed the 'call' button.

He rejected the call instantly.

Josh:
I'm with a client right now and can't talk.

...

Josh:
Saskia will be in touch.

Saskia?

> **Josh:**
> Sorry to hear about The Helix btw. Gotta
> go.

Saskia did indeed message me a few minutes later – I didn't
even have her number saved in my contacts.

> **Saskia:**
> Hey, Mally. Are you back from Scarnbrook
> yet? Josh and I wondered if you wanted to
> come over for a (long-overdue!) lunch
> soon. Ideally before Christmas if you could
> squeeze us in?! S x

What the hell was happening?

> **Mally:**
> Sure, when works for you guys?

> **Saskia:**
> How about Monday at 1ish?

> **Mally:**
> Yep, that's good for me. Is everything OK?

I re-examined the exchange again – our very first messages
to each other.

Chat about what? This month was getting more
perplexing by the day.

I checked my train app and found one that'd get me
into London Bridge at 11.37 a.m. on Monday, which
would give me just about enough time to negotiate
the awkward Underground / Overground journey to
Imperial Wharf without having to drag my suitcase –
and myself – home, first. I'd never once stepped foot
in their Chelsea Harbour apartment – I couldn't work
out if I was intrigued or terrified by the prospect. More
than anything right now, I was monumentally shattered.
I unmuted the film, resolving to move from this position
as little as possible for the entire weekend.

Chapter 26

☑ **Seeing someone in a new light**

Three whole days later, I was *still* monumentally exhausted. I suppose drinking your way through almost an advent's worth of miniature whiskys would do that. As would surviving on a diet of mince pies and stale Twiglets while stress-updating your LinkedIn profile to the televised backdrop of fictional characters living their perfect Christmas movieland lives.

I hadn't heard anything from Elle, despite my repeated attempts to get in touch with her. I had a few missed calls and voicemails of my own from unknown numbers – Tom trying to alleviate his guilt? – but I was in nowhere near the right frame of mind to listen to them right now. I needed to get through this weird lunch thing with Josh and Saskia, first.

After leaving my parents' place as tidy as possible, I began my journey to Josh and Saskia's riverside corner of the capital. I emerged from Imperial Wharf station fifteen minutes earlier than expected, so I decided to take shelter from the rain in the nearby Tesco Express. I might as well buy them a bottle of wine while I was in there, though there was no way it was going to cost me forty-five pounds.

As I negotiated the narrow aisles with my suitcase in search of the alcohol section, my stomach dropped. Because there was Saskia, browsing the cold meats in what could only be described as a very wary fashion. I watched with silent amusement for a few seconds as she picked up another packet, looked at its label, grimaced and put it back again. I was just turning around to make what I hoped would be an undetected exit when she spotted me.

'Mally! Oh, thank God you're here.' We hugged awkwardly. She smelt of coconut, her shoulder-length Scandi-blonde hair still slightly damp from a recent shower – this morning had no doubt already involved all manner of yoga positions and liquified greens. 'Tell me which one of these to buy for you, please, because Josh has been no help at all and I'm totally out of practice when it comes to buying this kind of… stuff.'

I think she means 'meat'?

'What, for lunch?'

'Yeah, I'm so sorry, it was only this morning I remembered you weren't vegan and that I should probably give you something, I dunno, deceased, ha ha, to chew on in case you didn't like what I'd cooked. Josh told me not to bother and that you weren't fussy and would eat whatever but… argh, listen to me prattling on. Anyway, feel free to choose anything at all.'

As she gestured towards the packets of processed meat, I noticed her hand was quivering. Surely the queen of mindfulness and breathwork wasn't nervous about the prospect of little old me coming over? She definitely seemed on edge.

'Honestly, Saskia, I'll eat whatever you've made. I'm sure it'll be delicious.'

I had a flashback to Mum's baked polenta, and my stomach clenched in self-defence.

'Ha, I'm being ridiculous aren't I?' Saskia said. 'Sorry, it's just that, well, inviting you over has been such a long time coming and now the day is here and I'm apparently screwing it up before it's even properly begun, aren't I?'

Fuck, she wasn't just nervous, she was floundering. I'd forgotten I was almost ten years older than her. I needed to put her at ease.

'Hey, I've got an idea. How about we skip the sliced dead animals and get a couple of bottles of something instead? I don't know about you but I could definitely do with a drink after the last few days I've had.'

Saskia visibly relaxed as I took control of the mini shopping expedition. We selected a couple of mid-range 'certified vegan' bottles of wine and filled the silence with weather-related chitchat as I paid.

I bagged the bottles into a bag for life I had to fork out twenty pence for – Josh would no doubt have something to say about the reinforced plastic. The security guard bowed to Saskia as she left. She probably got this kind of worshipful attention wherever she went. I expected her to ignore him or smile politely. But, instead, she bowed right back. They high-fived as they rose in unison.

'Ha, see ya, George! Give my love to Marie.'

Oh, right, she just knew him. Fair play.

'Hey, we saw the news about *The Helix*. I'm so sorry – what a shitty situation. How are you feeling about it all?'

We emerged into the cold, the riverside wind whipping rain across our faces. I had to shout to make myself heard.

'Pff, it's been handled so, *so* badly that it almost doesn't feel real.'

'Yeah, just before Christmas, too. So horrid of them. I know a couple of people who work there.'

Huh, Josh had never said anything about that. Although I suspected that was likely because he didn't want to concede he knew other people who worked for the so-called 'mainstream media'.

'Oh really? I had no idea. Who?'

'Jessie Barker and Inga Andersen from the brand partnerships team – do you know them?'

Of course I did. They were tall and young and shiny, just like Saskia.

'I know of them, but don't hang out with them or anything. Have you heard from them since it all kicked off?'

'Not directly – I saw some Instagram posts of theirs when it all came out. Jessie's in a right state as she's here from Australia on a sponsored visa and is trying to find out whether she can even stay in the country.'

'God, that's awful.'

We arrived at the entranceway of one of the identikit apartment blocks. The rhomboid-shaped water feature at the heart of the clinical communal garden appeared to be out of order. Saskia presented a key card to the door and it clicked open. We rode the lift up a few floors in silence, exchanging awkward smiles. Her nerves were starting to rub off on me. I swore she took a deep breath as she opened the door to what appeared to be a modest-looking apartment.

I counted four internal doors off the compact, hexagonal central hallway, which itself was a heaving mass of shoes, coats and exercise gear. A double mattress was propped up against the only wall without a door. I spotted the TheVeganSleepCo logo on its edge – it must've been their freebie one. It looked floppy and sad. Saskia kicked her shoes off into the tumbling tower of footwear.

'Josh! We're here! Look who I bumped into!'

Josh poked his head out of the kitchen doorway – which was even smaller than my own back in Hither Green. He seemed taken aback to see us together but managed to rearrange his face into a more neutral expression. 'Hello. Wine?'

'Fuck yes,' Saskia replied, giving him a peck on the cheek.

He raised an eyebrow in amusement as I thrust the bag of wine in his direction. He said nothing about the bag for life, and saluted his obedience before putting them in the fridge, unscrewing a bottle that was already chilled and pouring its entire contents between three large glasses.

'Shall I take my shoes off or...?'

Josh and Saskia exchanged a glance and Saskia shook her head quickly. Josh looked back towards me. 'It's totally up to you.'

I looked down at their socks and took my shoes off, placing them next to my suitcase by the front door. Josh handed me my glass of wine and I followed them through into the living room, which had a giant gap in the wall to open the small kitchen up into a more sociable space.

'Ooh, that's just crying out for a game of hatch catch!' I said, without thinking.

Josh's eyebrows lowered as he took a sip from his glass.

Saskia looked to each of us, confused. 'Hatch catch?'

'Oh, it's just this silly game we used to play when we were younger. Though our hatch gap was a little smaller than this one, eh, Josh?'

'Ha, yeah.' He took out his phone from his pocket and started scrolling absentmindedly. Saskia nudged his knee with hers, and Josh looked up, re-pocketing his phone.

'So, er, sorry about the job stuff and everything.'

'Thanks, Josh. All a bit of a shock.'

As was discovering that you were in Scarnbrook.

Josh cleared his throat. 'Yeah, I bet. So, umm, if you need any help with money or anything, just let me know, okay?'

Blimey, Josh was offering to help me? This was a first.

'Oh! Thanks, that's really generous of you. I mean, hopefully it won't come to that. I've spent the whole weekend getting my CV up to date, but it's a shit time of year to be job-hunting.'

The three of us took synchronised slurps of wine. I deliberately extended my own so I wouldn't be the first one to take a breath and, thus, speak. Saskia lost the silent battle.

'It's just so great to have you here, isn't it, Josh?'

'Mmm, yeah,' he replied quietly.

Saskia squeezed his knee before jumping to her feet. 'Right then! I'll go and start dishing up. It's going to be a bit of a salady affair – hope that's all right? Josh, you were right – Mally *is* happy to endure a meatless meal!'

Saskia bounded into the kitchen, leaving me and Josh on opposite ends of the corner sofa that framed the window. A potted, living Christmas tree twinkled between us, though if the number of dropped needles that surrounded it was anything to go by, I wasn't sure the word 'living' applied to it any longer. A tiny fragment of the Thames was visible from the balcony beyond if you angled your neck in the right direction.

Of course, it fell to me to address the elephant in the room. After all, wasn't this the reason I'd been invited here?

'So, then. Scarnbrook,' I said, before sipping again.

'Scarnbrook.' The echoed word hung in the air for so long you could've hung tinsel on it. Neither of us had said it to each other for at least fifteen years.

'You were there, too?'

He nodded, drinking more wine, his eyes focused on the Christmas tree or the sliver of river beyond, I couldn't really tell. I sensed I needed to ease my way into this topic, rather than pour it over his head like the ice bucket challenge.

'Ooh, you'll never guess who I bumped into at The Star!' I said, desperate to find common ground.

'What, you mean beyond that Darren twat?'

'Ha, yeah. Christian Woods! He's trying to buy the pub and turn it into flats, believe it or not. It's the only pub left in the village.'

Josh groaned and rolled his eyes, and I cheered internally. It appeared that I'd stumbled across a rare nugget of mutual disdain.

'Not his biggest fan either, then?' I asked.

'He was always a slimy weasel with a flagrant disregard for the offside rule. He barely spoke to me back then – I don't think he spoke to any of us who went to state schools – but these days he's constantly DMing me whenever he's in London to meet up and discuss "our respective ventures". Frankly, I'd rather drink my own piss.'

I nearly spat out my wine. I couldn't remember the last time we'd connected like this. His eyes were lit up in a way that took me back to Saturday nights in Scarnbrook when we were kids, the five of us watching *Gladiators* together, and us taking the mick out of him for blushing whenever Jet appeared.

'Yeah, he seemed like a right twat,' I said. 'He was trying to shove a new offer to buy the place in the manager's face – my mate Becky, do you remember her?'

Josh nodded. 'One of the twins, right?'

'Yup. Well, I kind of stepped in and got him to take the contract away with him. For now, at least.'

'Ha. Nice one.'

'So… how about you? Did you… see anyone while you were there?' I asked.

He shook his head, the glint in his eye switching off like a streetlamp at dawn.

'Do you… go there often?' *Nice one, Mally: probably one of the most important conversations the two of you will ever have and you're somehow managing to make it feel like you're trying out pick-up lines on your own brother. Ick.*

Josh sighed, and closed his eyes, his jaw tensing. All of a sudden, he leapt up, his wine sloshing over the glass's rim as he plonked it down on the wooden pallet coffee table.

His voice crackled as he spoke. 'I'm sorry, I can't do this.' He took seven quick strides towards the door at the opposite end of the apartment, entered what I presumed was his bedroom and shut the door loudly behind him. Saskia watched the whole thing open-mouthed through the giant hatch.

'Josh! Mally, I'm *so* sorry. I'll be right back; please sit tight.'

I didn't know what to do. Should I leave? Should I knock on the bedroom door to see if they were okay? Instead, I opted to do what I was told and stay where I was, straining my ears to listen to their intense murmurings, which then escalated into shouting, until Josh yelled, 'You speak to her, then!', at which point he emerged, clad in running gear, mumbled 'I'm sorry' to me and left the apartment without looking back. *Shit.* I mean, I hadn't expected a perfect afternoon, but this was way beyond my wildest worries.

Saskia appeared a minute or so later, blotchy-faced, her eyes red and watery. She looked gutted.

'Mally, I don't know what to say. I can't believe that just happened.'

What *had* happened, though? I opened my mouth to say something, but the words had yet to take shape. I took another gulp of wine, as Saskia plodded towards me, shoulders slumped.

'What's going on, Saskia? Why am I here? And what the hell was *that*?'

I tilted my head towards the door that Josh had just vanished through.

'*That* was twenty years of pent-up grief, anger and guilt, directed in the wrong place, as ever.'

She burst into tears. I put down my glass and stood up to give her a hug. This was all my fault. If I hadn't gone back to Scarnbrook, Darren would never have posted that Instagram story, I would never have seen those chrysanthemums in the graveyard and me and Josh wouldn't have been forced into having this conversation, which he obviously wasn't ready for. We sat down on the sofa.

'Saskia, I'm so sorry for starting all of this, I—'

'Sorry?! Mally, *you've* got absolutely nothing to be sorry for; you must know that, right? Honestly, when you sent that message to Josh about the flowers it finally felt like the breakthrough we'd been waiting for. But, well, as you can see, we're finding this a little bit harder than we were expecting.'

I had no clue what she was talking about. What did she mean by 'breakthrough'?

'I'm so confused, Saskia. Why was Josh in Scarnbrook? And why didn't he tell me he was going?'

'I imagine for the same reason you didn't tell him that *you* were going?'

It was a fair point. I hadn't wanted to upset him. Or risk word getting back to Mum and Dad. It made sense that he would've had the same concerns.

'Sure. But I was there to catch up with some friends.' Of course, this wasn't strictly the truth, but it *had* ended up happening in a roundabout way, so I wasn't going to beat myself up about semantics at this moment in time. 'But Josh just told me he didn't see anyone. So what was he doing there?'

Saskia wiped her eyes. 'More wine?' I nodded, against my better judgement, and she fetched another bottle from the fridge, topping up our glasses.

'Right. Josh went there after you'd taken your parents to the airport. I'm sorry I couldn't make it to lunch the week before, by the way.'

'Oh, don't worry. But he told me he had a last-minute PT session with a client that day?'

Saskia shrugged. 'Well, he didn't. He went to Scarnbrook. Just like he does every December. And every June.'

Every December. Every June.

For Livvie. For Christmas. For her birthday.

'I... I had no idea he still visited.'

'Yeah, every single year since... well, since it happened. He doesn't see anyone or anything like that. He just goes to see Livvie.'

My heart didn't know whether to swell with love, or to break into a million pieces. Now it was my turn to cry. Saskia brought her wine over to my side of the sofa, squeezing my shoulder as I tried to collect myself.

'Why didn't he ever say anything?' I said, between tearful sniffs. 'I'd have gone with him!'

'It's a valid question, Mally. But I think, because of the way Josh is, this is just a very private thing he does for himself, and for Livvie.'

I suddenly felt awful for taking twenty years to visit my little sister's grave. Why hadn't I done it sooner? Was I really that heartless?

'He's never even spoken to me about what happened to Livvie. I wish he had, y'know?'

Saskia nodded sympathetically and placed a hand on mine. 'I know, I know. But I think you being here today – even after what happened just now – is such an important step. For both of you.'

'Does he storm out like that a lot?'

She blew her nose into an old-school hankie that she'd whipped out from her sleeve. She was full of snotty surprises. 'More often than I'd like, yeah. Whenever his comfort zone is challenged, he just clams up and runs away. Sometimes he runs away for real, like that, and other times he fills his head with dopamine hits from all the likes and new followers on social media. I suppose the fact that you've seen it happen now is, in a roundabout way, a good thing.'

I could see what she was saying. Because this was Josh's way of letting me in. Not just into his flat, but into his silent struggles that he must've been hiding from me for so long.

'Don't get me wrong,' Saskia continued, 'this isn't how I wanted this afternoon to go down at all. The plan was to be tucking into my famous flourless chocolate chilli cake around about now.'

I'd forgotten all about food. But the mention of it got my tastebuds tingling. 'Umm, yum.'

'Fuck it, shall we just eat?'

'What about Josh?'

'He's a creature of habit – I reckon he'll be back in a couple of hours. And if you stayed it would mean so much to him – even if he doesn't show it. What do you think – will you stay?'

I smiled and nodded.

The salads were tasty, even without the addition of wafer-thin turkey slices. And the cake was epic, too. I made a mental note to try some more vegan recipes in the new year. Maybe this Jamie Chops chap was onto something.

We chatted like old friends, to the extent that I could see the very moment Saskia's romance radar activated as I told her about bumping into some 'old classmates'.

'Tell me his name *immediately*,' she said, with a glint in her eye.

'It was just someone I used to have a crush on at school, that's all. We went out for dinner a couple of nights ago and it seemed to be heading in the right direction. But then, well, I found out he was stringing me along.'

'Fucker.'

'Yeah. Hey, I just realised I don't know how you and Josh met?'

I braced myself for a tale of DMs and digital courting.

'Oh! So, umm, bit of a funny one actually, because we met in a counsellor's waiting room…'

I tried my best to keep my mouth closed as she told me the whole story. How they'd caught each other's eye before their respective appointments – his for therapy, hers for a job interview. How they'd recognised each other from Instagram, but had never dreamt of saying anything there and then in order to maintain their mutual privacy. How they'd bumped into each other at a vegan cafe a couple of weeks later and struck up a conversation over their matcha lattes. How he'd presumed she was having counselling, too, before learning she was a newly qualified practitioner. How that had enabled them to be completely honest and open with each other about their histories from the very start. And how they'd basically been glued to each other ever since.

It took me a few moments to process all this new information. Firstly, the fact that Josh had been seeing a counsellor for goodness knows how long – not once had I thought he was the kind of person who'd be minded to talk to someone about his feelings. I also couldn't ignore the warmth I was feeling towards Saskia. For the last couple of years, I'd dismissed her as nothing more than an attention-seeking influencer. I'd never stopped to consider that she and my brother might've formed a significant and genuine connection – the kind of connection I'd been searching for my entire life.

'I adore your brother. I always have. He's got such a kind heart. He just wants to do good in the world. But, like all of us, he struggles with certain demons. And that's why having you here is *so* important.'

I was finding that hard to believe, since me uttering the word 'Scarnbrook' to his face had been enough to tip him over the edge.

'But he's just so cold with me all the time! He seems to have a better relationship with his Instagram followers than he does with me.'

'Why do you think he might not want to get close to you? Or to anyone for that matter?' Saskia was trying to sound compassionate but I could hear the exasperation in her tone. 'He's scared of losing you, Mally! He's petrified of losing anyone he loves. The fitness and this social media obsession of his – they're nothing more than controllable distractions from all the uncontrollable things he's too scared to think about.'

I took my mind back to the in-jokes that Josh and Livvie had shared. The way he seemed to defrost around her. She used to curl up in his lap and convince him to put on her favourite cartoons. He relented every time. They were polar opposites in so many ways, yet their bond had always been strong.

I thought about how he must have felt when she died. When he *saw* her die. And how his natural barriers would've shot up even higher so he'd never have to experience that horrific kind of loss and trauma again.

'So, you're saying that social media is just some kind of security blanket for him?'

'Yeah, burying himself in online comment threads and confrontations brings him this weird sense of comfort. It's his way of doing everything he can to not have to think about his pain.'

'I get it. You're saying he's hiding in plain sight. Whereas I've just been plain old hiding. Like my parents.'

She rested one of her hands on mine. 'I'm not going to pass judgement on any of your coping mechanisms. But please understand that this is why it's been so hard for me to spend any time with Josh when he's in his family's company. Because his defences shoot right up. It's so hard to see him like that.'

'We were all convinced you thought we were dull or something.'

'Dull? God, no. When we first met at our engagement dinner, I remember being so relieved that you were so funny and nice. But it quickly became obvious that Josh was uncomfortable as hell and I had to help him through it.'

I felt thankful that Josh had Saskia in his life. God knows what would have happened to him if he hadn't.

'Why haven't we spoken about all of this before?' I asked.

'I didn't know if you were ready to listen. But, because you went back to Scarnbrook, we wondered whether you might be ready now. Which is why we invited you here – to make a start. But, instead, I'm worried I've pushed Josh into it and it's all still too soon. Oh God, I hope I haven't fucked this up. I really thought getting the two of you together like this might help him make some more progress.'

Before travelling back to London that morning, I hadn't known it was possible to feel any more untethered than I already did. But, right now, I felt as if everything I'd ever known was just beyond my grasp. I laid my head back onto the arm of the sofa and placed a scratchy hemp cushion over my face. Saskia sensed my internal existential unravelling.

'Shit, Mally, I'm sorry – I keep talking about Josh when this is as big a deal for you as it is for him.'

I kept the cushion over my face as I replied, 'don't worry, I'm pretty used to coming bottom of the pecking order.'

Saskia had nothing to say to that, although I heard her take a large slurp of wine, followed by a shaky exhale and some fingernail taps on her phone. I wondered how much longer I could tolerate the rough fabric on my skin, although I was quite enjoying the relative peace under there.

'Hey, Mally?'

'Mmm?' Still muffled.

'Are you ready for a slice of chocolate cake?'

I nodded my head in an exaggerated motion so the movement could be detected via the medium of the cushion. I added a thumbs up into the mix for extra clarity.

While Saskia took the plates into the kitchen and prepped our puddings, I removed the cushion from my face, along with some rogue strands of hemp.

'Do you mind if I put the telly on?' I called to Saskia.

'Go for it – the remote's in the drawer under the TV.'

I switched it on and flicked to Channel 5 by reflex, letting the Christmas movie fill the silence.

Saskia set down two plates on the coffee table – with an enormous slice of rich, gooey dessert on each one – and curled up in the nook of the corner sofa.

'Ooh, I love this one,' she said, gesturing towards the screen with a forkful of cake.

'You know this film?' I asked, not even recognising it myself. After a while, they all merged into one. Which was absolutely no bad thing.

'Yeah, it's called *The Road Home for Christmas*. This is one of the 2019 Lifetime movies that mentions Winter Storm Meghan, which is this fictional megastorm that gets brought up repeatedly as if the stories are happening concurrently.'

'Hang on a second. You love cheesy Christmas movies?'

'Fucking love them, Mally. You?'

'Yes, oh my God, I've never met anyone who loves them as much as me before! Or possibly even more than me by the sounds of it.'

'Ha, yeah, I'm a total nerd when it comes to the Hallmark cinematic universe and its adjacent cinematic universes. I could talk about them all day.'

'So could I! I've even created my own bingo game!'

Saskia's eyes widened in delight. We squealed in unison and squeezed each other's hands.

'What's your favourite one?' she asked, not able to contain her glee.

'All of them!'

'That's the correct answer! Right then, let's turn off this big light and settle in for some Christmas movie magic. I'm sure Josh'll be back soon. I'll grab us a blanket.'

Dusk was falling by the time the credits rolled. Josh still wasn't home, but he'd messaged Saskia to let her know he'd be back before dark.

'You were right, that *was* a good film. Can't wait to watch more Winter Storm Meghan ones now.'

'See? I know my made-for-TV movies. What is it about them you love so much, do you think?' Saskia asked.

I thought about my bingo lists as I fiddled with our shared blanket's tassels. 'The formula. They're so predictable and familiar.'

'Yeah, I love all the tropes so much.'

'I guess it also helps that lots of them are about finding love a little later in life.'

Saskia smiled. 'What else?'

I thought about the article I'd ended up writing for *The Helix*. All the narrative elements that tied Christmas movies together.

'The themes: community. Family. Home.'

My voice splintered as I spoke the final word. Saskia scooched up even closer and put an arm around me.

'Yeah, I suppose all the families in these films end up happy and together, don't they?'

I nodded, the sobs coming thick and fast now. I couldn't believe I'd never connected these movies to my own existence before.

'I always know what's going to happen,' I added. 'There aren't any nasty surprises – and there's always a happy ending.'

'The predictability makes you feel safe.'

I got goosebumps as I nodded. Because 'safe' was how I wanted to feel all the time. But after all the seismic shifts that had taken place in my life in the last week, I felt the opposite. It was as if the ground was dropping away, with everything I'd ever relied upon as secure crumbling beneath my feet. My friendship with Elle. My ties to the people I'd naively trusted in Scarnbrook. My job – or lack thereof. My non-existent relationship with my brother. Even my lack of respect for Saskia, who I'd previously dismissed as nothing more than a pin-up wife for Josh's Instagram grid.

Had I really been wrong about everything?

'You can always turn to me, you know that, right?' Saskia said, squeezing my hand gently.

'I do now. Thank you. I wish we'd got to know each other sooner. And with Josh here.'

'He's come so far. But he's on the edge of the digital rabbit hole right now and I was kind of hoping you could help me pull him away from it.'

'How?'

'Well, I suppose it boils down to this: if you stop hiding, maybe *he'll* stop hiding, too.'

Chapter 27

☑ **Festive train journey**

I boarded the busy train, which was full of spirited office workers heading home after Christmas parties, and found a spot near the door where I could gaze out of the window. Josh had come back almost exactly two hours later, as Saskia had predicted, although he'd gone straight to his room after a quick glance and a tight grin in my direction. Again, exactly what Saskia had told me to expect.

Talking so openly with my sister-in-law had been incredibly helpful but, at the same time, I couldn't shake off a sense of sadness that I'd never bothered to get to know her before now. In fact, I'd barely given her any thought at all beyond the bitching sessions with Elle about her latest Instagram posts, which always dripped with earnestness. I felt guilty for laughing at her now. Because she was bloody nice. And clever. And so obviously head-over-heels in love with my brother. A part of me was jealous of what they had – the same thing I'd believed I'd had with Tom just a few days ago, which was absurd.

The train jolted suddenly, so I reached for a nearby pole to steady myself, only to grab a fellow passenger's tube of festive gift wrap poking out of their backpack by mistake. They must have detected the brief change in pressure, as they spun around fast to look at me, just as I removed my hand in what must have come across as a pick-pockety manner.

'Sorry, I thought it was the pole!' They looked at me as if I was mad, which was fair enough, backing away slowly as if I might make another grab for it. Why did this kind of ridiculous thing always happen to me?

The Bermondsey rooftops flashed past the window, the *blink blink blink* of Canary Wharf's summit in the distance. That familiar flashing had always felt like a beacon beckoning me home after a long day in the office, but right now it felt like its relentless pulses were piercing my skull, each blink reminding me of something else that was lacking or collapsing in my life.

Flash: No job.

Flash: No sign of my best friend.

Flash: No Tom Brinton.

Flash: No fucking clue about anything any more.

I leant against the upholstered bum ledge next to the door – designed for a six-foot man, of course, so too high to be of any use to short women like me – and, with one hand permanently attached to my suitcase, closed my eyes for a few moments. I rubbed my eyebrows with my thumb and forefinger, hoping it would somehow sculpt all my mashed-up thoughts into some kind of recognisable form. But all it succeeded in doing was making my head pound even further.

The rain was whipping around cruelly as I exited the station at Hither Green. I'd only been away for just over a week, but it felt like much longer. I abandoned my wet luggage and coat in the hallway and went straight to the kitchen to put the kettle on. But something wasn't quite right. There were a few mugs piled up in the sink, and an unfamiliar box of herbal teabags was open on one of the countertops. I picked up the box and sniffed it, as if I was a dog trying to catch a scent. I dropped the box back down, turned slowly and looked around the living room. The fibre-optic Christmas tree was switched on. I had *definitely* switched it off before I'd left. And the radiators were hot to the touch, when I'd adjusted the central heating to the lowest anti-frost setting or whatever it was called. What the *fuck* was going on?

I poked my head into the bathroom. All seemed normal – no freaky messages written in lipstick on the mirror. My bedroom was undisturbed, too. The door to the spare room at the front of the flat was closed, as always. I pushed it open... and found Elle, curled up in bed, awake but vacant. The room stank of stale farts.

'Elle? What's going on? Is everything okay?'

She sat up but said nothing. This figure didn't feel like Elle. For one thing, rotting in bed had never been a habit I'd associated with her for the entirety of our twenty-five-year friendship. That was *my* specialty. And, when I switched on the bedside lamp, I noticed her eyes had zero sparkle, as if her spirit had retreated deep inside.

'Why are you here? Aren't you meant to be heading to Stevenage round about now for Christmas?'

More silence. I sighed, and opened one of the windows to try and freshen the room up. She continued to say nothing.

'You're scaring me, Elle. I'm calling Rory.'

'No! Don't. Please. He thinks I'm with you in Scarn-brook.'

'What?'

'I… really don't have the energy to explain right now.' She collapsed back down onto the mattress and turned away from me.

'Snap out of it, Elle. I know this job stuff is shit for the both of us, and we need to talk about it, but we also need to talk about the strings you've been pulling for my article.'

'It was a good article,' she whispered, although it was muffled by the pillow.

'Say that again?'

She turned over and glared at me with misplaced defiance. 'I said it was a good article, all right? Happy now I've given you your little nugget of praise?'

I was so used to seeking her approval that I couldn't help but feel wounded. My automatic response in this situation would be to fawn and fix. But fawning and fixing had only led me here. And, now I really didn't have anything else to lose, it was time to try something different: confrontation.

'Happy?! I'm anything but happy. The last few days have been horrific, not helped by the fact you've been completely ignoring me.'

She sat bolt upright again, this time throwing aside the bedcovers and standing to face me, her eyes regaining some of their fire, although her legs appeared to be a little shaky.

'*Me* ignoring *you*? I've barely heard from you all week! I *needed* you, Mally! Frannie's been sick, Rory's been working around the clock covering for a colleague, and I've been having to deal with angry freelancers who are demanding to be paid for articles that will never be published… you're not the only one with problems, you know!'

314

'If things were that bad, you should have called! Or sent another message! I'm not a mind-reader.'

She pushed past me and ran to the bathroom, locking the door behind her. I could hear her sobs echo off the tiles. It must've only been the second time she'd cried in my presence. I tapped on the bathroom door gently.

'Elle? I'm getting really worried. Let me in, please? Otherwise, I'll have no choice but to call Rory.'

I was tempted to phone him regardless of whether she let me in or not. Because I was fast realising I didn't know Elle as well as I thought I did.

But then I realised something else: Elle had undoubtedly made some bad decisions, but she'd come *here* in her moment of need. Because I was still her safety net, even though I was paying way too high a price for that, and this friendship was anything but equal. I'd call Rory when the time was right, but for the time being this was up to us and us alone to resolve.

Elle unlocked the door and I immediately put my arms around her, tightly. The last time I'd seen her this upset was when I'd told her about the conditional offer I'd received from Bristol University, and my plan to stay in Scarnbrook for my degree. I'd been taken aback by her reaction that day, and she'd eventually confessed that she'd been banking on me coming to Cardiff with her.

'We need to escape this place, Mally!' she'd said, with seemingly zero awareness of how much the village meant to me and my family.

As I held her now – conscious that she was refusing to relax into the embrace – I wondered how my life might've turned out if I'd stood up to Elle back then and accepted the place at my local uni. Whether we'd still be friends.

Would Livvie – would my entire family – have made it if I'd stayed?

Tears stung my eyes as I murmured, 'It's okay, it's okay. We'll figure this out and make everything all right.' I had no intention of changing the course of my life for her any more like I'd done back then – and countless times since – but right now, in this moment, both of us needed to feel better before things could move on. She extracted herself from my arms.

'Fuck, Mally. I'm sorry, okay? I guess you know the truth about me now, hmm? I'm a cold-hearted bitch who doesn't deserve good people like you in my life.'

'Stop talking like that, Elle. I know what you're trying to do. You're trying to push me away so I don't get too close. But this isn't the kind of relationship you can deliberately sabotage with a throwaway comment about my bad breath. We've come too far for that.'

'Huh, you and Tom Brinton really did hit it off, didn't you?'

'I'm sure you know all about it. I can't believe you set me up like that. It was really cruel. I genuinely thought he liked me.'

Elle sighed. 'I wasn't in touch with anyone else – just Ryan. I only heard about what was going on between you and Tom from him.'

'Yeah, but you know what Scarnbrook's like. Everyone talks to everyone. I swear the whole village knew I was back before I'd even stepped foot in that shitty Airbnb. Hang on, did you book a dodgy place on purpose?'

'Umm, I may have done…'

'Elle!' Despite everything, I couldn't help but admire how bloody good she was at her job. After all, the depressing nature of the accommodation had inspired the final angle for my piece.

Elle looked at the floor and wrapped a strand of her dark hair around her forefinger, just like she used to do at school. 'You uncovered a good story.'

'Even though it won't get published now.'

I grabbed a tissue from the loo roll holder and blew my nose, sitting on the closed toilet seat. Elle sat opposite me on the edge of the bath, and I handed her her own wad of bog roll.

'Yeah, about that...' Elle looked sheepish, yet another out-of-character facial expression for her.

'Oh God, what now? You haven't pitched it to *The Sun*, have you?'

'No, nothing like that. But... it may very well end up being published by *The Helix* next December.'

'How? I don't understand. We'll both be working elsewhere by then, surely?'

Elle climbed into the empty bathtub, which in usual circumstances would've been a strange thing to do but right now felt weirdly appropriate. She lay back with her eyes closed and replied in a whisper. 'I'm moving to New York, Mally. To work for *The Helix* there, instead. I've known about it for a while.'

'Sorry, what?'

'Back in the summer, I got approached by the US team. The new owner had heard good stuff about me. Made me an offer I couldn't refuse. They're paying for all three of us to relocate. We've found the cutest kindergarten for Frannie, and we've signed a lease on an amazing apartment in Brooklyn, too.'

'That's... amazing. Congratulations. But why didn't you tell me this sooner?'

'I literally couldn't. They made me sign an NDA, because part of the reason why they wanted me to move over there was because of what was about to happen with the London office.'

'Wait, you *knew* The Helix was shutting down in the UK?'

'Yeah, I'm so sorry.'

'Shit.'

I clambered into the bath with her, forcing Elle to tuck her long legs under her chin to create space.

'Shit!' I repeated. 'You're really leaving?'

'Yeah, next month.'

My mind jumped back to what Rory had said to me after I'd stayed over at the start of the month – he'd seemed to be probing me about something unspoken. I'd assumed it'd been about the usual work stuff, but there'd been a whole extra layer I'd been oblivious to.

'Next month? Jesus, Elle. What am I going to do without you all?'

We locked eyes, our broken faces – our shared histories – reflecting off each other. Elle grabbed my hands and started talking quickly.

'But that's the thing, this doesn't have to be the end. I've got it all figured out, and that's why I'm here, to talk to you face to face. You can move to New York, too! Not next month or anything, but once I'm there I can keep my ear to the ground for job leads. And I can definitely commission you to write more stuff for The Helix as a freelancer – you've proven you've got the talent. And then you can find an apartment near us and—'

'Elle, stop. Please. I'm not going to move to New York.'

She released my hands. 'But you've only just found out! Surely you need to think about it some more? Imagine how amazing it would be!'

'I don't need to think about it. If the last couple of weeks have taught me anything, it's that I need to stay put. I need to fix things between me and Josh. I need to try and rebuild my family.'

She looked at me with wide eyes before standing up suddenly. She battled with the shower curtain for a moment, clambered out of the bath and walked through to the kitchen. I followed quickly behind. She was crying again. Angry, furious tears that she removed any trace of as soon as they escaped. She yanked open the fridge and grabbed a bottle of vodka from the freezer compartment, and downed a huge gulp.

'As soon as you got this Scarnbrook idea in your head, I *knew* this would happen.'

I grabbed the bottle from her and took my own swig. 'You knew *what* would happen?'

'That you'd want to move back, even though there's nothing left there for either of us any more.'

'How do you know what's there if you never look?' I challenged, the harsh burn of the vodka emboldening me.

Elle sighed. 'There's no need for me to look. My life is here.'

'And I respect that. But I'm a separate entity to you; I can make my own choices.'

Elle scoffed and flopped down on the sofa, but I kept talking.

'You've honestly never been tempted to return?'

She shook her head. 'Me and Scarnbrook are done, for good.'

'Tell me why, Elle. I've never understood why you hated it there so much.'

Elle sighed, curling her legs underneath her and tucking herself into the corner of the sofa.

'A ton of shit went down before I met you, Mally. Did you never wonder why my dad wasn't on the scene when we moved next door?'

'I always figured you'd tell me when you were ready but, well, you never did.'

'That's typical of you, though, isn't it? You wait for things to happen *to* you, instead of making things happen for yourself.'

'Ouch.'

'Am I right, though?'

'Perhaps. But we're very different people. Not everyone has ambition and drive built into them. Some of us are happy to stay smaller.'

'Yeah, well, I'm not prepared to stay small. I want to be as big as possible. I wanted to show him – *Dad* – he'd made the wrong choice.'

'That he shouldn't have left you and your mum?'

'He didn't just randomly leave us, Mally. We found out he had a whole other family. Another partner, two kids, a mortgage, package holidays overseas when we thought he was away for work – the whole shebang.'

'Fuck. Fuck!'

'Yep. And when Mum found out, she didn't even give him an ultimatum. She just let him leave us. She allowed herself to be made small by him. And I promised myself I'd never reduce myself to that, for anyone. So there's my villain origin story. Satisfied?'

'Of course I'm not "satisfied", Elle. And you're not a "villain", for fuck's sake: you're just a messed-up human, like the rest of us. All this stuff you've been dealing with is huge. I'm so sorry you've been carrying all of this for so long. Does Rory know?'

'Yeah, he knows.'

'Good.'

'And I did *want* to tell you, so many times. But it was just easier for me not to.'

'Sometimes the easiest choice isn't the best choice, is it?'

'I guess not.'

'It wasn't easy for me to go back to Scarnbrook, you know. In many ways, it's the hardest thing I've ever done.'

'So why did you want to go?'

I collapsed onto the sofa next to her. 'For closure, maybe? I dunno. It just felt like the right thing to do after all this time.'

Elle nudged herself along the sofa and curled up next to me. 'You really like Tom, don't you?'

'Yeah.'

Elle blew all the air out of her lungs, as if she'd been holding her breath for decades. Perhaps, in a way, both of us had been.

'I just thought we'd moved on, you know? But you were so insistent, so I got in touch with Ryan on Facebook to let him know you were going to be in the area, mainly so he could keep an eye out for you, at first. But then, well, my stupid fucking brain got to work and I got this idea to get him to set you up with someone for the article. And I swear, Mally, the Darren thing was all I did. But then you bumped into Tom and the two of you seemed to be hitting it off if Ryan's reports were anything to go by, then you didn't reply to me for *days* and I just... couldn't deal with that. I started to spiral.'

'Why did me getting along with Tom Brinton bother you so much?' I asked, stroking her hair.

'Because… I don't want you to leave me. I want you to come with *me*. To New York.'

I heaved her into a sitting position and looked her in the eye. 'You're my best friend. You'll always be in my life – and, trust me, I have absolutely no intention of moving back to Scarnbrook. But you shouldn't be here. You should be with your family.'

'You're my family too, y'know.'

My breath caught in my throat before I responded. 'I know.'

Neither of us spoke after that. There'd be plenty more to say down the line, but right now, sitting here together – both of us exposed and exhausted – was enough.

I reached for the remote control and switched the telly on. It was tuned to the Christmas movie channel, and – if the unfolding Christmas cookie decorating montage was anything to go by – the film had around two-thirds to go. Elle stared at the screen blankly, her wide eyes red-rimmed.

I opened the drinks cupboard underneath the TV and took out a bottle of sloe gin. I held it aloft in her direction and raised my eyebrows. She nodded grimly. I fetched two tumblers and poured us both decent measures, sitting down beside her.

I reached into my backpack and removed the bingo sheets I'd angrily stuffed inside back in Scarnbrook. I smoothed them out and grabbed a couple of pens from the coffee table drawer, marking fresh columns of tick boxes next to all the tropes. I handed her one of the sheets and a pen.

She remained silent, but as the film continued, the protagonists winning an ice-sculpting contest, we silently played, drinking the gin as we did so. Just as we'd innocently done a couple of weeks ago before everything had shattered. Elle eventually reclined to get more comfortable, resting her head in my lap. I stroked her hair once more as the characters climbed onto the stage to accept their trophy, the woman making a heartfelt speech about having rediscovered the magic of Christmas before she and the chiselled chiseller kissed, dryly.

By the time the credits had finished rolling, Elle was asleep. I turned the TV off and sat with her for a few minutes longer to make sure she was properly conked out.

Eventually, I got up slowly, laid a blanket over her, crept into my bedroom and called Rory.

As soon as they'd left, I pulled on a screwed-up pair of pyjamas that had been under my pillow for goodness knows how long, clambered up onto my bed, wrapped myself up in my covers and turned out the light. It was still way too early for bedtime, but the last twenty-four hours had felt like twenty-four days and I was exhausted. But, just as my eyes started to close, my phone rang. It was Josh. I couldn't remember the last time he'd called me.

'Josh? Hello?'

I thought the line had disconnected, but after a few seconds I heard a long, shaky breath.

'You're scaring me. Are you all right? Are Mum and Dad okay? Is Saskia with you?'

'Everything's fine and, yeah, Saskia's here.' His voice sounded younger. Vulnerable, even. I got the impression he was lying in a dim room, just like I was. For some reason, it felt easier to talk to him in the dark.

'Okay, Josh. What is it?'

'I'm, uh, sorry about earlier, Amelia. Mally, I mean.'

'You can call me Amelia.'

'And, umm, I'm sorry I didn't tell you I'd been in Scarnbrook.'

'There's no need to say sorry. Saskia explained everything.'

'Yeah, I know she did. She's much better at that kind of thing than me.'

'Ha, yeah, and me.'

Pause.

'Livvie was always great at that stuff, too, wasn't she?' he said.

He'd said her name.

I bit my quaking bottom lip before replying, everything bursting out of me all at once. 'I miss her so fucking much, Josh.'

'I know. Me too.' He was practically whispering now. 'She was, well, she was everything to all of us, wasn't she?'

A moan of pain erupted from my throat. I muffled it as best as I could with my pillow, which was fast becoming sodden with tears.

'She was,' I eventually managed to whisper back.

Neither of us said anything for a while, and for once I didn't feel the urge to scrabble around for something to fill the pause with. Being together in this shared moment was enough. Josh spoke first.

'It was my fault, Mally, all of it. I shouldn't have been late picking her up.'

His voice cracked, and I just about made out the sound of Saskia's soothing hushes in the background. I could picture her next to him in their bedroom, rubbing his back, giving him the safe space he needed to release his guilt.

'Josh, it's okay, it's okay,' I said. 'I feel just as guilty. If I hadn't cancelled her trip to Cardiff, none of it would have happened. But it wasn't our fault.'

It wasn't our fault. It wasn't Josh's fault. It wasn't *my* fault. Before Tom had said something similar to me the other night, I'd never even put those words together in my mind, let alone spoken them aloud.

'We were just kids ourselves,' I continued. 'There was no way we could've known things would've panned out so horribly. It was all a totally unpredictable, fucked-up accident.'

I knew that these were the words that Josh needed to hear right now. But, in using them, I felt as if two decades' worth of my own guilt and shame were physically dissipating. I felt rawer than I had done in years, but with that rawness came a sense of peace, too. Of respite. And, there and then, the love I felt for my brother was fiercer than any love I'd ever felt for anyone else before. By hiding ourselves away from each other, we'd somehow got stuck at opposite ends of the spectrum of coping strategies. I had a feeling that we could make more progress by meeting in the murkier middle. Perhaps we would even go back to Scarnbrook together at some point.

Maybe not next June, or next December, but one day.

After we'd hung up – Josh having given me the number of a counsellor recommended by Saskia – I'd had a sudden and uncharacteristic energy surge, and had spent a couple of hours beginning the big job of sorting out Elle's old bedroom ready for a future lodger and a much-needed stream of additional income, thanks to my impending redundancy.

But my energy was eventually overtaken by a sensation I couldn't pinpoint. I returned to my own bedroom and perched on the edge of the bed, catching my reflection in the full-length mirror on the opposite wall. I tried to figure out how I was feeling. I couldn't really pinpoint any emotion at all. I certainly wasn't feeling any Christmas tingles.

I was aware that I was absolutely wiped out – emotionally and physically. But it wasn't just tiredness. I felt as if my spirit had been sucked out of my body, leaving behind a me-shaped shell. But the shell was flaking away into countless fragments and drifting upwards, a bit like when Marty McFly's hand begins to disappear in *Back to the Future*. I lifted my hand to check that some fluke event in an alternative timeline wasn't in the process of erasing me, but nope. All looked normal.

I had thoughts inside my head but they were echoey and distant, as if they didn't belong to me. 'Me'? I didn't even know if there was a 'me' any more, if there ever had been in the first place, or if there ever would be again.

I'd felt – or not felt – like this once before, when Dad had called me to tell me about Livvie. When a nameless family liaison officer from the local police force had continued the sentence he couldn't bring himself to finish.

My mind had left its casing that Saturday afternoon, and seemed to watch from above as my soulless body crumpled to the floor of my poky en-suite room and howled like an animal.

Elle had burst in from next door to see what all the commotion was about. She'd picked me up from the floor that day. She'd carried me ever since.

At the time, it felt as if her endless distractions and permanent presence had gradually brought me back into myself. Now I wondered if I *had* ever truly returned. Or whether I'd simply trailed along behind her ever since, like a helium balloon on a string. Mindlessly bobbing along, my insides full of nothing but an instinctive desire to be taken away from myself, tugging upwards, away from the gravity of grief. And, for quite some time, I'd been content – grateful, even – to do just that. After all, we'd both been so young with limited tools and experiences. And, apparently, no idea about what the other person was truly feeling and thinking underneath it all.

Over the years, my hollowness had festered, rather than filled in. It'd evolved into something that resembled a life to fool everyone around me that I'd healed. To fool *myself* that I'd healed. Then I'd arrived in Scarnbrook. For a few days while I was there, the healing had felt real, for once. Painful as fuck, yes, but necessarily so. But even that tiny bauble of hope, presented to me by Tom Brinton of all people, had shattered. And, right now, it felt like the black hole had finally consumed me.

I rested my head on my pillow, fully clothed, blankly wondering whether, if I slept, I'd maybe wake up tomorrow and somehow feel pieced together again. After a couple of hours of non-existence, a quiet, unrecognisable voice inside me told me that I needed to do something to knock myself out.

I took a big swig of Night Nurse followed by an even bigger swig of whisky. I climbed back into bed, the covers pulled neatly up to my chin, my hands by my sides. My usual sleepy instinct to curl up into a tight foetal position with a very specific amount of duvet tucked between my knees for optimum comfort seemed to have deserted me.

Slowly but surely, the chemicals blended together in my bloodstream and the grim echoes of the day, of the week, of the last twenty years, gradually ebbed and flowed out of reach, like a dark, silent tide.

I didn't know if minutes or hours had passed since I'd neutrally instructed my eyelids to close, but I did know that the nothingness that eventually enfolded me was sweet, blissful relief.

Chapter 28

☑ **Small-town guy falls for big-city woman**

The next thirty-six hours or so passed by in a blur of dry Coco Pops, a continuous conveyor belt of Christmas movies thanks to the dedicated channel on Freeview and a medically inadvisable amount of Night Nurse. By the time Christmas Eve rolled around, I felt sluggish rather than refreshed when the toddler upstairs began bounding about at 5.47 a.m. The void that had opened up inside me after Rory had collected Elle felt smaller today, but it was definitely still there. I stretched and automatically reached for my phone before stopping myself. There was nothing within that device that would improve my day today. I needed to get up, otherwise I could well imagine myself spending another entire day in bed. At the very least I had my advent calendar to complete.

I flung back the covers to coax myself into an upright position. I finally swung my legs off the bed and allowed my feet to find their slippers and padded to the kitchen.

I flicked on the kettle for a cup of milkless tea before placing a rank-smelling food waste bag that had been festering since pre-Scarnbrook on a tray to carry outside. I opened the interior door and squeezed myself past the buggy.

It was then that I spotted the note on the communal doormat. I placed the food waste down and scooped up the piece of paper. In Tom's distinctive script, it read:

> *Mally,*
> > *Don't freak out, but I'm outside.*
> > *T*

Tom was here?

I peeked through the letterbox. Sure enough, there was Tom's immaculate car parked directly outside my flat. I could see his silhouetted figure in the passenger seat. It looked like he was asleep with his head resting against the window.

I grabbed an umbrella from the rusted stand in the hallway and approached the car. Draped around Tom's shoulders was an emergency foil blanket. A Nutrigrain wrapper had been placed neatly on the driver's seat.

I knocked on the window next to his head. Tom jumped awake and attempted to open the door, which was locked. His car erupted into a wail. Well, if the rest of the street weren't awake already, they certainly would be now. I noticed Sophie peering out through a gap in the curtains from the upper flat, Oscar attached to her hip and waving frantically at me in an elf onesie. I mouthed 'sorry' with my fingers in my ears, then gave them a thumbs up to indicate everything was fine. After a few seconds or so of fumbling, Tom managed to silence the alarm and step out of the car while rearranging his shoulders.

'That stash of Nutrigrains came in handy again, then?' I asked.

'Yeah, turns out I should add "overnight drive in pursuit of unresolved issues" to the list of permitted cereal bar emergencies.'

I noticed that Tom was shivering, despite the fact he was still sporting his silver blanket.

'Shit, you're freezing. Come inside. You should've just rung the doorbell.'

'Would you have answered the door at four o'clock in the morning?'

'You've been out there for two hours? Bloody hell. That means you must've left Scarnbrook at...'

'About two fifteen, yeah. I couldn't sleep, Mal. Ryan sent me your address after he eventually told me what had been going on between him and Elle.'

I pressed my inner front door closed and walked with Tom along the narrow hallway to the living room. By then I'd remembered about the information Ryan had needed for his garage records.

'He really shouldn't be giving out my address.'

'I know, I know, data protection and all that. I'm sorry. I know this is... intense. But you haven't been receiving any of my messages and I couldn't even call you. I've been so fucking worried, Mally – so's my mum, and Becky and everyone, really – especially after we saw the news about *The Helix*. We tried calling you and leaving voicemails but you never answered. I had to check you were all right after, y'know, what happened back home.'

'*This* is my home, Tom. And here I am, alive and well.'

I busied myself washing the rotting food juices off my hands and making my cup of tea, grabbing another mug from the cupboard and chucking a bag in it for Tom. I poured in the boiling water, annoyed my hands were trembling. I grabbed a teaspoon from the drawer and drowned each floating teabag in turn while I spoke. 'To be honest, I don't know why you're here. What's motivated you to just turn up like this? Guilt for stringing me along? Pity for poor old Mally and her pathetic, lonely life?'

'No, neither of those things. I hope you realise that I had absolutely nothing to do with whatever plan Ryan and Elle had concocted between themselves.'

A bubble of hope broke the surface, but I smothered it down, just like the teabags.

'Oh, come on, so Ryan never told you he was keeping my dad's car hostage at Elle's insistence?'

'Absolutely not. Like I told you in Scarnbrook, me and Ryan have been drifting apart for ages now. Calling him about your breakdown was the first time I'd spoken to him all year.'

I threw my hands in the air in exasperation, the teaspoon clattering to the ground. 'I just don't know who to believe any more! My life suddenly feels like *The Truman Show*. For all I know, the constant appearance of Nutrigrain bars could be a paid-for product placement situation.'

'Now you come to mention it, did you know they bring together all your favourite breakfast ingredients into one tasty bar…'

My mouth dropped open and Tom's voice faded out as it dissolved into laughter.

'Sorry, I couldn't help myself,' he said, his shoulders still shaking with amusement.

I whipped him with a tea towel and tried very hard not to smile.

'Ouch! But, yes, I deserved that. Listen, Mally, please. I spoke to Ryan earlier. Or last night. Or whenever it was. I shouted at him if you want to know the truth. He told me everything. It was only him who was in touch with Elle, and she'd sworn him to secrecy. Apparently, the plan all along had been for Ryan to bring Darren to the pub quiz that night in an attempt to set you up on a disastrous date for your article. And she'd booked that poky rental purely because it was so close to The Star.'

'Yes, I know all of that. But did *you* know I was going to be in Scarnbrook last week?'

'No, I didn't. I swear. When I'd ended up calling Ryan from the petrol station disaster, he and Elle couldn't believe their luck. She convinced him to hang on to the car for as long as possible to keep you in Scarnbrook so you could gather more material for your piece. I feel so awful for what's happened, Mally. And I'm so sorry that I seem to have inadvertently fuelled the flames of their deceit.'

Fuelled the flames of their deceit. Gosh. Despite everything, I couldn't help but feel a little wobble of longing triggered by his turn of phrase.

'What about Carly? And Becky?'

'They had no idea, either. In fact, Ryan has begged me not to say anything to Carly for fear of what it might do to their relationship given his history with Elle.'

'Yeah, he asked the same of me.'

'Well, there you go then.' Tom's teeth chattered as he spoke.

'Shit, you're still cold.'

I felt the nearest radiator. It was freezing – the heating wasn't scheduled to come on for a couple of hours. I boosted the thermostat on the mantelpiece but the warmth wouldn't kick in for at least thirty minutes. And the wood burner would need hours of fuel – and actual logs, which I hadn't restocked for at least a couple of years – before it finally threw out any kind of heat into the room.

'Right, don't argue with me but I'm going to run you a bath. It's the quickest way to warm you up. You can take your cuppa in with you.'

'Um, yeah, okay.'

I glugged a decent amount of Feel Relaxed Radox into the running water, wondering to myself exactly when I'd last Felt Relaxed, and sloshed it about with my hand while Tom watched on in the increasingly steamy room.

'There you go. Have a soak and just shout if you need anything.'

'Thanks, this is… all a bit embarrassing.'

'Tom, you were mopping up my vomit not long ago. I think my shame still tops yours.'

'Yeah, fair enough.'

I stepped out into the hallway and started panicking internally. I was acutely aware that I was looking my absolute worst while Tom Brinton's naked skin was absorbing the warmth of the water mere inches away. In *my* bathtub.

I crept into my bedroom and examined myself in the mirror. Argh. So bad. I hadn't changed out of my tatty pyjamas for over a day, let alone crossed paths with any shower gel. I changed into my 'best' PJs under my dressing gown (so it didn't look like I'd made an effort), slapped some nice-smelling moisturiser onto my face, ran a brush through my hair and sprayed some Impulse down my pyjama top. I was about to scrabble about for something minty to chew on when Tom called out from the bathroom.

'Umm, Mally, can you hear me?'

'Yep!'

'It's just that I need a towel.'

'Shit, yeah. Hang on.'

I fetched a soft beach towel from the top shelf of my wardrobe, deducing that my standard towels probably wouldn't be big enough for him. I tapped the bathroom door, which opened a crack, his long, damp arm poking out. I pressed the towel into his outstretched fingers.

'Ta.'

The door closed and I made my way back to the living room to make a start on my cup of tea. He joined me on the sofa a few minutes later.

'Warmer?'

'Yes, thanks.'

But I could still detect a tremor in his voice.

'You're still shivering, though. Let me grab you a blanket. Or I can see if I've got any tin foil if you prefer?'

'I'm never going to live that down, am I?'

'Never.'

'A blanket would be good, but I'm not cold any more, Mally. I think I'm just a bit… nervous.'

Time seemed to slow down a little. The thing was, I believed everything Tom had said about his lack of involvement in Elle's machinations. In a way, it would've been simpler if I hadn't, leaving me no choice but to draw a neat little line through Scarnbrook – and all the people there. But, as I was fast learning, life wasn't about 'yes' or 'no', 'right' or 'wrong', 'good people' or 'bad people'. It was about all the messy places in between and finding the chinks of light among the chaos. It was about the choices we made, and the care we put into them. It was about 'and' not 'or'.

'Nervous? Why?'

'Why do you think? Because I'm here. In your flat. With you. I've barely slept since you left, thinking about what I would say at this very moment.'

'Oh.' I noticed that I was shaking a little bit, too.

'And now I'm here and, well, I don't really know what to say. I really like your flat, by the way.'

'Thanks.'

'Yeah, it feels like you, somehow.'

'Really? In what way?'

'I dunno, it just feels... nice.'

Nice. I was coming to think of that word differently. I always thought that I could place myself squarely in the 'nice' column, but now I wasn't so sure. And that was... okay. No, I'd not been the perfect sister to Livvie – or Josh, for that matter. I'd not been the kindest mate to Becky when I was younger. And I'd never lived up to Elle's massive expectations of me in terms of how a best friend should behave. But I'd always done the best I could according to what I knew at the time. But I knew more, now. And I'd never stop learning and growing and striving to do better. For myself as much as for anyone else.

'Don't you think it's weird that Father Christmas only has two lists: naughty or nice?' I asked, sharing my interior thoughts aloud, somehow knowing he wouldn't run a mile.

'You're pretty good at these out-of-the-blue existential questions, aren't you?'

'My brain's an annoyingly busy place.'

'So's mine. To answer your question: I've never liked the notion of "naughtiness", actually. I don't think any kid – or adult for that matter – is inherently bad. They've just maybe not been loved or cared for in a way that supported them to become the best version of themselves.'

'Wow, that's... pretty deep, Tom Brinton.'

'Huh, is it? What were you expecting me to say?'

'Oh, I dunno, something about how people can be nice and naughty at the same time…?'

I hadn't meant to lace my response with innuendo, but Tom's raised eyebrows and detectable swallow suggested his mind had leapt there, too. I looked forward to having more deep but flirtatious chats with Tom in the future. Shit, there was a future? Yeah, there was. I could feel it stretching out from each of us, converging, from this very room.

I nudged his thigh playfully with my knee and grabbed the biggest, softest blanket I could find. I draped it over him before touching the radiator behind the sofa, leaning over him to do so. I heard an almost inaudible intake of breath. I was suddenly aware of how close he was. And of the fact that I was wearing an old, tatty dressing gown that probably hadn't seen the inside of a washing machine for the best part of a year. But I didn't care about that any more.

I lingered over him for a second longer than I needed to, trying to gather my thoughts and feelings together in one place, but they were swirling around all manner of bodily regions. The *click click click* of the radiator pipes was the only sound, until Tom said my name.

'Mal—'

I spoke quietly. 'It's warming up. Shouldn't take too long to get going, now.'

I sat back down next to him. Not quite touching. But close enough to notice that the aroma of Radox had clung to his skin.

'Mally, I…'

I looked up at him and allowed my eyes to drink him in. His hair was still wet, his eyelashes stained darker with moisture. And his eyes seemed to be searching mine for some kind of permission. I wasn't nervous any longer. I was ready for my life to change.

'I want you to know that I didn't come here for—'

'This?' I asked, as I kissed him softly on the mouth. I mean, it was right there. It was the only thing I could do.

'Yeah, this,' he murmured as he kissed me deeply in response.

I pulled away gently. 'But is this what you want?'

'It's what I've always wanted.'

'Always?' I probed, kissing him again, finally getting to run my hand through that thick mop of hair. He hummed in appreciation.

'Definitely.' He created a filament of space between our lips. 'Hey, I need to tell you something: you know that time Elle and Ryan went to the cinema together?'

'Mmm.' I was rubbing the base of his neck with my thumb, just like I'd fantasised about doing on our first date.

'The reason I brought that up was because… well, I'd asked Ryan to set up a double date with the four of us for the following weekend. I never knew whether Elle had mentioned it to you. Or if you just thought the idea of it was so laughable that you concocted the bad breath plan between you.'

I was expecting to feel a rush of hurt at the revelation of yet another micro-betrayal by Elle. But it didn't arrive. I couldn't bring myself to be angry with her, because all of her poor choices – as well as my own – had brought me to this moment. And, in this moment, I could finally see what it was I needed to do. Who I needed to become. And the many people who would be by my side as I made the shift, instead of Elle and Elle alone. Plus, her decision to snub out my connection with Tom back then had only resulted in an even deeper one all these years later. And Tom Brinton, I knew, was so worth the wait.

'She never told me, Tom.'

'Yeah, I gathered. Oh well.'

'Oh well,' I whispered through a drowsy smile. 'I would've said yes, for what it's worth.'

'I know.'

We kissed again. For longer this time. The room was definitely getting warmer, but I couldn't tell if it was the central heating kicking in or the igniting embers inside me. I shrugged off my dressing gown as things began to move into a more horizontal direction, but felt a sudden vibration from Tom's pocket.

'Sorry. Hang on.' He placed the phone on the coffee table and began to return to me. I glanced at it.

'Umm, Tom, your mum's calling you at seven o'clock in the morning. Don't you think you should answer?'

'Argh, yeah, you're right.' He cleared his throat before answering. 'Hey, Mum. Yeah, all good...'

His voice trailed off as he wandered into the hallway, gently closing the door behind him.

I reclined on the sofa in a state of flustered arousal. I couldn't believe this was actually happening. I mean, years ago I'd played out countless imaginary scenarios of how me and Tom Brinton would finally declare our undying love for each other. Strangely, none of them had involved a reportable data breach and an emergency foil blanket.

Tom wandered back through after a few minutes. I scooched up on the sofa to create space where he'd sat before. He perched on the edge of it. Oh. Bugger.

'Sorry about that. She's been panicking about you almost as much as me. She needed to know you were okay.'

'She knows you're here?'

'Yeah, there's not much she doesn't know, to be honest. Is that weird?'

'No, it's lovely. I just hope you didn't tell her that I'm currently way more than "okay"...'

We kissed again. More urgently this time. If this'd been a cheesy Christmas movie, the film would've ended the instant our lips had touched, unopened, for the first time, our 'happily ever after' set in rock-hard gingerbread house frosting. But this wasn't a cheesy Christmas movie; it was a real, messy life. And, in my very real brain, I had a thought that made me stop. Once it was there, there was no shaking it off. I pulled away.

'What's the matter?' Tom asked.

'This is doomed, isn't it?'

'What, us?'

'Yeah. Us. Think about it. I can't see myself living in Scarnbrook again, Tom. It was home for me once. But, for the time being, this flat in this city is my home.'

'Yeah, of course it is.'

'And you couldn't ever move away from your mum, could you?'

'No. Never.'

'Exactly.'

'So, what are you saying?'

'I don't know. I know what I want. I just don't know how it could ever work.' I moved to the other end of the sofa, finding my dressing gown and wrapping it around myself tightly, placing my head in my hands.

Tom perched on the coffee table opposite me, and tenderly took my hands in his. 'Look at me, Mally.'

I raised my damp eyes to meet his.

'I'd be lying if I said I hadn't been trying to dismiss the same thoughts myself. But the simple truth is this: I like you. A lot. I think I always have done. And I have no idea where any of this might lead us, let alone how we might get there. But I do know that I just want to keep spending time with you. Things feel lighter when I'm with you. What was that word you used the other night to describe your family Christmases? Oh yeah: *tingly*. Well, that's how *you* make *me* feel. You make my face ache from smiling. And, well, it's hard to explain, but you've made me realise that home doesn't have to be a place. It can be a feeling. Or a person.'

The tears that fell from my eyes this time were happy ones. These were the nicest things anyone had ever said to me. And every nerve ending in my body told me that this was right. This was different. Billy, and the others before him, had helped me to forget myself for a while. But I was done with forgetting, now.

I squeezed his hands. 'I make you tingle.' It wasn't a question but a statement. I rubbed the nub of his neck again as he nodded, his hair follicles rising in appreciation. It was our thing, already. 'So, what do we do now?'

'Take it slowly, day by day, I guess.'

'Slow sounds good.'

'Yeah… so, on that note, I reckon it might be best if I head off. Not that I want to, mind you, but if I don't get going soon I, erm, might not ever feel the urge to leave. And Mum definitely wouldn't be able to eat that whole turkey by herself tomorrow.'

'Ha. Yeah, I think that might be wise.'

'You should come with me.'

His statement took me completely by surprise. Planning to spend Christmas with Tom and his mum while I was a temporary Scarnbrook resident had been one thing. But spending it with them so soon after what this sofa had just witnessed was quite another.

'That… doesn't sound slow, Tom.'

'Yeah, I know. I'm sorry, I shouldn't have said it. But… it feels right. And we can still take things slowly even if we're together, so thought I'd throw it out there.'

It feels right to me, too.

'I'm… just not sure,' I replied tentatively.

Yes, you are.

'Wouldn't it be a bit weird staying at your mum's place given all of… this?' I waved my hands wildly in the space between us as if the gesture somehow did the physical ache I felt for him justice.

He grabbed my flailing hands decisively but gently, and pulled me onto his lap on the coffee table, tucking my greasy hair behind my ears.

'Trust me, Mal, she'd be bloody thrilled to have you come back – she's been so worried. Plus, she knows how much I care about you. I think it would be a nice thing – for all of us. I'm driving straight to hers from here to stay there for the next few days.'

I thought about my barren fridge and my near-empty box of Coco Pops. I never had got around to picking up any shopping – not even that Pret Christmas sandwich – what with everything that had been going on.

This is risky, Mally.

'I… think I need to recalibrate here for a bit. But give her my love and tell her I can't wait to see her again soon.'

I knew these words were the safest words, so why did they feel so unnatural in my mouth?

'Of course, I totally get it. And I'm sorry again for putting you on the spot. But if you change your mind, at any time, call me – yeah? And please unblock my number so I can call you when I get back?'

I extracted my phone and did the honours. 'Consider yourself permitted.'

Tom kissed the top of my head before standing up and gathering his things. 'Hey, I totally forgot to ask what's happening with your article now that *The Helix* is closing?'

'Long story.'

'I want to hear all of it. Talk later, yeah?'

This was all actually happening, wasn't it? I could feel hope fizzing underneath my skin. It'd been a long time bloody coming.

I walked him to his car and we kissed a drizzle-dappled kiss before he climbed in. He wound down the window before he drove off.

'Oh God, please don't tell me you're going to roar again?' I asked, though I wouldn't have minded at all if he had.

'Ha, no. But there was one thing I forgot to give you.'

'Oh?'

He leant over to the glove compartment and extracted an ancient ball of once-orange fluff with two wonky eyes attached.

I gasped with delight. 'Marmalade!'

Tom passed his precious childhood comforter to me through the window.

'Sorry I didn't have time to wrap him, but I thought he could keep you company?'

'You're sure?'

'So sure. You know where to put him, right?'

I nodded. 'Of course.'

We kissed briefly once more. As he drove off, I carried Marmalade back into the warmth and stood in the communal hallway for a while. I hadn't even cleaned my teeth yet – I'd never imagined the most gut-wrenchingly romantic moment of my life would be infused with the stale flavour of Night Nurse.

This was what falling in love felt like, then. Knowing these thoughts and urges of mine flowed both ways without any shadow of a doubt. Knowing he'd never leave me hanging on two blue ticks. Knowing he'd already seen – and mopped up – the most dissolvable parts of me.

I sighed a happy sigh as I headed back inside.

I carried Marmalade into the living room and squeezed him onto the glowing branches of my tiny Christmas tree. At this angle, he seemed to be looking over my shoulder. I turned to follow his gaze and caught sight of the London snow globe on the mantelpiece. I lifted the glass orb off the shelf and carried it to the sofa with care, using a corner of my dressing gown to remove the thick layer of dust. The water was clearer than I remembered, the glitter flakes more iridescent. I turned its crank, gave it a good shake and placed it on the coffee table. As the music played, my mind began to swirl with everything that had changed in such a short space of time. All the truths that had been spoken – by me, and to me. There was one line in particular that kept repeating on a loop – something that Elle had said to me a couple of nights ago: 'You wait for things to happen to you, instead of making things happen for yourself.'

And then it all clicked.

My Christmas was about to be safe. But it *could* be incredible.

Why in the hell had I said no to Tom about going back to Scarnbrook with him? It was almost as if I was denying myself a piece of guaranteed joy in favour of…

what, exactly? More wallowing and solitary overthinking? What was I hoping to achieve by staying here by myself?

The safety of predictability.

I sat upright quickly – too quickly – lightheaded thanks to my empty stomach.

Just go to him, Mally!

I'm not sure if it was my voice, or Livvie's, that was screaming inside my skull. But, whoever it was, I loved them – and knew they were right.

Chapter 29

☑ **New year ahead, new life ahead**

Two hours later I was dressed, packed – if sweeping whatever clothes and Christmas gifts happened to be within grabbing distance into my suitcase counted as 'packing' – and driving an unfamiliar Zipcar back towards Scarnbrook. Marmalade was on the passenger seat, making the opposite journey to the one he'd made in the middle of the night. He was certainly clocking up the miles today.

I hadn't told Tom I'd changed my mind; I knew he'd probably insist on coming back and collecting me. But it felt important to do this by myself.

Pulling off the M4 for the final stretch of the journey, I yelped with delight as 'Driving Home for Christmas' by Chris Rea came on the radio. If this were the final scene of a made-for-TV Christmas movie, it would absolutely be the most appropriate track imaginable for this climactic romantic scene. Although they probably wouldn't be able to afford the rights to such a recognisable song.

The familiar roads began to unfold before me once more. It'd ended up being a cold and crisp Christmas Eve once the early morning drizzle had passed, and the buildings that had been dull and damp when I'd made this very journey ten days ago were now glistening with early-evening frost. It might not be a white Christmas tomorrow, but it could end up being a satisfyingly clear and crisp one.

Driving past The Star, I was thrilled to see the car park full and the place radiating festive mirth from every window. I took a mental note to text Becky later to let her know I was back – again.

In the fading dusk light, Scarnbrook's Christmas trees and fairy lights seemed to get brighter and brighter as I neared Jo's bungalow. And then I felt it: the full-on festive tingle I hadn't experienced for decades.

It was the physical feeling of love, wasn't it? That blissful, unconscious sensation that tells us we're part of a special, reciprocated connection. An unbreakable one, even. That's why losing someone is so fucking hard – because having that tingle unceremoniously ripped from our insides leaves our outsides mockingly unscathed, as if it had never existed in the first place.

Is this why people seem so obsessed with nostalgia, especially at this time of year? Maybe all they're trying to do is recapture that tingly feeling – of comfort and safety and predictability – that had once been the most tangible, natural thing in their lives. Yet, the older we get, the less reliable and uncertain the world seems to become, and the more fragile our safety nets feel. Looking back is often so much easier than looking forward. And, for some of us, opening ourselves up to new people, new experiences and new uncertainties is simply too much to contemplate.

Because that tingle – that sense of love and belonging – is addictive. And, as stupid as it sounded, I'd been filling that craving with my cheesy Christmas movies. Because the characters always re-discover the childhood joy and comfort they'd once taken for granted. And, up until right now, parking up a few houses away from Jo's home in one of the few on-street spaces available – evidently lots of people had descended on this pocket of the world for Christmas – I'd never even known that's what I'd been searching for.

I stretched in the driver's seat for a few seconds, before noticing a message notification from Tom on my phone from about forty minutes ago:

> **Tom:**
> I'm back at Mum's, safe and sound!
> Stopped off at Membury services on the way back for a cheeky Burger King.

I tapped out a quick reply.

> **Mally:**
> Yum! Btw, I have a surprise for you.

The ticks turned blue instantly, and I looked over at Marmalade.

'Right then, Marmy. Are you ready?'

Maybe the question was more for me than him. I scooped him up and slammed the hire car door closed just as Tom replied:

> **Tom:**
> ?

I responded by pushing his mum's doorbell.

He took a few seconds to come to the door, Jo calling, 'Who is it?' from her front room as he pulled the door open towards him.

'It's us,' I said quietly, holding out Marmalade to him. 'We both missed you.'

'You… came?'

I nodded, and he pulled me into the best hug I'd ever had in my whole life, which swiftly turned into the best kiss I'd ever had in my whole life. By the time it had ended, Jo had rounded the corner of the hallway, Chippie poking his head between her ankles inquisitively, her entire face beaming as she looked between our oxytocin-filled faces.

'Oh, Mally, sweetheart! She came back, Thomas! Oh! Let me leave you two lovebirds to it for a minute or two, I'll just…'

'Ha ha, Jo, it's fine. We have plenty of time for… all that.' I squeezed Tom's hand and he squeezed mine right back, along with an invisible sweep of the inside of my wrist with his thumb, before tugging me over the threshold of home.

Unpacking in Jo's spare room an hour or so later after more hugs, a mug of hot chocolate and a hefty slice of Lidl Christmas cake to tide me over until a 'picky tea' in front of the telly later, my phone buzzed, the word 'Mum' flashing on the screen.

'Mum! Happy Christmas Eve!'

'Happy Christmas Eve, sweetheart! Oh, you sound nice and chirpy! What time is it there? I can't keep up.'

'It's coming up to… six o'clock in the evening.'

'Gosh, it's not even lunchtime here and I've already been awake for what feels like a whole day. Your dad's been sleeping like a log on Sandra's enormous spare bed. It's wider than it is long!'

'Very posh! Are you both having a nice time?'

'Oh yes, it's lovely here. Though I must admit, it's a bit odd wandering about in T-shirts in December. It just doesn't feel like Christmas without one of my big, woolly jumpers on.'

'Oh, Mum. I love you.' The words slipped out automatically. I couldn't remember the last time I'd told either of my parents I loved them.

'Gosh. Well, we love you very much, too. We wanted to call you today instead of tomorrow as Sandra's taking us to some swanky place for Christmas lunch and your dad warned me I won't have any Internet signal for most of the day, whatever that means.'

I heard the background sound of a toilet flush, followed by Dad's muffled voice: 'Like I keep telling you, love, it's a different mobile telephone system in America! You'll need a Wi-Fi connection to use your phone!'

'Did you hear your father, Amelia?'

'Yes, I heard.'

I imagined them perched on the end of a giant bed together.

'Put her on speakerphone!' Dad sounded happy. They both did.

'You do it, Bob!'

I heard some rustling noises and then Dad's voice: 'Right then, here we both are, Amelia!'

'Hey, Dad! Happy early Christmas!'

'And to you, kiddo.'

Should I tell them about Tom? Not quite yet. But the news about The Helix?

My instincts were telling me to say nothing, to shield them from the worry, but I couldn't risk them finding out through a third party.

'Hey, Mum and Dad, don't panic, but just so you know, you might see some news doing the rounds about *The Helix*.'

'What kind of news, Amelia?' I could hear Mum's frown in her voice.

'That they're closing down the UK office…'

'Oh no! But what does this mean for…'

'Please, let me finish. Absolutely nothing is set in stone in terms of my job, but even if the worst happens, I'm kind of… excited for the first time in ages. I think it's time for a bit of a fresh start.'

'If you say so, Amelia. You promise you're not putting on one of your brave faces?'

Huh, she knew about my 'brave faces'?

'I promise. In fact, I think the hope about the future I'm feeling right now is the bravest thing I've done in years.'

'That's my girl,' said Dad.

Mum continued, 'Yes, we're so proud of you, Amelia. You'll get through this, sweetheart. You've gotten through worse.'

'We all have,' I said.

There was no response to that, and as she swiftly changed the subject and they told me more about their trip and their plans for tomorrow, I knew there likely never would be. Anything Josh and I would work to understand and mend over the coming weeks, months and years would be our journey, and our journey alone. This knowledge made me sad. But I had to make peace with the idea that sorrow and joy can – and must – co-exist if any of us stand a chance of finding happiness and hope in among the chaos and heartache of life.

After hanging up, I tipped a canvas bag upside down over the bed, allowing my small collection of presents to tumble out. I figured I might as well open them now, since each of them carried a shit-ton of emotional weight that I wasn't quite ready for Tom and his mum to witness tomorrow. My parents had given me a beautiful, personalised notebook and pen. I looked forward to discovering what creative avenues these fresh pages would open up, vowing not to fill them with lists for once.

Then there was a present from Elle, which she'd given to me on our last day in the office. It was my PE effort award – but it'd had a makeover. The engraved label on the base of the cup no longer read: *PE Effort, Year 9 Girl*. Instead, it said: *Best sister from another mister, forever.*

Sister.

Over the years, Elle had placed so much pressure and expectation on our friendship that, for her, it had mutated into something completely different and borderline unhealthy. But the love and care with which I'd cradled her a couple of days ago was real. I knew I wanted to be a part of Elle's life – and Frannie's life – forever, regardless of what continent they happened to be living on, but 'forever' didn't have to mean 'exclusively'. I'd been her safety net ever since she'd moved next door, but safety nets need to be anchored to something, and I'd been drifting from the moment Livvie had died.

Right now, I had to focus on anchoring myself to my own life, not to someone else's – and standing next to Josh as he did the same.

Which brought me to my final gift: the one from my big brother and my amazing sister-in-law. I untied the cloth wrapping, which doubled up as a beautiful tea towel. Pretty handy in itself, to be fair. Enclosed within was a VHS tape of *The Princess Bride*. I clutched it tightly to my chest.

I took out my phone and tapped out a message to Josh:

Mally:
Happy Christmas for tomorrow! Couldn't resist opening your present just now. Thank you, it's INCONCEIVABLE!

Josh:
You keep using that word. I do not think it means what you think it means.

Mally:
Lol. When did you last watch it?

Josh:
Couldn't even say. Fancy a NYE movie night next week to refresh our memories?

I smiled a watery grin as I collected up the presents and stacked them on the dressing table next to the window, risking a review of my appearance in the mirror as I did so. God, I looked unkempt. But also kind of... glowy and alive? I thought back to the numbness that had washed over me back in London after Rory had collected Elle. Perhaps, instead of emptiness, it'd actually been my brain and body resetting itself for the next phase of my life. Because, right now, I had a clear and unshakeable under-standing of what I needed to do: I needed to let go of my small existence of easy comforts to find true peace, despite all the complexities that would inevitably come along with that. Coming here to spend Christmas with Tom was just the first step of many, but I was finally ready to take every single one.

I tucked my hair behind my ears, smeared on some lip balm and sprayed each wrist with a random perfume Jo had left in the room for me. I rummaged through my backpack in search of a Polo mint before re-joining Tom, Jo and Chippie in the living room for their traditional Christmas Eve re-watch of *Santa Claus: The Movie*. But my hand landed on something else, instead.

It was a spare copy of the Christmas movie bingo sheet I'd tucked in an inside pocket when I'd packed for my first trip to Scarnbrook. I pulled it out along with a pen, and began neatly ticking off all the tropes I'd inadvertently achieved over the last couple of weeks once more. My life was nowhere near as straightforward as a Christmas movie, but I had to admit I'd experienced quite the character arc this month.

My hand reached the final trope on the page, but I suddenly felt unsure:

New year ahead, new life ahead.

I looked at myself in the mirror and bit my lip.
You've got this.
I nodded, and added my final tick.

One year later

Hey, Livvie,

I can't believe it's been more than a year since I last wrote to you.

My therapist (yeah, check me out!) thought it might be helpful for me to write to you again, after I stopped so suddenly when I got that bounceback email last December. At first I wasn't convinced – I thought it'd be too hard – but I finally felt like I was ready to give it a go today.

Shit, I don't even know where to start.

Maybe some life updates? OK – that's doable.

I have a new job! The Helix shut down suddenly at the end of last year in the UK, which was a bit of a shock but a bit of a relief at the same time, if that makes any sense at all?! But then my two bosses there, Lauren and Maggie, decided to set up their own comms consultancy, and I'm their copywriter! It's home-based, which means I can squeeze in some creative writing on the side, plus work from wherever suits me, which means I've been able to spend quite a bit of time with…

…MY BOYFRIEND! WHO IS TOM BRINTON!

Yeah, I know I buried the lede there, but I kind of wanted to build up to the reveal.

He's amazing, Liv. He's so fucking funny and goofy and kind and clever. Quite ridiculously, he seems to feel similarly about me (my therapist would probably berate me for the self-deprecation but, what can I say, it's a built-in coping mechanism).

Tom still lives near Scarnbrook, where he runs a really successful business (he lives in a BARN CONVERSION. In LANGWOOD!!), but they've been gradually expanding east this year, so we've been able to spend loads of weekends together in various Premier Inns off the M4 – not exactly the most glamourous of locations, but that's the price we must pay if his dreams of Southern England facilities management domination are to become a reality. Ha ha, nah, it's been lovely. Honestly, the hotels could be Fawlty Towers for all I care, it's just so fun hanging out with him. It feels easy.

I'm staying with him at his mum's place in Scarnbrook for Christmas this year – that's where I'm writing from now, in fact. It's been so nice to reconnect with this place after way too long. Can you believe that the only reason me and Tom got together was because of those Hallmark Christmas movies you used to love? 'I only went back to my hometown for a random work assignment, but ended up discovering so much more' etc etc – honestly, you couldn't make it up!

Tom makes me so happy, though. I... I think he might very well be The One.

Oh, more big news: Elle moved to New York at the start of the year! She got offered a fancy-pants management role at The Helix's HQ – they paid for her whole family to relocate, and Rory is apparently now a happy house (apartment)-husband in Brooklyn! I haven't made it out there to visit them yet, and I miss them loads, but a trip (with Tom!) is definitely on the cards for next year sometime.

Speaking of the USA, Mum and Dad are currently in Florida for Christmas for the second year running. They had such a blast there last year with Auntie Sandra that they've decided to make it an annual thing. I do miss Christmases with them, but we've been spending loads more time together as a family this year, and that includes Josh and Saskia.

Josh himself is doing… OK. His mental health is wobblier than I ever realised, but he's spending way less time on social media these days and I can see the sparkle returning to his eyes. We're doing Dry January together next month – wish us luck!

I know I used to bitch about Saskia in my emails to you, but I was wrong. She's so lovely and so perfect for Josh. And they're having a baby, Liv! I can't believe I'm going to be an auntie.

You would've been an auntie, too.

Oh, God. Now I'm crying (I can just imagine my therapist cheering me on – why am I like this?!). OK. Deep breath.

I found out recently that, in France, they say 'you're missing from me' instead of 'I miss you', and, yeah, that feels about right to me. There is, and always will be, such a massive, you-shaped hole in our lives, Livvie. I still can't believe you're gone.

You were my whole world, you know that, right? My person.

I'd give anything to go back in time to hold you in my arms again when you were a tiny baby. To watch The Snowman with you at least 57 times every December. To lift you up at our bedroom window and wish Scarnbrook good night, together. Even if the Zoltar Speaks fairground machine from Big produced a card to warn me about everything that would happen, I'd hit the rewind button right now, without any hesitations at all.

I am so, so sorry I never replied to your last email. It's my life's biggest regret. But I know that, if you'd made it, you would have forgiven me instantly. So perhaps it's finally time for me to forgive myself?

Ever since you died, I've been trying to recapture the joys of my past, but now I know it's possible to find different joys in my future. I can't wait to find out what they'll be. And I'll savour every last one of them, and live my life to the absolute fullest.

For you – and for me.

I loved you so much. I still do and won't ever, ever stop.

Your sister, always,
Amelia xxx

I chose not to read back what I'd poured out, totally unplanned, in my handwritten letter, instead folding it up immediately and sliding it inside the envelope. I'd place it on Livvie's grave later that day, with Tom, Josh and a heavily pregnant Saskia by my side. We were heading to

The Star afterwards for an early Christmas Eve dinner, where Josh and Saskia were staying in one of the pub's newly opened boutique hotel rooms.

But, right now, I had a couple of hours to fill with Jo before Tom returned with some last-minute bits from the Big Tesco.

I plonked myself down on my sofa spot, Chippie immediately curling into my lap in his cat-like way. I stroked him absent-mindedly, sitting in comfortable and contented silence while Jo focused on finding the home for her latest puzzle piece.

'There!' she proclaimed with satisfaction. 'You okay, lovey?'

'Absolutely,' I said. 'Hey, fancy watching a film?'

'Ooh yes, let me just see what the *TV Times* says is on.' She thumbed through the pages and dragged her forefinger down the relevant columns. 'Ooh, would you look at that – perfect timing. Can you guess what it is?'

'I probably can't tell you the title, but I reckon I could guess the channel…'

'Go on, then!'

'Channel 5?'

'Yes! It's called *Christmas Ever After*. And it's just about to start!'

I picked up the remote control, switched to the right channel, and waited for it to begin.

A Letter from Hayley

Thanks so much for reading!

If you've made it this far, hopefully that's a good sign...
If you enjoyed reading *It's Beginning to Look a Lot Like Christmas* anywhere near as much as I enjoyed writing it, it would be a huge help if you could review it online. Goodreads and Amazon (even if you didn't buy the book from there) are great places to leave your ratings and share your thoughts and feelings.

How this story began:
It was winter 2020, the country was in lockdown, all festivities had been cancelled and the only activity making me feel even vaguely human was watching formulaic cheesy Christmas movies. As I devoured them, I began to imagine how funny and potentially interesting it would be if a less conventional woman returned to her underwhelming hometown to try and have her own 'Christmas movie experience' against a backdrop of British drizzle instead of picture-perfect snow. The idea wouldn't leave me alone, so I wrote a scene to get it out of my head... and I never stopped writing.

This story, originally called *Fake Snow*, has been the subject of so many re-writes, and so many (very kind) rejections, but I stuck at it as it has never brought me anything but delight. I followed my joy, embraced my weirdness, and wrote a book I wanted to read. And now I get to share it with the wider world. I am so, so happy that I can.

Psssst: this book is also a game!

In case you haven't worked it out, this book isn't just a story featuring a Christmas movie bingo game, it's also a game of Christmas movie bingo in and of itself.

As well as all the chapter title tropes, there are many other tropes hidden throughout the story. The bingo cards themselves – the same ones that Mally uses – are at the very back of this book, or you can download them from www.bit.ly/CheesyChristmasMovieBingo and see if you can tick them all off (and you can also play along with your favourite cheesy Christmas movies).

Some clarifying facts about this book:

Scarnbrook is a made-up place, but it's very much inspired by my happy experience of growing up in the South Gloucestershire suburbs between Bristol and Bath.

Spaghetti Tree, however, is very much NOT made up. My teenage memories of that place are a mixed bag, but I'm happy to report that the establishment in question is now (at the time of writing) a lovely bar called Blame Gloria. You should pay it a visit! For the purposes of this story, I reimagined it as a cosy, subterranean tapas restaurant.

The chocolate factory anecdote is true, although it happened to family friends, not my own grandparents.

All the cheesy Christmas movies named in this book are real films.

Just like Mally, I 'won' a PE effort award at school when I was fourteen. Thankfully, I didn't have to give a speech, although I did have to collect it from an actual stage. CAN YOU IMAGINE.

Join in with my annual Cheesy Christmas Movie Watchalong!

Every December, I host an advent calendar-style cheesy Christmas movie watchalong on Instagram. Since 2021, a growing community of 'watchalongers' and I co-watch twenty-four (or as many as we can manage) Hallmark-style Christmas movies in the run-up to the big day. Visit my Instagram page (@HayleyJDunlop) if this sounds up your street and you want to get involved with the geekery.

The soundtrack to the story:

The soundtrack to this book is an alternative festive playlist, and is available at www.spoti.fi/3W2sgos. Plot twist: it *doesn't* feature the song 'It's Beginning to Look a Lot Like Christmas'…

Stay in touch:
If you want to know about future books, and learn more about my journey to publication (including *why* the above playlist doesn't feature the song this book is named after…!), you can subscribe to my newsletter at www.hayleyjdunlop.substack.com. You can also follow me on Instagram @HayleyJDunlop or find out more about my other writing at www.hayleyjdunlop.com.

A note on AI:
I have not used any generative AI technology at any stage of the writing process for this book.

Acknowledgements

In a country pub in January 2019, holding a small baby who refused to leave my side, two friends gave me a notebook for my birthday. Inside it, they'd written a brief inscription:

> *Our lives are punctuated by different chapters, but it's the story we write that matters.*

I was in a tough chapter back then, as a mum of two young children, and having completely lost touch with so many things that made me feel like myself. I didn't know it at the time, but that gift was a turning point. Over the coming months and years, as COVID kicked in and lockdowns changed everything, I turned to that notebook more and more. And, almost exactly six years later – with two much older children – I'm writing the acknowledgements section of my debut novel with that notebook still by my side. To Kim Perkins and Laura Kenning: thank you for that gift.

It's taken me many years to write and hone this story among the chaos of parenting and working, and I couldn't have done it without the enthusiasm, sturdiness and love of so many people.

Firstly, I owe a huge debt to Georgina Green, whose lockdown co-writing group – later co-hosted by the wonderful Lucy Beckley – provided me with the creative connections I never knew were missing. There's no way I would've entertained the idea of writing a rom-com without the magic and safety of that weekly ritual. As my book coach, George's continued insights and encouragement as this project developed gave me such an incredible springboard for everything that has since followed. Thank you so, so much. And to all the women who I've co-written with online over the years: you are all so inspiring.

Thank you to Laura Williams, my agent at Greene & Heaton, who immediately grasped what I was trying to achieve with what was originally called *Fake Snow* beyond the festive sparkles. Your wisdom and expertise over the last few years have been so appreciated.

Thank you to my editor, Jennie Ayres, at Hera. From the moment we met in 2023, I could feel your love for Mally and her story. Your care and kindness throughout the editing process meant that all of Mally's complexities and layers only got deeper, somehow with fewer words, and I'm so proud of where she ended up as a result of your guidance. I can't wait to keep working with you.

I also owe a big dollop of gratitude to the wider publishing team who worked behind the scenes, with particular thanks to Kate Shepherd and Dan O'Brien for their publicity and marketing help, Becca Allen for her impeccable copyediting, Rachel Sargeant for the excellent proofreading catches and Emily Courdelle for the cover design.

Thank you to Alexandra Sheppard, who sensitivity-read a very early draft and provided incredibly valuable feedback and advice. Much of the story has changed since then, but everything that's no longer on the page is still very much part of this book's foundations and my own journey as an author.

My amazing pal and graphic designer extraordinaire Hazel Tilley has helped me every step of the way with digital assets and general cheerleading. And thank you to Ana Sampson McLaughlin, Katie Sadler and Nicola Washington for all the behind-the-scenes expertise and support. I am so lucky to have many other creative enablers who fill my cup with laughter and glimmers at work (especially chief enabler Serafima Serafimova), in group chats (looking at you, Book Babes) and at gigs (my gig sister Louise Tilsley provided much Christmas movie factchecking): I couldn't have kept going without all of you.

I'm very grateful to local mechanic Rob Armour, who answered my (many!) questions about misfuelling. Any errors that remain on that front are definitely my own.

To all my early readers not already mentioned: Holly Harris; Buffy Handslip; Sarah Walters; Holly June Smith; Katie Huttlestone; Halina Johnson; Sabrina Russo; Hannah Raymond; Hellin Stacey; Ndéla Faye; and Anna Madley. Reading your early 'reviews' were some of the most magical moments I've ever experienced as a writer.

To my parents, Adam and Janet Dunlop. You instilled a love of stories in me from the very start. You always supported me to choose my own paths – and there have been many of them! I feel so lucky to have had such a laughter-filled upbringing, as part of a huge and loving extended family whose own stories and anecdotes have inspired so much of my own writing, in this book and beyond. You're the best parents – and grandparents – I could have wished for.

To my brother Alex. You're not a big reader, and haven't read any early drafts of this book. But that's because you were waiting for it to be an actual book rather than a Word document, which gave me even more motivation to keep going. Thanks for always having my back. Maybe one day we'll finally write that alien story together!

To my children, Elliott and Maisie. Being a mum isn't easy, but being *your* mum inspires me every single day. Elliott: your in-built confidence, magnetic charisma and unshakeable instincts continue to astound me, and everyone you meet. Maisie: your spectacular ideas, endless inquisitiveness and deep care for everything you do light up the lives of everyone who knows you. Being able to witness you both grow into such wonderful, uncompromising humans is my life's greatest achievement.

And finally, thank you to my husband, Andy. Along with the support of my family, our partnership is, and always has been, one of the most solid things I've had in my life. Over the years, that solidity has meant I've been able to allow my own edges to soften, my silliness to seep out and my ideas to take shape. Without you, none of this would exist. Reading the very first draft of this story aloud to you every evening while you ate biscuits – our children sleeping upstairs – remains one of my life's loveliest memories. I'm so happy that we get to keep writing our story together.

Cheesy Christmas movie

Bingo

Fake snow	
Reconnecting with the past	
A man and a woman wearing red and green	
Cosy fire	
Christmas concert	
Story opens in city	
Annoying best friend	
Baked goods	
Unexpected reunion	
Decorating a Christmas tree	
Small-town guy is secretly talented	
Awkward farewell	
Festive-themed contest	
Relatable klutz	
The actress Lacey Chabert	
'Inn' or 'lodge'	
The lure of Manhattan	
A festive freebie	
Seeing someone in a new light	
Bad news piles up	

@HayleyJDunlop

Solo Christmas ahead	
Steaming mug of delicious cocoa	
Car drama	
Festive train journey	
Sentimental item from childhood	
Little white lie	
A hasty departure	
Failing family business	
Character confronts loss	
Old family home	
A Christmas wish	
Near-miss kiss	
Creativity rediscovered	
Small-town guy falls for big-city woman	
A cold house	
Outsider saves the day	
Local scoundrel	
Coming together to solve a problem	
Mistaken identity	
New year ahead, new life ahead